Like a Song

Dallas White,
Book Two

SUSAN RODGERS

Join the *Drifters/Dallas* family by signing up at
www.susanrodgersauthor.com.
As a welcome gift, I'll send you a free bonus/deleted chapter
from book one of the *Drifters* series, *A Song For Josh*.

Happy reading!

Contents

Seen my share of broken halos,
folded wings that used to fly.
They've all gone wherever they go,
broken halos that used to shine.

Don't go looking for the reasons,
don't go asking Jesus why.
We're not meant to know the answers,
they belong to the by and by.

—Chris Stapleton

Chapter One

*N*ights like this, Matt Kelly could melt right into the door frame, he was so relaxed.

Indulging in the luxury of letting his shoulders sink a little lower and his breath exit in a nice, easy exhale, he took a few seconds to reflect and slow his breathing even further before taking the time to survey the space around him. Not that he really needed to lay his eyes on anyone in order to get a sense of what was going on and how people were feeling—the nearby laughter alone was enough to coax a genuine, bashful smile from his lips, although after his scan Matt was careful to focus his restful gaze on the perfect polished cap toes of his Salvatore Ferragamo Oxfords so nobody eyeballing him would suspect him of letting his guard down.

Letting himself 'chill,' as the kids would say, was not always easy for Matt. Most times, on the job and often not on the job, he was meant to be alert. Lives depended on him—not just the talent he was contracted to watch, but also the talent's closest loves—spouses, children, babies. *And pets too,* he thought with a cringe, remembering a day a few years back when protecting a child and the child's mother meant having to let a beloved puppy go. That terrible choice was necessary, but it resulted in great despair for a long time afterwards.

Matt's job was not always easy, not on the nerves and most certainly not on the heart. Yet the heart was why he stuck with it. For better or for worse, Matt was good at his job, and hell, these people—the *talent*—needed him.

He looked up from his spit-shined shoes when a chorus of guffaws and easy laughter echoed from the spacious dressing room to his left. Clinks of glasses and footsteps added to the happy voices within. The first person Matt spotted when he looked inside was the woman he'd saved instead of the puppy back in the dark days of watching over her full time. A superstar the world cherished for her music and for her acting, Jessie Wheeler was, at this very moment, nestled into the corner of a deep, soft couch, leaning into the relaxed curve of her husband's arm while holding lightly to his hand, laughing at something someone across the room said.

People of all shapes and sizes dotted the dressing room, sinking into soft white leather couches or sitting on the arms, as was Jessie's husband, Josh, who smiled and quietly took in his wife's joy as she nuzzled into him from her corner nest.

Someone was at the big bar fridge in the corner. *The drummer,* Matt thought, craning his head nonchalantly to take a closer look at the long haired, jean clad guy clearly rooting around for beer. Back by the clothing racks on the far side, two guys and a woman were digging into chip bowls on the craft table. Matt recognized them as the fiddler (the woman) and tonight's keys and bass players. The far end of Jessie's couch was occupied by Jessie's manager and pseudo-mother, Deirdre, aristocratically poised, her Christian Louboutins delicately balanced around crossed ankles.

There were more adults in the busy room too—Deirdre's husband, Charles, deep in conversation with a wiry guy Matt knew as Phil, a talent manager known for taking country singers to the top ranks of the biz. Jacob, a pop singer, and his pretty blonde dancer wife, Kayla, Josh's sister, were snuggled into an oversized matching white leather love seat positioned perpendicular to the couch.

At their feet, their young daughter Lily played on a bright Navajo rug, driving a plastic car up and down a jagged black line. Juggling for space on the rug, Lily let go with an occasional piercing shriek when another small child sharing the rug continuously crashed her car into Lily's. Micah, Jessie and Josh's youngest, was at the adults' feet too, constantly wiping straight long Josh-like chestnut hair away from his eyes. Micah adored his slightly older cousin and was helping Lily out by driving interference against the car that kept getting in her way.

Matt lingered a long time on the second child, the one ruthlessly shoving a miniature handheld car, a red one, into Lily's blue one. This child, a bouncy blonde, required more than an occasional glimpse from Matt's direction. The pretty wide-eyed youngster had been one of Matt's responsibilities for the last three months, and before then from time to time as well depending on the schedule of her very busy country singer father, the much loved Dallas White. At only three years old, Jade was written into Matt's contract for the entire duration of this tour. He'd had eagle eyes on her over the past few months, which led him to believe that, now, Micah and Lily would not win their mini-car battle. Jade had a stubborn streak. The child had long ago proven to her tired parents, and to her tense security, that she was not one to give up easily.

As supervisor of the other security on the tour—some here in the dressing room and some outside the room, hands folded in front of their muscled bodies and eyes carefully scouting the space around them despite the light-hearted air—Matt had done a lot of scheduling and surveying and discussing and organizing. Tonight's concert marked the last of it, of this exhausting round of touring, at least. Tonight the country singer who always chose to employ Matt when their schedules coincided, was celebrating.

Dallas is on his third beer, Matt counted as, in the back of the room, Dallas' drummer's hand finally emerged from the fridge, a cold beer staunchly gripped in the fingers. Matt watched as, with an air of sneaky pride, the drummer made a show of tossing the unopened wet bottle into Dallas' jubilant hand by spinning it end over end, the same way he'd spun a stick on stage earlier. Matt smiled openly while everyone inside the room cheered. *Dallas is celebrating,* he thought, watching the singer laugh and rag at his drummer before haphazardly screwing the cap off the beer and putting his lips to the foaming end of the bottle. *He's relieved because tonight was the last of the tour, and he's exhausted. Dallas needs a break.*

The end of the tour. Hence the presence of Jessie Wheeler and Jacob Ryan and their entourage, who were sharing in the celebration tonight. Hence Matt's frequent secret smiles down at his cap-toed shoes. Hence his glance now from the persistent three-year-old who was driving Lily crazy on the rug, up to Jessie on the leather couch. He watched her tuck a lazy light-auburn curl behind an ear before leaning her tall, slim body forward to softly scold

Micah, who'd yanked on one of Jade's many baby-soft blonde ringlets when his car got smashed instead of Lily's, this time. Jessie had been Matt's main charge for years, starting long before Dallas. In her early forties now, Jessie was a busy, happy, married mom of four. Discreetly watching her, Matt let himself sink into the bliss of knowing she was his soul mate. Their mutual adoration stemmed from years of shared pain. From the deep kind of love that came from knowing one another from the inside out. Their connection was a soul-to-spirit kind of thing. Josh was aware; hell, even the kids all knew just how much Jessie and Matt meant to each other.

As if she could feel his gentle eyes on her, Jessie turned and treated Matt to a peaceful smile. It was a long time coming, that kind of peace between them. Having Dallas around to often watch over these last few years was a sincere and welcome relief for Matt, most times.

The country singer might be a newish friend, if one considered the decades Matt had spent with Jessie, but Dallas had become a good and trusted presence in Matt's sometimes lonely life. Cassie, Dallas' petite, elegant wife of four years, and the mother of feisty little Jade, was more acquaintance than friend. Reserved at the best of times, she was hard to get to know, and Matt knew his serious, guarded work ethic was intimidating despite his attempts to engage her with kind eyes and careful smiles. She had a surfer blond son from a previous marriage. Ry, barely a teen, worshipped Dallas for far more than his ability to bring an audience of thirty-thousand to its knees. The security team called Cassie's son 'Shy Ry.' But from Matt's perspective, the kid—already a skilled guitar player, thanks to Dallas' patient lessons—was far easier to engage in a chat than Cassie.

At least she was around. At least, for the most part, she took time off work in theatre management to accompany her husband on his tours. Matt's celebrity actress wife, Shanda, was at the mercy of her work. She bounced in and out of his life like a rubber ball.

The last few months—hell, the last few years—were often lonely. When Dallas wasn't doing sound check or performing or just plain delighting the media, he was behind closed doors with Cassie and their two children. Hence why tonight was special for Matt. Hence why tonight was surreal, to him, a man who'd stood in the wings during a gazillion shows over the last many years. He'd practically drooled with a stoned kind of joy earlier when Jacob and Jessie, two people for whom he cared deeply, took the stage as guests of his current boss. They were logical choices for Dallas in this age of genre-hopping music because Dallas' tour was ending in their home city of Vancouver, Canada. Still, it was a huge coup for Dallas' team to snag the duo. Jacob and Jessie were busy celebrities. It was no secret that the reason they said yes was because of their mutual affection for Matt.

Hence Matt's profound joy. Tonight, the usual numb loneliness was replaced by sheer bliss. Here, under his watchful eye, all in one place, were most of the people he loved.

Reflecting on this, a grateful light settled into Matt's hazel-grey eyes. He looked up at Jessie again, probably for the millionth time since he'd taken up his post at the doorway. Dallas noticed and grinned carefully at Matt, who caught the look out of the corner of his eye but since Jessie was actually blushing sweetly back at him, he ignored his current boss and kept his eyes on his old one.

Yep, this was it—pure joy.

It might be temporary, but it sure as heck was sweet.

Chapter Two

A low strum wafting upwards from a collection of lazy couches in a wide part of the hallway caught Matt's ear. It was coming from two guitars, his experienced ears told him, but he didn't look away from Jessie to see who was playing. One of the more trusted members of his security team was over there, watching over the older kids, who were 'too cool' to hang out with the grownups. Big Dan was what the kids (and sometimes the adults, too) called the tall, robust Scandinavian man whom Matt and Charles had hired to help watch over Jessie back when superstardom first came calling.

They were all aging, these watchful men who dedicated their lives to keeping others safe. Thankfully, the kids kept them young. Like Matt, Big Dan practically raised Josh and Jessie's children. Like Matt, Big Dan suffered for it. Matt had an older daughter in her twenties, who he raised until she shut him out after he and his first wife divorced, so although it hurt, he could at least recall the best parts of raising a daughter. Dan and his wife were childless. For all intents and purposes, the Sawyer children filled a lot of holes in the lives of the toughened men who watched over them. No doubt Dan was in his glory right now, hanging out with Josh and Jessie's oldest, Emily-Grace, her brothers David and Dylan, and Dallas and Cassie's Ry. All musically talented, the kids were on a high after the show, no doubt in part because Ry had sung his first big song on stage with Dallas tonight.

Dan didn't have his hands full with ornery kids in the widened part of the hallway. Nope, he was being treated to brand new tunes in that small lounge at the far side of the hall.

The kids. Yep, Matt was feeling his age these days. In the old days, it was nothing to work the late shows with Jessie, hit the sack well past midnight, and rise at the first light of dawn for a run or an hour at the gym. Sometimes they'd board Charles' gold-trimmed private jet after a show, fly to a new city on only a few hours' sleep, and settle into a hotel for a few more hours if they were lucky. Bright and early, Matt'd be up supervising the security in a new venue, which was often a large stadium.

It got harder when the kids came along. Hell, everything got harder. Jessie's acting gigs were a little less nerve-wracking for Matt but often were the reverse of the stadium gigs. Sleep was still a luxury most nights, but heck, the film shoots were boring. Watching multiple takes of a scene was like watching a kettle come to a boil. Now, Matt would gladly take any private time at all with Jessie if he could get it, even just a shared run in the morning with maybe a stop afterwards for coffee. Hell, Matt'd run as far and as fast as Jessie wanted, despite the inflamed knees he'd have to suffer through afterwards; despite seizing pain that sometimes accosted his tired lower back.

One of the young guitarists in the hall cut into his wistful reverie with a holler. "Matt! Matt, come here! You need to hear this."

It was Emily-Grace. She lived life surrounded by three younger brothers, so hanging out with her occasional friend Ry was not something to get nervous about. To her, having another boy around was as simple as adding another bump on a log. She was a child who lived an insular life right from the get-go; she was used to being hauled around from place to place. She, Ry, and her brothers were used to the kinds of friendships that started on the road and that continued on the road, often picking up exactly where they'd left off.

Emily-Grace was gifted with her mother's musical talent. Her brothers were equally blessed. Ry was not Dallas' biological son but he may as well have been; the kid could write songs far beyond the ability of most kids his age. His ability to pick out melodies on the guitar was awe-inspiring.

There were essential differences between what Ry wanted to do with his talent and what Emily-Grace wanted to do with hers—they had to do with the stage. Ry wanted to conquer the world. Emily-Grace preferred to play privately.

Because of everything she's been through, Matt caught himself thinking as another holler forced him to finally break his lock on Jessie, who had long ago turned a subdued kind of attention back to the folks in the dressing room.

Pushing himself away from the door frame, Matt signaled one of his security minions to watch over the dressing room. A dark-skinned woman who kept trying to stuff the wild ends of her frizzy hair into a not so tidy bun took his place at the door. Matt thanked her with a formal nod before starting to saunter casually over to the small group of kids huddled around two guitars.

Dan met him halfway. "Blows my mind what these kids can do," the big guy mused as he took up pace next to his boss. "Ry picks out a melody and Emily-Grace chimes right in with harmonies. They're perfectly in sync and they haven't even seen each other since the Grammies. Even then, they only played together that one night at the hotel, the night before the awards. They remind me of somebody."

He broke out into an easy grin that might've come with a wink if Dan felt more grounded in Matt's daunting presence. The nervous vibe wasn't just because Matt was his boss. Everything about the man was intimidating. Hell, his polished shoes and finely cut blazer unnerved Dan, who stuck one set of large fingers in the pocket of his own droopy blue blazer, absently wondering as they walked whether he should ask how the tour with Dallas had gone overall. Despite the small light Dan detected in Matt's eyes, it was plain to see that the man just looked beat.

Maybe it was because Matt was walking away from Jessie. Matt was like a puppy, he lit up the closer he got to his old friend, and faded as they parted. Dan could never hope to crack whatever shell it was that encased the two; all he knew and needed to know was that they'd been through hell and back together, that Josh was as grateful as Dan to have Matt in their lives, and that what held Matt and Jessie together was a sacred, impermeable kind of magic.

Matt was just that kind of guy. The enigmatic, larger-than-life sort. The dependable, loyal, smart kind who practiced the gospel every day by putting everyone else before himself.

Dallas was already finding that out about Matt. And Dallas, Dan could see from short times in his presence, was as captivated by Matt as was everyone else in the man's circle. Why else would Dallas hire an aging security chief to watch over the most precious people in his life—his wife, Cassie, plus shy Ry and their busy little daughter, Jade?

Matt was the kind of man who saved lives. He'd saved Jessie's physical life twice—even taking a bullet for her—and for sure he'd saved her ailing spirit many times too, when Josh's addictions got the best of him and he went off the rails back when their family was being stalked.

Matt wasn't just the kind of man who watched over people. Matt was the kind of man who healed people.

Dan stood back and grinned widely as Emily-Grace, once so shy and scared, exuberantly reached for Matt's deeply trusted hand and pulled him closer. "You can be the first to hear this song all the way through, Matt. The very first!"

Unable to help himself, Matt chuckled and snuck a sideways look over to Dan, who tossed his head back and laughed outright. Emily-Grace was a mini Jessie, right down to the dusty old cowboy boots she'd worn special for tonight's big country music show. How many times had the two men heard Jessie say the very same thing? *The first to hear my new song. You can be the very first.* Years of experience had taught them that every time Jessie got excited about a new song, the whole world soon got to know it.

Magic. That's what this whole music-making thing was. That's what being around these talented people was all about. It was pure magic.

Emily-Grace was more confident than Ry. As her younger brothers watched—Dylan with his dark curls bouncing as he nodded in time to the catchy tune, and quiet David with his soulful brown Josh-eyes lit from within in awe of his sister's talent—she counted them in and started to play.

Ry was alight. Exuberant and jittery with adrenaline after his successful big-time stage debut, and still just a kid, he knew from being under Matt's care that the man was the kind of person you were meant to shut up and listen to. Not just kids, but adults too, always bowed to Matt's almighty word. But as Ry looked up from his perch on the top back of the big chair and planted his feet more securely, nervously, on the cushion, he looked closer at Matt and was surprised to see something he wasn't used to seeing on the man's face. It was closely guarded emotion, a less demanding expression than usual in the kind but often distanced eyes. It was soft. Tender, even. It struck Ry as odd to see Dallas' hardened security chief let his guard down. A happy, peaceful aura seemed to wash over Matt, which helped Ry relax and settle his feet more comfortably into the cushion of the big chair.

Ry let the corners of his lips lift just slightly and glanced shyly at the pretty young teen beside him. He couldn't help but tremble just a little at the way her light chestnut hair kissed her shoulders; it landed there the same way her famous dad's hair landed around his shoulders, depending on the part he was playing and on what was expected of him, looks-wise. Emily-Grace resembled her dad in a lot of ways, although the highlights in her hair were more auburn like her mom's than chestnut like her dad's. Her big curls moved when she did, which would have passed under the radar of most folks, but which delighted Ry, who was finding himself more and more devoted to all the little things about his musical friend that added up to make Emily-Grace unique and special in his young, star-crossed eyes.

Matt noticed the awestruck look Ry gave his singing partner. Rocking onto his right foot, he dropped his hands under his blazer and rested them on his hips, over the expensive black pants he'd worn for this reunion-like show. Studying Ry, he wondered what Jessie would think of the boy's obvious affection for her cherished daughter. It didn't seem to go both ways— Emily-Grace was still immune to the power of boys since she was so used to being around them, and she had a predisposition as to how annoying they can be.

Also, she was like her mother. When Jessie was tuned into her music, nothing and nobody got in her way. They were all there, anyway, all of the people in Jessie's world—inside the lyrics and imbued in the melodies. But nobody really got through to Jessie until she was ready to let them back in. Music was her safe place, and it guarded her well—it provided better security than Matt ever could. Music was Jacob's sacred place too, and Dallas' as well. A sad little pang rocketed over Matt as he considered that. It hit him that music was also Emily-Grace's safe place, and likely David's and Dylan's as well. And, by the shy look of Ry on stage tonight and here with the children of Jessie Wheeler, music clearly also gave him a place to hide as well.

Matt thought it was sad that they all needed a place to hide in the first place.

He had to bite his tongue to keep from ordering the kids down off the furniture. He focused on the music. The kids' song was, as Dan had alerted Matt, special. Matt's shoulders straightened and he had to force down a concerned frown before the kids even got the song to its second verse. He focused on Dylan's hands. Jessie's third child could take any instrument and make it sing, but his musical toy of choice was a set of drums. And like every drummer Matt had ever come across—and he'd come across many—Dylan couldn't keep his hands still when someone nearby was urging chords from a guitar. Like Ry, he was perched on the top back of a large stuffed and upholstered chair with his sneakered feet on the seat cushion below. Unlike Ry, whose hands were busy with a guitar, Dylan's hands were free. And so his thighs became drums and his fingers held invisible sticks.

Emily-Grace's harmonies nudged themselves quite contentedly underneath and over Ry's vocals. Sometimes both kids hummed, as it became apparent the song was so new that neither had decided on all the lyrics yet. It was rusty. A few times they stopped playing and giggled instead, before starting right up again.

Anyways, Matt decided as he lifted a set of fingers to slide them through his stylish, tidy, side-swept hair, *it's not about the song. It's like Dan said. It's about the singers.*

He almost groaned.

It was easy to picture where this friendship was going to go, especially when the kids looked up at each other after they brought the simple tune to a satisfying, exceptionally pleasing finish, and lost themselves in each other's eyes. It took Dylan jumping off the back of his chair and hopping up and down in excitement before Emily-Grace looked away from Ry, likely surprised at the intensity of the affectionate feelings that passed over her. Matt wasn't sure Ry would have averted his eyes from her at all if Dylan hadn't thumped him on the forearm and begged him to play another song.

"It's beautiful," Matt croaked finally, the lump in his throat hard to swallow. "Really special, Emily-Grace." He glanced at Ry. "Nice job, Ry."

Ry's cheeks blazed red. Averting his eyes from Matt, he shyly picked at a tuning peg on the guitar. Emily-Grace wiped a loose strand of hair off of her cheek and started to twirl it in one finger.

Like mother, like daughter, Matt thought, his heart doing a little hop-jump thing. Jessie had twisted her hair like that since the day he first met her.

"Do you think Momma will like it?" All four kids stopped moving and looked hopefully at Matt. None of them cared what Dan thought. Matt was a God in their eyes and he definitely, without a doubt, ranked well above any normal human in their mother's eyes as well. His opinion mattered.

"She will." Matt buried himself in Emily-Grace's pale blue Jessie-eyes. He had to push an icy spear of fear down deep into the darkest recesses of his chest. *Don't change, Emily-Grace,* he breathed inwardly. *Do not take your music to the stage.* It was not lost on him that he didn't concern himself with the wishes and dreams of the boy he'd been hired to watch over these last few months. Always, always, always, Josh and Jessie (Wheeler) Sawyer and their children were Matt's first priority to keep safe, not that he'd always done the best at that sacred job. Still—always. The Sawyer children were, as far as their parents were concerned, never to be lured to the sometimes false charms of the spotlight. Ever. Over the years, Matt took extra caution to ensure the kids were protected from cameras and from prying eyes in general. But this music...

He looked over at Ry. The boy's cheeks were a soft, healthy pink. His eyes, pale mirrors of the calmest, most serene water, were glowing from within. Like the Sawyer kids, Ry was not immune to pain. As a toddler he'd lost a father to a tragic fire. After, Ry lived a quiet life with his grieving mother until the day Dallas met Ry and Cassie at a Prince Edward Island campground and took a chance on love. Ry dreamed of taking his music to the big stages. He worked hard at it. Tonight he had charmed a whole lotta folks who were still talking and tweeting about a young prodigy they saw on the world stage for the first time. Matt had a feeling Ry was setting his sights on bringing Emily-Grace to those big stages with him. Matt knew. He just knew. Because Matt knew love, and hell, what he was seeing in these kids' eyes might be puppy love right now, but there was a trust there that both needed in their crazy lives, and from this point on it could only grow.

Nodding politely at the kids, Matt managed one last smile in Emily-Grace's general direction, then pivoted slowly around, hoping against hope that Big Dan didn't hear his tired knee crack when he turned. Hoping against hope that Emily-Grace didn't see worry streak across his face.

He moved one shiny shoe in front of the other, able only to give Dan a cursory half-lift of his lips as he passed. Beckoned by happy laughter, he headed back towards the open doorway of Dallas' dressing room. Not that Matt would go into the room. No, he knew his place. He belonged on the line between the older generation and the new; a line marked by a hard wooden door frame and a digital sign next to the door that, tonight, relegated the luxurious space with its comfy white leather couches and sublime atmospheric lighting to Dallas White and friends.

From inside, Dallas watched Matt take up his usual post again. Something had changed in Matt's eyes. Raising a beer to his lips with one hand, with his free hand Dallas touched his wife's elegant fingertips. Cassie raised her eyes and followed her husband's curious gaze over to Matt. Sometimes the sadness in Matt's eyes was profound, and both Dallas and Cassie wondered what had brought it to the surface tonight.

Jessie, Dallas thought, watching Matt. *It's because Jessie is in the room. Jessie, with her pain and her scarred past and her cherished husband, Josh. Josh, who Dallas knew Matt respected and liked but who would always be Jessie's number one.*

Settling back against the door with a sigh, Matt refocused on his shoes. This time his body telegraphed exhaustion. The earlier joy had disappeared into a haze of remembrance and loss.

Helpless, Dallas looked away and tipped back his bottle for another drink.

Chapter Three

*I*t was well after midnight when the families started to gather up their children and say happy-sad goodbyes. Small children were folded tightly against warm, tired bodies, and older ones, grouchy now because the over-tired bug was also nipping at their droopy eyes, were corralled in the direction of the backstage exit.

Matt was watching the melancholy parting of Ry and Emily-Grace with concerned interest when the venue's stage manager approached with a brisk walk and called him aside. The forty-something woman, a crusty gal named Lydia, skipped over any small talk. She held a cellphone out in front of her black low-cut Rolling Stones T-shirt. Like a trophy, it hovered between her and the man who held all the cards when it came to gatekeeping the stars in their midst.

Matt knew the look. He'd been about to say, "We'll be out of your hair within the half hour," when Lydia's wide brown eyes stopped him short. Fear—there was fear inside those eyes, darting back and forth across their watery surfaces like a sea serpent.

"What?" he asked, his voice brusque and deep. It was a forgotten voice, one he buried long ago. Fear had entered Matt's life many times. It came and went in relentless waves like fire and left its unforgiving mark in the eyes of frightened children, in the nightmares of the woman he'd watched over for so long, and in his own broken, charred, somewhat healing heart.

This new nightmare predator, as yet unknown, was not welcome.

He took a backwards step.

"Is it Jessie?" he barked at the harried, thin woman in front of him. Everyone knew about Jessie's turbulent background. The lone stalker, first; then the man who would do anything for his wife, even try to find her a new family...

Matt sighed heavily. That was old news. What could this harrowing look in Lydia's eyes possibly mean to him, to them, to...her?

Lydia blinked back rare tears and, at the same time, shook her head. "No," she managed. "This doesn't concern Jessie." She was a tough cookie, she never crumbled, not at the cruelty of unfeeling audio or lighting techs or because of the heartless managers of stars who tossed out orders the way they handed out off-colour, sexist jokes.

Although sometimes the sad videos of abandoned animals that populated social media got to Lydia.

But this was different. Tonight Lydia had, like Matt and everyone else present, been on the inside track of something real special. Dallas White's last concert on this tour had, here at Rogers Arena in Vancouver, featured beloved guest stars Jessie Wheeler and Jacob Ryan, and Lydia had ridden high atop the thrilling crest of it all by stage managing the event. Shows like this were a breeze. These stars were the epitome of kindness—no egos got in the way. Not even the hangers-on were troublesome. The managers were terrific, and even the stars' kids were well-mannered and sweet.

And Josh Sawyer—oh Lordy, Josh Sawyer had ridden in on his Harley after a workday on a movie set on nearby Burnaby Mountain. Lydia herself had witnessed the man casually strolling in to greet his wife and kids, unzipping his classic red and white leather motorcycle jacket as he walked, a black half-helmet dangling from his strong fingers. Lydia saw his famous churlish grin lift the corners of his mouth the second his wife danced out of her dressing room to greet him with their youngest, Micah, too big to be in her arms, but there anyway. And the music—the onstage stuff? Hell, it was surreal. Guitar solos and ballads and up-country rock tunes galore! The music could have gone on forever. Nobody wanted to leave the arena, not even the crew. Three standing ovations and multiple bonus songs were the reward. Lydia was on such a high she almost forgot to call 'go to black' for the light technician at the end.

And Dallas White. Lordy, when he sauntered off the stage at the end to shake Matt's hand and then wandered over to his petite, elegant wife for a hug and a kiss, Lydia thought she would just have to melt then and there. She'd worked some pretty big shows back in the day when Dallas was romantically linked with his Georgia singing partner, Deborah, but never was joy apparent on the man's face in those days. Nope, not ever. Tonight Lydia saw the look of a contented man in every move Dallas made. Lydia'd watched him affectionately tousle the hair of Ry, the boy she'd heard he'd taken on as his own, before reaching over to take his young daughter from his wife's arms. Lydia'd had to force back a tear when Dallas, a beloved country star whose faltering career rocketed back to the top after he found true love, bent to leave a lingering kiss on his pretty blonde wife's head.

"You need to tell me what's up," Matt demanded, curling his hands into fists at his side, which worked to call the usually crusty stage manager back to him. "Lydia? Talk."

She couldn't. Lydia could not say the words that she knew would destroy the peace these people had found tonight in music and in each other. She'd come to the one man who, over the years, had proven his worth to all of them—to the stars, to their families, and to the crowds who came to the big shows in the hopes of leaving their own worries behind. She trusted that Matt Kelly would know what to do, would know how to handle this new darkness, but still, she couldn't bring herself to speak.

Instead, she flipped her phone around and held it out higher in front of Matt. A tear annoyed her by slipping past her guard and sliding down a cheek. Glistening in the lights of the bright hallway, it was followed by another in a tiny rivulet.

Nearby, Dan had Micah in his arms. The little boy was snoring contentedly against his shoulder. Concerned at the brisk interchange that had Lydia in tears and Matt on guard, Dan, his eyebrows raised in an arc, glanced at Jessie behind him before he faced Matt, whose stare was locked on Lydia's phone, eyes darkening and lips curling downwards.

"What?" Dan prodded, at the same time wishing with a vengeance that he didn't have to know, that he would never have to know. "Jessie?" he gulped. Always, their collective fears were based on Jessie. What might hurt Jessie, what might send her spiraling into bed for days, what might catapult Josh back into addictions, what might endanger the Sawyer children.

"It's not Jessie," Matt managed. A twinge of guilt that this new hurt wouldn't directly wound her ripped up his spine and landed in his throat so that his next words emerged gritty and low. "It's Dallas."

"Dallas?" Dan moved lithe, chestnut-haired Micah to his other shoulder and gave Lydia a questioning, sympathetic look as he asked. The usually composed stage manager was outright sob-choking when Matt handed her back her phone.

Matt reached for the words. They hurt like hell to say, even though in his bones he was screaming with gratitude that Jessie and Josh would remain for the most part unaffected despite the awful news that Matt would have to deliver to Dallas in just a moment's time. "His brother. He died."

"Dale? Dale's dead?" Dan whispered back to Matt while Lydia turned away. Too many folks in the hallway were starting to notice her raw emotional state.

Taking a deep breath, Matt looked over at Jessie, who started to tiptoe towards him. Years sharing each other's lives meant they could read each other. Words were almost not even necessary. The pain and accompanying guarded relief in Matt's usually gentle eyes were enough to raise alarm.

"Suicide," Lydia choke-whispered to Dan just before she walked away. "They're saying it was suicide. And it's all over the Internet. For God's sake please tell Dallas before he checks his phone."

Jessie touched Matt's elbow while Josh watched, his liquid brown eyes narrowing. She didn't speak.

"Get Dan to take your family home," Matt ordered simply. "Tell Josh to watch the puddles on that monster bike of his. The city's sopping wet tonight." Pushing past her, he stopped suddenly. Josh's eyes were on him, no doubt of that. Josh was always reading Matt and Jessie and their unspoken words, but all was well between the men these last few years. The connection Matt and Jessie shared was old stuff now, entrusted to the history books and to occasional cuddles when they found themselves overseas together, which was more and more rare these days while Jessie mostly stayed at home to focus on her family.

Turning back around, Matt slipped his fingers into Jessie's and pulled her close. "Beautiful," he whispered. "You, on stage tonight. Just beautiful, as always," he breathed as he let her go. After a few precious seconds more, her warmth melding into his, he started to back away.

She grabbed his arm. "You need to tell me, Matt. What is it?" Insistent, Jessie vice-gripped him, squeezing tightly and not letting go even when he tried to pry her away.

"Circle of life stuff," he told her finally, his eyes misting over at the grand, precious mystery of life and death and the finality Dallas would have no choice but to accept. Allowing a finger to touch Jessie's cheek, Matt smiled sadly. "It's Dallas this time, sweetheart," he murmured. "I need to tell him."

"Someone in his family?" A low bubble of pain started in Jessie's gut.

Matt leaned in and planted a soft kiss on her forehead. "His brother. Dallas' brother is gone."

"Aw, hell. Jesus, Matt. I'm so sorry."

"Me too, sweetheart."

She sighed heavily and let go of him. "You're that guy, Matt. You know— the one who has to pick everyone else up. All the time, it falls on you. The weight of it all, it always falls on you."

A small, sad smile wriggled its way forth. Matt crooked his head to one side. "I'm okay, Jessie. Don't worry about me."

"You big lug. I always worry about you." Taking hold of his shoulders, Jessie started to turn him around to face the others. Watching them, Dan sighed quietly, put a big hand on Micah's small back, and stole away. "I'm here for you, Matt," Jessie continued. "Call me if you need me. K? Now go be you. Go be there for Dallas."

"You bet. Nite, sweetheart."

"Nite, Matt." Folding her arms, Jessie frowned as Matt, shoulders hanging low, limped tiredly towards Dallas.

Passing Josh on the way, Matt spoke with a quiet reverence. "Get your family home, Josh. And watch the goddamn puddles on that big bike."

Swiveling at the waist to watch him go, Josh exhaled slowly before turning a confused eye back to Jessie.

"Let's get the kids," she said softly, approaching her husband. "We need to go home."

Josh slipped his hand in hers. Together, they headed over to a yawning

Dylan and a weary Emily-Grace and David, who were hovering around Charles and Deirdre. They all referred to the Keatings as the kids' grandparents, even though Charles and Dee (as they affectionately called Deirdre) played that role by virtue of history and not of genes. With Micah in his arms, Dan followed close by.

Dallas was just pulling his phone out of his pocket, while cradling his daughter in his other arm. He held the phone up to Matt. "It's always a thrill to see what the fans have to say after a show like that. The energy out there was off the charts tonight, eh Matt? Don't you think?"

Cassie was at her husband's side. Unlike Dallas, she'd had little to drink at the dressing room after-party. Her eyes widened. She was about to ask if everything was okay when Matt did a quick air-snatch and grabbed the phone right out of Dallas' hand.

"What the hell?" Dallas retreated by stepping back a foot, which jarred his sleeping daughter.

"Let Cassie take Jade," Matt insisted, reaching for the delicate child so he could hand her over to her mother.

"What? I stopped drinking after four brews," Dallas shot back, alarmed at the sorrow he discerned on his friend's face.

"S'not that. Give her to me."

Reluctantly, Dallas let Matt take Jade and ease her into her mother's arms.

Nearby, Ry watched with a growing nausea. Something was wrong—he could sense it. Matt was intimidating as hell at times, but Ry had never seen him take Jade from either parent, nor had he seen him shove Dallas forcibly into a room, as he was doing now.

Cassie followed the men, with a frightened look back to her son first. "Go to Jessie for now, Ry," she said. "Give us a few moments."

The door closed in Ry's face. Slowly, he teetered around and leaned against it. Emily-Grace was watching him. He shrugged, and hoped he looked less scared than he felt.

Shortly, the door opened and Matt came out, closing the door behind him. He stood next to Ry for a few seconds before he spoke. His eyes were moist. Nervous, unsure, he touched his nose a few times before he looked sideways and locked Ry in a steady gaze.

"Son," he said quietly. "Dallas will need a little time. He's just had some tough news."

Steeling up his shoulders, Ry prodded him. "What kind of news?"

Matt hesitated. "The kind that hurts, son. The loss of someone you love, kind."

"Who?" Ry gulped. "Who did Dallas lose?" Ry had grandparents on Dallas' side now that they were all a family. There was a ranch and animals and cousins and...

"His brother, Ry. Your Uncle Dale."

"Oh." Ry took that in. Uncle Dale was not someone he knew well. But Uncle Dale did have kids—two boys—and that was sad, because Ry was once a kid with no dad. And that plain sucked. The loneliness memory choked him, and he took a deep breath to make it go away.

He looked back up at Matt, who was watching him. "So I suppose we'll be going to Alberta instead of home, then."

"Yes, Ry. I'll be helping Phil get that sorted out tonight." Phil, Dallas' longtime manager, had left hours ago in a limo with a backup singer he was soft on. Matt would have to call him right away.

Shifting his weight, he contemplated the need for sleep and the impending absence of it. And then he considered something he hadn't thought of before, at exactly the same time Ry said it out loud.

"At least Alberta's close to, uh, B.C. Right?"

"Ah. Yes. Yes, Ry, it is." Matt glanced over at Jessie and allowed himself a small smile. He couldn't be with her the way he wanted to be, but at least this way maybe he could get Dallas' family settled in Alberta, help with the security for any funeral arrangements, and then jet back to Vancouver for a while, or visit Josh and Jessie at their ranch near Canmore, Alberta, if they went there as he'd heard them consider. It'd be a better option than Matt flying to Ontario to meet with Phil at his office to plan the next phase of Dallas' busy life, as had been the plan. Even a few extra days would be nice to have. Maybe Shanda, Matt's wife, could get some time off so they could be together.

Emily-Grace stole up alongside Ry. She took his fingers in hers. Matt raised his eyebrows. "Ry? Did I hear you say you might be going to Alberta?"

"We might." Ry tried to act tough. And awake. Both were hard this time of

20

night. He stared at his fingers, the ones now interlocked with Emily-Grace's. His spirit started to soar, which seemed entirely inappropriate, considering Dallas' bad news. "Dallas' brother died. He lives, uh, lived there."

"Oh. That's sad."

"Yeah."

"It's almost summer. We're going to our ranch soon. It's in Alberta. We need to fine-tune that song."

"We do," Ry agreed, giving Emily-Grace's fingers a squeeze. "We really do."

Suppressing a grin, Matt turned towards Jessie and nodded at the small intertwined fingers beside him. Apparently she had already noticed and was trying to suppress a giggle at a suddenly nervous Josh, who was unable to move over to the kids because Jessie had a vice-grip hold on him.

The door behind Ry, Emily-Grace, and Matt swung open. Dallas emerged, which instantly sobered everyone up. Cassie was at his side, one hand resting on his lower back.

"I called my dad," Dallas announced, sucking in a breath for courage. "There's a kid. A little kid. A boy. I think he's maybe four, according to some social worker?"

Ry straightened. Matt tensed.

Another breath. Dallas swiped lanky fingers under his nose and inhaled yet again. Adrenaline made his words almost run together. "Nobody knows a thing about this kid. He just got dropped off by that social worker about an hour ago, at my dad's new place, a touristy sort of ranch my dad bought not all that long ago. It's near Sundre. Nobody wants him, this kid. His mother dumped him on Dale, I guess, and Dale bailed."

Cassie closed her eyes.

Dallas deflated. "I mean, like, Dale really bailed. The ultimate all-time bail."

The hall went silent. Nobody spoke. The only sound was from Lydia, the stage manager, who was crying softly in the corner for the country singer she adored but whom she would never really know.

"I gotta get to Alberta," Dallas suddenly declared. "I gotta go see about this kid."

After a few quick seconds to digest the news about the boy and how his unexpected appearance might change things in Dallas' world, and therefore also in his own world, Matt spoke to Cassie. "Your ride's waiting outside."

With a nod, he signaled to the security gal with the frizzy hair, who was waiting to jump in and help. "It's time to go."

Chapter Four

"Your mother's late. She should have been home two hours ago."

Dallas barely heard his worried father. Seated on a worn floral couch in his parents' small bungalow with his father kitty corner to him in an unmatched overstuffed chair, he was focusing on an image peering out from a worn photograph clenched between his strong fingers. Staring at it, he announced, "I know her."

The snapshot in Dallas' hands was faded and creased. He ran a callused fingertip over the image, over the serene face of a young woman sitting casually next to a teen version of his brother Dale—Dale, handsome and tanned, brown hair a little too long over the ears, jean jacket open, plaid shirt peeking out. Alive. Vibrant. Just bursting with life, Dallas thought, although Dale was not smiling in the photo, and looked about as serious as Dallas ever saw him.

Dale's arm was slung overtop the woman in the photo; he was leaning into her, his eyes were locked on her. Her hair was pulled back in a long ponytail that set off dark eyes and an aquiline nose. Most striking of all was an eagle feather, hanging loosely on her right side, just in front of her ear. Although the photograph's colour had long lost its vibrancy, it was easy to make out that the long-ago woman staring up at Dallas had Indigenous blood. *Cree*, he thought, trying to pull up a vague memory of her from what seemed like a lifetime ago. Or from many lifetimes ago.

"Maria. I dated her until—" Dallas fell silent.

His father picked up the story that, for all intents and purposes, was aired for Matt's benefit but really meant for Dallas. "Until she decided hard muscles earned on the farm were the real deal. Not fake like the kind manufactured in a gym for the benefit of the girls at school."

Dallas cringed. "I didn't go to a gym back then. I lifted hay bales same as Dale did."

"Ten times slower. You were a skinny runt. Useless on a working ranch."

Hovering at the doorway, Matt straightened.

In the three days since Matt had accompanied Dallas, Cassie, Ry, and Jade to J.I. Outfitters in the mountains an hour from the small farming town of Sundre, Alberta, he'd learned a few things worth noting about Dallas' father. Initially the older man had reluctantly come forward, shaken Matt's hand, and introduced himself as Boone White, saying White like Whoo-ite. His overt reticence caught Matt off guard. Also, Boone spoke with such a gentle tone that when Matt remarked on it to Dallas, he was told *all cowboys out here speak that way*. Oddly though, Boone's quiet manner did nothing to hide the sometimes caustic comments he tried to roll over his son like stones.

It bothered Matt, the way Boone couched his aggression with an easy cowboy lilt. It was obviously getting to Dallas, too, who right now was making a point of avoiding Matt's stare.

The tension in the room was as thick as the layer of dust on the lid of a long-forgotten shoebox Dallas' mother had dug out of storage. Sitting still wasn't working for Dallas. He stood and laid Dale and Maria's photograph on top of a pile of pictures tumbling out of the thin cardboard box. "It's for the photo board," his mother whispered when Dallas found her going through the cherished, faded photos at three in the morning during his first full night at the rustic new-old ranch. "The one they always put up in the lobby at the wake."

The picture with Maria in it had not made the cut.

Pointing at the photo, Boone sliced the sudden quiet in two. "It's her boy that was dropped off here the evening we got word of Dale…that Dale…" He coughed back sudden emotion. Covering for it, but not fooling either of the two men in his company, he added, "The boy's the government's problem now."

A kindly distant neighbour dropping off apple pie had taken the child under her wing and driven him to the police station in Sundre late on the night he was dropped off to the grieving parents. In the neighbour's mind, neither Doris and Boone nor their daughter Dawn and her husband, Johnny, were in any state to care for a mystery child, especially one too traumatized to speak. The neighbour figured she was doing everyone a favour. It seemed the right thing to do, especially when Dale's brand new widow, Jenny, landed at the ranch with her two sons and had to promptly eyeball her newly dead husband's supposed love child.

Dallas went to the window, and looked out over a dusty, dry property spotted here and there with forsaken looking trees in need of a drink, and about a half-dozen moldy plastic white lawn chairs scattered haphazardly on the bank of a mostly dried-up riverbed. Three of the chairs were tipped forward. One lay on its side a good fifteen feet from the others, a dead branch caught up between its back rungs. A neglected fire pit sat in the middle. Its main feature was a rusty metal barrel re-purposed from a derelict clothes dryer, meant, Dallas thought absently, to help keep a tall stack of firewood burning.

"Is there a fire ban?" Dallas asked, hands on his hips, eyes locked on what he thought was a poor excuse for a campfire pit. His words emerged dusky and low as if he had no real care or concern if anyone actually answered. "If there isn't, there should be. It's dry as a bone out here."

His father, stooped and weary, dropped an arthritic hand on the arm of his overstuffed chair, a behemoth Dallas remembered from his childhood as his father's favourite. The right arm's best feature was a bald spot with tufts of stuffing showing through, thanks to some serious chewing by one of the family's dogs, Corky, one Sunday while the family was at church when Dallas was ten. Boone raised himself slowly. Watching from the doorway, Matt had to talk himself into not launching forwards to help the older man. That would have been frowned upon—even after just a few days, it was clear the only person Boone ever allowed to help him was his longtime wife, Dallas' mother, Doris.

"We want a fire, we'll have a fire," Boone answered roughly, his usually quiet voice the texture of sandpaper. "Don't matter what the government says." Grasping the shoebox lid with his left hand, he clamped his fingers onto it and shoved it on top of the photos. He stared at it long after Maria's much younger face disappeared from view.

25

"I don't get why she'd say it's Dale's kid if it's not." Dallas turned around and faced his father. The room was small and dark. Its only other window was blanketed against the day, which made it easier for late afternoon naps, Dallas figured, when the old man got tired and needed to close his eyes. Squinting in the dim light, Dallas added, "Dale wouldn't have turned a blind eye to his own kid."

"Who says he did?" Picking up the shoebox with both hands, Boone hovered next to a shelf filled with dog-eared books about the old west. Poking at a few of them, he made space for the shoebox and set it on top, so it teetered at an angle. Again, Matt had to restrain himself from vaulting forwards. He figured the last thing either of these men would want to do is get down on their hands and knees to pick up pictures of Dale from happier days. The day they could do that—together, at least—would be a long day coming, given the tense nature of the last few days.

It seemed the favoured son was the one who died. Not the wealthy star revered by country fans the world over.

Matt cleared his throat. An older model sedan was rumbling down the short, earth-packed driveway. Both men turned to look at him. He trained his eyes on Dallas. "It's your mother. I'll go see if she needs a hand with the groceries."

Doris had insisted on going into distant Sundre alone for the groceries, despite the overwhelming reams of food dropped off by neighbours near and far after word spread of Dale's passing. They'd be eating lasagna and apple pie for a year. Johnny'd had to sit on the deep freeze's lid to get it to close, and even then they had to put a tattered trunk on top of it to get it to stay shut.

Dallas acknowledged Matt's gesture with a quiet mumble before addressing his father. "So you think the boy is his."

"The social worker says so. Papers say so," Boone answered brusquely. "Your brother used every excuse under the sun to go into Calgary. If he wasn't actively involved in the boy's life, then I think he at least knew he existed. Maybe this woman thought she could get some money from him. From you, I mean, indirectly. Everyone's motivated by money, ain't they? Maybe that's why Dale did what he did. To get out of it. Cause he couldn't fight it anymore. Or to get out of feeling like he was less than you. Ranch work is hard. And our rinky-dinky little tourist operation don't always pay all the bills."

Outside the small living room, Matt stopped his trek to the door and twisted around to look behind him. Dallas was three-quarter on to Matt from this perspective, and there was no mistaking the lowering of his shoulders as he exhaled in one long breath. A garage full of sports cars, women sending panties through the mail, a beautiful wife, sweet son and daughter, a new album skyrocketing up the charts, sold out arenas—and here he was a high school kid again, one who, he'd once explained to Matt over expensive whiskey, was a facade at home. Who couldn't wait to escape the ranch he'd grown up on in Cochrane, just outside of Calgary. So he could be who he always felt he was meant to be—a songwriter. A singer. Someone who lived and breathed music.

Not someone living a life he didn't want.

Dallas' father still rejected Dallas' dreams and success, which was evident in the beat-up excuse for a ranch Boone was trying to build into a thriving tourism business without the aid of any of the money Dallas offered him over the years.

The property was dotted with five tiny wooden guest cabins and a spattering of older fifth-wheels and trailers. Horses milled about in a nearby corral. Last summer, the first summer the Whites owned the aging ranch, they ran three guided horseback trail rides a day, plus catered to weddings and family get-togethers, all for international or domestic travelers seeking 'old west adventures.'

The extended family had moved from the Cochrane area as a unit. Dale brought his wife and two kids along, and the brothers' younger sister, Dawn, also took up residence in the remote mountain setting with her boisterous husband Johnny and their three kids, all ten and under—Ruby, Cooper, and Colt, aged ten, seven, and five.

Boone had one last thing to say. Squaring his shoulders, he stared Dallas right in the eye. "Don't make sense to me. A hard working man like that, thinking he's less than a trained monkey the likes of you. Running to the city all the time in search of something better when he got a good life, a good family, right in front of him. Might be plain, but it's fine by the standards of most of us normal people."

"You're angry right now about Dale, Dad. I get that," Dallas said quietly, before leaving the room to follow Matt out to his mother's car. "I have to tell you, though, that all these years you've only been hurting yourself with your stupid pride, turning down my offers of help. Mom and Dale and Dawn suffered collateral damage. I could have helped all of you. I could have made things easier for all of you if you'd let me." Over his shoulder as he left, he added, "You get a pass for your shitty comments today. Today you get a pass. But you should know that tomorrow is a whole new day."

He left his father stooped over the shoebox of photos, leaning on the shelf for support. His free hand was on his hip and he was staring downwards, breathing heavily from the emotion of having to suddenly bury one son, while knowing he'd figuratively buried the other the very day Dallas first left home.

Chapter Five

*O*utside, Dallas had to stop and pace in a circle a few times before he gathered his wits enough to face his mother. He was trembling so hard he thought he might fall down or puke, and he didn't want his mother to see him do either. Nor did he want Cassie or Ry to see him lose his shit. Jade was too young, she wouldn't know the difference, but Cassie and Ry were quick studies of Dallas, and right now both were in sight down at the nearby riverbed, passing the time by picking out pretty rocks with Jade.

Matt summoned up his courage to speak to Dallas' mother. Already he could see that she was the determined sort who buried her pain in a hard day's work. In one quick movement she had opened the trunk and was pulling out bags of groceries. He took a deep breath. "How was the drive, Mrs. White? Sundre's a good hour away."

"Drive was just fine, Mr. Kelly. We saw a herd of wild horses just down the road from here, and there were three or four elk soaking up the sun near the river. Earned me the only bit of life I managed to squeak out of my little visitor the entire trip. And then it was nothing more than a twist of the head and a look of longing. Care to interpret?"

"Uh…we?" Matt was fairly certain Doris had gone into town alone. He knew another woman that always tackled her troubles with long drives—Jessie—but he pushed her from his mind when Doris dropped four heavy bags of groceries and a twelve-pack of double toilet tissue rolls at his feet, grabbed the remaining three bags for herself, and slammed the trunk shut.

Sidling past the back passenger door of her cranberry sedan, she expertly balanced her groceries on one arm and swung open the door with her free hand.

A small set of troubled dark eyes blinked out at Matt from the back seat. Not wholly surprised, Matt rocked back on a heel and studied the mystery child Doris White had retrieved from children's aid and brought back to her grieving household.

He was small for his age if he was actually four, Matt thought. Always Jessie's kids were the comparative factor for Matt, and this youngster was smaller than all of hers at four. Yet there was an intelligent, resigned aura about the boy, as if he was well aware that he had to take whatever life chose to fire his way, and that the good stuff was already long, long gone. His clothes were simple—just denim shorts appropriate for the hot summer day, topped by a Paw Patrol T-shirt, which made him seem even younger and more vulnerable in Matt's eyes, who couldn't imagine any of Jessie's children—or Dallas' two—ever being dumped on some stranger's doorstep before he or she was even old enough to understand what was happening.

The boy's name was Hunter, although rarely did anyone at this beat-up excuse for a ranch ever call him that. They mostly just referred to him as 'the child' or 'the boy.'

Hunter didn't budge. It unnerved Matt that he maintained eye contact. And it wasn't like he was pleading for help, no; instead, Hunter seemed to be taking Matt in and making assessments the same way Matt was doing with him. As if Hunter was the adult—the wiser of the two—in an old soul kind of way.

A voice broke into Matt's thoughts. In her brusque no-nonsense manner, Doris officially introduced the two of them. "Matt Kelly, meet Hunter. Or so we've been told his name is. Hunter, this is Mr. Kelly, to you. Mr. Kelly works with my second son, Dallas. Your uncle."

Spinning around on one work-booted foot, Doris walked a determined path to the steps of the rustic bungalow she shared with her husband, and disappeared inside.

Matt and Hunter stared at each other for a good many more seconds before Matt heard footsteps in the hot caked Alberta dirt behind him and was jarred to action.

"Uh, hey Dallas," Matt managed, taken aback at the way Hunter was bringing Jessie to mind again because of the way Hunter was silently studying him. Jessie had done the same thing all those years ago, at age twenty, when Matt was first hired to watch over her. They'd been standing in the hallway at La Casa, the grand yellow Spanish villa Charles and Deirdre owned, and she was studying Matt with an almost complete absence of emotion, as if nothing and nobody really mattered, anymore.

It had taken a long time for Jessie to come out of her shell, a shell that all of them instinctively knew was some kind of post-traumatic stress state. Yet the music she brought forth spoke for her. And for gazillions of others who became Jessie Wheeler fans the first time they heard her sing. And how did Jessie's walls finally break down? Little by little, in painful steps, and never fully until one day she met Josh in a garbage pile. It was only after meeting someone as traumatized and hurt as she that she finally let go—really let go—and allowed herself to fully bloom, to open up to friends and love and family.

So…Hunter. What would it take to help a frightened child open up? To love and to trust? Certainly not a family suddenly thrown into chaos at the loss of a beloved son. A slow nausea worked its way into Matt's belly. He was a keeper of children. He was a man responsible for keeping the children of celebrities safe. For keeping the celebrities themselves safe. Boone had moved his family out to the middle of nowhere, partially to try to keep curious onlookers at bay. Everyone wanted a piece of his son, Dallas White, especially a few years ago when Dallas broke up with his fiancée and married sweet and elegant Cassie Keough. Boone was done with those kinds of predators. J.I. Mountain, visible from a plateau on the mountain across the dusty road from the rustic outfitting company he bought, was always a favourite place to visit. You could only get there by following the Panther River on horseback. When the ranch came up for sale, Boone grabbed it with both hands. It wouldn't save the family from all of the curious gossip mongers, but by sheer distance alone it would at least mitigate the steady flow.

Now? Dale's sudden passing would raise a whole new curiosity about Dallas. A weird kind of messed-up sympathy. Bringing a mystery child with soulful, sad Hunter eyes into the mix—piercing, dark eyes with Cree blood in them—would only ramp up the gossip train more.

Good thing Matt was used to helping people. Good thing he'd had so many years with Jessie and Josh and their kids. Good thing his wife Shanda was busy doing her own thing these days. Good thing Matt had nothing else planned for the immediate future. Vacation, shmaycation. He was already running scenarios through his head, things that would need to be done in coordination with Phil and his team of word jockeys, otherwise known as publicists.

Funny thing was—Matt wasn't terribly concerned about Dallas or his family. The child peering up at him from behind a too-big seatbelt in an adult seat in a rambly old car had Jessie-eyes. Not in colour, but in sorrow. There were no tears, because Hunter's ran too deep to shed, just like Jessie's once did.

Matt had an odd feeling that the only person he would have to really watch over and protect, the way he once watched over Jessie and her family, was Hunter.

A lonely child left at the mercy of complete strangers.

A lonely child whose resolute expression re-focused beyond Matt, on the pale eyes of a country singer the world adored.

Matt turned to see Dallas standing just behind him. Dallas raised a thumb and finger to his lips and pinched lightly again and again in a kind of absent, curious wonder. "Hunter, is it?" he asked nobody in particular. Hunter's eyes were locked on his now and, Matt thought, were maybe widening just a little bit. Dallas and Dale had similar features, although Dallas wore his hair long, all the way to his shoulders, much to the disdain of his ranch-hardened father and church-going mother. Dallas had a ring tattoo around one bicep, too. *Devil's ink*, his father said at dinner yesterday. *Dale would never ink up his body.*

A long, low sigh escaped Dallas' lips. He dropped the nervous hand to his hip and glanced over at Matt. "I wonder if he's hungry. Do you think he's hungry?"

Matt studied Dallas. "Ask him, Dal," he said simply. "Just ask him."

"I would," Dallas replied, toeing the ground with his boot, "but I hear he doesn't talk."

"He talks," Matt grimaced. "Just not in words. You'll learn. And then one day he'll surprise you."

"Not me." Dallas shook his head. "I've got my hands full, Matt. Jade takes up most of the space in my family." He was pretty sure Matt growled when he said that, but his friend was the respectable sort who avoided conflict whenever possible, so to his credit Matt didn't offer any more rebuttal than the almost silent growl. If Dallas could have read Matt's mind, he would have heard him say, *if we all felt that way, who would care for our elders? Our forgotten people? Who would bring apples and blankets to the homeless amongst us? Or medicines to our sick and dying? If we all felt that way, we wouldn't have the music of Jessie Wheeler to rock us to sleep or to heal us when we are in pain.*

"I'll see that he gets fed," Matt conceded, inwardly trying not to fume. "Then he can bunk in with me tonight. There's an extra bed in my cabin."

"I'd appreciate that, Matt," Dallas managed. "I know Mom means well but it's gonna take her a while to get her head straight. I don't know what the hell she was thinking today, picking up a stray child and bringing him home. There's no way Jenny will have him around, I can guarantee you that. Even if she could get past herself and whatever the hell Dale did to bring this on their family, she's got her own grieving to do. And Dawn and Johnny already have three kids, I can't see them wanting to -"

"Jesus, Dallas," Matt cursed impatiently. "Shut it, will you? Hunter might not feel much like talking just yet, but the kid's got ears. Cool it."

A loud whinny from the corral beyond the car saved Dallas from more of Matt's harsh warning. In the car, Hunter perked right up.

Matt noticed. He gestured towards the small boy. "Either he's used to horses or he's never been around them before."

"If he's Dale's kid, he'll practically have been born on a horse. Dale goes to—uh, went to—horses the way I went to a guitar, growing up." The reminder sobered Dallas. "We had some things in common, but as brothers go we were oil and water a lot of the time."

"Horses not your thing? Hell, you're a country singer, Dal." Matt almost laughed, despite knowing that most country singers likely never ride a horse their entire lives. Sometimes it was fun to get Dallas going. Today was not one of those times, though, so Matt chilled and rolled up a sleeve of his fitted white button-down shirt, although he couldn't quite erase the grin on his face.

"Don't be an ass," Dallas chided him. "I rode me plenty of horses, growing up. I can't help it if I liked riding women better. There were some hot cheer-leaders at my high school."

"Dallas, what did I just tell you? Big ears, buddy." Finishing off his sleeve with a final tug to ensure it was secure, Matt reached into the car to loosen Hunter from the seatbelt. "First thing we need to do," he spoke directly to Hunter in a soothing voice, "is feed you. Second thing we need to do is get you some fresh clothes for tomorrow."

"She left a bag," a voice behind them said. It was Cassie, who hooked an arm through Dallas' elbow and smiled down at Hunter. "The social worker who left him here," she whispered to Dallas so Hunter wouldn't hear her. "She left a bag. Your mother must have grabbed it, it's likely in there somewhere."

It was. Matt fished it out from the floor of the seat next to Hunter. It was a homemade duffel made of plain denim cotton and decorated with hundreds of tiny coloured beads in a pattern that none of the adults recognized right away.

Ry came running, following his little sister, who Dallas swooped up in a big bear hug that had Jade laughing with delight. Braking with a skid on the loose dirt overtop the hard packed clay, Ry squinted at the bag. The pattern in the beads jumped out at him. "Cool horse," he said to Hunter, who Matt swore almost smiled with relief. "Really cool. You like horses? There're horses here. Want to go see them?"

Sliding down from the car, Hunter shyly took Ry's outstretched hand. Ry grinned up at his mother. "I think I found a new friend." He wandered away with Hunter at his side, talking quietly while Hunter kept pace and looked up at him with a sense of outright wonder.

Jade wriggled to get down from her father's arms. "Fwend, fwend!" she shouted. "I want to go wif my new fwend!"

Dazed, Dallas let her go. Cassie gave his arm a gentle squeeze and trotted off after the kids, calling, "Don't let Jade sneak into the corral, Ry! Keep an eye on her!"

Amused, Matt gave the car door a little push. It slammed shut with a loud *thwang*. Almost gleefully, he faced Dallas, who was staring after his family with undisguised surprise.

"He can't be Dale's son. My brother wouldn't have abandoned his own child. Dale was a good man, Matt. I wish I would have been around more, you know? Maybe if I'd been around I'd have seen this coming. I could have stopped him." He swiped a knuckled fist under his nose and sniffed.

Matt clapped him on the arm. "Nobody really sees this kind of thing coming, Dal. We think we can watch for signs, but we don't really know." Josh came to mind. Matt's own dark days wishing he could change a helluva lot of things in his own life, came to mind. "The kind of darkness that drives a person to suicide is the kind that buries a man so deep he can only see one way out. If Dale was anything like you, but was around your father a lot, I'm guessing he'd have buried the tough stuff pretty deep and would have kept his pain to himself."

"I don't think he would have talked to Jenny, either. She's a feisty thing in her own right. She and I never mixed well. Maybe she got angry at Dale for refusing any help from me money wise, you know? I could have splintered them right in two."

"Your success is not the reason for your family's troubles, Dallas. You worked hard for what you got. Your talent got you there and your hard work kept you there. The only thing worth dwelling on now is that little boy and what's best for him. Maybe we need to find his mother. Or maybe we need to give him a home."

Dallas was thoughtful for a moment as he took that in. "I don't see Boone and Doris getting past this, Matt. I don't see them coming out the other side of this thing."

"Your parents?" Matt asked. "They will always be a little bit broken, Dallas. I'm real sorry about that. I'm real sorry for you too, pal. I'm glad you have Cassie to help see you through this. But don't forget that your parents have each other. Doris has Boone, and Boone has Doris. They're tough old coots, your mom and dad. They'll find their way through."

"Farm folks," Dallas sighed, watching Ry lift Hunter up on the bottom rung of the split rail fence that housed the dozen horses J.I. Outfitters owned. "Farm folks are tough as nails. Too bad their offspring are not."

Reaching for the groceries at his feet, Matt handed two bags to Dallas, who set one down for a sec so he could poke a hole in one of the toilet tissue packages and hook a finger inside to make it easier to carry.

Once the groceries were delivered to Doris, the men started a slow walk over to the kids and Cassie. Dallas laid a hand on Matt's arm. "I'm pretty sure taking on this kid is not part of your job description, Matt. I'll settle him in with Ry for the night. He can sleep with us until we figure out what to do with him. I have a feeling he'll stick to Ry like glue, anyway. Ry's shy but he's a good kid. He'll take care of the little guy."

"I appreciate that, Dallas. Just keep in mind one thing. Someone hurting as bad as Hunter is now can't help but affect those around him. Let me be frank." Matt stopped walking and faced Dallas, who halted and twisted slightly around to meet Matt's troubled eyes. "Ry lost his biological father when he was a few years younger than Hunter. This'll connect the kids, but it may also bring back a lot of sad memories for Ry. Are you sure you're up for that? Ry's at an age when kids start to rebel."

"And I'm not his real father. I know. It's crossed my mind that Ry might act out, but he hasn't yet. I feel like we're good."

"And as for the concert the other night, and Ry's stage debut, he is now a media darling. Take my advice. Keep him off the stage for now. I've seen what it can do to kids. They grow up too fast, they lose their privacy, they don't make good judgment calls. They think they're infallible."

Dallas squinted at Matt and cocked his head. "You're not talking about the Sawyer kids. None of them have been on stage."

"I don't need to talk about the Sawyer kids. Not yet, anyway," Matt replied with an air of uncertainty. "At least not from the perspective of being stars in their own right. They've had their own troubles via their parents, as you know. No, there are lots of examples out there of kids who took the stage young and grew up far too fast. Ry has enough to deal with. Keep him off the stage as long as you can. Trust me."

Raising his hands, Dallas started to walk backwards. "You're preaching to the choir, Matt. The last night of the tour was special. There are no more immediate plans to let Ry sing publicly. And as far as Hunter goes, Cassie and I will make sure we dialogue with Ry about what's happening with him and about the implications of all of this."

"Let me know if I can help." Matt started walking again. Dallas waited until he caught up, and they approached the others together.

Dallas grinned. "Matt the psychologist. Thought you were my security."

After a loud *harrumph*, Matt managed a small chuckle. "I learned a very long time ago that they're one and the same."

"I figured. I take it to mean you're sticking around until we sort this out. I'm not paying you double just cuz you're doing two jobs."

"Three jobs. Triple." Matt held up three fingers. "Babysitter. Even Jessie would agree."

"Bullshit. We get sitters for the kids when we need them."

"Who said I'm talking about the kids?" This time, Matt grinned so widely that Dallas gave him a half-assed shove, which caught Matt off guard. He went tumbling towards the fence and almost landed on Hunter. As it was, Matt grabbed Hunter at the last minute to prevent him from toppling over too.

The little boy tensed at first, but then let himself lean into Matt, who held him carefully and helped him settle his small feet securely on the rail again.

Hunter pointed at a palomino horse he couldn't take his eyes off of. "Stawbuck," he said in a whisper so quiet that Matt almost didn't hear him.

Ry, however, was listening closely. He bounded up onto the rail next to Hunter. "That's right!" he cried. "That horse's name is Starbuck. Cooper told me! He was Uncle Dale's favourite horse."

A long silence took over the adults at the corral. Jade's was the only voice for a good few minutes. Her singing and humming seemed to calm Hunter even more. He laid more completely back against Matt and said the horse's name again, as if he was trying it on for size.

"Stawbuck." He added a short phrase. "My daddy's howse."

Dallas whistled, a low whistle that caught the horse's attention. The palomino raised its graceful head, gave a quiet whinny in salute to its solemn watchers, and seemed to bow in majestic courtship before it quietly moved away.

Chapter Six

*J*enny couldn't stem her curiosity. The homemade bag that came with Hunter was lying in plain sight, in the porch just off the kitchen. Stewing on it, Jenny started shooing everyone out of the door after a filling farm breakfast of fried eggs and bacon, and thick slices of buttered bread baked from scratch by Doris early this morning, or more like overnight, since Doris couldn't sleep and was up kneading dough by four.

With one eye on the bag, Jenny sent Doris for a nap with the promise that she herself would finish the dishes that Doris had half done anyway. It was worrisome that Dallas' mother wasn't sleeping, but seeing Hunter's bag dropped in a corner and left there to rot trumped Jenny's concern. Her curiosity about her husband's love child was getting the best of her. The ache for the privacy to go through Hunter's bag alone was a damnable itch she just had to scratch.

Last night, Boone had finally gotten up the manly courage to ask Jenny some tough stuff. She'd brought the boys over yesterday after supper so they could be around their grandparents and try to feel a little closer to their dad. While Shane and Cormac wandered the riverbed with Ry and with Dawn's ten year old, Ruby, Boone cornered Jenny, who was running a broom around the tiny kitchen just for something to do. She needed to keep her hands busy and her eyes on the floor.

Being forced to answer to her father-in-law about Dale's deception had been downright humiliating. Boone stood behind a chair, gripped the top rail, and point blank huffed out, "Did you know about this?"

Helluva thing to ask a brand new widow, Jenny fumed now, drying her hands on a checked dish towel and staring at Hunter's neglected bag in the corner, sprawled over the scuffed and scratched toes of a pair of Boone's old cowboy boots. Her answer to her husband's father last evening was short and to the point. *No, sir.* She hadn't looked up from the broom.

Jenny spotted Hunter's bag early this morning at the same time Matt did, when Matt came up from his claustrophobic cabin for breakfast. She noticed his eyes land on it, and then filter over to the child it belonged to. Hunter was wearing the same clothes this morning that he had on yesterday.

Unaware that Jenny was fuming close by, Dallas caught Matt staring and followed his narrowed gaze back to the porch. "Oh, so that's where it landed. We were looking for it." He touched Hunter's long, dark hair. "All right kid, after breakfast it's bath time and fresh rags for you." Hunter curled up into a ball on the chair he had to share with Ry, since there were only so many mismatched chairs in the White kitchen.

Now, dropping the dish towel next to the sink, Jenny tiptoed over to the homemade bag. Dallas' off the cuff concern about Hunter needing a bath had landed flat. Nobody seemed to be in a hurry to get the little fellow bathed and dressed. After breakfast, Dallas and Cassie had retreated to their small cabin without Hunter. It was taking the two of them to tend to their wild daughter, who was hauled from the table when she started screaming something about wanting a different kind of bread than the thick homemade slices slathered in fresh strawberry jam that everyone else craved.

When Matt left the table, he took Hunter by the hand. Hunter went along willingly.

Maybe Hunter senses that Matt is alone here too, Jenny considered. She peeked outside the kitchen window. Matt and Hunter were making their way to the corral. Ry, and Jenny's two boys, Shane and Cormac, were running on ahead.

Biting her lip, Jenny turned and faced the bag.

Nervous, she reached out a tentative hand so she could finger the fabric handle on Hunter's elaborately decorated duffel bag. Taking a deep breath and gritting her teeth, she scooped up the bag by hooking it under one finger, and held it aloft as if it stunk before dropping it on the newly wiped kitchen table. She stared at it for a while, studying the colourful beadwork horse before summoning up the courage to pull the zipper back. Jenny wasn't the first to go through the child's few things, but that was of no consequence to her. Dale was her husband. The boy was supposedly Dale's offspring. Discreetly going through his child's things barely figured at all in the realm of Jenny's social conscience; not when compared to the travesty—travesties—her husband committed. Not when held up against the realm of wrongs she felt he wrought against her and their two boys.

What mysteries lay inside Hunter's bag?

The usual little boy stuff, at first. Underneath assorted T-shirts and shorts, a denim jacket, jeans, and one long-sleeved western-style plaid shirt, Jenny's fingers landed on something soft to the touch. It felt like worn flannel. Grasping it, eyeballing it when she pulled it out into the light, caused Jenny's heart to do a little hop-jump thing. When she tried to breathe, she found that her throat was almost fully constricted.

Dangling from her fingers was a stuffed pony, sewed with some re-purposed soft caramel brown fabric. Homemade, Jenny figured, taking a closer look at the uneven stitches around the pony's hooves. She held it aloft at eye level. A wide set of frozen embroidered eyes and a tangled yellow yarn mane and tail wounded her. Resentment bubbled instantly to the surface. With a careless toss, she threw the stuffed pony to the side with barely a thought as to whether the small boy who'd landed in her midst missed it, needed it, or depended on it for comfort.

The spurned toy landed on the pale linoleum floor with its legs splayed out in all directions like an awkward, newborn foal.

"You're the ugly puppy nobody wants, kid," Jenny said to the bag, loud enough for only a spider in the corner to hear. "You want comfort? Ask your father for it, you little runt."

She was just reaching in again, her skin touching something that crinkled under her fingertips—like paper, she figured—when a tired voice from behind stopped her cold.

"He's Dale's son, Jenny." It was Doris, too anxious and worn out to get to sleep.

Caught off guard, Jenny whipped around and stood. "You look like death warmed over, Doris. I brought you some Melatonin. That'll set you right side up."

Doris had to literally focus on putting one foot in front of the other in order to make her way across the small space to her daughter-in-law. She used the chair backs to help support her and guide the way. "Jenny," she tried again, "that boy is your husband's son. He's my grandson."

Jenny was clutching the paper she'd felt at the bottom of Hunter's bag. She looked down at it, and wrinkled her eyebrows as if she were surprised to see it there.

Reaching out a tired arm, Doris took it from her, gently opening Jenny's fingers one by one in order to get a grip on the envelope held solidly in the younger woman's grasp. When Jenny finally let go, she paced the floor a few times, swiping at a cascade of loose strawberry-blonde hair as she moved. After three tries to get the annoying hair off of her cheek, she set her small frame staunchly in the middle of the floor and re-did her loose ponytail, which fell in a frizzy mess to her shoulder blades. Crossing her arms and rocking her weight over to one foot, she faced her husband's mother. "We've been married since forever, Doris. I think I'd know if Dale was having an affair."

Doris wriggled her index and middle finger into the envelope. She extricated a letter. "It says right here, Jenny, clear as day. That little half-Indian boy belongs to Dale. Boone says Dallas knew the mother too. When I shake the cobwebs from my old head and think way back, I kin recall some bitter words between my boys one summer, over her. It was back before Dallas left for Toronto. She was a right pretty lady. Maria, her name is. She hails from the Cree community. Was working at a service station when the boys were fighting over her."

Now the enemy had a name.

"Maria." Jenny let her tongue try it out; let her lips form a toxic ribbon around it. The name emerged strangled but soft, as if saying it made the woman who belonged to it real, and reality wasn't something Jenny much felt like dealing with these last few days. "He never talked about ever dating a Maria. Then again, Dale didn't talk about much."

"They must have picked up with each other again." Shuffling forward, Doris held the letter up in front of Jenny, open-faced at eye level so Jenny would either have to look away or read the offensive thing. It was an official form letter with letterhead from some government agency Jenny could barely make out for the tears bubbling in her eyes. "I guess Dale had the sense to get a paternity test done," Doris continued. "This letter says that Hunter is his. He's our blood, Jenny."

"Yours, maybe, but he sure as hell ain't mine." Spinning around, Jenny sidestepped the sprawling boots and shoes overflowing the porch. Shaking, she pushed open the door to the bungalow. The plain house faced the struggling river, which was over yonder past a spattering of uneven older campers, just beyond a few wasted, patchy stands of dried-up Jack Pine resilient enough to grow in the tough soil. In contrast, hovering in Jenny's peripheral vision were the half-dozen small wooden cabins Dale, Boone, and Johnny so carefully repaired over the last while, the ones Dallas and his family, and Matt, were staying in. These were hugged by tall, straight, lodgepole pine, which nestled around them in casual repose.

Turning her head to stare at the closest cabin, Jenny shuddered. Someone had draped a towel on an outdoor chair, over the wide arm of a low wooden Adirondack that Dale had painted blood red just over a week ago. It was bizarre to see—Jenny's husband's work was glaring her in the face like a big ole red stop sign. His touch was on everything around her, right down to the metal coat hooks he'd personally screwed into the outside wall of every single cabin.

Doris followed Jenny outside. Stopping at the top of the steps, she stood above Jenny, who crouched over and tried not to puke as the world around her spun and swirled. Unseen, children's voices drifted up from the riverbed in hollow, ghostlike echoes. To the right, a horse whinnied, and another answered eerily back.

"Jenny, we got two choices here," Doris determined with an air of righteous certainty. "Either we find this boy's mama to see what's up and maybe get him back to her, or one of us households takes him in."

"You can't be serious, Doris." Shoving aside the gooseberry bushes behind the rail by the bottom step, Jenny leaned over and retched. When she was done, she waded out of the bushes in two furious steps, stopped, planted her feet in the sparse, heat-bowed grass, and stood proudly with her shoulders back as far as she dared, given the whirly, sick state of her gut. Unconcerned about the new jags of light blood with which the bushes' sharp branches had marked the skin on her pale face, she started in on her mother-in-law. "My husband routs a vacuum into his truck that puts him to sleep forever, leaving me with a ton of debt and an eight and twelve year old to raise alone, and you're seriously thinking of taking his love child in?"

On the top step above her, Doris' eyes darkened. She raised a stubborn chin. Only the tremor in her right hand gave her fear away. Jenny noticed it when Doris lifted the hand to grip the rail and tighten her fingers around it, needing it for balance and to root her to the quickly spinning earth.

Doris pressed her lips into a firm line and waited for Jenny to go on. Her tough veneer didn't slow her grieving daughter-in-law down one bit.

"What kind of life would that boy have with us? With me and my anger?" Jenny stuck a pointy finger in her chest and jabbed until it hurt. The fierce gesture seemed to poke a hole in her resolve. Curling her shoulders forward, almost shrinking into the tough grass, she begged her mother-in-law to understand. Changing her weight to her left foot, she choked, "I might not be the warm and fuzzy sort, Doris, but I'm a good person. I'm a hard worker. Me and Dale have been working our arses off to help make this rundown excuse for a dude ranch profitable. I was counting on him! Countin' on him to pick up your husband's slack. Boone ain't getting any younger, you know. He snores up a storm in late afternoon while Dale's out hanging signs and hammerin' in all the tired, stuck-out nails around these rundown shacks. He repaired the fences. He takes—took, goddamnit—load after load of cowboy wannabes on horseback up one side of the mountain and down the other. Face it, with everything there is to do around here, you and your man are too old to raise a child as young as that bastard kid, and I don't want to."

Doris didn't miss a beat. "Dawn and Johnny will help. You don't give them enough credit."

Jenny harrumphed loudly, pulled at her frizzy ponytail, and sob-talked her way through that false promise. "Ruby's slow, you and I both know it. She's gonna need a lotta help to get through school, and Cooper and Colt are so busy learning rodeo in summer and playing hockey in winter that Johnny can already barely keep up with the travel, much less filling the truck up with feed and hauling straw. Dawn is your daughter and I love her, but she don't know the space bar from the letter L on the computer, and she can't cook a pork chop without it coming out harder than a slab of concrete. Slathering burnt chops with cans of cream of mushroom soup don't fool nobody but the real cowboys, so although I know you mean well, you ain't thought it through, Doris. What'll happen is that the boy's care will come to me, because I'm the capable one, I've always been the capable one, and all I'll see when I look at him is my failure to keep my husband happy, and all I'll feel is hot pain tearing up my gut. I don't want that boy around here, Doris. I don't want to see him, because if he's in my line of sight I can't be held responsible for what I'll do."

She stomped a foot and bent over double again, speaking from half upside down so that Doris had to creep down the steps and sidle in closer in order to hear. "Doris, I got nothing against a little boy whose got no real cause to hurt anyone. What I got something against is what got him to us in the first place. And what I want to see is that child in my rearview mirror." Forcing her body as upright as she could, Jenny leaned on her thighs, inhaled slowly, and added, "What you ought to do is give the kid back to child protective services and make high and mighty Dallas step up and take on some of this failed excuse for a tourist operation. Sit him down and talk it out now, because you know Dale's brother. Dallas is always ready to run. He'll have that society wife and that vixen of a little girl of his on his private jet before Dale's body cools. I hope he leaves Ry," she said almost as an afterthought. "I like that kid. He gives Shane and Cormac an outlet to air their grief. I wish Ry could stay." The adrenaline was fading, weaving its way to a thin and bitter end. One last pronouncement put a final exclamation mark on Jenny's angry morning rant. "Your country music royalty will be gone before Sunday. You'll see."

Limping past Doris, Jenny pooled what was left of her strength and took the steps to the bungalow two at a time, heaving her small, lean body up with the rail's help. "Now if you don't mind, someone's got to clean the bathrooms and put a menu together. I'll be taking some of those lasagnas out of the freezer. Did you remember to get romaine lettuce for Caesar salad yesterday? I wonder if Dallas' little woman has ever done her own laundry."

"Cassie's just like us, Jenny," Doris snapped at her daughter-in-law's back. "She was raising Ry on her own when she and Dallas met."

"Well, ain't that somethin.'" Jenny stopped at the top step and swung around at the waist to look below her. "I wonder if her memory is short, or long." A final snort, and she disappeared inside to root around for cleaning rags, the bounce of her frizzy ponytail the last thing Doris saw before the door slammed.

Chapter Seven

"This can't be happening." Wheezing from the effort to stay calm and steady, Doris turned her heavy body around and eased herself down on the bottom step. She could see Boone moving slowly over by the barn. It worried her to see him moving in a way that made it seem like every step hurt. He was stooped over a set of rounded shoulders; that much was evident even from a distance. He stopped by the corral fence. The way his head was raised, Doris could see that he was watching something or somebody. Sure enough, when she craned her neck she could make out Matt in the corral. Dallas was just approaching. Matt had a hold of the palomino's halter. Doris saw Dallas stride over and lift Hunter down from the horse's bare back. Shane and Cormac were lounging a few feet away, laughing at something Ry apparently said, which irked Doris because she felt they should all stay as sad as she and Boone.

Maybe forever.

The three older boys took off running towards the riverbed. Ry braked and looked behind him, hollered something at Hunter, and waited while Hunter pedaled his small legs into gear and caught up. Doris watched Ry give Hunter a hand when they got to the bank. The two boys slid down its craggy side together.

Forcing herself back up, Doris trundled off to greet her remaining son and Matt at the corral. She was just about to lean on the top rail of the fence when Boone moved into sight again. She saw him retreat back into the barn, his arms full of some practically antique cracked leather tack in need of repair.

Inside the corral on the opposite side of the fence, Dallas stopped near his mom and rested his forearms on the rail, elbows out to the sides. Matt, hovering close by, struck what he hoped looked like a casual pose by raising a foot up on a bale of straw and resting his arms on his bent thigh.

Dallas opened the conversation with a surprised reverence. "That little guy's pretty attached to Dale's horse."

"Maybe he saw a picture of it?" Matt speculated, leaning down to graze a finger over the bale so he could grab a sprig of straw to chew on. In the distance, the older boys' giddy laughter floated up over the bank. Matt cocked his head to listen for the sound of a small child laughing along with them, but it never came. He turned his attention to Doris, to try to get a read on how she was doing. A covert sideways glance seemed most appropriate. He stuck the straw between his lips and listened to what she had to say.

"I expect Dale brought his love child out here when your father and I were at church," she stated matter-of-factly directly to Dallas. "It's the only time we were guaranteed not to be here." Weariness and a hangover from the heavy emotion Jenny's words brought on were starting her body down a whole new strange path. It was troubling—Doris was trembling. It was the strangest feeling, like she was made of jelly on the inside, like her knees were about to let go.

She gripped the rail a little tighter and hoped the fellas wouldn't notice. Pity and tender care were not on Doris' agenda unless they were initiated by her and aimed elsewhere. "Maybe he brought the Indian woman out here too, for all I know," she added. "Jenny always brought her young fellas to church with us. She never missed a Sunday, unlike my incorrigible son. Dale missed every Sunday. I expect you miss your share of services too, Dallas. Where did your father and I go wrong? Where does that leave Dale now?" She pushed away a renewed need to weep. That kind of emotional outpouring was reserved for the privacy of her bedroom.

"Indigenous, Mom," Dallas chided gently. "We say Indigenous these days."

"She looks Indian to me. And so does her son. How are we supposed to take him to church with us? The community will talk."

"They're already talking, Mom. They were talking the second Dale got pulled out of his truck."

Clenching her teeth, Doris leaned into the fence. A mahogany bay horse

47

was leisurely munching on a tuft of grass not far in front of her. She gave it a long, unsteady stare.

Matt sent Dallas a warning look. It was evident by the teetering in Doris' posture that she was beyond exhausted.

Dallas muttered an apology in his mother's general direction.

Rustling up some courage, Matt started them down what he hoped was a new, safer road. "Did I hear a helicopter take off from the ranch next door?"

"You did," Doris answered wearily. "The owner flies into Calgary for work plus he uses it to take tourists on private alpine outings. Romantic champagne lunches and the sort. Hired hands do the ranch's daily heavy lifting. We're the poor kids on the block, or haven't you noticed?"

A quick, nervous thrum started in Dallas' ears. "Mom, I could buy Dad ten helicopters. The stubborn old coot has no interest in anything I have to say or offer."

She cut him off with an annoyed air palm to the face. "Your father believes in a hard day's work. In his mind, fancy-pantsying around a stage in tight jeans is not a respectable way to make a living. I'm surprised you were able to father a child in jeans that tight."

Incredulous, Dallas wondered if he should bother trying to fight back. Close by, Matt pulled the straw out from between his lips and rubbed a finger thoughtfully over his chin. Dallas toed a hole in the ground and said weakly. "You're gonna need some help around here, Mom. Let me hire you some help. Why don't you ever ask for help?"

For the first time since she approached the guys, Doris looked Dallas straight in the eye. "Help." She threw her arms out to the sides. "Stay. Help."

Dallas maintained her eagle-eyed stare until he got so uncomfortable he had to look away and appeal to Matt.

Matt sighed and gave himself an easy push away from the bale. "I'm going to take a walk and then head into Sundre to try to get on the Internet." He paused before leaving Dallas to deal with his mother. "Mrs. White, Cassie said Ry told her some of J.I.'s campers were asking questions about Hunter, and about how long Dallas is staying here. I want you to know that Phil and I will be discussing the need to post more security out here, a few regulars, especially by the office near the road, at least for the interim."

"Pshaw." Doris waved an arm in the air. "We moved out here to the boonies to eliminate the need for such foolishness. Besides," she maintained, "Jenny figures Dallas will be gone by the weekend." Pointing her nose up in the air, she challenged Dallas. "Is that right, son?"

It hurt Matt to see the question posed that way, in a confrontational tone, from a mother who'd just lost a son. It hurt to see sorrow land in Dallas' pale eyes and settle there like lily pads on water, moist and helpless. He tried to fill in the blankness threatening to swallow them up. "Hey Dal, why don't we plan to go for a ride when I get back? Your father would probably like to get out on the trail."

"Oh, Dallas don't ride," Doris jumped in. "He never tell you that? Despite what he wants all his women to believe, he's a big city boy now. Even in the old days, he rarely rode. It was Dale who did the rodeo circuit. Dale was the one who went out on the trail with Boone, not Dallas."

"I went too, Mom. I went out a lot. Too."

"Despite your fear. Yes, I remember that, Dallas. You sucked it up pretty good back then but you never fooled your father. You know that, right?"

Dallas recoiled. "I was never trying to fool him. That was never my intention." A sideways look to Matt preceded an explanation. "I got kicked when I was a kid. Horses and me have had a precarious relationship ever since."

"Dale was a rodeo champ," Doris said to Matt with a proud toss of her head. "He's got real buckles to prove it, not just fake ones handed out at music awards shows."

"Dale never got kicked, Mom."

"Sure he did. He just never whined about it. He got right back up in the saddle and carried on."

"Did he. Carried on."

"Jesus, Dal," Matt groaned. "Come with me to Sundre. You need a break."

"He gets lots of breaks," Doris tossed in airily. "Dallas has had all the breaks."

"And to think I missed your Sunday pie, Mom. What the hell was I thinking?" Shoving himself away from the rail, Dallas bent and tucked his lanky body through it. "Jesus Christ," he muttered when his mother was out of earshot. "I'm gonna fucking kill Dale for putting me through this. Oh hell, wait. I can't. My stupid brother's already gone and died. The ass."

"Take it easy, Dallas," Matt cautioned. "There's been a lot of distance between all of you over the last few decades. You can't expect to just pick up where you left off, especially in these circumstances. This kind of sorrow brings out the worst in people."

"Pick up where we left off? Hell, Matt, that's exactly what we're doing. To them I'm still the skinny kid who hung on his brother's every word, who followed his every footstep. I was so damn in awe of Dale that I forced myself to go on those rides, to groom the horses and muck out the stalls." He tapped Matt's bicep to get his undivided attention. "Back in Cochrane our summer jobs were taking tourists on trail rides. You think I wanted anything to do with that? Do you know how many times I almost shit my pants because there was bear or cougar shit on the trail? That kind of stuff didn't even phase Dale. There was a reason he never let anyone see him sweat. It was because he didn't sweat! Fear was not a word in his vocabulary."

"Fear's in everyone's vocabulary, Dallas. Everyone's just got a different way of showing it, that's all."

Dallas shrugged off Matt's attempt to even things out. "As far as Maria goes," he said instead of rebutting, "she got the better White brother. It killed me when she chose Dale over me, but I always understood why. They were good together."

"Why'd they split up?" The guys were at Matt's cabin door now, facing out over the sloping riverbank, which was visible across the small clearing. From this vantage point they could see shallow water rushing over jagged and polished stones like mist over diamonds. The boys were having a grand time, splashing and playing with some of the kids from the campground side of J.I.'s tourist operation.

Before he answered Matt, Dallas gave a holler in the boys' direction. "Cougars and bears live around here, Ry! Do not, I repeat DO NOT go wandering. Stay close by. And keep your eyes open." He turned to his friend. "Dale and Maria split up because our dad could not tolerate Dale dating a Cree woman. Dad grew up in a strict Christian family. He knew kids who got hauled off to residential schools. He witnessed the results, saw the pain of being a kid from the res first hand. It wasn't pretty. Misplaced pride notwithstanding, I suppose our dad did not want to see Dale dragged into something that maybe he wasn't prepared to deal with. Love can do that to a guy. Rose coloured glasses and all that, you know."

"You're preaching to the choir, Dallas." Matt chuckled and reached for his cabin's doorknob. "Should we give Cassie the option to come along? Is there any good coffee in Sundre?"

Dallas grinned. "Is there any good coffee in Alberta? I'll ask her. I can't see her wanting to stay here, that's for sure. Everyone's too preoccupied to give my wife the time of day."

"You won't have to look far to find her." Matt pointed to one of the rustic public washrooms they all had to use, that were meant for the cabins' paying guests at better times. The opening and closing of the door had garnered his attention. Bucket in hand, Cassie was stepping lightly over the hard ground towards a second washroom, her sleek blonde ponytail bouncing as she walked. In a breezy, carefree kind of way, she wiped her free hand down over the floral print of her sundress, and smiled down at Jade tripping along beside her. From where Matt and Dallas were standing, it looked like Dallas' two girls were singing.

"Huh," Dallas muttered, dropping his hands to his hips in curious wonder. Jenny was watching from the top step of the bungalow with undisguised, open-mouthed astonishment. Dallas gave her a boisterous wave. To Matt, he said, "Someone's peeing her panties right about now. They all probably think we don't even wipe our own butts."

"Dallas, let's be honest. If you wanted a Starbucks, you and me both know you'd have one driven in."

"Ouch, Matt. I'm not that shallow. It'd be lukewarm, anyway, by the time it got here."

With a laugh, Matt went inside to hunt down his toothbrush.

Dallas, in the meantime, started to hum, and wandered over to his wife and daughter for a chat.

Chapter Eight

*W*ith Hunter buckled into Jade's rented child seat in the back, Matt and Dallas pulled out of J.I. just as Dawn and Johnny were driving in with their three kids. Ruby and Cooper spilled out of the back seat of the truck before Johnny even had it in park, leaving five-year-old Colt alone, hollering to be let out of his car seat. Johnny's window was down, so Matt and Dallas got an earful when Dallas lowered his window to call out a greeting as they passed by.

"Give that kid a microphone," Matt said with a wry half-grin. "He's got a set of lungs on him. Were you like that as a kid?"

"I was the quiet, soulful type," Dallas replied, leaning back and crossing an ankle over a knee. "I hardly ever whined or complained. Dale and I left the tantrums up to Dawn, which maybe explains her kid." He pointed out his parents, who were making their way over to Johnny's big truck. His playful tone went down three notches. "They've aged twenty years this week," he lamented, watching Boone and Doris on their slow walk.

Ruby bounced over to Doris and took hold of her wrinkled fingers, which brought a sad but welcome smile to Doris' lips. Dallas' mother rubbed her ten-year-old granddaughter's hand between both of hers in warm welcome.

"They'll be okay," Matt said firmly. "They'll have enough to occupy their minds today to get through another day."

Dallas grunted in quiet agreement, and settled in for the drive.

An hour later, the guys found themselves in Sundre, stationed in a quiet local cafe with reasonable enough Internet for Matt to get his work done. Nobody bothered them except to lower their eyes with respect and offer mumbled condolences to Dallas. The only surprises on the trip were leaving Cassie back at J.I. (*They'll like me better when I bake them up some lemon jelly roll*, she'd stated) and having to bring Hunter with them (*Likely for the best*, Matt had said while Dallas remained silent on the matter. *Cassie has her hands full with Jade, and as great as Ry is, I don't think leaving a twelve year old with a traumatized child for an extended period of time is in anyone's best interests*).

Hunter was the polar opposite of Dawn and Johnny's youngest—no tantrums for him. The only challenge he presented was falling asleep in Matt's arms while Matt was trying to work on the computer.

Dallas sat across from them and unwound soft, doughy bites from a cinnamon roll. At one point, he prodded Matt's wrist with what was left of the treat. "Didn't you say that you and Shanda once considered having kids? A few years back, just after you got married?"

Without looking up from the screen, Matt shrugged. "We talked about it. It fizzled out somewhere between her becoming a major star and me helping raise someone else's kids. Then I got old. I'm no spring chicken, Dal. Kids are a lot of work, or haven't you noticed?"

"Oh, I've noticed," Dallas chuckled. "Ry's a breeze. Jade's a monster. I don't know how Dawn does it with three."

Matt was sending emails to some of his more trusted security. He clicked on *send,* sat back, cuddled the little fellow in his arms, and looked up. "For a time, Shanda and me actually thought about adopting an Indigenous child."

Dallas got quiet. He chewed before he swallowed and finally spoke. "Maybe this is your chance."

Thoughtfully, Matt rifled fingers through his hair before leaning forward to close the lid of his laptop. He stroked Hunter's long, dark hair. "He's a beautiful child, Dallas. Easy-tempered, it would seem. Just sad. Lost."

"He must miss his mother." It was almost a whisper. "And his dad too. If he ever really knew Dale, that is. I wonder if he'll be able to tell us some day."

"He will. Some day." Matt hesitated. "Dallas, you've got the means to raise this child. He's your brother's son."

"Yeah, Matt. I've got the means. I'm just not 'all-that-and-a-bag-of-nails,' you know?"

Puzzled, Matt cocked an ear.

"I mean," Dallas continued, "I may not be the best man to raise a mixed-up kid like Hunter." Leaning back, he tried to look nonchalant by stretching his legs under the table and crossing his feet at the ankles. The tips of his ears got hot, suddenly, and he was pretty sure his cheeks were reddening. It sucked to have to admit what he thought was his major weakness. *Matt's a trusted friend,* he thought. *He's an understanding guy.* He dove in further. "Ry was half raised when I got him," he conceded, nervously tapping his fingers on the table. "Even now I don't step in with parenting duties, not that he ever really needs much guidance. He and I just play guitar. He's an easy kid to raise. And Jade? She's Cassie's shadow. I just smile when she brings me her drawings, you know?" Staring down at his fingers, he hesitated. "I don't know that I could do Dale justice by trying to raise his kid. And it wouldn't be fair to Cassie to dump a troubled kid on her. I'm away a lot, how fair would it be to leave her on her own with three kids? You know?"

"You want to know what I think, buddy?"

"No," Dallas frowned. He unwound another strip of dough off the cinnamon roll and popped it between his lips. "But I have a feeling you're going to tell me anyway."

"I think you need to remind yourself that you are no longer a boy," Matt started, putting on the wise counselling hat that the people around him all depended on. "Your parents still think you're fifteen. Or younger. What they've been saying to you since we got here is swayed by grief. And there's no better formula than grief and anger to fuel a lot of things said out loud that normally would never see the light of day. Trust me. This I know." Without looking away from Dallas, Matt tipped the last of his tea to his lips. Dallas finally looked up and met his trusted gaze. "Remind yourself of who you are today, Dal," Matt tried gently. "Don't let your mother's and father's old time versions of who you used to be tell you what you are capable of now."

"I'm not gonna put my tail between my legs and run away, if that's what you think, Matt. They won't let me throw money at them, so I guess I better stick around for a bit and help out in other ways."

"Are you talking about helping out around the ranch?"

"Someone's got to fill Dale's muddy boots." His stomach wrenched. *As if.*

Matt let the angst that slipped through the cracks in Dallas' face slide. This was not the time to analyze old sibling worship. "You hate farm work."

The reminder sunk in. Dallas winced.

"Mucking stalls is not your thing," Matt added. "There's no worse damage to a man's spirit than the damage done by daily work that makes him bitter."

"This is my family, Matt. I'll do what I need to do to try to leave them better off than when I found them." The last of the roll—the moist, inner, luscious cinnamon bit—got picked up and shoved into his mouth. He chewed thoughtfully.

Matt filled the silence. "This little boy in my arms is your family too, Dallas. Just do the right thing by him too, okay?"

"He likes you better than me."

"Jessie's kids got me trained. They made me soft. Little kids recognize that, they see behind the armour. Now it's your turn." Surprising Dallas, Matt half-stood and rolled Hunter over into his arms. "Little boys are not much different from little girls, Dallas. And your daughter adores you."

"Tricky bastard."

"Easy," Matt warned. "Would you swear around your daughter?"

"He's sleeping! He can't hear me!"

"Shhhh! Would you raise your voice around your sleeping daughter?"

Rolling his eyes, Dallas growled at his friend. "You can be bossy. You know that?"

"It's my job. Be grateful."

Giving Matt a half-assed warning look that came with a hint of a smile, Dallas adjusted Hunter in his arms. Sobering, he tried to see Dale's features in the child, in the shape of Hunter's eyes or in the way he curled his fists in sleep.

Matt opened his laptop and went back to work.

Later, emails sent and work finished, Matt was opening the door to the rented SUV so Dallas could place Hunter in Jade's rented child seat, when Dallas paused.

"I think we should try to find Maria," he suggested. "I think finding her would be the best answer for everyone. If she'll take Hunter back, I can support him. Them."

"Jesus, Dallas." Leaning on the open door, Matt crushed the idea at the outset. "Are you talking about money? That's not always the answer. It's just an easy out. You know this. Besides, to my knowledge Maria hasn't asked for money. Which means…"

He stopped to ponder what it meant, to let the thought travel him down a new path.

"Which means?" Leaning into the car, Dallas placed Hunter carefully in the child seat. Reaching out a hand, he touched his brother's boy's baby soft cheek.

Hunter groaned, and his lips curled sorrowfully downwards, which almost brought both men to their knees.

"Which quite obviously means," Matt replied, forcibly looking up from Hunter as his heart twisted with grief for the child, "that she has another motive."

"I see." Dallas didn't move. Instead, for a full two minutes he watched Matt turn circles on the hot Sundre sidewalk, a thumb and finger rubbing his chin and bottom lip while Matt considered what Maria's motive might be.

Eventually Matt double-checked Hunter's harness, gave Dallas a curt nod, and slid in behind the steering wheel. After hesitating to give Hunter a long look, Dallas ducked into the passenger seat.

The drive home was silent until Dallas couldn't stand being alone with his thoughts. He flicked on the radio and proceeded to drive Matt nuts with a version of radio tag, pushing buttons and changing stations almost constantly. When his own songs filled the silence, the music changes were accented by harsh grunts.

About a half hour from J.I., Matt was ready to give Dallas a solid punch in the arm the next time he reached out to change the song, when Hunter let out a sudden piercing scream. The shrill cry instantly deteriorated into a series of agonizing, heartrending wails.

"Jesus!" Dallas cried out when the first howl startled Matt into almost skidding off the side of the road, which threw Dallas up against the door. Gripping the passenger side's high oh-my-Jesus handle, Dallas tensed his body and braced his other arm against the dashboard while Matt wrestled the large vehicle to a crooked stop on the dirt road. "What the hell?!" Dallas hollered, swallowing back the urge to close his eyes and count to ten while his heart resumed its normal pace.

He twisted around to eyeball the upset child in the back seat.

Grim, Matt shouldered open his door and jumped out from behind the wheel. He hauled open the rear door. Dallas sucked in a few steadying breaths and followed more slowly.

Frowning, the guys stared in at their distressed young passenger.

"I think he's still asleep," Dallas volunteered, somewhat astonished. Hunter was wailing full-on now, but his eyes were closed.

"I expect it's a night terror." Bending at the waist, Matt reached in and carefully undid the safety seat's harness. "Emily-Grace used to have these a lot when she was younger. Hunter won't remember anything about it when he wakes up. Whoa there, little guy!"

Hunter was writhing in the seat. Dallas had to help steady him so Matt could get a solid grip to remove the boy from the vehicle. It took another few minutes of Matt adjusting the small body in his arms and speaking peacefully before Hunter calmed down enough to settle down. Gently, Matt rocked him and pressed him close to his body, all the while keeping a steady pace back and forth next to the SUV. It was a good few minutes before Hunter allowed Matt to guide his flushed cheek to Matt's strong shoulder. The small eyes remained closed the entire time.

"You're good at this," Dallas said honestly, respect and pride creeping into his voice. Arms and ankles crossed, he was leaning casually back against the vehicle, watching closely. "Dale would be proud."

"Ha. Nice try, Dal. I know what you're getting at. Shanda and I are rarely in the same household. As much as we'd love to, we can't take Hunter."

Choosing not to respond to that, Dallas wagged a finger in Hunter's general direction to alert Matt. He spoke softly. "He's waking up."

True enough, Hunter raised his small head up from Matt's shoulder. Instantly he stiffened and stared across the dusty road.

"What's he looking at?" Dallas strained to see. Raising a hand, he shielded his eyes from the late afternoon sun.

"Horses." Matt turned his body so Hunter could see better. "Wild ones.

Josh told me about them a few years back. It's a breakout herd. They're protected out here, right?"

"Yeah, for the most part. Dale was on the board for a while. Maybe he still is, uh...was, I mean." He grimaced at the reminder that his brother was gone, and shoved himself away from the hot car. Moving was a way to distract himself from the heavy emotion. Needing something to hang onto, he rested a hand on his engraved belt buckle as he moved, hooking his thumb over the top edge.

Hunter started writhing again. Matt did a quick check for vehicles on the usually barren stretch of road before he set him down. Immediately, Hunter took off at a run towards the wild herd.

With a shout, Dallas bounded after him.

He jogged to a sliding stop when Hunter, ten feet ahead, planted his child-sized feet in the long, dry grass at the side of the road and stared.

Watching, Matt took two halting steps and held his breath. There was a startling peacefulness in the air out here, a real spiritual feel to the place. The snow-topped mountains held their own majestic appeal, for sure, but it was everything else that gave the place an undeniable mysticism—the whispering breath of the meadows, the communion of bordering trees, the optimistic, buoyant breeze that spoke if you took the time to listen, the bell-peal ripple of water flowing over rocks and under downed branches in some hidden creek, nearby.

And then there were the horses.

The herd was small, made up of maybe a half-dozen horses at most. The leader, the alpha-male, was all black—a muscular, midnight black that glistened with sweat in the baking sun when he moved. What was most striking about the black horse was the coarse untamed mane that cascaded down his neck in one broad wave, culminating at its top in a wild forelock that almost covered the horse's serious, wise eyes. It was a miracle the animal could see, the forelock was so long and thick. The wind helped; a feverish, steady breeze had come up. It lifted the horse's mane and forelock, and gave the statue-still animal its only signs of life, masking a quiet, quivering energy that, once ignited, was sure to explode.

It was ready to run; they all were. The breakout herd knew to be wary, to trust only themselves in these mountains, on this meadow. History taught them caution. Men taught them fear.

Even more astonishing than the beautiful animals poised in silent tableau in the meadow before Dallas and Matt was the little boy that had fallen into their care. Where only a few moments before, Hunter was lost in a nightmarish frenzy that had him bucking in fear, now he was the exact opposite. He was as still as the horses with which he was locked in soundless accord.

Hunter took a step forward, but Dallas and Matt were both too astounded, too lost in wonder, to even consider reacting. In harmony with the pastoral, bucolic pace of the wild land around them, their minds had slowed. Sounds were at once indistinct and addled, nebulous and dreamlike. Movements were amorphous and hazy.

The black horse broke the spell. With moist, solemn eyes locked on the small boy less than fifty paces away, it raised its wild head and whinnied. As one, the breakout herd stepped lightly over the long grass, turned in hushed unison, and galloped away in a stunning display of proud, natural wonder, their hooves ricocheting like thunder on the hallowed ground.

Hunter pivoted slowly back around to his awestruck caregivers. Shoulders heaving, black hair tossed by the wind in an echo of the black horse's mane— the horse a wild thing that entered and left his short life in as brief a time as it seemed his father and mother did—he planted his feet in the long grass and stayed across the road. Fists curled, head raised proudly, he seemed to be daring Matt or Dallas to have the balls to remove him from this extraordinary place...

The only place Hunter felt he belonged.

Matt strode forward but stopped six feet away from Hunter. He could hear Dallas behind him, choking out sobs he was obviously trying to stifle judging by the way he was gasping for breath.

Beauty will do that to a man, Matt thought, fighting back the overwhelming emotion threatening to disarm him too.

He took a good, hard look at Hunter.

Like Dallas, the child was sobbing too, but he wasn't making any sounds. He made no attempt to hide his pain but also, like Dallas, seemed to have learned to suppress the sounds of it. Matt had to turn away. He wished he could call Jessie. He knew he would, when he was alone in his cabin later. She would understand this kind of intermingled pain and beauty. Hell, she wrote it.

She sang it.

She lived it.

As did Dallas. He shared his pain when he felt safe, on the stage. Not in public. Not in front of his security buddy, and he most certainly would not in front of a child that confused and scared the hell out of him.

Behind Matt, Dallas walked around to the far side of the SUV so he could do his crying alone. Matt was actually relieved when Dallas stopped fighting and bent over to grieve outright.

A few moments later, a light tug on his jeans pulled Matt from thoughts of Jessie and Dallas and the kind of pain that had the power to completely derail a man. He looked down to find Hunter, face flushed and cheeks streaked with tears, begging with wet, saturated eyes to be picked up. The afternoon's spiritual break was over. Reality was beckoning—the hard, remorseless kind.

"Okay, little buddy," Matt said, startled by the sound of his voice as if it didn't belong out here with the wild wind and the powerful horses and the cleansing water in the creek. He bent to Hunter's level. Using the rolled-up sleeve of his white shirt, Matt wiped the small face clean. He picked Hunter up and sighed when the little boy, seemingly exhausted, collapsed fully into him. The skinny arms around Matt's neck were pure sweet relief and love.

Matt couldn't help himself. *Jessie,* he thought, *you would love this child. You would love everything this child stands for.*

Hunter was in need of a home. Jessie and Josh had often claimed they wanted five kids. They were currently raising four. The idea almost crippled Matt. Hunter and Jessie would likely be able to read each other the same way Hunter and the black horse just did. They were troubled creatures saddled with sorrow, each with a lot of wild still inside. Each staking claims on certain kinds of freedom that most people never ever recognized, or missed.

You can't miss what you've never known, Matt considered.

Dallas' sobs were hiccupping to a staggered halt. Matt, out of respect for him, waited. Dallas deserved some time to grieve for the brother he lost in such a terrible way, and for having to bear the weight of his parents' pain.

60

Add to those crippling hurts the traumatized child that had landed in Dallas'
midst amongst chaos and grief.

Matt leaned backwards against the SUV and just waited. Maybe he would
catch another glimpse of the wild horses.

But no.

The horses were gone, left to the breeze and to the mysterious meadows
beyond. Yet the magic remained. It imbued Matt's sagging spirit with longing and hope.

The entire drive home, he went over and over the gift of the wild horses
that he and Hunter and Dallas were given. He had no doubt there was something much, much bigger to life than most people ever dared dream.

Something spiritual.

Something extraordinary.

He was certain Dallas knew this now too, if he didn't already.

It just wasn't something they could talk about. There was no space for
spoken words on the rest of the drive back to the ranch.

Just before he pulled into J.I.'s parking lot, Matt took his foot off the gas.
He didn't look at Dallas when he finally said, "You okay, buddy?"

Other than grasping Matt's arm and giving it a brief squeeze, Dallas didn't
answer. His body was heavy, his mind numb.

After passing through the gate that Dallas pushed open so Matt could
drive through, Matt braked to a stop next to his cabin and watched Dallas
scoop up his daughter, who came running to greet him, with Cassie smiling
just behind her. Leaving Hunter for a second so he could catch his breath after
the surreal roadside stop, Matt wandered over to the riverbank and stared
down at the rushing water. Ry was around—the cozy, welcome strum of a
guitar reached Matt's ears. Turning, he saw Ry with his guitar in his arms,
sitting comfortably on the small deck outside Dallas' cabin. Nobody else was
in sight. Jenny's truck was gone. Johnny and Dawn had also apparently left
for the day. The older Whites were likely napping, Matt hoped. They sure
could use the rest.

Sighing, he waved to Ry and wandered back to the SUV. Opening the
back door of the SUV, he retrieved Hunter from the car seat. He set him on
the ground and looked down at him.

Hunter stared impassively up at Matt, his cheeks dry now, his coarse dark hair blowing in the breeze like the horse's just over a half hour earlier. Matt extended a hand. Hunter slipped his tiny fingers into Matt's larger ones.

"Do you want to go sit on Starbuck?" Matt asked simply.

A wide smile greeted him. Hunter led the way, pulling Matt along towards the corral.

I know a gal who would love you so much, Matt thought, and wished to hell he wasn't falling in love with this mysterious kid. In Matt's experience, love hurt, which was exactly why he figured Dallas and his family were all keeping their distance from Hunter.

Starbuck was waiting patiently in the corral. The grand blond palomino bowed its head when Matt lifted Hunter up to sit on its bare back. Matt bowed his when Hunter leaned forward, grasped the horse's creamy mane, laid flat out with his belly down, closed his eyes, and smiled.

In the clearing, Dallas set Jade down, and watched.

Chapter Nine

*C*assie tiptoed into the bungalow's small kitchen and jumped when she rounded the corner through the doorway from the porch and almost ran into Boone.

"Jumpins!" Instinctively, she threw a palm over her chest. Her heart was racing. "You startled me, Mr. White."

Dallas' father was standing stock still facing a window, both hands gripping the edge of the kitchen counter. Pale, his denim long-sleeved shirt wrinkled and messily tucked into his jeans, he hadn't bothered to take off his dusty cowboy boots, which Cassie knew was a big no-no in Doris' household. It worried her.

Gathering her senses with a swipe down her ponytail, she took a breath, counted to five, and moved past the older man towards the refrigerator. Retrieving a bottle of beer for Dallas, Cassie set it on the counter and twisted off the cap.

"You know," she tried softly, "your son is not who you've decided he is."

A sarcastic grunt from Boone raised a warning flag in Cassie's mind. She set the beer cap down quietly on the counter, raised an eyebrow, and took a sideways peek at Boone who, she discerned, was watching Dallas in the dry, hot open clearing that divided the bungalow from the cabins and trailers beyond.

"Would that be the dead son I'm starting to think I never knew at all, or the pussy live one who always hated the farm? Who ran from Doris and I at the first light of dawn shortly after his high-school graduation?"

"Hmm." Cassie's acknowledgement was more to herself than to Boone. It emerged in a whisper. "I see."

"What do you see?" Boone turned, pivoting slowly on one heel so that in the late afternoon light it took Cassie a few moments to decide whether the grey around his eyes, pooled underneath in even deeper hues of blue and black, was just a shadow, or bone-deep weariness.

Cassie melted. Letting go of the damp beer bottle, she left it on the counter, turned fully to her husband's father, and leaned back. "Sir," she started, but he cut her off.

"Boone," he announced heavily, shoulders caving. "Just Boone. A regular old man living a regular old life."

"Boone," Cassie echoed, ducking her head. A small upturn of her lips ignited a tiny flicker of light in her eyes when she spotted flecks of peeling polish on her toenails and couldn't help but feel grateful that in this humble company she would never have to worry about presenting a perfect appearance, like at Dallas' shows. "Thank you. Yes." Crossing her ankles, she exhaled in a whisper and looked back up at her host. "Boone, you and I are not so different."

"You don't say." Other than adding a disagreeable harrumph, the tired man didn't move.

Cassie dove in deeper. "I judged Dallas too, before I knew the truth of who he really was, what kind of man he has proven to be. I judged his career choice. His music. The second rate lifestyle I was certain he lived. I thought he had no ambition, that he eked out a living playing a string of roadside bars. But I was wrong about him."

Squinting at her as if he had to work to stay awake, Boone raised his hands just enough to clench the edges of the countertop behind him, and afforded Cassie enough respect to stay quiet and listen.

His silence gave her the courage to go on in a steady, firm manner. "He's the hardest working man I know. He likes a beer or two after a show, or sometimes before, to help him relax. He likes to build things, to work with wood, to putter around the outside of my house with a weed trimmer, to fill my bird houses with seeds." She smiled, remembering the rare quiet days the couple got to spend at her place in Halifax enjoying their new daughter, or playing board games with Ry. "Sometimes he puts sunflower seeds in his palms so the chickadees will land there for a bite. I think he does that more to entertain Jade than in any charitable hopes that the chickadees will get something to eat, but—"

Boone interjected. "He was always the softest of my two boys. Dallas wasn't much for cutting wood or hauling hay. He was always off in dreamland, thinking about God knows what, ten steps behind his brother. Drove his mother crazy in the mornings. That kid missed the school bus so often that we finally caved and got him a rusty old truck when he turned sixteen. We got tired of driving him."

"Oh, well, he still drags his butt sometimes. When I have to go looking for him I usually find him jotting song lyrics down on a scrap of paper. Once it was toilet paper—can you believe that?" Cassie's laugh was contagious. "I don't know if he was ever able to read what he was trying to write down, but I do recall I liked the song that came out of it. It's one of my favourites, actually. I've learned that when inspiration strikes, I need to let my man be."

Boone chuckled before he shook his head. "He's lowered himself to writing songs on toilet paper. That don't surprise me one bit, missy."

Unsure how to take that, Cassie retreated back into herself and thought about what to say to this unpredictable man. She hoped it was just the grievous loss of Dale that was reducing him to his lowest common denominator, and that his ability to wound would pass. Boone was emerging as a cantankerous, sour sort, which disturbed Cassie because he'd had so much influence in the early parts of her husband's life, and seemed to have retained the power to hurt Dallas now. It surprised her; Dallas had only ever spoken of his parents with affection, and she hated to think that anyone, much less Dallas' father, would want to throw knives at the man she loved.

Her mind wandered to Dallas as a child—to him and his brother. The boys must have lived out of each other's pockets on the ranch in Cochrane back in the old days. "Boone," she asked with a dose of caution, lest she open a round of bullets, "were Dallas and Dale close when they were kids?"

Boone angled his head around to glance out of the window behind him. Dallas was standing still, his eyes locked on the corral. Although Boone craned his neck further, he couldn't make out what his son was looking at, but knowing that Matt had wandered over there with Hunter, he figured rightly it had to do with a kid and a horse. It unnerved him. Dale was the same way when he was a boy, always gravitating towards the horses. Dallas was no different in those days than he was here, today—more often the watcher than the rider.

"One was the protector, the other the protected," he said without looking back at Cassie. "I'll let you figure out on your own which one was which. I suppose they were close in the sense that they trusted each other. Dallas was the weaker of the two. He needed Dale. That's why this whole thing…" Boone's voice faded out before he rebounded and said, louder than he intended so that it came out gruff and careless, "I just thought if one of my boys was gonna end his own life, it weren't gonna be Dale. That's all."

The end of the sentence was abrupt and final, which intensified a sudden sting that tore through Cassie's insides at the callous, insidious statement. Whipping around, she grabbed the beer bottle from the counter behind her and clenched it between both sets of fingers. The kitchen counter was a good thing; it provided the necessary stability to keep her from spinning down onto the old linoleum and curling up into a ball.

She spoke over her shoulder. There was fight in her words. "Dallas is much stronger than you give him credit for, Boone."

The older man had to talk her down off the ledge she was climbing up onto. "Easy, girl," he cautioned. "I'm just tellin' it straight up. We're talking about the grown man who hightailed it to the east coast and hid in a tent, leaving a lot of people high and dry. Fans, crew, band members…I read the papers."

Dropping the bottle back on the counter, Cassie turned back around to him. "You went looking for news about him. You've been following his career."

The observation went unnoticed. Boone hoisted himself away from his piece of countertop and stood facing Cassie with his feet apart. He spoke in his usual lilting Alberta cowboy way, but because of his message, the tone was abrasive in Cassie's mind. "Think about the amount of money that Dallas is responsible for. Only a yellow-bellied sapsucker would leave that on the table, and I'm not talking about the outrageous sums he pulls in and chucks into multiple bank accounts. I'm talking about the venues—the festivals, the stadiums, the hardworking people who paid good money for tickets, who maybe booked hotel rooms and had to pay for meals, many who in lots of cases likely couldn't afford his show in the first place. I'm talking about all the extra people who were countin' on him for work. He just walked away and left them all in the lurch."

Cassie opened her mouth to speak but there didn't seem to be much to say. She and Dallas had not discussed that bit of history in detail, but there was a reason why they didn't open that old wound. It hurt Dallas to think of it, to bring it back into the light of day, the same way any man's weaknesses have the ability to rise up and haunt him.

Dallas did that, yes. He left people in the lurch but he accepted responsibility for it. He did what he could to make it right. The fact remained that although Dallas' actions were necessary at the time in order to buy him some desperately needed healing time, there were deeper, layered hurts that made him push a big 'ole stop button on his career in the first place.

Those hurts, the things that wounded Dallas, were becoming crystal clear to Cassie now. It was like some unseen force was wiping grease off a filthy window. Only problem was that as the window was clearing, the sun coming in was far too bright. It was shocking to try to stare through it—at it.

In fact, it was blinding.

This is the sense that Cassie was getting from her brief time with her man's people. Dale's passing was so much more than just a family tragedy. His death had opened nasty, angry sores in the spirits of the living.

Those sores were starting to fester. Caught in their crossfire was a child everybody seemed scared to let into their hearts.

There was one other child at risk here, exposed right down to the bones. It was a long ago child, buried deep in the soul of a man.

"He did the same thing when he was a kid." Dug in, empowered by the armour afforded by standing upright in his own home, almost towering over petite Cassie—who didn't look strong enough to withstand an Alberta wind much less the kind of ear-splitting thunderstorm the Rockies were famous for—Boone didn't hold back. "Dallas whines about his fear of horses coming from getting kicked when he was a kid. Well, missy, his brother got kicked too, more than once. Dale got bucked off, he got bit, he got shoved hard between a horse and a fence one time, and he wore a limp for months after a string of bad wrecks at rodeos. I say string because he kept on competing when he was hurt, Dale did, even though he had to do chores on a leg so sore he had to fashion a crutch out of a tree branch in order to make his way from the house to the barn. My boy was not a quitter."

"Dallas plays shows when he's sick. I've seen him with a fever, vomiting all day and night before a show, so sick he can't stand upright, and still going on stage. He had a bad time for a while and it just caught up with him, that's what happened that one time—"

"Don't give me that. A man can weather a fever for what, a ninety-minute set, when there's gold at the end of the rainbow, girl. Specially when he's coddled and ushered off in a cushy limo to some luxury hotel right after. Ask Dale how many fevers he worked through, all day long, in the biting wind and in the cold rain. Every day, animals got to be fed and cared for on a ranch. The barn work's got to be done no matter how bad a man wants to lie down in the straw and curl up into sleep."

Withering, Cassie bit her lip to keep from crying. This attack on Dallas was going to go in Dale's direction no matter what.

Sensing her breaking, Boone decided then and there that he ought to put the final nail in his second son's coffin. Clearing his throat, he started down a dark road. "Dale broke his arm when he was thirteen," he said, haltingly at first. "Fell out of the hay loft one night, out of the open door up high in the barn where we brought the hay in back in the days when we used conveyor belts and rectangular bales. He fell clear to the ground."

Unable to help herself, Cassie leaned slightly forward. Stories of Dallas as a kid were rare; he never talked details when the old days came up at dinner or when Ry got curious and poked away at Dallas during one of the long flights or bus rides from show to show. As far as Cassie knew before coming here for Dale's funeral, Dallas' life on the childhood ranch was all sunshine and apple pie.

"Dallas used to pretend the open door to the hayloft was a stage," Boone said, a distinct darkness wading into the story and edging his voice. "This one night in summer—it was a hot one, we were always in a cloud of smoke cause of so many forest fires burning in the mountains, it got so bad it hurt to breathe—well, Dallas was out there acting the shenanigans all fired up pretending he was Tim McGraw or Garth Brooks, who the hell knows, you couldn't see him for the smokey haze all around us, you could only hear him. Stupid ass kid standing at the edge of the loft, belting out country songs at the top of his lungs."

Cassie was startled at the disapproval spreading over Boone's face while he recounted what sounded like a sinister day more than thirty years ago. Swallowing, she tucked her hands behind her butt against the counter, and hung on every nefarious word.

"Doris got all worked up. She was worried about her weak boy on account of the smoke. The hay loft was high enough up that a fall could break a fella's neck. We were always careful up there to keep the boys and Dawn well away from the edge. Well, Doris knew her middle child. Always in a fantasy world. Hell, we were worried about him not seeing the edge and wandering over it on a *clear* day." He shook his head, remembering. "This day was a bad one for the fires, so bad that law enforcement was knocking on doors asking folks to evacuate. Sirens going up and down the road all day and night long. You can imagine the state Doris was in. Trying to pack things up, worried about the animals, little Dawn at her feet crying about a new batch of kittens that'd likely have to be left behind. And Dallas up in the hayloft, oblivious. Probably thinking the smoke was fog from one of his dream shows."

Cassie looked past Boone out of the window behind him. Dallas was no longer in sight. Fear gnawed at her throat. A dry ache started there, and she prayed he'd taken Jade into the barn.

Boone was too far in to stop. Making Cassie comprehend the depth of Dallas' childhood failures was a way to raise Dale up on the pedestal Boone felt Dale abandoned when he left so abruptly—forever—without saying goodbye. "Doris sent Dale out to get that stupid kid. I never knew exactly what went on between the boys, but I always figgered Dallas wouldn't listen and so they got into a tussle. We were all beat from the long day of worry and fire prep and I was busy keeping the kids' mother calm plus I was on and off the phone, trying to get places set up for the larger animals—there was no animal rescue in our neck of the woods in those days. Fire come up, you dealt with it the best you could. Most times, you either stayed and fought, or animals got left behind. I had a wife and kids. I had to do what was best for them."

Is he choking up? Cassie wondered when Boone abruptly stopped talking, looked away, and swiped at his nose. *Did animals get left behind? Horses, a dog, cats, kittens, and did Boone have cattle in those days?*

Her answer wasn't long in coming.

After clearing his throat twice, Dallas' father started in again. "Next thing we know, an hour has passed and no sign of either boy. Doris comes out of the bedroom wondering what they got up to. I'm ready to blister a couple of behinds when I go out looking for them. And what do you suppose I find?"

Cassie blinked. A shadow had darkened the doorway that separated the porch and the kitchen.

Dallas.

Awed and subdued after the mystical experience with Matt and Hunter and the wild horses, Dallas had left Jade with Ry and walked on muted boots up to the bungalow. He was in need of the calming, loving presence of the one person he trusted most in the world. He'd opened the door without a squeak, afraid to disturb the quiet of the place and the strange, confused beating of his heart. With an introspective push, he'd closed the door behind him with the same reverential care.

From the kitchen came his father's voice. Stepping forward, Dallas had cocked an ear. As always, Boone was speaking in his usual soft cowboy lilt.

It didn't surprise Dallas to hear it laced with disgust.

He leaned against the door frame, avoided Cassie's searching eyes, and turned an ear to his father.

Anxious to see how this childhood trauma played out, yet afraid of what Boone might say in Dallas' presence, Cassie reached behind her and slid the beer bottle off of the counter. Gripping it in both hands, she let the condensation soak her fingers and rested concerned emerald eyes on her man. Pearlescent water dripped from the bottle's wet base and landed on the linoleum Doris scrubbed so hard the night after Dale died that it was almost bare.

Cassie had no clue whether Boone knew Dallas was behind him or not. If the older man knew, he didn't blink an eye. Instead, a steel curtain washed over him. When he spoke again it was from an inner coil of anger, the words oozing out like hot lava from a vicious volcano, gaining momentum with every heated syllable.

"I found Dale on the ground outside the barn, out cold, his arm twisted at an odd angle. It took me a while to realize he was there. It was well after midnight by then, the world shadowy and strange as blazes with the eerie hazy glow from the fires all around, and I'd checked the hay loft first. There was no sign of Dallas, by the way. When we finally got away, after me looking for that crazy kid all the while Doris was nursing Dale, it was near sunrise. Doris left in an ambulance with Dale, which we had to wait for because of all the craziness around us. I took Dawn and the cat and kittens in the truck." He hesitated. "We left more than just the rest of the animals behind that night."

Cassie was watching Dallas. He didn't blink. She saw him swallow and curl a fist at his side. Dallas' father had his grown son caught and bound. Imprisoned. To Cassie, it seemed Dallas was afraid to move forwards or backwards at this critical, tense time. Movement would be jarring. Retreating would be unacceptable and weak. Striding forward would surely bring a cataclysmic, irreversible end to the telling, and maybe even to the tenuous relationship.

Boone was as powerful as a spider. He'd just wrapped malignant silk memories around his only remaining son, leaving Dallas sticky and paralyzed. Yet the White patriarch was equally caught. Cassie shivered at the baleful way Dallas had his father fixed in a dark, cool stare.

Whistle-like, Boone sucked in a breath. At the same time he changed his stance, leaned a hip sideways against the counter, and turned his back even more to the son he in all likelihood didn't even know was in the house. "You can imagine the chaos, Cassie," he continued, drawing up his chin, thick hands fitfully opening and closing with the distressing memory. "Emergency responders were already done-in fighting the fires and begging folks to evacuate the area. Now they have a badly hurt boy and a missing kid to deal with. Now I ain't one to frown on a kid's fear—it's a very real thing, I know that. Like I said, I still don't know what really happened, whether Dale just fell or got shoved. What I do know is that Dallas likely run off because he'd heard his mother say time and time again that the boys ought to watch themselves up in that hayloft cause if either ever went over the edge, they'd likely break their neck. I expect Dallas was scared of what happened to Dale." An outright strangled sob snuck out. It was a reminder that this time, these last few days, they all had reason to grieve Dale.

Recognizing that, yet unable to let Boone off the hook for bringing up a disastrous family memory that so badly stung the child in Dallas, Cassie spoke softly. "He must have been so scared."

Ten feet away, Dallas blinked, but kept his gaze locked on his father's back.

Boone's eyes, pale like his son's, deepened. "I didn't give a shit. If he had any sense, he'd have gone to the road and flagged down a police car. There were plenty of those around. But no, Dallas did what Dallas always does. He sucked up a lot of attention and a lot of important resources that were needed elsewhere, and worried the hell out of his mother, and Dale too, once he was conscious and on the mend. We didn't find Dallas until three days later, when we were given the all-clear and moved back home. Where do you suppose he finally turned up?"

"I-I don't know. Maybe near a river? Were there any creeks near where you lived in Cochrane back then?"

"No, Missy, water had nothing to do with where we found him. Dawn heard him singing. He was sitting on the edge of the hay loft, legs swinging over the side, singing away, oblivious to all the shit he caused."

From behind Boone, a thin voice cut through the air. "I fed the horses. While you were gone, I fed and watered them."

Although visibly startled, Boone didn't turn. To Cassie, he warned, "You better watch him, he ducks and hides when things get rough. No care or concern for others. Dale would have faced what he done, if it'd been Dallas that went over the loft's edge. Dale woulda come running for help."

"Yeah, Dad," Dallas offered, defeated. "Dale sure knew how to ask for help when he needed it."

"Dallas," Cassie chided softly, new spots of pink high on her cheeks telegraphing her discomfort and concern.

He glanced up at her, just long enough for her to shake her head in warning.

Boone, slowly and with effort, his shoulders rising and then caving from the effort to breathe through the blanket of muggy air left swirling around the room after the release of the horrid memory, swiveled around to Dallas. "You ever think that maybe that whole disaster got the stink of abandonment on Dale? You ever get out of your own way enough to think that maybe your brother needed you? You bailed on him, Dallas. You bailed on all of us."

Then? That night during the fires? Cassie wondered, confused. *Or years later, when Dallas took off to Toronto in search of a singing career?*

Dallas raised his eyes to meet his father's. "I was a far from perfect kid, Dad. I know I did things wrong."

"You push him?"

Wincing, Dallas replied stoically, "No, Dad. Did you?"

Boone flinched; his eyebrows arched into a question mark as a loud guffaw escaped from between his lips. "I wasn't up in the barn with you boys. I was too busy trying to outrun the fires. Trying to figger what to do about the horses."

"I'm not talking about when we were kids."

Cassie sighed and turned her head away. Pivoting around, she set the wet beer bottle back on the countertop.

The sudden silence was overwhelming. There was a low rustle in the bedroom down the hall—Doris was stirring from a desperately needed nap. They could hear her padding to the washroom, then closing the door.

Dallas and his father were on lockdown. Neither budged until Ry came bounding in the door, Jade's little feet wheeling along behind.

"Hey Mom, do you think I could start riding a horse? I'm thinking that I'd like to learn to ride. Emily-Grace just texted me; she invited me to her family's ranch and they have horses. She told me her dad said if I wanna be a real country singer I ought to learn to ride a horse. He was just teasing her, but still…" Ry stopped talking when he realized some kind of old west standoff was happening in the small kitchen.

Cassie grabbed the beer, flipped back around, and started to walk towards her children. She covered the few paces quickly, touching Dallas' hand with the damp bottle when she started by him, shooting a look of concern over at him when he refused the beer and pulled away. Unwanted, the bottle hung between her fingers.

Boone broke the silence. "The only thing that could have pushed Dale over the edge this time was loneliness, Dallas. Despite what this place looks like to your rich pretty-boy eyes, it's breaking even and we only been in business a short time. So it weren't finances. A man can be lonely even if he's got a wife and kids. I gather that's why your brother took up with that Indian gal. I expect when that went south, Dale couldn't stand the sight of himself in the mirror. He couldn't find a connection to you. You bailed on him when he was a youngster and you ran away, and you ain't stopped runnin' since."

Cassie was near her children, almost at the door, ready to reach out and poise a hand over the handle. The accusations in Boone's voice stopped her cold. It sickened her that Ry and Jade heard the judgment on Dallas too. The confusion in Ry's eyes was evident in the way his vision darted from Boone to Dallas and back again, finally landing on Dallas, who'd gone pale and started to tremble.

The long ago abandoned horses and the fear of what the fire would do to them if it burned unhindered through the Cochrane ranch was on Dallas' mind. *If they survived, they'd be hungry. That's what I was thinking back then once I saw that Dale would be okay. That someone ought to stay and take care of them. Dad needed time to calm down. I just didn't know it would take him forever.*

Dallas' brain clicked from the horses he loved in childhood, to Hunter. Abandoned. Lonely. *Like me. They left me.*

Shoving the black-haired child from his consciousness, and shoving the terror of those childhood days and nights during the fire into musty corners of his brain, he cornered right. "Dale used to lie down amongst wild horses. From the time he was a little kid he knew all their special meadows, the favourite places where they liked to graze. He'd lie on his back and stare up at the sky and they'd all just calmly graze around him while he picked out formations in the clouds. Dale was every bit as much a dreamer as I was, Dad. Only he dreamed in horses while I dreamed in music. And this is the thing about dreamers."

Dallas took a step forward, seemingly oblivious to the fact that his young family was in the room, standing in shocked silence behind him. Even little Jade was quiet, after instinctively clueing in to the tension. "Dreamers are, by nature," he said, "the loneliest creatures on the goddamned planet. If it was loneliness that did my brother in, it was a long—time—coming." If Dallas had the nerve, he might've jabbed a finger into his father's chest, but as it was, he just stared a little longer into the man's tough-guy eyes before spinning around and plowing past Cassie, Ry, and Jade.

The door slammed behind him before his footsteps' staccato rhythm going down the steps gave a marked finality to Dallas' painful exit.

Ry took Jade's hand.

Cassie grasped Jade's other set of little girl fingers in hers and looked back over a shoulder up at Boone. It seemed the man was not all metal and thunder, he was just skilled at lashing out in anger in order to keep the hurt in. There was no question that his eyes were floating.

"Please, Boone," Cassie tried, appealing to the kindness she sometimes heard in the quiet cowboy modulation of his voice when he spoke to his wife. "You need to give Dallas a chance. Cut him some slack. He still bleeds, the same way he did when he was a child." She grazed the door handle with her fingers and then looked back. "He's always talked about you guys. About your family. About what he's missed out on by not being out west to help run the ranch. I think..." She paused and thought for a second before completing her sentence. "I think you should consider that Dallas' fear the night Dale broke his arm—during the fires, I mean—is what's kept him from coming back to you. To all of you. I think a little boy left behind for three days while forest fires rage around him, especially one who cannot ever seem to win his father's approval, and who is terrified of his part in his brother's injury, likely retreats so far inside that the fear takes over. I know Dallas. He shut off after that, didn't he?"

Boone sank deep against the cupboard. His mouth opened and closed like a fish searching for water. No sound came out.

"I thought so," Cassie whispered, as Jade tugged ever-so-slightly on her hand. "Boone, after living three days in terror, the only thing that could have brought that child fully back to you and your family would have had to be Jesus himself. I'm glad Dallas had music in him. It's likely what saved him." Another pause. "I would have liked to have known Dale better. Truly. His connection with horses, you know? Wow."

With that, Cassie tossed her head proudly, gave Jade a little nudge so the child would move in front of her, and followed her daughter through the door. She let it close with a curious, soft click behind her, when she realized Ry was still in the house.

Cassie almost sank to her knees when she heard what Ry said to Boone.

"My dad died in a fire. An Alberta forest fire. Did you know that?"

Boone's answer was unintelligible to Cassie's ears. She clung to the rail until Jade pulled her down the stairs with a whine about looking for pretty stones in the riverbed.

Inside, Boone had acknowledged that he did know that. He wondered to himself if he'd used the fire story to hurt Cassie, to on some level warn her away, to start a fracture between her and Dallas.

To punish Dallas.

He was not proud of himself.

Ry glossed over it with a deep inhale. He scrunched up his shoulders. "I'm serious about learning to ride. Do you think you could teach me while I'm here? Just get me started and all? I could maybe be of some help around here, mucking out stalls and all. Emily-Grace helps her dad."

That got Boone's attention. He answered with a question just as his wife made her way into the kitchen and unwound a twist tie from a bag of gingersnap cookies. "Isn't this Emily-Grace you like to talk about the daughter of a couple of famous actors?"

Ry shrugged. "Yep. Her mom's both an actor and a singer. Big time singer, like Dallas. Not country, though." He brightened. "Although Emily-Grace's dad likes country. It's mostly all he listens to, she says. Drives her nuts." Ry grinned. "I'm trying to win her over. To bring her over to the country side of things."

"She mucks out stalls?"

"Emily-Grace? Yep. Says she does."

"Doesn't her family have hired help to do that sort of thing?"

"I dunno. Some, I suppose. It's probably like us. We do our own stuff most times. Mom doesn't want strangers around."

Doris piped up. "How long are you staying here, Ry?" The teen with the surfer blond hair was starting to grow on Doris. She needed people to take care of.

Ry lit up. "Do I have a choice?" The rundown Alberta ranch, to him, even if it was hours away from Emily-Grace's family's ranch, was at least in the same province. "I'm useful. I can do stuff. I can chop wood."

"In this heat?" Doris allowed a small smile to tug at the corners of her lips while she pulled out cookies and dropped them on a plate. She couldn't stop herself from ruffling Ry's long, layered locks when he wandered closer. "Who wants fires?" Wiping sweat from her brow, she idly wondered why her husband seemed so downcast.

Boone was sizing Ry up. It was as if he was noticing him for the first time. "How'd you learn to chop wood? Your dad?" To his wife he said, "Plug the kettle in, Doris."

"Shush," Doris cautioned him. "Ry's father passed away when he was just a baby. And it's too hot for tea."

"You don't have to talk quietly around me about my dad," Ry announced. "I barely knew him. That's why, um," he recalled the angry words he heard Dallas and Boone tossing around earlier, "I love having Dallas in my life. He taught me." He looked at Boone. "The wood, I mean. Dallas taught me to chop wood. He makes a real good dad."

Boone was speechless. Doris smiled outright, a rainbow in the storm. It was faded, but the colours were starting to form.

"He's teaching me guitar, too. He teaches me lots of things."

"Son, there's no point in trying to right our son's wrongs by telling us what you think he does right. The water's already run under the bridge, if you know what I mean."

Doris stopped in her tracks. "Boone! For Heaven's sake."

Ry forced a grin. "When my mom met Dallas, she was scared to bits to get to know him. And that was before she found out he was a big star. Seems to me that people get too hung up on all the extra stuff about people, and they hang onto things that shoulda stopped mattering a long time ago. People just gotta let go of all that extra stuff, and look at the person the way they are now. It'd make life a lot simpler."

"Well now, that's a wise way of looking at things." Doris was humming now, actually humming. Which surprised Boone and lifted his spirits. There was nothing he liked better than seeing his wife happy, and although happy was relative these days and perhaps would never fully be a thing in their household again, this was a tiny, wee, little start. He allowed himself the pleasure of a cleansing sigh while Doris rewound the twist tie around the cookie bag and said to Ry, "Where'd you learn to think like that?"

"Oh," Ry chuckled, sliding into a seat at the table for a longer chat with Dallas' parents, whom Ry suddenly felt he wanted to know better. "Mostly they're the lyrics in one of Dal's songs. One of his biggest hits, actually. He helped a lot of people with that one. Don't you know that song?"

Doris smiled even wider. The colours in her rainbow got brighter. She set the plate of cookies on the table and waved a practiced, impatient arm at her husband of many decades. "Sit," she ordered, "and since when do you wear your boots in the kitchen? Take them off." With a lump in her throat, she said to Ry, "Of course we know that song. Now, young man, what can I get you to drink?"

Ry answered honestly. "Ma'am, I'll take a lemonade for now, but for later I'd like to borrow your husband. I've asked him to please teach me to ride." He grinned roguishly at Boone. "Give me the wildest horse you got in your stable. Please."

"I'll teach you all right," Boone agreed, the weariness of the afternoon's emotions finally lifting a little from his voice. "But I'm holding you to your promise to help muck out stalls."

"I'm in!" Ry lit up. "But Boone—can I call you Boone? Or maybe..." He stalled and puckered a lip. "Maybe someday I could call you Grampie? Kind of in an adopted grandparent kind of way?"

Boone ducked his head with pride. He liked this kid.

"Oh, call the old man Grampie now," Doris instructed in her forthright kind of way. She was hauling out bowls and flour, despite the piles of bread and cookies already taking over her countertops and the top of the fridge, the gifts from well-meaning neighbours after Dale's passing. "That'll keep things simpler with all the kids around here." Her cheeks were a happy rosy pink when she stopped her baking prep and opened the refrigerator door to pull out a glass pitcher.

"All right. Deal." Ry accepted the glass of lemonade she poured. "Thanks." He waited a moment before trying a hesitant, "Grammie."

Doris positively glowed. She set another glass of lemonade on the table, this time in front of her husband. "I said it's too hot for tea," she admonished, and winked at Ry.

Lifting the cool, homemade drink, Boone eyed Ry over the rim of the glass, took a tentative sip, and in his mind's eye picked out a suitably tempered horse for the lessons. They'd start as soon as he finished his snack. To Ry, he said, "Drink up, son. You're gonna need your fluids today. Mucking out stalls is going to be hot work in this here almighty Alberta heat."

Beaming, Ry set down his glass. With two fingers, he extricated his cell phone from a pocket in his shorts. He held it up high. "I'm not allowed to use electronics at the table," he told them, "but with your permission, there's a certain girl I need to text. Like right away."

"You're going to tell her you're going to learn to ride?" Doris dumped a cup of flour in her bowl. She was humming again.

"Nope." Ry was bouncing. "I need to learn about mucking out stalls. What does mucking out even mean?"

Outside, Cassie was mystified at the laughter discernible through the kitchen window. Holding Jade's hand, she was standing still in the clearing, watching Dallas' back as he made his way over the polished stones edging the riverbed.

"Bears," she murmured anxiously to herself. "Elk, cougars, and who knows what else. Wolves, maybe. Don't go far, please, Dallas."

Out here, folks sometimes took knives and even guns on their mountain walks. Dallas had neither. Cassie's shoulders drooped. Tipping back her head, she took a long draw on the beer she'd gotten for Dallas.

Alongside the riverbed, Dallas forced songs through his lips so he could numb his brain and not have to think. He closed his eyes and sang a rowdy song he knew Dale had liked. Before he made it over the smooth stones to the second bend, he sank down onto a driftwood log and begged his brother to come home.

Chapter Ten

"*Y*ou never said a word, Dal. You knew about Eddie, the forest fire. You must have been terrified. What were you, ten?"

"Something like that." Dallas' response was barely audible. He'd muttered it facing away from Cassie and down towards the floor while packing a few things to take into Calgary—an all weather coat in case the overhead clouds broke open later, a full water bottle, a couple of apples, a ball cap to pop on his blond layers in case he decided to go walking publicly.

Today of all days, Dallas did not want to be recognized. On the cards was an investigative excursion to try to find Hunter's mother. The media hype over Dale's suicide, his abandoned child, and the mysterious mother was tremendous news in Alberta, Dallas' home province. Diligent, curious fans who figured out where Dallas was staying were starting to make pilgrimages out to J.I., which was pissing Boone off to the nth degree since he moved the clan out to the boonies in the first place to dissuade star struck fans from stalking the family ranch. Many were leaving flowers and cards by the roadside, craning their necks for a view of Dallas, and then leaving. The braver folks tried to take walks around the ranch, purportedly sussing out the rental cabins and the small camping area. They didn't get far. Matt had uniformed security now in place. Johnny was around a lot too, hunkering up his shoulders and policing the ranch. Between him, Matt and his rotating crew, Boone, Dawn, and Jenny, Dallas and his small family were somewhat protected from the growing ranks of gawkers.

For now, the cabins were only being used by Dallas and Matt and a three-man road crew who'd been at J.I. all summer and who were, for the most part, so exhausted at the end of their long shifts that they grabbed quick dinners at the central canteen and immediately begged off to sleep. The trailers in the camping area mostly belonged to trusted known seasonal renters. Most of those only made the drive out on the weekends, and some barely came out at all. Less than a dozen regulars were around. They cared about Doris and watched over her, bringing food, and warm, dependable shoulders.

A few nights ago after dinner, Matt had taken Boone and Johnny aside and strongly suggested that for the next little while no new camping reservations be taken or trail rides be booked. Ornery Boone took it about as well as Matt thought he might. He made it clear that J.I. Outfitters needed the steady income it'd come to rely on from renters and trail riders. Boone hated being told, however cautiously, what he should do. After that heated discussion with Matt, he made a point of avoiding him whenever possible. He wouldn't speak to the newly hired security at all. Some of the cabins and rides were booked up before Dale's passing; that helped ease Boone's anxiety in the short term but was not a long term fix, especially since cancellations were made to accommodate Dallas and Matt.

Matt was coming along on the Calgary trip with Dallas, purportedly to have a confab with the security company that he and Phil hired to post the rotating sentries at the entrance to the ranch and on the grounds. The canteen was the obvious place for the main grounds security to hang his or her hat; from where Dallas was standing near the chalet's front window now, he could see a guy in a black T-shirt weave his way between white plastic chairs to set up camp for his shift underneath the open-air partially roofed picnic area.

Dallas was thinking about his father. The memory of the horrific childhood fire, told in Boone's bitter words, had left Dallas with festering, open sores. Now that Dale was gone, maybe the 'middle child grudge' Boone couldn't seem to let go of would never stand a chance to heal. Dale was always the buffer in the old days. Now Dallas and Boone were just metal on metal, rubbing against each other, shooting sparks into the sky. All Dallas could do was try to prevent the sparks from igniting another fire.

Maybe it was time to go home.

"Did you sleep okay?" Cassie's tender touch on Dallas' fingers should have been welcome, but for some reason it grated on him this morning. Her simple presence was grating. The claustrophobic cabin was grating. Jade was jumping on the double bed, screaming, trying to out-voice Ry, who was already at the guitar at this early hour, playing the same chords in a repeating pattern, again and again. Hunter was the only quiet one. He sat in silence next to Ry, eyes locked on Ry's changing fingers on the fret board, small legs hanging over the edge of the bed.

With a disapproving grunt, Dallas zipped shut a sturdy, frayed knapsack he'd borrowed from Johnny. Hoisting it up onto a shoulder, he headed towards the door without looking back.

"Dallas!" Cassie grabbed the door just before it closed in her face. Striding through the doorway, she trotted after her husband. Last night was torture—Dallas didn't eat dinner with the family, he didn't join them at a campfire, he didn't speak to her or talk to the kids, and he slept with his back to her. No way was Cassie going to spend a full day alone at somewhat hostile J.I., wondering what kind of state Dallas would be in when he got home.

She didn't catch up to him until he got to the rented SUV, hauled open the back door, tossed the knapsack in, and slammed the door shut.

Matt had stopped at the canteen to chat up the new security, to fill the guy in on what to expect today. Dallas eyed the two of them from underneath angry lowered lids. If he had the keys instead of Matt, he'd jump behind the wheel and spin out of this godforsaken hole alone. *Nothing here but rabbits and naysayers who never believed in me in the first place,* he muttered inwardly.

Cassie stood in his way when he tried to go around her to the passenger side.

"You're not helping things, Dallas," she complained, throwing one leg wide so he couldn't go around her without rudely pushing her out of his way. "We said we'd always talk about stuff and never leave each other mad. We promised each other! You can't freeze me out this way."

Dallas shifted his weight to one foot and reached an arm out to balance himself against the SUV. A rush of willful resistance overtook him. Crooking the opposite elbow so he could hook his thumb over his wide leather belt, he forced himself to meet Cassie's nervous eyes.

Swallowing, she crossed her arms and tried to drum up some strength to fight back.

Dallas stared her down. "Call Phil and get his office to sort out crew for the jet. It's time to go home."

"Okay," she replied. A hesitant flash of uncertainty flickered across her pretty face.

"What?" Dallas demanded, scaring Cassie into retreating back a step. "What was that look?"

Her response was tentative, as if she wasn't sure it was her business to weigh in on ancient family troubles. "Your father just needs some time, Dallas. He's a good man. He's got a lot of weight on his shoulders right now."

"Who doesn't." It wasn't a question, it was a simple, angry declaration. Dallas didn't move.

"The kids like it here. They're getting to know your parents, your sister and sister-in-law, their cousins."

"All the more reason to pull out of here as soon as we can."

"Dallas, come on. Give it time. You always raved about your mother's cooking, your life out here in Alberta under the big sky. I know you miss this kind of laid back life."

"I missed something I started to romanticize once the thrill of the 'big show' wore off with greasy spoons and faded lights. Now I see why I left here in the first place. It wasn't the place that scared me off, Cas. It was the people."

"If you had the chance to go back, you'd spend more time with Dale. I know you would. The same applies to your parents, your sister. And what about Jenny? Huh? She's walking around in a daze. Her boys could use some quality time with their uncle. I know your dad is not making this easy for you, babe, but you gotta grab those old hurts and try to let them go. See them for what they are—a father's pain making itself known to someone he feels can take it. That's all. This is bigger than you. You can fly away and go back to your life at any time, but your family can't. Right now they need you. Us."

"Us?" Dallas' laugh emerged sardonic and sharp. "You've got to be kidding, Cassie. Look at you."

Biting her bottom lip, Cassie smoothed the thighs of the butter yellow silk sundress she put on that morning. Her voice was quaking when she spoke, and not from anger. "The clothes I packed were for the tour, Dal. I need to go into Sundre and find some more suitable things to wear. Jade needs some work boots or something better than sandals, too."

"So go. Get Dawn to take you into town."

"Okay." She hunkered up her shoulders. "So we can stay a little longer, then? Ry says your dad started giving him riding lessons. He's thrilled."

Out of the corner of his eye, Dallas spied Matt sauntering their way. He spoke quietly, but Matt was close enough to overhear anyway. "You can stay. You want Jade to get to know her relatives? All the power to you. Personally?" He jabbed a finger in his chest while Cassie wrinkled her eyebrows and struggled to interpret the choice of words that did not include Ry. "I can't promise I won't hop a jet in Calgary today—any jet—and fly the hell away from here. My dad keeps reminding me that I'm a runner, and that I've got no respect for money. Well, Boone, you bejeesus old bastard. Fucking watch me go."

The outburst ended with him slamming a palm on the SUV, taking two steps back, and storming off behind the rear bumper so he could hop in on the other side.

Carefully, Matt approached Cassie. He turned his back to Dallas in the big car.

"Matt," Cassie said softly, eyes filling. "Did you hear that? Apparently Dallas' people will never belong to Ry. Which kind of feels like Dallas just turned his back on him too. And maybe on Jade and I too, if he's seriously considering taking off and leaving us here."

Matt's knowing sad half-smile tipped Cassie off to the notion that either she or her husband might be overreacting. She wasn't sure which was the guilty party.

"He won't," Matt affirmed. "Dallas is not your usual egocentric star, Cassie. All the time I've known him, he's been as down-to-earth as they come. He might threaten to pull that power card, but he won't follow through."

"I hope you're right. Geez, Matt. This is going to be a long day."

"Think about it, Cassie," Matt suggested kindly. "When the two of you have a fight, what does Dallas normally do? What's his usual response?"

Cassie pondered that before answering. "He retreats. Usually he disappears into his studio, or if we're in Halifax he rents a place for a night and cools down there. The nerd."

"Right. And on tour he takes a seat at the back of the jet."

"You make it sound like we fight a lot!" She swatted him.

He chuckled. "That's not what I'm saying at all. It's just that there's very little privacy in public life. Not that I'm spying on you two," he was quick to add. "It's just that it's my job to notice things, to be aware of patterns in the people I watch over."

"Fair enough. And thank you for not intruding just now. I guess that's why Dallas is so attached to you. You've become a good friend to him."

"He's a good guy, Cassie. The busy life he leads under constant public scrutiny has been wearing on him. You and the kids have made it a whole lot better. You brought real joy into his life. Still, he needs this, this time at home, to reconnect with his roots. It's just that he's come at a troubled time. And he's changed. Often the families of stars are as in awe of them as their fans are."

"It's funny though, because he's still the same person on the inside. In a dream world half the time, lost in song."

"But he has money and power now. A lot of both. Boone is trying to stay right side up. His pride won't allow him to accept help, and he's just lost a son he depended on to carry a lot of the workload. Boone wants and needs Dallas, but he doesn't know him anymore. He doesn't know how to bridge that gap between hardworking rancher father and creative, musical, and let me add famous, son. Sounds like he never did. And maybe he never will. But the way I see it, Cassie, being here gives the two of them a chance to mend their fences. It's never too late to try, at least."

"I wish they could," she sighed. "I just don't know how to make that happen."

"You're already doing it," Matt smiled.

"What? How?"

"Easy. Dallas brought some very special people into Boone's life. The old fella softens right up when you and the kids are around."

Cassie's cheeks pinked up. A tentative smile crossed her lips and widened. "Thanks, Matt. I can see why Dallas is so fond of you. You're very wise, you know that?"

"Wise, am I? Wise enough to know that you are the only person here that is likely capable of caring for Hunter while I'm gone?"

"Ah. The true side of Matt Kelly emerges. The soft, sweet side. You're handsome, but you can be intimidating. Why do I never see this side of you on tour or at shows?" She held up an index finger. "Forget it. I know. You're working then."

Matt laughed and reached for the driver's side door handle. "Ask Jessie Wheeler if I'm intimidating. She's seen me on the floor curled up in a fetal position."

"So I've heard. From her lips to my ears. However, in that very same wine-fueled conversation, she also said there are limits as to how far she can push you. Your word is stone, she said." Matt's smile eased back, and the light in his eyes faded, which prompted Cassie to take his fingers in hers. "Jessie's a special gal, Matt. I see why the two of you are so connected. I'm sorry that she can't be who you'd truly like her to be, in your life. It must be lonely, sometimes."

"I'm not sorry. Not always." The words were husky but strong. "She and Josh went through hell and back to be together. That kind of love is sacred. I watched them struggle for a very long time. The kids, too." He paused. "Now when I see that family together, my heart is full. That kind of love is worth fighting for." He brightened, but Cassie sensed that he was not telling the whole truth, at least not how being witness to that kind of love—a love that he so obviously shared with Jessie too—hurt him. His eyes clouded over, but he rebounded and blinked the pain away. "I'll bring Dallas back to you today, Cassie," he promised, his voice no less husky.

"Matt the security chief a.k.a. love guru, huh?" Cassie gave his fingers a squeeze. "Shanda rides horseback, right? She did on that old show of hers, Sacred Peace, and in that western she made a few years ago with Josh. Why don't you invite her up here, Matt? Things are still good between the two of you, right?"

"I just might do that." All this talk of Jessie was bringing Matt down. And Hunter…he hated leaving him. The kid had a way of getting under a guy's skin. Shanda would love the little fellow. Hunter would adore her.

Maybe…

Matt shook the thought away. Hunter belonged here, with this family, in this place. The idea of him and Shanda taking him in, or of asking Jessie and Josh to consider taking him in, was just a couple of possible backup plans.

A few minutes later, Cassie watched the black SUV disappear down the mountain road in a cloud of dust.

Ry jogged up behind her. Cassie glanced around. Jade and Hunter were out in front of the cabin, poking with a stick at something on the ground. Both were still in their pajamas. Cassie sighed and smiled at Ry, who was growing so fast he was just about as tall as her.

"Mom," he said earnestly, "will you hurry up? I'm not a built-in babysitter. Grampie's probably waiting for me."

Ohhhh, Cassie breathed. *Grampie.* Dallas' earlier comment about Jade getting to know her family—intentionally excluding Ry—jarred her. She wrapped an arm around her son's shoulders just as Boone left the bungalow and waved to Ry.

"Do you mind if I watch?" she asked her son.

"You can if you promise to keep Jade out of the corral. My little sister's a menace."

An outright laugh complete with a tip back of the head surprised Ry. His mother seemed so concerned earlier. Sad, even. Ry's excitement over his new riding lessons got dampened all last night and this morning because Dallas and his mom seemed to be fighting. He didn't understand people in love behaving that way. Heck, Ry couldn't imagine ever fighting with Emily-Grace.

He grinned and did a half hop-step. He just couldn't help himself. This place—ranch life, grandparents, cousins—it was all a dream after all those years of being alone with a sad mother. It was just too bad about Uncle Dale. Ry liked him the few times they'd met, usually for only a brief few minutes backstage at one of Dallas' shows. Making a quiet promise to himself, Ry swore he'd do better watching over Jade—and now Hunter, it seemed—so that his mother and Dallas wouldn't have to worry, and maybe it would keep them from fighting. If Dallas walked away from him and his mom, everything would change. It would all go to shit again.

A tremor passed through Ry at the memory of a despondent mother who often took to her bed and left him alone, even when he was little. His mom never did that anymore. Thank God for Dallas.

"Are you okay, Ry?" Cassie asked, frowning. She'd felt the quiver pass through him.

He rallied. "I'm fine, Mom. Hey!" Stopping, he turned to her. "Why don't you take riding lessons with me? We can surprise Dallas when he gets home. The other day he said he wanted to get out on a trail while we're here. You can come too!"

"He said that?" A furrowed brow accompanied the remark. Riding was the last thing she thought Dallas would want to do. She added, "I have no interest in getting on an unpredictable large animal and traipsing off through a wild forest littered with bears and other wild creatures."

"Mom. Yeeesh. You're such a mom. And yep, he said that. He was helping me with the new tune Emily-Grace and I wrote. You were with Aunt Dawn, I think, doing laundry or something. Dal said Johnny told him there are tons of trails here. They go right up the mountain. Apparently there's a spectacular view from a clear-cut up there."

"A view?" Laying the back of a hand across Ry's forehead, which he promptly swiped away, Cassie joked, "Who are you and what have you done with my son? Since when do you care about views?"

Ry hemmed and hawed. He toed a hole in the dirt. "I just thought that maybe Emily-Grace's parents might come for a drive up this way some day. She'd likely love it up here. She knows how to ride, and she appreciates the little things in life. Like views."

"Does she. Hmmm." Cassie winked at Boone, who was sauntering in his easy cowboy way over to them. "I think someone's got a real good case of puppy love."

"Seriously, Mom. Get a grip. We're songwriting partners. We just want to write songs together."

Boone harrumphed. The disapproval faded quickly when Cassie said quietly, "Someday soon we'll need to talk about you and your music, Ry. For one thing, I know for a fact that Emily-Grace's mother and father are strongly against their daughter having any kind of public music career."

"She wants to be a dancer, not a singer. But that doesn't mean she can't still write songs behind the scenes, Mom. She's real good at it."

"Okay, honey," Cassie capitulated. "Well, you've both got some more growing up to do before either of you need to worry about careers, so for today how about you go riding with Boone here, and I'll watch for a bit and then see if I can corner Dawn or maybe Jenny to take me and the two little ones into Sundre."

Boone chipped in. "Did you clear that with Mister My-Shit-Don't-Stink-In-My-High-Falutin'-Gucci-Shoes, Cassie?"

She laughed. "Oops, no. I forgot. Matt and I got talking about other things. We'll borrow one of the two fellas stationed here, or Johnny. We'll be okay. There aren't that many people around, and Sundre's a small place. Besides, it's Dallas who they want to see. Most people don't even know what I look like."

"They'll know you if you have a little Indian boy trailing along behind ya. A white woman, a white girl, and an Indian boy."

"Um, Indigenous, Boone." Cassie shrugged. "Most people say Indigenous now."

He took the gentle reprimand well. "Ask me if I care. I'm tired of being told what to do and what to think. I'm ready to be back to the one giving orders." He grinned at Ry. "You ready, kid? Lesson number two?"

Ry whooped, which brought the two smaller children in question, running.

The problem of taking Hunter along on the shopping trip was easily solved when Hunter refused to leave Ry's side once he found out that Ry was going to take another riding lesson from Boone. Reluctantly, Boone saddled a small paint, and lifted Hunter up into the saddle. The child was small on the large animal, so the stirrups were rejigged to fit his tiny feet. Soon, Ry and Hunter were both listening attentively to Boone, which suited the older man very well. In fact, Boone had to stop and wipe his eyes a few times.

Doris was watching from the back step of the bungalow. "The Lord giveth and the Lord taketh away," she whispered to Dawn and Cassie, who were alongside hanging laundry on the line. "And then He giveth again."

Cassie and Dawn shared a small smile. When the laundry was fully out and drying in the gentle breeze, the two loaded Jade, along with Dawn's ten year old, Ruby, into Dawn's truck. Johnny followed in his truck with Cooper and Colt.

Doris settled into a low camp chair near the corral to watch the riding lesson. Dale and Dallas as youngsters flitted through her mind, and suddenly

Boone was decades younger, handsome enough to make her catch her breath, and a lot less ornery.

Like her husband, she caught herself having to wipe her eyes. *Where do the years go,* she wondered.

She smiled, and settled in with a sigh to watch.

Chapter Eleven

*H*ighway 2 on the approach to Calgary was an easy drive; the opposite stretch, heading northwest, was cluttered with RVs and fifth-wheel trailers on this warm summer day, all pointed towards scenic Sylvan Lake or a myriad of other mountain lakeside destinations. Since Matt and Dallas were heading south, they bypassed most of the big rigs and made good time on the road.

What they were less successful at was chatting in the easy manner they were accustomed to, and neither considered turning on the radio to provide a backdrop for the heavy thoughts running around their heads.

Matt, left elbow perched on the door, was steering with a light touch on the smooth-flowing highway, just using a few fingers on his right hand. Jessie was turning over and over in his mind. The chat with Cassie had him missing his old friend, missing their days together, their old routine. Like when they used to hang out on film sets or cozy up together on the flights between stops on one of her tours. Shanda was in Matt's thoughts too; in his head, the women he loved were flipping around each other like socks in a dryer.

Dallas, in the meantime, was going over what he knew about the woman they were heading to Calgary to search for.

Maria. Her name was Maria. She would've been pushing forty when she became pregnant with Hunter. Dallas had no idea if Maria had other children. Did Hunter have siblings? Jesus, did Dale have other children with Maria? Dallas told himself that was unlikely, or all of the kids would have landed on J.I.'s doorstep.

It was Dallas who knew Maria first, not Dale. Late one night just after high school he stopped for a piss at a service station on his way back from Calgary, grabbed a chocolate bar from a rack near the cash, looked up, and instantly disappeared into the most soulful eyes he'd ever seen. *Mahogany-bay,* he thought at the time, equating their shade of brown to the good-natured dark horse he liked to ride at his family's ranch. *Bottomless.* Desperate to dive into the expressive, enigmatic pools so he could get to know the girl they belonged to, he pushed the chocolate bar across the counter, hoping she would touch his fingers when she picked the bar up to scan it.

She didn't, he remembered with a wistful grin, recalling that her fingers were slender and feminine, and that he longed to feel them graze his skin.

Reaching up now, Dallas touched his hair. *An eagle feather,* he thought with a start as a new memory from that inaugural meeting grabbed him. *She had an eagle feather braided into her hair.* He'd pointed to it.

"It carries my prayers to the Creator," she'd said simply, her voice barely a murmur.

"It's sacred, right?" he'd answered stupidly, scolding himself for not filtering his thoughts before he spoke. "For you, your people…I guess I'm just surprised that you can wear it in your hair on an ordinary day. Like to work, I mean."

"I do what I want," was her response. It wasn't said in a critical way, nor was it in any way defensive. It was a simple fact. Dallas was to learn that Maria was driven by what felt natural to her, and not by any higher decrees or rules handed down over generations or through society. She was her own person. If she wanted to wear an eagle feather in her hair, she wore an eagle feather in her hair.

The feather exuded a spiritual power Dallas was helpless to understand back then; even now, thinking of it laying against the silken black strands of her long hair, he recalled its power translating to Maria, absorbing her, drawing him in. When she lay coins in his palm that night, the change from the five dollar bill he handed her, her touch was as electric as he initially thought it might be. She seemed to know it, Dallas recalled, leaning an elbow against the window glass of the SUV now, oblivious of the slightly undulating terrain flying past. She'd let her fingers linger in his, blinked in a sort of quiet appeal for rescue (or so he interpreted), and didn't smile.

Most girls smiled at me back then, Dallas reminded himself, in some desperate attempt to build himself back up into the teen he thought he was, and not the skinny loser his father made him out to be. He brought his arm down from the window, leveraged his hands on the seat cushion, and hoisted himself up taller.

The movement startled Matt out of his reverie. He looked over, and Dallas mumbled a quiet, "Sorry," before disappearing back under Maria's spell.

The night they met, Dallas was on his way back from a Calgary honkytonk. He'd fought with his father about going, stormed out of the house, won the bar's big Stampede Week talent contest, and was on a high. At the time, he thought he deserved Maria. She was the prize, the cherry on top of soft serve ice cream. Remembering her now, it struck him that she was tall in stature, almost as tall as him, actually, although she was diminutive and restrained, personality-wise. Maria was a woman of few words. When she did speak, Dallas listened. When her quiet voice was heard, it was as powerful as the eagle feather. What she had to say was almost always as sacred as the great bird itself.

Dallas tucked away a mental note to pay more attention to Hunter. Perhaps when the little boy finally started to speak regularly, his words would have solemn meaning too.

That long ago night, he waited for Maria to get off work at midnight. Knowing his father would be pissed and his mother would worry, once he had his mystical girl in his truck, he turned left instead of right when he pulled out of the service station's parking lot. *I ran away twice that night,* he remembered. *Twice that night I temporarily escaped.*

Nausea gripped his throat, clutched at his stomach. *Why is all the bad stuff coming back now,* he wondered. *I gotta reset the energy around my family. It needs to be swapped out for the good stuff again.*

That crazy night was one of the last nights of Calgary's famous Stampede. All the local cowboys and cowboy wannabes were partying and Dallas was only too happy to take his exotic girl with the quiet power into the heart of the storm. But not until after they pulled into the parking lot of an abandoned factory and did the sex thing first. Amazing how strong their connection was after just a few hours of serious flirting.

What Dallas didn't count on was running into Dale later, around two in the morning—Dale, his rodeo cowboy brother.

And who was with Dale?

Boone. The boys' father.

Dallas caught hell. While Boone publicly ragged him out, Maria stood quietly at Dallas' side and sized up Dale. Who, Dallas recalled, stood in a kind of exhausted silence at Boone's side and sized her up right back.

Boone took Dallas by the scruff of the neck that night and stuffed him into his truck, on the passenger side. Went around the hood, whipped open the driver's side door, and slid in behind the wheel. Waved an arm outside the window at Dale and angrily ordered him to drive Maria home.

Dale later told Dallas that their father was concerned for Dallas and so they went looking for him. *He said you are too young and naive to be in the city, to be in the bars at night. He said you don't know what sharks are out here, what kinda trouble you can get into, a good lookin' kid like you. Specially during Stampede, when all the cowboy riff-raff is in town boozin' up and lookin' for trouble.*

And you do? Dallas had answered Dale, throwing his gloves down and furiously kicking around loose hay. *You know about that kind of trouble? Does knowin' about it make you infallible, Dale?*

It was late afternoon the day after the Stampede contest; the boys were in the infamous, nefarious hay loft when he and Dale had words. Dallas was under orders to work for the day organizing the rectangular bales to make room for the fresh hay they'd have to stack in the airy space later in the summer. He was tired. Despite the protective gloves, his hands were blistered, and he could barely breathe for all the hot dust floating around, sucking its way into his lungs. Worse, he was hungover as hell and desperately wanted to make a hasty exit to go see Maria, to apologize, to beg her forgiveness for his father's nasty interception in what had surely promised to be a perfect night.

In the loft, Dale, in all his big brother know-it-all grandeur, was pissing him off.

Dale didn't answer Dallas' question, the one about knowing about being infallible. All these years later, the image of his brother standing with sunken shoulders amongst the hay, silhouetted by the open door he'd once fallen through, and telegraphing what seemed to be some kind of deeper dejected unspoken concern, struck Dallas, who all of a sudden caught himself wondering what it was his brother kept inside that day. At the time, Dallas was too pissed and sick to really care, although he had looked twice at Dale standing so close to the open ledge where he had fallen during the big fire years earlier. In the light of day, he could see that Dale had been in some kind of fight. Bruised knuckles peeked out below long sleeves, which struck Dallas as odd because why in the heck in the heat would Dale cover his body with the long sleeves of a plaid shirt? He ought to be wearing one of his usual T-shirts.

Now, thinking back on it, as the taller buildings of the city came into view, Dallas instinctively realized that somehow that night at the bar, Maria must have picked up on something about Dale that Dallas plainly didn't see. Dallas was too lost in his own misery and embarrassment to fully understand that Dale was not himself. Only in later years did he get stumped at the dull gloom on his brother's face, and at what he thought was unrealistic anger on his father's part—an anger which seemed to simmer under all of Boone's later interactions with Dallas.

Perhaps there was more going on back then than Dallas had originally understood. Maybe he was too selfish to see past himself and his passion to write and to sing, than to really see anyone else. Things changed after that night, between the brothers. Dallas had always blamed Maria and distance for coming between them. Boone and Doris were old school—Maria was a no-no. She was barely acceptable as a friend, and was absolutely not girlfriend or wife material. If he could have, Dallas would have hung on to her anyway—her exotic eyes beguiled him. And always, always there was that mysterious eagle feather in her hair, on the right side, its centre just in front of her ear, a conduit right to Heaven, Dallas thought. She was everything he wanted to be—free, enigmatic, wild. The romantic in him soaked up her sadness, which he learned was earned from a history of loneliness and sorrow.

The choice of keeping her in his life disappeared the day he found Dale with her.

In the hay loft.

Two weeks after Dallas was escorted, shame-faced, away from Stampede. Two weeks after he knew true love for the first time.

Now, the memory of finding his brother with Maria caught up to him.

"Pull over, Matt," he commanded, the earlier nausea no longer bearable, fueled by a growing anxiety he could no longer suppress.

A quick look to Dallas, and Matt obliged, swinging the car so hard to the right that it swerved and almost fishtailed. Dallas bailed, and retched into the long grass bordering the highway's shoulder.

In the distance, Calgary loomed under a grey sky hazy with threatening rain.

"I thought I was done with my teens a long time ago," Dallas said after, curving his body frontwards when he leaned against the car and stared at the dusty toes of his boots.

Somber, Matt got out from behind the wheel and traipsed slowly around to face him. Cars and trucks raced past, leaving overheated, humid air stirring in their wakes.

Dallas looked up at his friend. His eyes were bright, moist. "I never thought those days would come back to haunt me. I guess it's got something to do with losing Dale like that. It makes me think about all the wasted days and nights when I should have picked up the phone, or come for a visit…all this shit has opened old sores." He wrapped his strong arms around his stomach and stared back at the ground. "I don't get it, Matt. Maria meant something to both of us in a first love kind of way. I suppose it makes sense that Dale would still be curious about her if he ever ran into her. She was rare. A sensitive, wild thing caught in a whirlwind kind of world too big and fast for her. Like one of those horses Dale coveted. Meant to run free in meadows, not live in this kind of urban nuthouse." Absently he waved an arm in the general direction of the city.

Matt chose not to respond in words. His allegiance, and reverence for Dallas' hurt and confusion, was clear in the way he stood at ease at his friend's side, until Dallas suddenly hoisted his lanky body away from the vehicle and got back inside.

A few minutes later, Matt swung open the driver's side door, and eased the SUV back into traffic.

They were absorbed by the city a short time later.

In a while, after navigating through a few different neighbourhoods, Matt drew Dallas back to the present with a voice gravelly from lack of use on the quiet drive. "There," he remarked, pointing to a two-story white duplex that displayed, in black numbers by the front doors, the address he'd found when researching Maria. Releasing his foot from the gas, he drew the big car to a cautious halt at the curb.

In front of them was an inconspicuous, lower scale dwelling with the kind of beauty that's only found if it's looked for.

A row of pretty pale pink flowers with wide petals dotted the duplex's perimeter. Its simple presence was incongruous in this dry, plain neighbourhood, by this house. They'd passed a school just down the street. Its crowning glory was broken glass and boarded-up windows. A basketball net in what passed for a playground was either well used or sadly neglected— like a spiderweb, net remnants hung eerily from a lopsided, unpainted ring.

Both men had shuddered at the idea of little Hunter playing on a school ground that stank so strongly of decay and thwarted dreams.

They focused on the house in front of them.

A parallel set of small cement slabs led the way to matching, uneven wooden steps, steps that led up to two doors, presumably into the duplex's two residences. Patches of wilted, dried grass poked up between the slabs, which were, for the most part, incomplete and broken. Forgotten. That's the sense that the guys got when they eased out of the vehicle and glanced warily at each other before trudging in the muggy heat up the forlorn walk that led to number 211A.

The door was once a vibrant red; flakes of paint chips lay on the top step. Some, at the mercy of the wind, had made their way to the tired greenery alongside the steps, landing gracelessly on the leaves and on the petals of the pink flowers, which lent an eerie careless indifference to the place.

Matt caught a glimpse of someone pulling back a dark curtain covering a small window just left of the door. By the time he cranked his head and got a good look, that someone had already peeked out and thrown the curtain back into place. Nobody answered when Matt knocked. He tried the door while Dallas fidgeted alongside. "Nada," he announced. "Locked. What do you want me to do, Dallas?" Clearly, someone was inside the home. Clearly, that person did not want company.

"You're the ex-cop. Figure it out, Dick Tracey."

Matt forgave him for his sarcastic temper but ragged at him for forgetting to put on his ball cap.

Dallas ragged back. "Once again, that's really your dominion, old man." Secretly, he'd thought of the hat but shoved aside the notion to grab it. Part of him wanted to laud his success over Maria. She broke his heart; she'd be sorry when she saw the famous Dallas White at her door.

If she answered it. Which—if it was her that peeked out at the fellas—she was choosing not to do.

Matt jumped ship and sidestepped over to 211B. Knocked. Knocked harder. Was reaching for the door handle when the door squeaked open on dry hinges. *Oil those things,* Matt almost said aloud, wishing for the lush coolness of Kits Beach in Vancouver or the pool at Jessie and Josh's house. This sticky, damp heat was too much for a man accustomed to the restorative vitality of refreshing swims and luxurious, soft towels to dry off with afterwards. He was fairly certain Dallas felt the same way, judging by the way Dallas was frowning and pulling his sweaty shirt away from his body.

A small wrinkled face stared out at Matt. He almost jumped when his vision adjusted and he discerned a pair of dark eyes within the gloom of the place.

"Are you looking for Maria?" the person, an elderly woman, asked outright, in a voice that seemed far too voluminous for the body it came from.

"Yes. Yes, Maria. You know her."

Dallas stepped quietly up behind Matt. The woman who belonged to the wrinkled skin and piercing—yet gentle—eyes pondered him. She smiled in recognition. Matt and Dallas expected her to say *I know you. You're that country singer.*

"You're Dale's kin," she announced instead. The warmth she exuded upon recognizing Dallas was Dale's doing.

"Wh-what?" It had been a long time since anyone said as much to Dallas. Always it was a simple proclamation—*You're Dallas White*—usually accompanied by squeals and requests for autographs. "Okay," Dallas answered, a little awestruck at the throwback to normalcy. "Dale. Yeah. He's, uh—he was—my brother. He died. Like—just. Died."

"I'm aware," the old lady said, reaching a gnarled, leathery hand out to Dallas, who hesitated before taking the thin, almost weightless fingers in his. "Please accept my sincere condolences."

"You knew him."

"I most certainly did." Backing up, she moved aside so her unexpected visitors could make their way inside. "Come in, gentlemen. We'll talk over tea, if you have a mind to sit for a bit. You," she said, pointing to Matt, "are a wise, sweet man, aren't you? I know such things. I read People."

"You're intuitive?" Dallas asked. An admission that she was psychic wouldn't have surprised either man. This fragile, bent-over woman seemed to have a calm, unearthly wisdom about her. And Dallas needed wisdom. He yearned for it. Or a spiritual connection to Dale, maybe she had that? A direct line? Maybe she was someone who could tell him *why*?

He held his breath.

"Nooo, dear," she replied amicably, tottering into the dark abyss of the tiny place and heading straight through to the back, presumably to a kitchen to put the kettle on. She waved an arm towards a rectangular seventies-style coffee table. "I read People," she said. "The magazine. There was a story on you a few years back. About how you and Jessie Wheeler have this special relationship. You saved her life once."

"Twice, actually," Matt muttered under his breath, tucking his hands into his pants pockets, raising his shoulders, and bashfully rolling over the side of one foot.

Dallas fired a playful grin over to him. "You and me have a special relationship too."

"Really," Matt said dryly. "Do we." A happy light danced across his eyes.

"Yeah, I mean, you haven't exactly saved my life but hey, I'd be worth saving, wouldn't I? If it came to it?"

"Depends."

"On?"

"On how much vacation time you're planning to give me."

"If you save my life, or now?"

Chuckling, Matt said, "Always."

Contemplating that, Dallas snapped a thumb and forefinger on Matt's bicep. Matt yelped and took a step back before Dallas said, "None. You'd just go running off to work for Jessie. It's my duty to keep you away from her."

"Crossing the line, man." Folding his arms across his chest, Matt glowered at Dallas. "Not your business."

Dallas gave him a look. "Is that sour face for real, or are you just putting me on?"

"Sit, gentlemen. Sit." With the kettle on to boil, their hostess toddled back into the room.

Still facing Matt, Dallas asked, "Are you three? As in years old?" He was pretty certain he heard Matt growl in response. Dallas grinned and clapped his friend kindly on the arm.

The woman dropped into what was likely her favourite chair, a sturdy rocker with round wooden arms and faded grey-blue needlepoint seat and back coverings. Matt followed her example and stepped behind the coffee table to settle into a not-so-comfy under-stuffed couch with weird bulges. Dallas sat on the opposite end.

Since he was facing the old lady, Matt officially introduced himself and Dallas.

"I'm Ethel," she told them in return. "A proud widow of a Calgary fireman." She winked conspiratorially at Dallas.

"True?" he asked, unable to hide his astonishment.

"Very much so," Ethel answered, adjusting an afghan over jeans.

Dallas raised an eyebrow when Matt leapt up to help her. "Always the white knight," he joked, which brought a small smile to Matt's lips. "You're making me look bad, buddy."

Ethel brightened. The casually happy rapport ricocheting between her two nervous visitors was a sunny light in a dark time.

Matt sat back down and waited respectfully for Ethel to offer more. In his mind, a necessary grace period had to pass before he got into the tough stuff.

"Thank you, young man," Ethel said graciously to Matt before she looked back at Dallas. "I know your story," she said, a slight, uncertain flicker quivering over her aged face when she fixed him solidly in her gaze. "Your brother was thrilled to bits when you jumped ship on that Deborah vixen and married a fireman's widow. He couldn't wait to tell me. We toasted your union with champagne."

"My union." Dumbstruck, Dallas shook his head slowly from side to side. "You and my brother."

"And Maria." It was laid out as a simple fact, said matter-of-factly with a slight raise at the end, suggesting that Dallas should have figured that part out already.

Matt leaned back, crossed an ankle over a knee, and listened. Maybe he wouldn't have to do any asking of the tough stuff after all...

"My wedding was, like, four or so years ago now," Dallas said, doing the mental arithmetic in his mind. "Dale was at it."

"Yes, darling. When he came back, we celebrated. He was over the moon for you. He had a lot of nice things to say about your new wife and he didn't hesitate to announce how relieved he was that you finally saw the light and married a nice woman."

"It sounds like you knew my brother well."

"Maria and I were neighbours for many years. I had a lot of opportunity to get to know Dale. He was very helpful around my place."

"Around your place..." Dallas echoed. He found himself at a complete loss for words. Just how long had Dale been coming around here? Jenny flitted across his mind; Shane and Cormac, too. Dale's boys adored their quiet, hardworking father.

"About Maria," Matt tried, wondering if it was Hunter's mother that had pulled the curtain back next door. He had to wait to push any further when Ethel wriggled her way out of the needlepoint rocker and went for the tea. Following, Matt assisted her but she didn't speak again until everyone was served and resettled.

Matt was just getting comfortable on the lumpy couch when he noticed that Dallas' attention was focused on something along the wall to the men's right. Following his gaze, Matt saw that it was a framed photograph that was taking up a central place of pride on the mantel below Ethel's wall mounted flat screen television, which seemed completely out of place amongst the older style furnishings. Staring out from the photograph was a stunning ebony horse with intense eyes—maybe even the same wild black horse the guys saw that day with Hunter.

"About Maria," Matt tried again, retraining his eyes on his hostess. He waited.

Uncertain, Dallas let his mind drift away from the framed photo. He looked nervously over at Matt before lacing his fingers together on his knees and sitting straight up to target Ethel in his vision.

She smiled and took a sip of tea. "Dale and Maria shared one of the most beautiful love stories I ever bore witness to."

What? Dallas had to drop his focus to his interlaced fingers, concentrate hard, and count to ten. Twice.

"Apart from my own," Ethel was adding hastily. "How blessed am I?" The teacup rattled in her hand, ever so slightly. "*Was* I, I mean. Of course. Past tense, gentlemen. Past tense. Hold your women tight. Love slips away like a wilted flower."

"They had a child," Matt offered while Dallas sucked in a breath and tried not to hyperventilate.

"Wee Hunter. Yes, a beautiful child. A special child. They waited a long time for him to come along."

"What?" Without intending to, Dallas' abrupt reaction was borderline rude. Matt sent him a look of warning. "How long?"

"Years, honey. At first Dale felt it prudent to be cautious, at least that's what he said. I really think the reason he wanted to wait was because he didn't want to be away from his child. The way he and Maria were living, there was no way around it. Your brother could not be a full time father."

"Dale *was* a full time father. He has—had—two boys. Cormac and Shane. And a wife, I might add."

"Jenny. Yes, I know, son. I know about Jenny. I met her once or twice. Fiery thing. Exact opposite of your brother."

"Here?"

"No. Around. At Stampede one year. Maria wanted to meet her. Dale set it up. I went along for moral support. The second time wasn't planned, it was random. At the mall, of all places. Maria was always calm but she took that time hard." Ethel leaned forward. Matt straightened, ready to rescue her tea, which was close to overflowing its decorative, old fashioned ceramic brim. "Jenny had the boys with her. They were only about four or five. Maria was strong and accepting, but it hurt her to actually see Dale with another family."

"Ethel, I don't understand. H-how long were my brother and Maria seeing each other?"

Ethel pondered that for a moment. She put a quivering finger to her lips. "Oh," she said after a while, "I think they met when Dale was in high school. Or he had just been out of school a year or so. Something like that." She smiled, a mostly toothless smile. "You should know, you were there, son!"

Dallas was getting frustrated. Jenny crossed his mind again. By her behaviour these days, it didn't seem like she had a clue that her husband had another woman on the side. Hunter, for certain, was a complete surprise. "I don't mean when they met, Ma'am," he said, trying to corral the urge to holler questions, one after the other. His celebrity media training held up well, especially when Matt, who had already figured the puzzle out, fired him another look of caution. "I mean, this last time they got together. How long?" To accentuate the serious nature of the question, he sat further forward and clenched his fingers so tightly together the blood ran from them and they turned white.

His determined stare would have unnerved most people, but Ethel had the advantage of Dale's descriptions of Dallas. Dallas, the misunderstood son, the dreamy poet, the child who once carried fear with him everywhere he went on the working ranch that was his home. The ranch that had large horses and mysterious machinery and such wicked thunder and lightning storms that the house shook, and that got fires burning in the mountains.

She answered with a knowing, understanding smile. "Why, son," she said, lifting her delicate teacup to her lips, "they never broke up!"

Chapter Twelve

"Jesus Christ," Dallas cursed as he paced up and down the gravel parking lot of the treed park Matt had swung into shortly after their visit with Ethel, "Dale had a second family. His whole married life, he had a second family! He stayed with Maria all those years! Right from Stampede on up!"

Matt was perched atop a picnic table that bordered the parking area, elbows on his thighs, doing his utmost best to keep his friend calm. "I'm sure you've figured out why he kept her a secret."

"Hell, yeah. Boone. My bastard, racist father." Rifling fingers through his long hair, Dallas lit the air blue again. "I can't goddamn believe it. I mean, Dale was a good guy, I thought! How could he do this to Jenny? To his boys?" He swung around to Matt. "We're no longer talking fly-by-night here, Matt. This is serious shit."

"Your record is on the wrong loop here, Dallas. Try putting it on a new loop."

"What the hell you talkin' about, Matt?" As an afterthought, Dallas added, "Explain. Please."

"They loved each other. They 'got' each other. They wanted to be together but life got in the way. Done."

Rocking over on his left foot, Dallas paused and tried to realistically consider what Matt was telling him.

Matt added an addendum, albeit he uttered it in a quiet, humbled way. "I'm real glad Dale and Maria got that time together, Dal. A lot of people can't find a way to make true love work."

"Well, hell, Matt," Dallas griped arrogantly. "A lot of people shouldn't get that time together. They have responsibilities to others. Maybe not meaning you, of course," he countered too quickly, contemplating Matt's situation and trying to wrap his head around it. "I know it hasn't been easy for you. With Jessie, I mean."

"With Shanda too, when you throw Jessie in the mix, buddy. We're making it work. All of us are, in the best way we can."

"Which means?" Dallas pushed. "Come on, tell me, for real. Do you sleep with Jessie? Is that a thing or is it just a rumour?"

Matt hesitated. "Not often," he admitted, with a touch of longing. "Just once in a very blue moon."

"But you do. How come..." Raising his right hand, Dallas scratched his head. "Jesus, I see you in a similar boat as Dale, apparently, and I think to myself that I want you to be happy, because I've seen you really suffer over her, Matt. But then I think about Josh and about their kids, and about Shanda, and I think, hell, that's just wrong. I mean, does Josh know? Does Shanda know?"

"That Jessie and I are sometimes together? Yes. They know."

"So it's an open marriage."

It took Matt a minute to answer. He scratched at a raw mosquito bite on his hand before he spoke. "Not exactly, Dallas. There are no other partners involved. Josh and Shanda choose to stay faithful, as far as Jessie and I know."

"So you get what Dale did." The pronouncement was loaded with accusation.

"I do, although I'm not saying he made all the right choices along the way—"

"Yeah," Dallas considered, cutting him off. Adrenaline was ripping through his brain. He started pacing again. "Like he should have damn well divorced Jenny and let her move on, and he should have gotten the hell away from my father. Salvaged what he could, if he loved Maria that much. He's done now. His life is kaput. Finis. Dale has no more chances to do things right and live his life the way he obviously wanted to!"

"Maybe he couldn't. Maybe he couldn't let your parents go."

"Of course he couldn't. Jesus, this is perfect Dale we are talking about here. He was not the runner in our family. Remember?" Dallas jabbed at himself.

"Or Jenny. Maybe it was more about her," Matt offered. "Maybe he was afraid she'd take the kids and run."

"I dunno. I don't know what the hell to think." Gazing out over a nearby bubbling brook, Dallas considered another baffling thought. "If he loved Maria so much, why would he do what he did? Why would he end his life? He had a kid to consider!"

"That's a question only Dale, and maybe Maria know, Dal. And, I suppose, the universe at this point. Knowing what I've learned lately about Dale, and about Maria, I feel like there was a reason. I feel like this was somehow planned."

"Like maybe Maria was supposed to go too, but couldn't go through with it?"

"Maybe. I don't know, Dallas. I don't suppose we'll ever know."

"Unless…"

Matt shook his head. "If Maria was the person next door, and wouldn't see us today, and Ethel was reluctant to talk about her, I don't think we'll be getting inside her door any time soon."

"She must miss Hunter. She's got to be going crazy, wondering how he's doing."

The quiet, reflective boy passed through the men's minds. If it was Maria that packed Hunter's bag, she had not left a personal note. Yet she'd put a worn old stuffed animal in there, presumably for comfort. She loved Hunter's father. She loved Hunter. Unless…

"Maybe Dale cheated on Maria. Maybe he wanted to end things with her and be with Jenny full time."

Matt slid off the picnic table. "Stop, Dallas. This constant storytelling in your own head is not going to answer any of your questions. Only time will. Maybe." He slapped his friend on the shoulder. "Let's go. I still need to drop in and have a chat with the security firm."

"But Matt, it doesn't make sense. I feel like I never knew Dale at all."

Turning back around, Matt poked the bear a little. "Maybe that's not what's bugging you."

Dallas threw his arms out to the sides in frustration. "What else could it be?"

"Dallas," Matt tried. "Look, buddy. Love is just not always cut and dry."

"What are you saying?"

"I'm saying that Maria was someone you once cared a lot for. That's what I'm saying."

"Seriously. You think I'm more upset about all this because Dale stuck with her despite a helluva lotta trouble. Whereas I wasted a good chunk of my life chasing unicorns! You think I'm jealous. That's what you think."

Annoyed at the overbearing waves of mosquitos in the park, the stifling muggy heat, and the lack of resolution to their visit with Ethel, Matt fired back in a voice far louder than he meant to use. "What I think, Dallas, is that this is far more complicated than you likely understand at this point. Let it go. Let your brother rest in peace."

"And what about his kid?" Dallas cried. "His mother is alive. We saw her peeking out from behind that curtain!"

"We don't know for certain that it was her. We couldn't get in and we couldn't convince Ethel to say one way or the other."

Dallas shoved a finger in Matt's chest. "There are no death records for Maria. You checked."

"Correct. We'll send a social worker out. Maybe that will open some doors. Maybe she already has a relationship with someone she trusts."

"In the meantime, my family—Cassie, Ry, and Jade, I mean—are getting awfully close to this kid."

"And you and your parents are keeping your distance. Smart." The accusing look in Matt's eyes stopped Dallas' barrage of questions cold.

Dallas sighed. His shoulders caved. His voice lowered and slowed. "And you, my friend," he said, dropping his hands to his sides, "are the closest. I'm sorry. Hunter's crazy about you. Dumbass."

A lump formed in Matt's throat. "This might not end the way we want it to," he said. "In all likelihood, Maria is experiencing remorse. Especially if she's angry at Dale, if she's grieving. She could demand Hunter back any day."

The thought was sobering. Regardless of all the chaos and uncertainty surrounding Dale's passing, Hunter was a part of him. Dale's sudden passing had left a Grand Canyon sized hole. And Hunter, despite almost everyone's attempts to remain carefully detached, was starting to fill it.

Chapter Thirteen

*H*unter and Ry were on their second horseback riding lesson of the day when Matt swung the SUV into the public parking lot and braked in front of the closed swinging gate. He expected Dallas to hop out and pluck off the rope that held the two parts of the gate closed, but his buddy didn't move.

No curious fans were lurking. Colin, the burly salt-and-pepper-haired security stationed out front by the small barn today—the barn that served double duty as registration office and camp store—sauntered over to Matt's lowered window and told the fellas that the day had been quiet overall.

Matt put the SUV in 'park' and took his foot off the brake.

"It's just been damn hot and muggy," Colin said. "We could use a good old fashioned mountain thunderstorm to crack open the sky and let some breathable air in." He put his hands on the window frame and leaned casually on the door. "And some rain along with it. The earth is so dry the ants bounce when you walk by. The land needs a good soaking."

"I expect Doris' vegetable garden could use it," Matt said amicably. "She makes ten trips a day down to the garden to move the hose from the corn to the carrots and back again."

"Yessir, I've seen her at it. She's wearing a path straight into the ground. I suppose it gives her purpose these days." Colin got somber and mopey at the thought. Doris was good to him. She'd brought him homemade biscuits and strawberry jam just this very morning. He rallied. "I'll get the gate for ya, boys."

"I got it," Dallas said. "No worries." He didn't budge.

Colin went back to the weather. "We need a storm the likes of the one we had last summer, the big one that shook the planters clean off my deck in Calgary." Punctuating the seriousness of the storm with a hand slap on the door, Colin didn't wait for an answer, and instead strolled off with an air of righteous certainty.

The SUV was still idling in front of the swinging gate. Annoyed, wondering why Dallas wasn't moving, Matt looked over. He was just about to unbuckle his seat belt and get out and open the gate himself when he caught a glimpse of quiet hesitation in his friend's eyes. Following Dallas' gaze, Matt sat back in his seat and exhaled thoughtfully. Cassie was seated on a hay bale in the corral, watching the boys listen to Boone. At Cassie's feet, Jade was bent over the patchy hard-packed earth trying to entice one of the barn kittens into playing with a piece of straw she was holding between her fingers.

"He's got their undivided attention," Matt observed respectfully as both boys lifted the reins at the same time, seemingly in response to some order Boone barked at them.

Dallas contemplated the busy corral before answering. He was lost in some age-old memory. When he eventually spoke, his words seemed to come from some deep, inward place. A sad place. "I'm not seeing myself so good in their eyes right now, Matt."

He's thinking about him and Dale when they were kids, Matt figured. *He's remembering his father teaching them to ride.*

The corral was a dozen hay wagon lengths away. Nobody other than Colin from security had acknowledged their arrival back at the ranch. Dallas and Matt had the luxury of watching Boone, in a rare light moment given the tough events of the past while, call out something to Cassie that made the younger boys and Cassie all break out into laughter.

Even Hunter. Matt held his breath. The child seemed to light up from within. Still laughing, his head thrown back in delight, he bent to reward his patient horse with a sweet child-sized scratch on the neck.

Dallas spoke again, this time with more reverent restraint than outright self-loathing. "Why is it that coming home reduces people to being kids again?"

"Is that such a bad thing?" Matt pointed to the activity in the corral. "Don't you remember any happy times with your dad?"

Blowing out a long *pffftt* first, Dallas said, "Apart from my mom's home cooking, all I seem to be able to recall these days is the awkward me who could never seem to do anything right. The dreamer. The kid who couldn't wait to escape. I think that's all my dad remembers too." Rifling his fingers through his blond hair, he went on in a humbler, quieter voice. "I suppose there's no love lost there, having a kid who you know can't wait to get out from under your feet."

"That brings back memories," Matt chuckled.

"You? Or your daughter?" Looking briefly sideways at Matt, Dallas raised his eyebrows. Matt rarely talked about the days when he was married to Julie, a petite woman Dallas knew about but had never met, with whom Matt had raised a daughter.

"Katy. She wanted a frog tattoo on her leg." Matt grimaced, remembering. "She had this thing about frogs. I used to bring them to her after travelling with Jessie. Teddy bear frogs, decorative ornaments for her bedroom, sticker books with frogs on the cover. It was our thing. A way I could feel better about myself, I suppose, since I was away so much."

At the memory, he smiled. It came out crooked, and quickly flipped over altogether. Shaking his head at the absurdity of the passage of time, Matt absently started picking at the bottom of the steering wheel so he could train his eyes there instead of at his friend. Katy was in her twenties now, and rarely a part of his life since his divorce from her mother. "I didn't mind the idea of a tattoo so much," he continued, finally looking up and taking a quick glance at Dallas, who was listening attentively. "It's just that she wanted this behemoth big thing, not some small discreet bit of ink. I had a helluva time weighing in. Julie kept trying to force me to take a stand. Katy and I were already growing apart. She used to babysit for Jessie and Josh. When things, uh, changed, with Jessie, it got so I could barely face her. I was a mess back then. Dallas," he said, twisting to the side so he could face his buddy more fully, "my point is that it's not always all about the kid. Sometimes the parents are more messed up than the kids. They project their problems, you know?"

Dallas grunted. "That doesn't bode well for me as a dad. Thank God for Cassie."

Trying to keep him on track, to get his point across so Dallas wouldn't be so hard on himself, Matt eased him further down the parent path. "Do you think your dad had dreams?"

"Dreams?"

"Dreams. Delusions some people aspire to their whole lives. Pie in the sky stuff."

"Hell, I don't know." Dallas thought for a moment. He rubbed a finger back and forth over his bottom lip and stared out at the sloped, treed mountains on the not-so-distant horizon. "Yeah, sure," he ultimately replied with confidence. "Not the money-making stuff, though. Not the big time. Just… what you see. Mountains, green space, blue sky. A good horse. My mom." Dropping his finger, Dallas licked his lips, softening at the realization that his dad had acted on what he wanted out of life. Boone was living a life that had meaning, for him.

Without looking at Matt, Dallas announced, "This is it. This is my dad's dream." Taking a moment to let that sink in, he scanned the world around them.

Matt followed suit.

Beyond the rundown tourist outfitting operation with its tiny cabins, plain bungalow, bits of rusty tractor and farm junk here and there, moldy white plastic chairs that seemed to be forever flipped over, and the dry, thirsty Panther River that served as a border to the property, were mountains. Mountains, lush and vibrant, alive with variegated green trees cascading with summer splendour, brimming with mysterious, unseen wildlife—cougars, bears, wolves, deer, elk, all picking out trails, dancing over branches, and climbing over the rocks that peeked out here and there through the trees.

Ubiquitous wild horses spotted occasional meadows here and there, vital waterways flowed down over polished stones in creeks and via little falls. Above all, there was finally a cloudless blue sky today, the earlier grey clouds having given up without ever splitting open, and moved east. The sky was now a perfect backdrop to a blistering sun so full of energy it practically hummed. The guys caught sight of a bald eagle floating, dipping, soaring, in search of small prey that also called the mountains home, nesting amongst hillocks and hiding under rocks, themselves feasting on even smaller suppers—insects, or grubs.

This place was alive, bursting with life. If one looked close enough, he or she could almost see it breathe. On the windy days the trees sang, the leaves in their branches rustling with glee, calling out joy, proclaiming hallelujah to those taking sanctuary in their midst. To those smart enough to say *bah* to city life and venture into the wild.

Dallas' father was one of those. If you placed him in some kind of order of those looking beyond civilization for the biggest kinds of secrets, the kind only found in nature, he'd be in the forefront, poised to run, ready to hop on a horse and just go wherever the wind took him—to explore the crevices, the flora, the fauna, the crystalline water, the hidden essential natural treasures the Rockies offered in spades.

Dallas had gone in the other direction. He'd run *to* civilization, instead of away from it. He countered Boone's dream; when the boys and Dawn were young, Dallas' dad counted on his love for the mountains filtering down to his kids the way water trips lightly over rocks, downhill. The chasm between Dallas and his father widened substantially the day Dallas left behind what his father most revered in favour of a hyped-up life on the fast track.

"I do see what he loves about it," Dallas said simply to Matt, as the eagle above surfed some invisible air current and saluted them with a graceful, elongated dip of a wing. "I love it too. Nature, green space, bubbling brooks. All calling us, begging us to lay down our arms and relax into the bosom of a peaceful, stress free existence. Sometimes I want that. Sometimes I friggin' need it. My dad's blinded by it, though. I think he forgets about all the work it takes to live out here. Hell, it's an hour to the nearest hospital. What if one of the kids takes an attack of appendicitis? That'd make for a hairy 'ole drive, especially in the wintertime. And out here, winter starts in September and sometimes goes til June."

Matt clenched his jaw tightly shut. It wouldn't do to raise the simple fact of how much more work Boone was being forced to take on now that Dale was gone.

The heavy workload was on Dallas' mind though. "I expect Dad's feeling the weight of everything these days, Matt," he admitted. "I know I am. Leaving my parents here, leaving Jenny and the kids? Hell, it's gonna be harder to go knowing what they all have to cope with. Damn Dale. What the hell was he thinking? It was easier to leave when he was around. Come to think of it, it was easier to be here, too, even just for short weekend visits. I coped better in his shadow. With Dad, with everything. Dale was my buffer. I'm lost without him watching over me."

Dallas was watching Boone again, and the happy tableau in the corral. For the first time since they stopped at the gate he stopped looking everywhere else, and turned his head to attempt a protracted bleak smile at Matt. "I'm glad I have you, buddy. I'm glad you're here."

Matt stopped picking at the steering wheel, met his friend's eyes, and waited while he considered what to say. "I'll help you as much as I can, Dal. You know it. I draw the line at shoveling horse shit, though."

Snickering, Dallas said, "What, you never shoveled horse shit with Jessie and Josh at the ranch? I find that hard to believe."

"Oh, I shoveled lots of shit for those two. A helluva lot more than just the smelly kind, too, believe me. I'm done shoveling shit."

"Yeah, so'm I." Dallas wrinkled his eyebrows and watched Boone lift Hunter off of Starbuck. The horse's back glistened with sweat in the heat of the day. Even from here, the guys could see that Hunter, too, was glowing, and not all of it was coming from sweat. "Hunter must have worked his magic. Boone's graduated him already from the little paint. Or maybe it's more about Dale, lettin' Hunter up on the big horse. A memory thing for my dad."

The guys watched quietly for a moment.

"You're not done shoveling shit if you take Hunter in," Matt offered cautiously. "That kid's all about horses. So's Ry, for that matter."

"Then Hunter belongs here with his granddaddy." Dallas reached for the door handle. "Ry can come visit as often as he can handle good 'ole Boone. Mom'll put some meat on his skinny bones. He'll have to do his guitar playing in the barn, though. Boone's not a fan."

With that, Dallas slid out of the comfortably air-conditioned vehicle, slammed the door, and hightailed it for the gate. Lifting the rope that held the two sides together, he gave one side a shove so it swung open, and he hauled the other side open himself.

Matt piloted the big car through, gave Dallas a thank-you wave, and parked next to the small cabin he was using while at J.I. Sliding out from behind the wheel, he looked back over at the corral and saw Cassie rise up from the bale she was sitting on and take Jade's tiny fingers in hers. Jade went running, and leapt into her father's arms. Matt smiled, and wandered over to the public men's room to freshen up before searching out the hired security based at the canteen for an update on how the family's day had gone. From his perspective, it actually looked like it was probably the best day they'd had since the news of Dale's passing saturated the media, at least as far as unwanted curious interlopers go.

And Boone? Having the small boys around seemed to be some comfort for him. Either he was recapturing old memories by teaching the two boys to ride, or he needed to be around the horses, and the boys gave him a reason to be there.

Or a reason to get out of bed, at least.

The boys were gonna learn fast at this rate. For all Matt knew, they were at the corral the entire live-long day.

Doris was nowhere in sight. Matt had passed by two trucks before he parked. One was Johnny's big rig, which meant that he was somewhere around the property, maybe fixing fences or feeding animals. Dawn and the kids, on the other hand, were not around, or Matt figured the kids'd be hanging around the corral, since kids attract other kids like magnets.

Jenny's truck was nudged in close to the bungalow; Matt was grateful she was still coming by. Jenny and her boys were a tangible link to Dale. He wondered if Dallas would try to talk to her about Maria. He hoped not, at least not yet. On the way home, they'd discussed telling Boone and Doris about the longevity of Dale and Maria's relationship. Matt had cautioned Dallas against going there just yet, if in fact ever. Dale had kept that part of his life secret for a reason. What would be the point in tearing open wounds that already gaped?

Jogging up the few wooden steps to the men's restroom, Matt pulled open the door and disappeared inside.

At the corral, Dallas tossed a giggling Jade up in his arms. Like warm butter on a hot day, the little girl's blonde hair shone in the afternoon sun.

Cassie bent over and ducked through the split rails of the fence, touched her husband's arm, and welcomed him with a chaste kiss.

Inside the corral, Ry, exhilarated from a two-lesson day, slipped off his horse with the reins in one hand and started to follow Johnny and Starbuck. Johnny'd come out of the barn to take the big palomino and lead him into his stall. Head down, Hunter trucked along behind them.

Boone was sauntering alongside Ry. He grinned down at him. "You sore, kid? Your legs?" He ignored Hunter altogether.

Ry lit up. "Heck, yeah. Feels great."

"You'll be cowboying up in no time. You're a natural, son." Boone snuck a surreptitious peek to the side, beyond the fence, where Cassie and Dallas seemed to be flirting with each other like newlyweds. "You'd think they hadn't seen each other in days," he remarked curiously, unaware of the morning's fight and the couple's attempt to reconnect in a conciliatory way.

Ry noticed, and leaned forward so he could see around the front of Boone while they walked. Dallas' renewed presence at the ranch sparked a new conversation. "What is it you don't like about country music, Grampie?" he asked.

The unexpected question caught Boone off guard. At the same time, the tips of his ears bloomed red with satisfaction at Ry's use of the word Grampie. Cassie was a doll and was growing on Boone and Doris in leaps and bounds, turning out not to be the prissy wife of a country star by any means. She pitched in where she could and had a bright, sweet nature. Her son Ry had a mature, wise quality about him that shone through his shyness. The combination, along with Ry's sheer excitement at learning to ride and to help out around the place, even hunkering down to shovel manure earlier between lessons, was completely and unanticipatedly endearing.

"Country music?" Boone frowned, slapping his gloves against a thigh. The heels of his worn boots kicked up dirt as he pondered the question during the easy ramble towards the barn. "I like country. What makes you think I don't like country?"

Ry puckered a brow. "You don't like the stuff Dallas plays. You didn't even come see him last time he played in Calgary."

"That's because the stuff Dallas plays don't qualify as country in my books."

"So you don't like *new* country."

Boone kicked a hay bale when he walked by. It bought him some time, although it startled Ry's horse and made it jerk the reins, which Ry responded to by grinning at the horse and loosening his grip. Boone took a breath and dove in. "Here's a part of your musical education, Ry. There's good solid country music, and then there's stuff that has no business even bein' on the radio. I like me some Patsy Cline and Merle Haggard. Now, bein' fair, I'll go as far as, say, 2001. Way before your time. Some George Strait, mebbe. I do like that fellow—he's classy, the cowboy hat he wears is well deserved, I'd say. But these new fellas, they throw pop songs in their sets, wear sneakers and ball caps, and the crap they play has no substance. I don't know where my son got the idea to write that kind of stuff. He may as well be a pop singer."

"Dallas is real good, Grampie. He's one of the biggest country stars there is. Bigger than Keith Urban, even, and that guy can riff on a guitar!"

"Keith Urban. Pshaw. An Aussie's got no business even calling himself a country singer. Dallas'll never be a George Jones. He ain't in that class of musician and he never will be." A thought bounded through his brain. Boone narrowed his eyes. "I know you're good on the guitar, son. Can you sing?"

"Uh, yeah, I think so. I like singing, anyways."

"Do you play the real thing or the hopped up pop-country my son plays?"

"Um, well, I mostly just play my own tunes but I do like trying out The Hunter Brothers' stuff, and sometimes I play Kip Moore ballads or Blake Shelton. Those kinds of guys."

"That Blake Shelton thinks he's all that and then some." Boone would have let out a *grrrr* just for fun, if he'd had the nerve. This little music battle was fun, unlike when he argued over music with Dallas, because then the verbal sparring was always laced with arsenic. With Ry, it was harmless banter. "And what man in his right mind would walk away from Miranda Lambert?"

Ry winked. "Ah, so you've heard of them. If you know who they are, then you've heard Dallas on the radio too. You can't listen to those guys on the radio and not hear a Dallas White song. Plus he duets with a lot of artists; they're all dying to record with him. My favourite is the one he did with FGL."

Busted. Boone chuckled and delicately swung the conversation away from having just gotten caught listening to new country. His heart felt ten tons lighter. Next to him, Ry was bouncing. "FGL?" He played dumb.

"Florida Georgia Line. I want to be just like them. Only a soloist. I don't want a singing partner." *Except maybe Emily-Grace,* Ry thought, his cheeks blooming pink at the pleasant thought of sharing the stage with Josh and Jessie's special daughter.

They were inside the barn now. Reaching over, Boone took the horse's lead and tied it onto a metal loop on the outside of the horse's stall. He tossed Ry a wooden brush. "Set that close by. You'll need it when we get the saddle off."

Johnny was already pulling off Starbuck's saddle. Ry nudged sideways when a small body squeezed by. Hunter went to Johnny's side and ran a finger over the leather saddle as Johnny hoisted it onto a saddle rack. Whistling, the affable guy earned a tentative smile when he tossed Hunter a brush.

Thoughtful, Ry set down his brush on a nearby bale and followed Boone's instructions to remove the saddle and bridle from the tired horse. After, picking up the brush, he started an easy movement following the natural direction of the horse's sweaty hair. After a while, he said quietly, "I like hanging out with you. Thanks for giving me and Hunter lessons today."

The kid was leading up to something, Boone suspected. He narrowed his eyes. "Get up at sunrise tomorrow and you'll get another. I got to get this place up and running again. Can't wait forever. We need the income."

"Dallas could help you." Ry kept his eyes locked on his work. The man at his side grew quiet. After a bit, Ry looked over at him. "Why won't you let him help you?"

"I prefer to work for my living, Ry. A man's work, not stage monkey stuff. Now switch brushes like I taught you this morning and do the mane and tail."

A burst of wounded pride rushed up Ry's chest and almost strangled him. He forced it down but changed his stance and picked up another brush, but kept it lowered to his side. "So do you mean you would never come see me play? It's hard work, Boone." He emphasized *Boone.*

Boone flinched.

"I did a guest appearance at Dal's last show," Ry said. "I didn't sleep the night before because I had a bad case of the nerves—good nerves but still nerves—then the day of the show I had a grueling sound check that took forever. All day long while I was waiting, all I could think about was my solo song, so I played it over and over and over, and that doesn't count writing it in the first place—music AND lyrics—plus revising this and switching that, and figuring out the right key and the bridge and the runs, plus rehearsing with Dal and the band, and typing everything out on the computer for what Dallas calls the business side of things, which I think means who owns the rights to the song and how I'm getting paid, plus there was a contract for the show that my mom had to sign. And after the show when I asked Dal what I should do next, he said to start all over and write a whole new song. And then another and then another." Collapsing against the stall behind him, Ry gave off an exasperated groan, colouring it with a happy grin. "I'm exhausted just thinking about it."

Boone afforded him the courtesy of listening. "I'll give you that it's a kind of work, Ry," he replied firmly. "I know my son, though, and he's got a lot of help hired to give him a hand with all the business stuff. What I don't like is him parading around some publicity agency or whatever it's called, showing off that tattoo around his arm by flexing muscles he had to pay to build in some gym, as opposed to being on the ranch with his brother and me doing a real man's work. Not trying to gauge his success by how many women send him their panties in the mail."

Ry threw back his head and laughed. "That happens. I've seen some. That's not what I'm after. I'm gonna be like Dal and stick to one beautiful lady. He sure loves my mom."

A soft look came over Boone's eyes. He took Ry's hand with the brush in it and led him back to the horse. Placing the brush over the horse's mane, he gave it a downward swipe so Ry would get the hint and finish the job. "Dallas is a grown-ass man on the outside, son. But his insides are all mush, that's all I'm gettin' at here. That big stage he likes to parade around like he's on top of the world? He hides behind it. What he's really doing is hiding. Hiding behind his music and this big image of who he wants the world to think he is. Don't let that happen to you, kid. Don't hide."

To Boone's annoyance Ry stopped brushing again, although this time he left the brush hovering against the horse's mane. "What's he hiding from?" he asked.

Boone took the brush from him and started a vigorous brushing. "Himself, son. He's playin' hide 'n seek from himself. Dallas is play-actin'. He can't be the tough guy in the real world so he puts on this act. Always has. Even as a little kid he was always tryin' to play tough but we all could see right through him. *Dale* could see right through him. Dale took the reins. Startin' when they were very young, he would take the tough jobs so Dallas could do the easy stuff. All it did was make one of my sons the wrong kind of hero, and make the other one feel forgotten." Boone's brushing was quick and deliberate. The horse snorted its disapproval.

Ry spoke with caution. "I think Dallas felt forgotten too, Boone. Until he met my mom. Why is that, do you think?"

"You're too wise for your own britches, kid." Pausing, Boone gripped the brush harder and leaned against the horse. "I don't know. Dallas has always been a weird branch on the family tree."

"I think," Ry tried, "that Dallas was lonely. He missed life out here. He always talked about you guys, like life on the ranch was perfect."

Boone looked down at Ry. His eyebrows arched up as he questioned that.

Gaining confidence, Ry went on. "During a guitar lesson one time he told me that he learned music from the radio in your kitchen. That it was always on while his mom was baking or cooking dinner. That she made the best strawberry jam on the planet. That he and his brother spent hours playing in the hay loft or riding around on horseback acting out westerns. The old milk house at the ranch in Cochrane where he grew up was always the jail," he added brightly. "Dallas may not always admit it, but overall I'd say he sure loved growing up on the ranch. And I can sure see why. I love being around horses. And around you guys."

Soft flecks of moisture dotted Boone's eyes. He gave one a swipe with the back of his brush hand and winked at Ry. "You won't when you do a full day's work around here. You'll sneak off and I'll find you asleep up in the hay loft, just a wussy-assed musician like my son."

Laughing outright, Ry grabbed the brush from him and started on the mare's coarse, wiry tail.

At the barn door, the light changed. Ry looked over first; Boone glanced over a moment later.

Cassie was there. She leaned against the open sliding door after Dallas, next to her, dropped Jade in her arms, pivoted carefully on a heel, and walked away.

Straightening, his smile turning upside down, Boone watched him go.

Ry ached to chase Dallas down, to run after him. Instead, he sucked in the hurt in his gut, and went to his mother's side.

Chapter Fourteen

*E*arly the next morning in the men's room, Matt had a hard time drawing a shaving blade down over his strong jaw without drawing blood, because he was still chuckling over Ry, whom Matt had passed in the clearing when he was making his way over for a shave. Early rising was a breeze for Matt these days, what with early ranch bedtimes and what he considered a lackadaisical schedule since none of his regulars—Dallas, Jessie, or Jacob—were touring. Ry, however, was not accustomed to seeing the sun come up. Matt wasn't even sure Cassie's son took notice of the fresh new day's prism'd blessings. It had rained last night, and today J.I. was anointed with enchanted promises of good things to come. Nascent pink and orange sun rays snuck through a glowing, hazy mist, backlighting the scattered rooftops of the small ranch with the golden new light of dawn. The leafy trees and even the horses were aglow with a touch so soft and magnificent that even the mourning doves stopped calling out greetings, and bowed with respect.

Matt saw Boone chuckle too when Ry stumbled out into the clearing after trudging down the washroom steps all bleary-eyed and stooped. When Matt, shaving kit cradled in his fingers, had walked by Boone a few minutes ago on his way to the public bathroom, he'd waved. Dallas' dad was outside on the bungalow's small landing, welcoming the new day with a stretch and a yawn, being careful not to spill a steaming mug of coffee. Like any mountain outfitter, the older man was exhilarated to welcome the sun, at least until reality caught up with him. Matt saw the exact moment when it did—when Boone remembered the loss of his eldest. His shoulders drooped and he paused and stared at something, something Matt couldn't see.

Not that it would have mattered anyway. Whatever Boone was looking at only had meaning for him.

And maybe for Dale, Matt thought as he dabbed at a tiny dot of blood on his cheek with a folded square of toilet tissue, wondering what it was that had caught Boone's attention. *Maybe it wasn't a thing. Maybe it was a whinny from a horse. Maybe Boone's eye latched onto a sign hung by Dale. Or perhaps it was just the way the newborn sun was lighting up the trees sloping up the mountains, like fire. Maybe the sunrise was something Boone and Dale had often remarked on—or never took the time to talk about at all.*

"I'll never know," Matt pondered out loud to his reflection in the mirror. After dropping the bloodied tissue in the garbage, he started gathering up his things for the short walk back to his cabin. He zipped the leather case shut, gripped it in one hand, and pushed open the door with a casual shoulder shove. "When a loved one passes, the oddest things can trigger grief," he considered. The thought was sobering. *I need to hop over to Vancouver. I need to touch base with Charles and Dee, to figure out my schedule for the next while, to see the kids. Maybe I can convince Shanda to meet up with me at home for a weekend. I can check in on Jessie and Josh, see how they're doing. Make sure Josh is doing okay, make sure he's staying away from 'the dirt,' staying clean. Unless they'll be at their Alberta ranch...*

He racked his brain to try to call forth the dates Josh and Jessie planned to be at their ranch. "I'll call Ulysses," he muttered, too embarrassed about not remembering to give in to making a call to Charles to ask. Ulysses, a handsome black man—another longtime member of the Keating security team—usually took over when Matt was busy with Dallas. Ulysses would know when Josh and Jessie would be on the move. Still, it unnerved the hell out of Matt to realize he'd lost track of the Sawyer family's movements. *Just another reason to step away from here for a bit*, he thought a little wildly.

His cell was lying on the lone bedside stand in the tiny space. Matt stared at it for a while before picking it up and dialing a Toronto number—Phil, Dallas' manager.

Phil answered on the first ring. Their discussion was curt and to the point.

Later, after a hearty ranch breakfast of scrambled eggs, toast, and hash browns, Matt checked in with the two rotating security staff, who were just coming on shift. All was well, so he went looking for Dallas. Matt spotted him down in the riverbed following Jade around, although apparently the country singer was lost in thought, since he didn't appear to be engaging with his daughter at all.

Matt vaulted forward to grab Jade when she slipped on a wet stone. He caught her by one arm just before she would have landed in the swiftly running shallow water.

Hunter was down there too. Like an older brother, he took Jade firmly by the hand when Matt let go of her, all the time eyeing Matt with a disconcerting certainty. The little guy's voice was rarely heard, yet what he managed to say with his eyes communicated far more than words ever could.

At a loss as to how to respond to what Hunter was saying, which was clearly *No worries, I got her,* Matt simply nodded and stuck his hands in the pockets of the black dress pants he was wearing for lack of time to pack proper outdoor clothes for this unexpected trip.

Dallas was more alert now that Matt was at his side. "Sorry," he mumbled, fixing his gaze on the point upriver where the narrow river disappeared around a bend.

"Not necessary," Matt managed, still watching Hunter. The boy pointed out a small frog to Jade, who giggled appropriately and earned a small smile back.

Matt turned his attention to his friend. He sucked up his courage. "Look, Dallas, I just had a chat with Phil."

"Oh?" Dallas looked over. "Why? What's up?"

"We were just figuring some things out. He said you're good to stay here for a while. Your schedule for the next month has been cleared."

"Oh."

"Sooo…things are under control here. The Calgary firm's more than capable of handling things for the time being."

"Oh."

"You okay, buddy?" Matt asked in a nonchalant kind of way. "Did you sleep okay last night?"

"Sleep? What's sleep?" Dallas grimaced, bending to grab a stone that he fingered absently. "This whole early-to-bed-early-to-rise thing goes against my nature. It's counterintuitive to the way I roll. I was finally falling asleep when Ry bumbled his way down the ladder from the loft for his riding lesson with my dad."

"Your dad had him cantering around the perimeter of the corral pretty much at sunrise."

"Well, ten minutes after Ry got up, Hunter must have realized he was gone. So—"

"You were just dozing off again when Hunter got up and wanted to go looking for Ry."

"But he'd peed the bed. Again. Cassie clued in and started rustling around looking for dry clothes for Hunter."

"Which, let me guess, woke up Jade."

"Who's like that rabbit, that battery rabbit—"

"The Energizer Bunny."

"She never friggin' stops. Matt, I'm too old for this." Dallas tossed the stone into the fast-moving water near his feet. It landed with a tired plop. "How'm I gonna get through the next twenty years?" As if to punctuate his point, he yawned so wide his jaw cracked. He rifled exasperated fingers through his messy, wild hair.

"Keep Hunter," Matt suggested. "He seems to be able to occupy her."

Dallas pshawed that idea without a second to think about it. "Not going there right now, buddy."

Matt waved an arm in capitulation. "Sorry," he mumbled. "I'll shut up about it."

They were quiet for a few minutes. The only sounds were the airy movements of leaves on shrubs and trees on the top of the bank, water trickling smoothly over stones, and an occasional happy squee from Jade.

"I think I need to go back to work," Dallas said eventually, in a low voice and without looking at Matt. "I'll call Phil and get him to rebook those shows. There are always a few good summer festivals I look forward to. I'd hate to let the fans down."

"Your fans get it, Dal," Matt retorted sharply. "They understand that you need a break right now."

"A break, is it? Matt, the break I need right now is, sadly, from my own daughter."

"And from Ry and Cassie," Matt reprimanded. "Since taking a break from Jade means leaving her mother behind as well."

Dallas fell into a glum silence.

Matt pushed his buttons. "And I guess you also need a break from the pressure to make a decision about Hunter."

"There is no decision to be made about Hunter. He is not my responsibility."

"Are you sure about that, Dal?"

Dallas' eyes narrowed. He stiffened, ready for a fight. Matt's hard tone was clearly confrontational. "I thought you were staying out of it. Not two seconds ago you said you were shutting up about it."

"Just let me throw this at you. You loved Hunter's mother once."

"Jesus Christ. Matt, are you out of your mind?" Sidestepping away from his friend, Dallas almost needed Matt's rescue too, when he lost his footing and slipped on a rock. He caught himself just in time and recovered by firing a death ray glare at his friend. "I'm not going to get into this with you right now."

Jumping deeper into the fire, Matt said, "This discussion needs to happen, Dallas. Not with me, no, but at least with your wife. I'll shut up about it if you promise to at least talk to her."

Dallas planted his feet a hip's width apart and stared Matt down. "Look, you know my dad's position on me. I'm not great at responsibility. I'm a runner. Dale was the stand-up guy who stuck around. Until he didn't," he added with a sad downturn of his lips.

"Dale, huh?" Matt rebutted. "Your brother was apparently as good at putting on a show as you are. We've discovered that he was not as tough as everyone thought."

"Maybe not, but he was tougher than me. Dale stuck around to deal with Dad. He took care of Mom and Dad, he did the farm work. He broke the horses. He was good at that—he was a rodeo cowboy. A horse whisperer. I ran away from the hard stuff, Dale ran towards it."

"Maybe it's time to stop running."

"Not interested, Matt," Dallas sighed, frustrated. "I've got all the family I can handle. Go take a break. That's really what you came down here to tell me, isn't it? That you want to get the heck outta Dodge?"

"You can be infuriating as hell, Dallas. Shutting down will solve nothing. Pushing one's family away just leaves a man lonely."

"Or dead. Apparently."

Matt had to fight to keep his temper under control. Little Hunter was an adorable, gifted child. The members of this crazy family ought to be falling over one another to take the boy in. "You see that little boy, Dallas?" he said through gritted teeth, pointing. "The one playing with your daughter right in front of you? Do you?"

Dallas shot him an angry look that read *I'm not blind*.

"Take a look in that child's eyes," Matt insisted. "That's your brother, right there."

Looking at Hunter, Dallas flinched, although it wasn't so much Hunter's features that brought Dale to mind, it was the child's actions. Hunter had stuck like glue to Ry at the corral earlier this morning, even though he was mostly ignored by Boone and had to content himself with watching. Dallas knew Hunter's actions were less about wanting to be with Ry than about needing to be near the horses.

Since Matt didn't get an angry reprisal this time, he went on. Lowering his voice, he said with conviction, "There comes a point when you have to stop running, even though it means things you don't like might catch up to you. I know all about that, I'm the master of that, and I was taught by an even better master of running away."

"Jessie."

"Yeah. Jessie."

Saying her name still had the power to take Matt's breath away, especially after such a long time away from her, with only that brief concert last week—was it only last week?—in Vancouver to see her, to touch her, to ensure she was happy. *Maybe I should wait to take a break*, Matt thought. *I don't have to go to Vancouver. Jessie and Josh will be coming out to their ranch soon. I can drive down, it's only a few hours from here, I can maybe take Ry down with me so he and Emily-Grace can finish their song…Dallas needs me right now. The kids need me.*

A jarring comeback called Matt back to Dallas. "Yeah, things are glorious in that ball park, right Matt? You just toured with me. You're still running. Maybe you ought to stop telling me what to do, and take a good hard look at yourself!"

A long sigh preceded Matt's tired response. "Hey. I said I was the master of running. I'm not denying that I'm all messed up. It's just that life isn't cut and dry, Dallas. It's not always about winning. Sometimes it's about just getting by the best way we can, with good music and good food and good company and good friends and—"

"Lovers on the side, huh, Matt? Regardless of how sorry I am to watch you suffer, I don't approve, just so you know. It was never my style to bed another man's wife."

"You bedded plenty, you hypocrite."

"Not to my knowledge, I didn't."

"Turning your back so the girls could pull off their rings doesn't count. Do you think I just got off the turnip truck? I've been around celebrities for a long time, Dal. I saw you in action plenty back when I worked full time following Jessie and Jacob around."

"Those girls were flings. They meant nothing to me, and I was just notches on their belts. You're willingly hanging onto someone who doesn't belong to you, and hurting a real good man in the process. As much as I respect you, and Jessie too, Matt, it's a shitty thing to do. It's a crappy life choice. For yourself as well as for them."

Recoiling, Matt fired back. "You think I have a choice? About how I feel about her, I mean? Do you think Dale could choose to cut Maria out of his heart? You don't get it, Dallas. There's a lot to my story that nobody but Jessie—and Josh—will ever understand. And I'm betting there's a helluva lot more to Dale and Maria's story, too. Maybe you should take a closer look at all of us. I bet if you did, my choices would make sense to you, and Dale's would emerge out of the fog too. You would understand me better. And Dale. You'd start to get what made him do the things he did. You just need to stop looking in all the wrong places. Take your brother off that pedestal you put him on and look him right in the eye."

"Ain't you forgettin' something, Matt?" Dallas drawled, turning such a fast, angry circle in the riverbed that it got the kids' attention. "As far as Dale goes, I can't. He's dead. My brother is a pile of ashes on my mom's dresser right now. My mom's," he added, "not Jenny's. For obvious reasons."

An instant red bloom coloured Matt's face. His eyes flashed. "I know that, Dallas. Your mom knows that, your dad knows it, Dawn knows it, the kids know it, and you can bet Jenny damn well knows it! Get off your high horse. Get over yourself and your narcissistic self-pity. Pay attention to your family. Listen to your dad for a change instead of bucking against him all the time. Open your eyes enough to see that everyone around you is falling apart! They spent every day with your brother and still didn't know him. You think *you* were deceived? Think about how they're all feeling right now! Especially your father."

"My dad's tough. He's a bronc. He always comes out fighting." As he said it, Dallas realized that was what he once thought about Dale—that Dale was as tough as nails. Paling, he gave Matt a quizzical look. "He's not, is he?" he said, almost inaudibly. "My Dad? He's not so tough, is he?"

"Those broncs, Dal, they're reacting to the pressure of flank straps that cowboys wrap around their abdomens. Do you think they always want to come out fighting? They've got no choice. They get conditioned to it."

Dallas stopped pacing and circling. Hunter and Jade went back to investigating. "I don't want to fight with you, Matt," he said, meeting Matt's eye, grateful that he seemed to be settling as well. "The choices you and Dale made might have come from love, and they're your business, same as choosing to leave Hunter in my parents' hands is mine. Go take your holiday, go be in Jessie's presence if it makes you happy and lets you breathe again." He started to pick his way back over the stones. "I've got a call to make," he hollered back over his shoulder. "There are plenty of good men and women working in security that I can hire for those summer festivals I'm going to get Phil to book me back into."

He ground to a halt when he remembered that he had two small children in his care while Cassie helped his family out with all of J.I.'s cleaning and cooking needs. With a heavy sigh, he turned back around and frowned at Hunter and Jade. "The kids," he said wearily. "Damn it."

"Go," Matt demanded, equally drained from the energy the fight took out of him. "I'll watch them."

"Keep 'em away from the cougars," Dallas grumbled, only too happy to step away. He hopped up the small bank and made a beeline for his cabin. For the second time that morning, Phil got a call from Alberta.

Afterwards, Dallas strode through the clearing towards the barn so he could fill his father in on his plans, all the while thinking *The old man'll be damned smug at me for running away again, but I could care less, because I'm packing my bags first chance I get.*

Boone cut him off before he got a word out. And he was beaming. "Thought we'd take these kids to some pro rodeo. Innisfail's this week." Ry, a fixture at his side, was practically hopping up and down.

Nearby, Johnny was putting a newly shined-up saddle on its saddle rack. He craned his head to listen. Further down in the barn, his young sons Cooper and Colt were trying to help their dad by patiently mucking manure and dirty straw out of stalls, although they were fighting more than helping, at this point, judging by their hollers.

"The rodeo? What? Is that such a good idea?" Dumbfounded, Dallas took a step backwards.

"Why wouldn't it be?"

"Dad, uh…"

"Because Dale would have been there if he hadn't called a final 'quits?' Is that it?"

Two fights in one short morning were more than Dallas wanted to tackle. Already he was feeling the loss of his pal Matt for the summer festivals. Matt was the one man Dallas needed around these days to help keep him sane, although lately he was on this annoying Hunter kick. Plus Matt's recent disclosure about still taking Jessie in his arms when the opportunity arose was grating on Dallas' nerves, given the revelation about Dale's secret relationship all these years.

Deflating, Dallas sucked back a sudden need to sit right down where he stood, right in the middle of the barn where Boone had Ry spit-shining tack for the tourists when they started coming back for trail rides.

"It's okay, Dad," Dallas capitulated, putting his hands on his hips. "Dale wouldn't want you to miss the rodeo. Especially Innisfail." Innisfail was Boone's home town. He grew up watching pro cowboys compete in that rodeo and eventually collected a ton of prize money and fancy engraved silver buckles himself, as did Dale in later years.

Boone backed down. "All-righty, then." The hackles on his back settled.

He grabbed an easy fistful of Ry's hair and shook it lightly, which made Ry laugh and paw at the thick fingers holding his long blond surfer locks hostage. "I think I still got some of Dale's old kid-sized cowboy hats kickin' around. Doris kept 'em all in a big box, in one of them blue Rubbermaid bins the wimmin like to stuff things in and move from place to place for no reason other than they don't have time to look in 'em, so why not just move 'em around?" He chuckled. "Let's go find you a hat, Ry."

"Got a small one for Hunter?" Ry asked as they started to saunter away.

Boone slowed. "Mebbe. We'll have a look-see. If not, we'll pick one up on the grounds. Dallas can pay for it." He tossed a 'you-got-that?' glance over his shoulder back at Dallas, who visibly shrank and had to take his hands off his hips and stick his fingers deep into his jeans pockets so as to prevent himself from giving his father the finger.

Johnny wandered up behind him. "Dawn thinks he's trying to replace Dale with Ry. Or maybe replace both of you, since he's got Hunter out there too."

"Both boys?" Dallas laughed, a hard-edged, sarcastic laugh that came out muddled and heavy in the barn. "He hardly acknowledges Hunter at all, Johnny. So I guess you're right." Slapping his brother-in-law on the shoulder, he started to walk away. "If crusty old Boone thinks he can relive the days gone by, he's got another think coming. He can't. He can't bring back our childhood, Dale and me. He can't replace the magic that once was Dale and Dallas. That went the way of the whispering wind the day Dale stuck a vacuum hose in his tailpipe and routed it into the cab of his truck."

He left Johnny at a standstill aching to tell his wife that Dallas was okay. Dawn had just lost one hero brother; she only had one left. Yet the way Dallas just spoke was rather grim, to Johnny's concerned ears.

Shaking his head, Johnny whistled at his sons, and put them to work polishing the tack Ry left behind.

Chapter Fifteen

"*I*t's not quite the 'Greatest Outdoor Show On Earth,'" Boone preened, proud as a peacock to be escorting Ry to his first rodeo, "but it's a good close second. And sometimes the smaller rodeos are even more fun—you can get closer to the competition. Feel the dirt in your face, hear the pounding of the hooves. You're gonna love it, kid. Some of these competitors are world champs."

Johnny's oldest, Ruby, jumped in like the experienced rodeo pro she was at all of ten years old. "There's saddle bronc, bareback riding, bull riding, and steer wrestling. And one day I'll be in the barrel racing but Mom says not yet."

"Best pancakes you'll ever have," Johnny winked at Ry. "Breakfast. Tomorrow." They had reservations in a local motel where, later, they'd tuck in overnight. Plans were afoot to attend the rodeo's barn dance and nobody wanted the worry of having a late drive home since it'd be about a two-hour drive back to the ranch. The biggest perk to Johnny for the overnight stay was the rodeo's famous pancakes. "They go down real good after a few brewskies the night before."

"It's not the pancakes, it's the greasy sausages," Dawn laughed. She hooked an arm through her husband's strong elbow and they marched off, as excited as their kids to be at the rodeo. The funeral and the days surrounding it were all about sadness; the lingering heavy grief that they all thought would never go away was finally opening up enough to form tiny cracks and let some light in.

Dallas was walking ahead of Matt, who'd very grudgingly hired extra security to accompany the large family group to a very public event Matt would have preferred they avoid. To everyone's surprise, even Jenny and her boys had come along.

"For the tribute they're gonna do for Dad," Matt overheard Shane glumly say to Ry earlier. "Mom didn't want to come. I think she's just going along with it for me and Cormac."

Jade was in Dallas' arms, and Cassie was walking next to Dallas. No words were passing between the adults. The entire two hour trip, Dallas had driven without speaking. Jade and Hunter rode in the back seat; Cassie was at Dallas' side in the front, idly noticing every time Dallas peeked in the rearview mirror to study his nephew.

Matt had followed closely in the SUV with Jenny and her boys—he didn't have much choice. Boone had pooh-poohed any security and spun out of J.I. before Matt even had a chance to mobilize the rest of the troops. Doris and an excited Ry were with Boone in his truck on the way to Innisfail. Johnny had his own immediate family with him—Dawn, of course, and Ruby, plus seven-year-old Cooper and five-year-old Colt. Matt's additional security in the form of a young twenty-something guy, Brett, and an older, red-headed woman, Rhonda, had followed along at the rear of the convoy.

They picked their way into the stands on the rodeo grounds and found seats on wooden benches. Ry settled in with Boone and Doris, who, everyone had to admit, were much brighter when Ry was around. Matt had Jenny on one side and Hunter on the other. Dallas flanked Hunter's left.

When Shane, Cormac, and Jenny were called onto the field during the opening ceremonies, a blown-up action photograph of Dale trying to stay seated on a wild bronc—right arm raised high for balance and a grin the size of J.I.'s entire spread—was projected onto a large monitor for the crowd's benefit. Matt and Dallas strained their ears towards Hunter. Barely discernible, the little boy said, "Daddy," and pointed one small finger at the action on the field.

Matt wrapped a protective arm around his shoulders. Dallas exhaled slowly and looked away while the announcer on the field told him, as part of the audience, just who his brother really was—a rodeo cowboy, a respected wrangler, a horse whisperer.

"I missed so much," Dallas said in a subdued voice to the dusty air.

"I never thought it would all be over so damn fast. I always thought there'd be more time."

Matt let the comment go with a quiet nod and a tighter hold on Hunter.

Later, the extra security came in handy when Dallas, with Jade in his arms, got waylaid in the barbecue lineup.

"That was a beautiful tribute to your brother, Dallas," a pretty young blonde crooned mournfully to him, nudging close enough that Matt, who was carrying Hunter, frowned and signaled Rhonda. Rhonda tucked a wisp of loose hair back into the tight bun she'd made up that morning. Like a chaperone at a high school dance, she stepped calmly between Dallas and the fan.

Cassie was used to the constant attention her man always got in public places. With a calculated eye roll, she whispered to Dawn, who was watching with interest in front of Cassie in line, "Take notice. Next she touches his arm."

"Check," Dawn announced brightly when the fan wrapped slender fingers topped by nails decorated with silver stars around Dallas' elbow. Jade stiffened. Recoiling, she narrowed her eyebrows and physically shoved the intruder away from her precious daddy. "Thatta girl," Dawn giggled, reaching a hand down to gently touch her own daughter, who was in front of her in line.

Cassie sighed. "He's Jade's private property. She doesn't often get her father to herself. Everyone wants a piece of your brother, Dawn."

As if to prove the point, the fan shrugged off Rhonda's rigid order to 'move along.' Jade started whining when 'starry nails' grasped at Dallas from both sides and got right in his face.

Cassie bent closer to Dawn. "Now it gets fun. I've discovered that there are different types of fans. This one's the worst. Your sexy brother once admitted that he gets a kick out of flirting back. In the old days he'd even take this kind to bed, he told me." Adorning a playful half-smile, Cassie sat back on a high wedge heel and winked at her husband, who groaned and petitioned Cassie with a muted *help* when Jade started trying to dislodge the annoying fan with a kick.

Tapping Dawn's wrist to be sure she was paying attention, Cassie went on. "Dallas hasn't decided whether Jade is a help or a hindrance. This is the part where he appeals silently to me so I will take Jade and let him flirt." She held up her hands and mustered up a wide grin for her husband. "As you can see, he won't be getting any from me today."

Dawn tittered. "TMI."

"What?" Cassie raised her eyebrows.

"Too much information. What's your man not getting from you today? You might want to clarify exactly what you're talking about."

Laughing, Cassie elbowed her sister-in-law so hard that Dawn had to sidestep quickly in order to remain upright. She grabbed Ruby's shoulders for balance.

Cassie elaborated. "Help with Jade is what I meant. He won't get that kind of help from Matt, either, because Matt's arms are full of Hunter, and Jade won't go to the new security, so Dallas is screwed. Now," she reached for and adjusted a paper plate in her hand so she could grab plastic cutlery, "phase three. Desperate measures. Watch and learn."

Dawn handed Ruby two sets of cutlery and levelled her plate at her waist. She tossed a spirited grin at her helpless brother. "Ah. This is way more fun than the hide-and-seek we played as kids."

"You see?" Cassie pressed the plastic knife to her lips and smiled playfully at Dallas. His discomfort at juggling an irascible child and an out of control fan was obvious.

"I do," Dawn answered. "The seductive blonde is going in for the kill."

"It usually starts with a pout, a pronounced batting of long, fake eyelashes, and a tilt of the bottled hair."

"Apparently."

"And then she begs for a picture and if she's really feeling bold she'll ask for a sweet little kiss."

"And of course she'll play on his personal loss." Dawn's eyes lost their coltish sparkle. "Will he give in?"

Jade was outright screaming now. Having a case of the 'hangries' wasn't helping, and the barbecue lineup was long. Eyeing her daughter, Cassie picked up a second plate and cutlery and watched Rhonda cautiously peek over at Matt for direction.

Leaning towards Dawn, Cassie smiled and kept her gaze locked on her husband. "This is where it's going to get really interesting." She pointed an elbow at Matt. "Months on tour with him, and that man still intimidates the heck out of me. There's a reason for that."

"Ah," Dawn responded, brightening. "The fun begins."

Cassie sobered. "I wonder if Dallas ever wishes he could go back in time and have his fun again. You know, pick up a few of these little buckle bunnies."

"Do you trust him?"

Without hesitation, Cassie nodded. "Yes. I'm glad I've been on tour with him, though, so I could see first-hand how he handles the starry-eyed ones who don't know where the line in the sand is. I worry, but ultimately I trust him. Maybe I'm just naive."

Dawn covered one of Ruby's ears with a napkin. To Cassie, she whispered, "Johnny cheated on me once."

Letting Dallas out of her sight for a second, Cassie whipped around to her sister-in-law. "No. Really?"

"Y-yep. Unfortunately."

"Aw, Dawn. I'm sorry to hear that. I like Johnny." The object of their conversation was just walking towards the end of the lineup with his two young sons in tow. They were on their way back from the port-a-potties.

"I decided to keep him. If it weren't for Johnny, think how much time I'd have to spend in those loathsome outhouses."

"Obviously you forgave him."

"He paid the price." Dawn gave her husband a wave. Innocently, he adopted a roguish, toothy grin, touched a finger to his cowboy hat, and waved back.

"You cut him off? No sex?"

"Hell no, that would have backfired. My man needs sex. I need sex. Nope, I learned a valuable lesson. I didn't want him to keep looking elsewhere. So no. That wasn't it."

"Hmm? I'm intrigued."

Dawn pointed to her daughter, who was otherwise entertained by Doris at the moment. "Ruby. She saw him kissing another woman. Johnny lost a lot of his daughter's trust. He's had to work hard to get it back."

Cassie got quiet. "Ruby's only ten. This was...recent?"

"She was eight at the time. Old enough to know what it meant."

Both women were momentarily silent. The splinters Dale brought to the White family as a whole—to Boone, Doris, their two remaining offspring and spouses and kids, plus Jenny and the boys—were indomitable. They were mountainous. They sucked up everyone's energy and monopolized the family's time. The regular stuff of ordinary days was getting shoved under the table, and old hurts that were once hastened into shady corners were resurfacing in the darkness like wolves on the prowl. The passage of time in Dawn's case had done little to dull the pain. The old wounds had the potential to rupture, especially with an unexpected love child like Hunter taking up space in the every day.

He was whiskey on an open sore.

"I'm so sorry," Cassie murmured to Dawn, as Dawn helpfully dropped a spoonful of coleslaw on Cassie's first plate.

Shrugging, Dawn averted her eyes, focusing instead on dishing plates for herself and Ruby as well as spooning food onto Cassie's two as they moved down the line. "Nobody's marriage is immune to bumps and bruises, Cassie." Softening, she met her sister-in-law's kind, concerned, emerald eyes. "Dallas is struggling with all of this. The coming home and 'not-being-treated-like-a-star-by-his-own-family' thing. It's hard to picture him as some superstar when we remember him as a skinny little dreamer who got picked on in school."

Cassie sucked in a breath. "He got picked on? How bad?"

"Bloody nose bad. The bullies got pounded on by Dale, so Dallas started to squeak by. When he started winning talent contests, the assholes eased off until their girls started wanting Dallas, then the whole cycle started all over again." Dawn was at the end of the line now. Grabbing a few pats of butter, she dropped them on Jade's plate, which wasn't as overflowing as the two ladies' plates, and she continued. "Not much wonder my brother hightailed it out of Alberta the first chance he got. I suppose being away from Dale's shadow, from the status quo that Dale had to fight his battles for him, made it easier for Dallas to reinvent himself."

"Was he close with Dale?"

Dawn pondered that. "I don't really think so, not in a tell-all kind of way. Their relationship was more about Dale protecting Dallas. I think there was some hero-worship going on. The kind that doesn't lend itself to baring one's soul, if you know what I mean."

"So Dale was okay with Dallas leaving."

"Hell, no. Dale needed Dallas too. Once Dallas left, Dale had to take all of Dad's shit. Not the farm work—that wasn't shit to Dale. He liked hard work. He put everything that made him angry into his work, into the physical release. Come to think of it, so did I after Johnny cheated on me. Monotonous farm work will break the angry in all of us. You're too damn exhausted to dwell on the bad stuff. No, the shit Dale had to take on was Dad as the bully, only Dad didn't pick on Dale the way he bullied Dallas as a kid. It was more of a silent thing, a hostile undercurrent that ran under everything they did from day to day."

"What do you think it was about?"

"I don't know. I've never really been able to put my finger on it. I always thought it had something to do with Dallas leaving, but like I said, I don't think Dale really minded the farm work, and he was good at it, and he was good at the rodeo too. He left a suitcase of shiny buckles behind to prove it. I know Dad built up a lot of resentment against Dallas for leaving and I think he always thought Dale was pissed at Dallas for leaving too, but I disagree."

She retreated inwards for a few seconds before she went on. When she was ready, she looked up and met Cassie's steady, welcoming eyes. "I knew Dale, Cassie," she said, "as much as anyone ever did. He was a quiet kid who grew into a quiet man. You never really knew what he was thinking. Often he was in a daze, in some distant place in his mind. I used to wonder whether he wished he'd gone to Toronto with Dallas. At first I know he worried about Dallas. None of us ever thought Dallas was strong enough to survive the big city; he was a farm boy, for God's sake, and bad at that, really! He proved us all wrong. Over time, Dale relaxed somewhat, but he was still distant at the best of times. He worked hard, he took care of his family, he paid the bills. He was an ordinary kind of man."

"You don't know why he would choose to…umm…why he…"

"Why he would take his own life? There were no real clues that I could see, Cassie. Dale didn't *get* quiet, he was always quiet." She pondered that. "He just got different. I know everyone thinks Hunter has something to do with it, and maybe he does, but Cassie, Dale changed not long out of high school. The distance thing, becoming hard to reach, to hold a conversation with. Needing to beat the shit out of a manure pile thing. Going from wild mustang to wild mustang, riding like the wind kind of thing. Throwing his fear and this—well, I can only call it inner rage, although you never saw it aimed at a person, thankfully—down in the corral, or in the rodeo ring, fighting like a crazy man to beat down an invisible enemy, that kind of thing."

Her voice got quiet as she prodded Ruby towards the seating area. They picked out spots at a weathered picnic table. "I don't know what it was with Dale, what changed. I just know that once Dallas left, that whole undercurrent that I can't put my finger on went back and forth from our dad to him, and it made our dad quietly angry, often in a verbal way. It always manifested by him putting Dallas down, like by making fun of him on stage, pulling out bits from the entertainment news on TV or from gossip magazines and the like. Dad's overt mistreatment of Dallas made Dale start to steal away from us." She sighed. "I guess what I am saying is that we kind of lost Dale a long time ago. I don't know how Jenny held onto him for as long as she did. Maybe she just kept hoping he'd come back to her someday. His spirit, I mean."

"Did they ever break up? Take breaks from each other?"

"Do you mean were there signs that Dale was cheating on her?"

"I suppose. I guess that's what I mean."

Dawn shook her head. "No. Not that I could see. Dale and Jenny were like any other couple. They worked, they raised kids. He had his interests and she had hers, but lots of couples are like that."

"Like music," Cassie smiled. "Our dissimilar tastes in music almost kept Dallas and I apart."

"For me and Johnny it's hockey and Hallmark movies."

"Too funny. You don't seem like the Hallmark type, Dawn. You're too down to earth. I wouldn't think any of you rancher folks ever stop working long enough to watch TV."

"You're right, I'm not the Hallmark type," Dawn corrected her with a giggle. "I'm all about the Calgary Flames. What does that tell you about my husband?"

"Oh God, does Johnny cook too? And vacuum? Can I borrow him?"

"He makes a wicked grape jelly and the biscuits to go under it, although I'm supposed to pretend I made them. He's all about keeping his grandmother's recipes in the family. That's my man!"

A vicious squeal from Jade drew Cassie away from Dawn, who chuckled and looked past Cassie across from her, over to the growing barbecue line up. Clearly Jade was calling the shots. Dallas had given up on grabbing a plate for himself and had stepped out of the lineup to deal with his angry child and the increasingly obnoxious fan.

"You'd think she'd get the hint," Dawn muttered.

"He's too nice. No way will Dal take a chance on upsetting his fans. The entertainment media has a one-eyed way of looking at things."

"Look, she's trying to take Jade from him! The nerve! Unbelievable! I feel bad for Rhonda, she's looking pretty flustered."

"Annnnd…"

"Matt swoops in. What took him so long?"

"He and Dallas have worked out the timing. Matt watches and waits until things get to a certain point, then he acts."

True enough, Matt had gone into action. Hunter was now in Rhonda's arms, quietly observing Jade and her hissy fit.

"I'd go over but this is far too much fun." Cassie forked potato salad between her lips. "Yum. Good stuff."

"You should try Johnny's," Dawn giggled.

Ry plopped down opposite them. "Jade ought to be a singer," he grumbled, digging into his hamburger with gusto. Shane and Cormac dropped down next to him, their plates heaped full of beefy Alberta ranch goodness.

Cassie elbowed Dawn. "Okay, watch this part. Matt's taking control."

"I'm drooling. Am I drooling? Omigod that man. Bummer that he's married."

"And you're not?" Cassie laughed.

Matt had 'starry nails' by the elbow and was quietly ushering her towards the main gate. At the same time, he quickly gestured to the third member of the security team, the young guy, Brett, to step in and keep other fans away from Dallas. When it seemed he felt secure enough to take his eyes off of Dallas, Matt wrapped an arm around the pushy fan's waist and bent closer so he could speak to her. She was tripping over the ground, he was sweeping her along so quickly.

"What do you suppose he's saying to her?" Dawn asked Cassie, who was teasing her husband by raising big spoonfuls of potato salad accompanied by deliciously satisfied eye rolls.

Cassie watched Dallas sink into an annoyed pout, take his screaming daughter from Rhonda's arms, and slink to the back of the barbecue line, flanked this time by both remaining security.

"What's Matt saying?" Cassie repeated, responding to Dawn's question. She kicked Ry lightly under the table. "He's saying Ry, go get your sister so Cassie's handsome man can fill his boots with food."

Ry fumed. "Mom, she's having a tantrum. Let Dallas deal with her for once."

Cassie's eyebrows shot up into a question mark but she chose to let the underbelly of the remark slide. "Ry."

The way she said his name with authority left no room for question. Grumbling, Ry shoved himself away from the picnic table but he took a huge bite of his burger first, giving his mom a hard stare over the top bun before tossing the whole thing back down on his plate. It landed in the coleslaw and tipped over sideways, the top bun sliding off into the creamy mess.

"Matt," Cassie sighed, going back to Dawn's question for real this time. "I know exactly what he's saying on the outside. The inside's a different matter altogether. He's telling her that he will have Dallas send her a signed photograph and a CD, and he's thanking her for being so sweet to him. And he's adding that Dallas needs to tend to his daughter right now, and also have some lunch before the bull riding starts. Matt's very diplomatic."

"He's going to leave a bruise on her arm."

"She won't care. She'll social media the heck out of it and whine about how close she got to getting a kiss from Dallas White."

"So what's Matt saying on the inside?" Dawn tapped Cassie's arm. "Omigod, he handed her over to the local security at the gate, flipped around, and put his sunglasses on. There is not a cowboy at this rodeo that can put a notch on Matt Kelly's belt. I am so glad he's let down his guard enough out here to throw on jeans and boots."

"He's trying to fit in. Last night he went into Sundre to shop."

"He'll be blistered up the yin-yang by day's end. New shit kickers. Ouch."

Ry reappeared with Jade, who he unceremoniously dropped in his mother's lap. Cassie wrapped her arms around her daughter. "You'll have to wait to hear my interpretation of what Matt is saying on the inside. It's not repeatable in mixed company. Small ears."

"Cover them." The closer Matt got to Dallas at the end of the barbecue line, the closer Dawn got to having an apoplectic fit.

"You can't crush on Matt, Dawn," Cassie reprimanded. "You're married."

"It's my turn. Don't we get turns?"

Tossing back her head, Cassie let out an elegant roar. "No, we don't! Stop drooling!" Laying her palms over Jade's ears, she said, with a sly look to Ry, who had been around Matt enough in work mode to know that he was a man not to be messed with when on duty, "On the inside, Matt was cursing Dallas for the depraved life he used to lead in the first place. Since he still attracts those kinds of women like honey attracts bees. And, I may add, Matt is also cursing over my husband's inability to control our wild daughter, who, as you may have noticed, has settled quite happily in my arms."

"Princess syndrome," Ry muttered to Dawn before frowning at his mushy damp burger top. "He can't say no to her."

"Oh." Dawn sat back. "My brother still has no spine?"

Both Ry and Cassie sat up straighter and looked over at Dawn. "He has plenty spine, Dawn," Cassie said, trying not to sound offended. "He's a new dad, that's all. He dotes on his daughter. And on Ry, too," she added quickly, unable to meet Ry's eyes. "He'll get the hang of it."

Dawn got quiet. Glancing over at Dallas, who was scooping spring mix greens out of a lime green bowl, she let out a slow breath. "I spoke out of turn," she said, apologizing. "I only have one brother left. I need Dallas to have some spine. He used to have Dale to watch over him. Even from a distance I'm sure Dallas always liked knowing that Dale always had his back, and now he—" She went silent when Matt reached Dallas and the two security flanking him. "Although I suppose it's all in how you look at it," she added, appraising Matt's serious security vibe. She shivered her approval. "I suppose he's got some spine again. Some mighty fine spine indeed." Her eyes lightened up just as Johnny and the two boys made their way to the picnic table. "And I have my big tough man. All is well. Right, Ruby?" Her daughter snuggled under her arm.

Cassie looked back over at Dallas. Matt needn't have worried about standing out amongst the rancher crowd. It was Dallas who stood out—Dallas, who was once again being approached by star struck fans, this time by two fresh-faced teens in plaid shirts and jean shorts. With three security close by watching the girls' every move, not taking lunch plates of their own to fill, and more brave fans lining up, Dallas was as much a magnet now as he was after a big show.

A lonesome, confused magnet, considered Cassie as she watched him give up trying to fill his plate and instead stand with his back to the buffet table so he could sign autographs and pose for pictures.

Handing Jade over to a surprised Dawn, Cassie pushed herself up and away from the wooden picnic table and sauntered casually over to the barbecue line. Taking Dallas' abandoned plate in one hand, she went through the line and filled it up, turning for a second to wink at Hunter in Rhonda's arms. "You're next, little guy," she said. "You must be hungry too."

Hunter was looking very concerned. His dark eyes were glistening. Cassie couldn't help but notice that his small hands were curled into fists and for the most part his eyes were stuck on Matt, who was busy ushering fans here and there.

Biting her bottom lip, Cassie followed Hunter's gaze over to Matt, who looked her way and caught her eye for a brief moment. Taken aback at the sheer intensity he exuded in this open, unprotected space, Cassie had to reboot her expression. Forcing a smile, she nodded, hoping the acknowledgement would come out looking like an understanding thank-you to Matt, for his work protecting her husband. She raised a clean plate. "Do you like potato salad?" she asked, and went to work piling food onto the plate without waiting for an answer. It was moments like this when she clearly got a sense of the stress of Matt's job. It added a new layer of worry for Dallas' safety and, by extension, the safety of herself and her children.

Behind her, Dallas posed with his arm hung casually over a middle-aged woman's shoulders, and blushed when she brushed her lips against his cheek and whispered something in his ear.

"Jesus," he grinned at Matt when the fan moved out of earshot. "I didn't even try that when I had the freedom to play."

"Loser," Matt shot back, barely cracking a smile. "You snooze, you lose."

The two men shared a chuckle and continued to please the fans until Matt finally put the kibosh to them and ordered Dallas to eat. Taking Hunter back from Rhonda, he set him on the ground and led him to the picnic table. Lifting him, Matt set him down next to Dallas, and then crawled over the bench to eat what Cassie had picked out for him.

Dawn watched Matt for signs of the intimidating man Cassie admitted she sometimes feared. She relaxed into a smile when she saw Hunter lean fully into Matt's side and tuck his small fingers into Matt's big, strong ones. A wave of peace washed over her when Matt lifted an arm, wrapped it warmly around Dale's son, murmured a blessing into Hunter's dark hair, and blissfully closed his eyes.

Chapter Sixteen

"Country music, I got used to. Rodeo, however, will never be my thing. Dallas, please don't ever take me to another one of these outdoor circuses." Cassie lifted a glass of white wine to her lips and took a sip.

"My mother's an animal lover," Ry chipped in, speaking to Dallas. "She feels sad for the horses."

They were sitting around a rectangular table in the main barn, waiting for a live country music act to take the stage for a traditional barn dance. Most of the older kids had chosen to opt out; the younger ones had the choice made for them. With the exception of Ry and Shane, the younger set was back in the motel with Brett watching over them from the parking lot, and Rhonda outside their door, in the hopes of keeping curious fans away. Indoors with the kids were a couple of sisters Dale and Jenny and Johnny and Dawn had made a practice of hiring each year to babysit while the White family was in Innisfail for the rodeo. Ry had acted all tough, stating that he did not require a caregiver, but Shane shushed him immediately. The sisters had started sitting for the White family when they were fourteen; identical twins, they were twenty-one now, and blonde and gorgeous. Once Ry set eyes on them, babysitting took on a whole new meaning. He immediately pushed his crush on Emily-Grace Sawyer under the proverbial rug.

Cassie was insistent that when the clock struck nine, Ry would have to leave the dance. He consented without argument.

"Your mother's a softie, all right," Dallas agreed, laying a hand on Cassie's thigh and giving it a gentle squeeze in response to Ry's comment about Cassie's love for animals. "I should have known better than to bring her to a rodeo."

"It's not that I'm soft," Cassie rebutted, getting her back up. "It's just that between screaming every time one of those cowboys got thrown, praying bucking hooves wouldn't land on him and slice him in two, and the whole idea of horses being forced into something they have no mind to do in the first place, it was a stressful way to be entertained." She raised a hand and air palmed Johnny, who, along with Boone as well as Dale's two boys, was the group's main rodeo defender. "Just to clarify, Johnny," she said, "I don't like horror movies either. To each his own, right? I just prefer not to be scared. I like my cozy little life the way it is. I'll take my entertainment in live music and rom coms. I'm not partial to watching men practically break their backs while the broncs underneath them buck and kick. Those cowboys' medical bills must be astronomical. Someday they'll pay for their addiction to adrenaline."

Dallas set his beer down on the table. It left a damp ring on the green and pink plaid tablecloth. The folks closest to them, all perched on wooden chairs, went silent, their enthusiasm dampened as well. It was no secret amongst the family that Dale had suffered multiple broken bones over the course of his rodeo career. The entire White clan all knew of older cowboys who had competed in rodeo. Some walked with limps, others suffered chronic pain from disintegrated discs on their lower backs, and a few grunted their way painfully through farm chores with scarred, sore shoulders. What drew the conversation to a halt, though, was the jarring reminder that Dale hadn't lived to complain.

Not that he would have complained anyway. He would have just sucked it up and carried on.

Jenny sighed and looked up into the shadowy rafters of the barn, where pretty white fairy lights hung in gently cascading waterfalls, giving the otherwise dimmed barn a rustic, whimsical feel.

Cassie shifted uncomfortably in her chair. "So sorry," she murmured almost under her breath. She was barely heard over the pre-recorded country tune booming through a nearby speaker, filling time until a live band was ready to down-strum its first chord.

Johnny broke the silence. "C'mere," he said to Cassie when the rollicking chords of an upbeat Florida Georgia Line tune started up. "Let's dance. You look too pretty to be hiding behind a table, and that rascally man of yours don't look to me like he wants to do anything about it."

"Oh!" A panicked look crossed Cassie's face. One glance to the dance floor cemented a new fear. The dancing area took up the whole centre of the massive barn and was already filled with cowboys swirling their cowgirls around, all anxious to get the party started after a busy, high-octane day.

The new anxiety zipped across Cassie's emerald eyes and telegraphed itself clearly to Dallas, who sat forward, focused on the wide board under his boots, and cleared his throat. "It's just the two-step, Cassie," he offered. It came out sounding like a gentle reprimand.

"Which we never get to dance since we never get to these kinds of parties, Dal," she admonished back. "We're usually stuck in hotel rooms while the crew goes out," she explained to the others, careful to keep an eye on her husband and her voice at an even timbre.

Dallas took offence. "It's not like we don't have a choice, Cassie. We choose not to join them."

"Because your fans won't leave you alone. Like today. Your life's a circus."

Surprised, Dallas stared at his wife. Cassie was not ordinarily a complainer. Fans came with the territory; he'd explained the issues they brought to the table back when he and Cassie first got together at their idyllic Prince Edward Island campground. Too bewildered to respond in words, he let his hand drift away from her thigh.

"I think it's high time I danced with my son." The declaration came from down the table, where Doris was sipping on a diet coke while she studied the suddenly bristly interactions between her famous offspring and his wife. Rising, she stepped behind her husband and reached for Dallas' hand.

Johnny stood too. "Cassie," he said with a cheeky grin, "I can teach you the two-step. I have a feeling you're a quick learner."

Obliging, Cassie blushed, took his hand, and forced a woeful smile back at Dawn as she trailed behind Johnny to the dance floor. "I hope you don't mind," she mouthed to Dawn.

Dawn leaned back in her chair and smugly folded her arms across her chest. Her response was a playful sideways look at Matt. "Don't you have to stay close to Dallas?" she teased.

Matt was settling into the country and western vibe, even going so far as to let Dallas buy him a stiff cowboy hat earlier. Giving it a low tug over his forehead, he acknowledged Dawn's question by standing and extending a hand to her. "M'lady," he offered, a serious bent to his head belied by a cheeky upturn of one corner of his lips, and a tiny light settling into his pale eyes. "Would you care to dance?" It wasn't lost on him that spunky, small Dawn had been watching him all day.

"Depends. Can you two-step?" Dawn remained seated, but her heart rate quickened and her knees went weak.

"Badly."

"Really? Where'd you learn? You're no more a country boy than I am a Lululemon girl."

He grinned. "Jessie Wheeler. I paid attention when she was teaching her kids."

"Jessie's not country—oh, wait." Unfolding her arms, Dawn crossed one foot over a knee instead. "I read somewhere that her husband's a big country fan. Do you think we could meet him some day? Could you make that happen?"

Jenny cut in. "Omigod, Dawn, you're a hopeless flirt. Either go dance with him or I will." She slammed her Bud Lite Lime down on a square of the green and pink plaid. "Dallas'll abandon your mom the second his slutty fans start circling like sharks. Matt, get your ass out there on the dance floor."

Matt's gaze darted over to Jenny. Frowning, he let his extended hand fall to his side. The light in his eyes cooled, leaving them a musty, cloudy hazel-grey.

"Oh," Jenny whined, souring by the second. "I see. Dallas' babysitter doesn't like being told what to do."

"Easy, Jenny," Dawn cautioned. "This is just a random small town barn dance. I'm sure Dallas has things under control."

"Oh, get over it, Dawn. These guys wear Givenchy on the ranch. They're all show. Look at Matt. His brand spanking new cowboy hat doesn't have a speck of turd on it." Eyes moist, she stared pointedly at the object of her derision. "You should have seen Dale's good hat. It was ripped and torn and covered in dried horse shit, just like any good cowboy's should be.

You're just playin.' You don't even ride. Dallas don't ride. There's only one thing left I can say for sure about my asshole husband—at least he was a real cowboy."

"Mom!" Eyes wide, Shane was aghast.

Jenny ignored her son. She was more surprised than Dawn when Matt had the audacity to reach down and take her hand. He physically pulled her upright and gave her fingers a tug. "I do need to be near Dallas right now," he assured her in a gruff voice. "Someone's got to dance with me so I don't look like an idiot, and you and I have a conversation to finish, so I guess that someone is you." Glancing back at Dawn, he used his free hand to give his new hat a gentlemanly tip. "Next song," he grunted.

Swooning in her chair, Dawn was too overcome to respond at first; then she threw her head back and laughed—a great, loud, infectious laugh that was almost too big for her small frame but which lightened up the moods of everyone at the table.

Jenny hung her head and obediently followed Matt out to the dance floor. When he turned and placed one hand almost under her armpit and the other at shoulder level in the country two-step style, and started moving to the music at a casual two-quick two-slow pace to match the beat of the Florida Georgia Line tune, Jenny obediently positioned herself backwards and went along with him.

After a while, Matt remarked on her smooth, practiced gait.

"I've been dancing the two-step since I was a kid," she bit off. "I ought to be good at it." Grudgingly she added, "You're not so bad at this yourself, City Man." Nodding at his feet, she added, "You're limping, though. Just sucking it up?"

"New boots," he admitted. "Dallas insisted. I guess he wanted me to fit in."

"Ha. You heard what I said about the hat. You're not ever going to fit in around here."

"I'm not arguing that point. Believe it or not, I have bruises around my head too."

"You gotta break things in out here. You can't just waltz in and figure you belong." Jenny was trembling.

Matt sensed her discomfort. "My job is to be a chameleon, Jenny," he explained. "I try not to be noticed, but it doesn't always work out that way. I'm trying to make the best of things here."

"Yeah, my husband suddenly stickin' a vacuum hose over the tailpipe of his truck must have made it hard to get your shoppin' done for this trip, huh?" The wet sheen floating across her eyes deepened into more of a pool. Letting go of Matt with one hand, she pulled at the back of her frizzy hair as if trying to smooth it down. She swallowed.

Matt's voice got quiet. "Jenny, my guess is that at this point you don't know who to be the angriest with. Dale, Dallas, me for invading your space, or maybe even Dawn because she still has a husband. Although overall I expect the person you are the most angry with is yourself." He couldn't help but think of how hurt and angry she would be when she someday found out the truth about Dale, that he had a longtime secret life that included a permanent lover he met before he even married Jenny. He blinked, and took in a deep breath so he could stay focused. The truth always came out, he figured. It was likely inevitable that Jenny would eventually clue in.

"Sunrise to sunset," she spat back at him, referencing her life before Dale died. "Dale and me. Up at the crack of dawn, always. We saw some glorious sunrises but were always too damn tired to care and we sure as hell didn't ever talk about 'em. Even when we went to Cuba, we just put our heads down and suffered on the beach, counting down the days 'til we could go home. That was once, that Cuba trip; we only took one vacation away in all the time we were married, and it sucked." She stopped moving, and Matt didn't nudge her to continue on. The other dancers just glided around them. "Dale and me had very little to say to each other when we got married," she said, "and it got worse as the years went on. He got quieter until I guess he got so quiet he just disappeared. Made himself disappear, I should say. He was on the open range but he may as well have been living in the city, for all the good it did him. It was like his soul just closed up and disappeared." She swallowed again, and somehow pulled up the guts to say, "And I think it was because of me. The boys. Boone. Being straddled."

Contemplating her, Matt didn't speak. Intuitively, he felt that the tense woman in his arms had more to unload. He snuck a look over to Dallas, who was waltzing by with Doris. Relieved, Matt saw that both were smiling.

Fans were respectful, giving Dallas and his mother a polite amount of space.

Stubbornly, Jenny raised her chin before she unraveled a little more. "A night out for Dale and me was rare and usually consisted of the boys' school things or hockey games or rodeos. When we did get out, once a year on our anniversary, we'd go to a steakhouse in Calgary. I was lucky if Dale could stay awake and not fall into his fried mushrooms and onions. I'd drive home and he'd sleep. I'd listen to the radio, catch Dallas on there sometimes and wonder what the hell kind of fancy life he was living. I figured he could have steak like that just about every night, if he wanted to. Not just once a year."

Her words mellowed with remembrance. "That'd be the Saturday night of our anniversary week. Sunday morning we'd have sex like always, regular as clockwork, neither of us opening our eyes to look at each other, both of us there just cause we knew we were expected to be. It got to be so we'd not get that Sunday sex sometimes—he'd have rodeo or a hurt mustang coming in to the ranch or whatever. We'd miss it once and then again and more and more, and before I knew it I couldn't recall the last time. Everything was good, though, or at least the same, the same routine. He'd go off for a load of feed or to an auction; he did his thing and I did mine. Got so I didn't ask him where he was, it was just routine. Sometimes Boone was with him, sometimes he wasn't. Sometimes Dale picked up the kids at school, sometimes I did, sometimes they took the bus. Didn't matter. We got by. I thought everything was fine."

It's because I'm a stranger, Matt thought, *that she is sharing this with me. She can't tell Dawn or Doris because they're too close. She's afraid they'll judge her.* It endeared Jenny to Matt, to have her open up to him this way. In front of the others, she was a tough old bird, the kind of woman who could drive any truck no matter how big, and haul a horse trailer along behind, and back the damn thing up without a second glance. Or chop a poisonous snake in half with a hoe without a whisper.

Yet in Matt's presence, for some reason she was vulnerable.

The piped-in Florida Georgia Line song was three-quarters through. On stage, the hired live band's lead singer looked about ready to take the mic. Jenny had started dancing again. Matt swept her around a turn and wondered if she had any idea just how imbued Maria was in Dale's life.

"Jenny, I know you're a capable woman," he said carefully. "Your boys have been hanging around with Ry. I overhear things. Dallas hears things. You should know that everyone's watching out for Cormac and Shane. Dallas wants to help them, to help you. I know it must feel like it, but you're not alone."

"I'm fine." A swing of the frizzy hair. A proud, upraised chin. "We're gettin' by."

"All right. S'good."

She threw in a wrench. "What about that boy?"

"Hunter?" Matt almost kicked on the brakes. As it was, he missed a few steps and had to do a little double hop-step to get back on track.

"You and Dallas went looking for his mother. How'd that go? Did you find her?" Jenny swiped a set of knuckles over one eye. The move left a wet sheen on the side of her face, shining in the overhead twinkling fairy lights.

Oh, we found her all right. Sort of. Matt sighed. "Jenny, Hunter is not responsible for any of this. He's a victim too."

Her hold on him tightened. "Let's get this straight. I am not playing the victim card here. I am not a victim nor was I ever any kind of victim." She spat it out like venom. "If you want to consider the boy a victim, then fine. I get that he's just a kid. However, I need to move on. My boys need to move on." She took a deep breath before turning a corner and wading in deeper. "City Man, as far as I can tell, nobody in the White family has expressed any interest in taking this child in. Unless I'm blind and deaf, it doesn't seem like anyone is going to step forward and do anything about him. They're all just wading in muck up to their knees at the moment. They're barely moving forward at all."

As are you, Matt thought.

"I've seen you with him."

Ah ha. Yes. Matt stiffened and his heart quickened. "He needs horses. He needs younger parents, Jenny. I'm about run out."

"Your wife is younger. I read in some gossip mag that she wants kids."

"Shanda's schedule is all over the place. Hunter's soul would cripple up. He needs the kind of freedom J.I. has to offer."

She didn't bat an eye. "If it didn't work for his…father…then what makes you think it would work for him?"

Gently, Matt said, "Freedom is different things to different people, Jenny.

For some, it's the ocean. For others, mountains. Some prefer the plains." He hesitated, and decided to throw a bone out to help Dallas as well. "Some need to be on stages, healing their souls with music."

She harrumphed. "Or raking in big paycheques."

Matt let that go. "Dale wasn't unhappy sharing his life with you, Jenny. From the tributes I've read online and what was said at the service, he was real proud to be a married guy living a rancher's life. He may have been a quiet man but he was tougher than you give him credit for. He was not the kind of man who would stay in a relationship that wasn't working for him. He loved you, his boys, his horses."

"The domesticated kind and the wild kind."

"Y-yes." Taken aback, Matt stopped moving. How much about Maria did Jenny really know?

Jenny's shoulders slumped and she raised a brave face to Matt. "It's really weird to say it, to admit it. But in a strange way I'm glad Dale had his fling. He worked so hard. It was never easy. Maybe that woman brought him some joy."

"He had joy." Matt paused. "The boy knew Dale, Jenny. Dale was a part of Hunter's life. Maybe right from the day Hunter was born," he tried, testing the waters.

"Oh. Of course." It took a moment for that to sink in. "All the better then, right?" Jenny whispered, this time not bothering to wipe away the tear that trickled down her cheek in a tiny rivulet, glistening like a mirror in the fairy lights. "I always thought Dale was lonely. I didn't want him to be lonely." She shook her head. "I had no clue how to reach him, Matt. Not really. None of us did."

Matt simply nodded. No words were big enough to cover the graciousness Jenny was showing now which, Matt had to admit, was also likely a truth she could never bear to share with any of the White family.

Dallas spun his mother around them, then wrapped an arm around her waist and led her to the family table. Jenny allowed a soft smile that gentled her features before she let go of Matt.

Matt smiled sadly back. "If you ever need anything, Jenny, from Dallas or from me, you call, okay? I'll give you my private number. You can ask Dallas for anything too. He's a good man. You all need to cut him some slack."

"Dale…really loved him. He missed him. A lot, actually, although he never said it. I could just see it in his eyes when one of Dallas' songs came on the radio, that's all. That's how I knew."

"I'm glad. Dallas' music brings peace to a lot of people, Jenny."

"It sure brought peace to Dale. Just not quite enough, I guess."

They walked to the edge of the floor, Matt's strong hand in hers until they came in sight of the others. Jenny let go, and made her way on shaky legs to her chair.

Dawn jumped up just as the band took over. The volume in the place increased, and rose up into the rafters. "My turn!" she cried, laughing over at Johnny when she grabbed Matt's hand.

Johnny had just delivered Cassie to her seat. He sat back in his own chair and put his feet up on the one vacated by his wife. "Have at 'er," he called amicably, and lifted his beer with a grin. "Cheers, Matt. She's a handful, I'm warning ya!"

Aren't they all, Matt chuckled. Tipping his stiff new hat to Johnny, he limped back out to the dance floor with his hand in Dawn's, this time right to the centre where country line dancers, thumbs in belts, were stomping and stepping in unison. He groaned.

"Oh, suck it up, Cowboy," Dawn chided with glee, hauling him right into the centre of the front line. "You can do this."

If Jessie could see me now, Matt laughed to himself, trying to follow Dawn in the rowdy dance. He sucked in a breath when everyone stomped again and he followed more than a beat behind. "Blisters," he mouthed to Dawn when she raised an eyebrow.

She brightened agreeably and hooked her elbow in his. "Ooohhh, muscles," she called out loud enough to be heard or at least understood over the music. "Just dance, Matt!"

He cricked a heel against the wooden floor, winced at the pain, and forced a grin in the general direction of the family back at the table.

"Save me," he mouthed to Johnny, who raised a beer in salute.

Jenny caught his eye, and smiled.

Matt closed his eyes, and let the music carry him away.

Chapter Seventeen

"*N*ow that the rodeo's over I guess you'll take off?"

Back in the cozy bungalow at the ranch, early birds Matt and Dallas were the first to hit up Doris for breakfast. It was a glorious morning, a few days after the family arrived back from Innisfail. Bright sunlight streamed in through the windows; the cotton curtains Doris made just after the family moved in were as still as statues, already wilted in the heat. It would be a scorcher in Alberta today.

Matt took his time answering Dallas. As far as he was concerned, he should have split after he and his buddy had words down by the river. The unexpected rodeo trip had put a real solid spike right smack dab in the middle of his plans. Seated at the table, he slathered homemade strawberry jam on a thick slice of still warm freshly baked bread and took the time to compliment Doris on its mouthwatering goodness before he responded to Dallas, who was at the counter by the stove pouring coffee into mugs. Most of the others weren't up yet, although Dallas had heard Jade stir before he wandered up to the bungalow for sustenance. The tiny kitchen would be bustling sooner rather than later.

Boone wandered in with a yawn and a stretch and dropped into a seat at the kitchen table. Having overheard Dallas quiz Matt on his planned time off, he watched Matt for an answer. There was something about having the quiet, steady man around that just made things go easier these days. Matt was dependable and easy-tempered. Wise. Smart as a whip. He'd become the family's sheltered port in the midst of a tempestuous storm.

When he was ready, Matt filled them in on the latest revision of his plans. "I had a message from Charles," he told them. He contemplated Boone and then looked up at Doris, who was bustling at the counter as always, trying to stay busy so she could outrun reality. "Charles Keating is my boss." He threw a half-assed apology in Dallas' general direction. "Well, he's one of them. Charles and his wife Deirdre took Jessie Wheeler in way back when. They managed her career, produced her music. As I'm sure you know, Charles and I usually work closely on Jessie's and Josh's security, although with Dallas' tour I've been a little out of the loop lately. Charles said they've got a break coming up in their schedules. Josh and Jessie want some time at their ranch west of Calgary, near Canmore. I need to head down and check on things, secure the area before they arrive tomorrow night."

"Today?" It was Doris who posed the question. She did it with two pieces of toast pinched between the fingers of each hand, held upright like flags. She stood still and held her breath.

"No, Ma'am," Matt replied cordially. "I can do a lot from here today. Tomorrow's fine, first light. I want things in order here before I go."

"Good luck with that," Dallas bit off dryly, immediately shrinking from the reprimanding look his father fired across the table at him. He slid down onto a chair next to Matt.

Doris bent over the table to butter the toast, then dropped it rather unceremoniously onto a plate in front of her husband. She gave Dallas an affectionate light swat on the shoulder. "We'd be in better order if you'd step up and help out. We've got guests arriving tomorrow."

Suitably chastened, Dallas mumbled, "Whatever you need, Mom. Just point me in the right direction." He couldn't look at Matt. Losing the man, even for a few days, was like letting a life raft slip from his grasp. Dallas pictured himself getting caught in an eddy out on some river, being spun around like a washing machine with no hope of ever coming out heads up.

Boone was still eyeing him. "We need to get out on the trail, Dallas," he said frankly. "Do you still remember how to ride?"

Dallas huffed and shoved his chair back from the table. Grabbing his mug, he stood and headed over to the fridge to grab the milk. "I don't know why I put up with this shit."

A smile played on Boone's lips. He winked at Matt. "What, nobody else has the guts to treat you like an ordinary lowlife human, Dallas?"

Dallas dumped some milk in his mug before he slammed the fridge shut and took his seat at the table again. "Just Matt." He held up his mug. With a grin, Matt matched the gesture. "He says it like it is. Cheers, Matt."

"Cheers back," Matt said sociably. "Cassie does too. And let's not forget Princess Jade."

"Phil too. Scratch that, I take it back. Phil sucks up to me."

"Because you make him wads of money," Matt offered. He tore off a chunk of strawberry soaked bread. Uncharacteristically, he licked his fingers after shoving the delicious homemade treat between his lips. Something about this cozy family home just made the childlike move seem okay. Blushing, he looked under lowered eyelids at Dallas and hoped Doris hadn't noticed.

"Fair enough," Dallas laughed, using two fingers to push a paper napkin towards Matt. "All right," he said, turning to face his father, "you're my dad. You get another pass but your passes are running out. No more sarcastic comments about me and ranch life, y'hear? Behave."

For once, a careful camaraderie fell into place between Dallas and his father. The two actually exchanged almost shy grins before Dallas looked away and took a generous swig of his coffee.

Cassie landed shortly afterwards. Jade ran into the kitchen ahead of her and leapt into her grandmother's arms. Hunter was tagging shyly along beside Cassie, his hand in hers. She smiled down at him before lifting him up and depositing him on a surprised Dallas' lap. "I'll get you some cereal, sweetheart," she announced to the little boy in her care. Doris was already pouring cereal into a bowl for Jade.

Unnerved by Cassie's presumptuous move, Dallas looked up at her. His wife was humming happily.

Sensing Dallas' body tense up when Hunter landed on his lap, Hunter froze and sent a scared, pleading look to Matt, who hesitated before handing over a generous chunk of his bread, which Hunter accepted without losing Matt's steady gaze. Hunter didn't crack a smile, but after a moment, Matt did.

"He looks good on you," he said to Dallas.

Dallas touched Hunter's small head; drew his fingers through the boy's coarse hair. "He looks more like his mother than he looks like Dale," he observed. In a moment of quiet reflection, he spoke to Cassie when she set a cereal bowl down in front of Hunter. "Thank you, Cassie."

She bent for kisses—a tender, lingering brush against her husband's welcoming lips, and a more thoughtful, chaste one on the top of Hunter's head. Hunter thanked her with a tiny smile meant just for her—for the woman who was taking care of him these days.

Dallas' heart warmed with gratitude at first, until he saw something in Cassie's eyes that frightened him.

Matt caught the look too. Taking a sip of his coffee, he realized he'd seen it many times—in his ex-wife's Julie's eyes when she looked at their daughter, in Jessie's eyes when she took a step back to smile at her children, in Deirdre Keating's eyes, when she—a childless older woman—stood back to reflect on Jessie, who for all intents and purposes stepped in to Charles' and Deirdre's lives to play the role of daughter.

Matt had seen this look in the eyes of his own mother. It was love—a deep, soul love expressed through the eyes and in softening lines of the face. In most women's eyes it was a warm sheen of light, emanating from an eternal, selfless, bottomless pool. The maternal love Cassie shyly sent over the still, invisible air to Hunter was multi-faceted. Her eyes became shimmering emeralds, which made the moment all the more mystical and divine.

Hunter accepted Cassie's love. Matt saw the exact moment the child opened his heart enough to let her in. Hunter dipped his head the same way the wild black horse had bowed to him that day in the meadow.

Intuitively as well as by sight, Cassie recognized the reciprocity in Hunter's slight movement. Her eyes deepened, and glowed from within, bringing to Matt's mind one of Monet's beloved lily pad paintings—weeping willows and blue sky melting into infinite violet-blue water, awakening a sense of mystery, beauty, and love...but most of all, life.

Oddly, the effect was as startling to Matt as it was to Dallas. For more than a few seconds, Matt tightly gripped his coffee mug in order to prevent himself from leaping up and grabbing Hunter out of Dallas' arms, running out of the door, and spinning off down the road in the SUV. *Shanda wants kids*, he caught himself thinking wildly. *Hunter is an easy child to have around. I've got some good years left...oh, Jesus.*

Dallas got scared when he spied the tenderness in Cassie's eyes, in the loving down-tilt of her chin, in the way she grazed a finger on Hunter's arm every time she came near, in the way she continued to happily hum. *Oh, shit. Jesus.*

Matt noticed that Dallas had yet to really lay a comfortable hand on the wise-eyed child who was spooning cereal into his mouth with one hand and taking bites of toast Cassie made for him with the other. Dallas pulled him away from the emotional roller coaster of thoughts Hunter's presence seemed to always spin Matt into.

"What's that song you're humming?" he asked over his shoulder to Cassie, who had turned her back to him so she could putter away at the counter.

Hunter stopped eating. Everyone's eyes locked onto him when Cassie said calmly, "Hunter was humming it this morning. It seems to comfort him." She lowered her voice. "He had a little accident this morning. He was overwrought when he woke." She was spreading peanut butter on a bagel for herself. Pausing the knife in midair, she twisted around and looked at Dallas. "The song's one of yours, Dal. Don't you recognize it?"

The room got quiet. Cassie pivoted around and leaned back against the counter. Tilting her head, she hummed a little more and finished with the bagel and peanut butter.

"Oh, geez, it is. It's an old one," Dallas acknowledged, surprised. "It's one of my first singles."

"Well, Hunter was humming it when he woke up this morning. He was just lying there in bed, eyes closed, lost in thought, humming the song."

Doris took a step closer to Cassie. "Hum a little more of it, Cassie."

"Um um," Cassie said, shaking her head. "Dallas knows it better than I do. Sing it, Dallas."

The shocked look that crossed Dallas' face was easy for Matt and Cassie to interpret. Patches of red high on his cheeks, a firm, straight set to his mouth, eyes moving into slits, eyebrows arcing down…the stubborn side of Dallas was generally, in their experience, not to be messed with.

Cassie pushed his buttons a little further. "Come on, Dal. Hunter obviously has some kind of special connection to that song. Sing it for him."

Doris revealed a possible reason why. "Dale used to play it in his truck, Dallas. He had that first CD of yours on repeat for years. Wore the thing plain out. It got to be a running joke around here to give him the same CD every Christmas."

"I don't sing that song anymore. I got sick of it."

Cassie held her breath. At this point in her marriage, she'd learned when to stop pushing her husband. She was getting close to that line. "It comforts Hunter. He needs it, Dallas. Look at him."

They'd all forgotten about Hunter. Without exception, everyone in the kitchen except Cassie, including a very quiet and subdued Boone, had looked away from the boy and were intent on watching the interplay between Cassie and Dallas. In Hunter's left hand now was the little bit that remained of the toast, drooping so that it rested on the table. Still clutched in his right hand, the cereal spoon lay flat on the table. Hunter's head was tilted down, his gaze focused on the cereal left in the bowl. Waterfalls of black hair partially shielded his cheeks from view. Something was odd about the cereal Hunter had left—big drops were falling into it.

Tears.

Into the cereal bowl big teardrops were falling, landing on the remaining flakes and melding into the milk, puddling, coalescing so that they instantly disappeared the way his parents had.

The tears of a lonely, abandoned child.

"Comfort him, Dallas. Please," Cassie begged in a voice so small she almost didn't recognize it as her own.

The only sound in the room was a child sobbing the way a child does when he does not want to be heard. Big gulps to try to keep the pain from leaking out. A four year old already feeling what it is like to be humiliated. To be the object of unwanted attention.

Dallas' forearms on the table framed Hunter's smaller arms, albeit from a very safe distance. There was still no actual contact between them.

A gruff voice cut through the room—a sarcastic, angry, not-so-steady voice. Dallas' voice. "What the hell would Dale want with all those CDs?"

"They were found in the glove compartment of his truck, Dallas. The police gave them to Jenny. She dumped the entire box of all the things that were in the cab of that truck on our step the day after Dale…the day after he died. By the pile of them, I think probably almost every last CD you ever made was there, including multiple copies of the one containing that song you got so sick of. I don't suppose Dale would have had the heart to give any away."

Dallas forced himself to look up at his mother. She was standing behind Boone, one hand resting on his shoulder. Like Hunter, and like Dallas before him, Boone was staring aimlessly at his food. "Almost every last CD?" he asked, biting off the words.

"Well, I know where one of them went."

Swallowing, Dallas waited. Still, Doris surprised them all. "Your father has one."

Boone tensed. His fingers coiled like snakes next to his plate. A pulse in his forehead started to throb.

"Still in its wrapping, I presume," Dallas grunted, eyes flicking across to his father. Yet a tiny, pleasing warmth formed in his stomach, pushing out a wee bit of the hot red coals that usually lived there when Dallas was around his father.

"No," Doris murmured into the silence, which was abruptly broken when Boone gently nudged his wife aside with an elbow and shoved back his chair with a loud thump.

Boone eased his tired body up. "Bring the kid on the ride, Dallas," he ordered, taking a good hard look at Hunter before speaking to Cassie. "We need to get some of these sluggish horses back on the trail before our new guests come. They get winded on the uphill trek. Tell Ry to get his lazy butt out of bed if he wants to come." He fixed a stony gaze on Dallas. "You can ride Starbuck. Bring the boy; he can ride with me."

Instantly, Hunter's sobbing stopped. At the same time, his head darted up. The wet, wide eyes captured Boone, lassoing their way into his heart. Letting go of his spoon, Hunter wiped his long hair off of his cheek and rested back against Dallas' warm chest.

Dallas almost stopped breathing.

Boone nodded at Hunter. "You can ride with me," he said again, his voice low and controlled. "But I don't want no shenanigans. It'll be about a two-hour ride. Think you can handle that?"

"He's four," Doris admonished. "He don't know the meaning of two hours, Boone."

She blushed happily when Hunter pointed to himself and said softly, "Stawbuck."

"Nope." Boone was firm. "Dallas hasn't ridden in a long time. You'll wear a helmet and you'll ride with me or you don't come at all." At that, he spun around, grabbed his cowboy hat from a wooden peg on the wall just inside the tiny porch, and left the house. The screen door slammed behind him.

"If I'm going, you're going," Dallas ordered Matt, who'd watched the whole interchange with interest. "You gotta go where I go."

"I have work to do before I head south tomorrow," Matt grinned with a casual wave. "Have a good time, Cowboy."

"You can take a few hours, Matt. I don't doubt you've ridden a few times with Josh and Jessie."

"Not often, if I could help it. Once or twice."

Dawn was just on her way in. "His butt's too soft for horses," she teased. "He likes, oh let me see, designer men's wear on his ass. Soft linens, virgin wool, cushy leather seats, not the tough leather of hard western saddles. Can't get that tender little ass bruised now, can we, Matt?"

"And on that note, since apparently I have something to prove, I guess I'm going riding." Matt shook his head when he passed Dallas' sister on his way out. "I can rope a steer with the best of them."

"Don't forget your bear spray."

"Cassie, are you going?" Doris asked, picking up Boone's plate and walking it to the sink.

Giggling, Cassie said, "I'm pretty sure I just heard the words bear spray. So that would be an enthusiastic no."

"Ry'd love to have you along."

"Nope. I'll stay here and do some baking that you can tuck into your freezer for your guests, Doris."

"Freezer's full, honey. Remember?"

Cassie coloured. "Of course. Sorry, Doris. I'll clean, then. And I see that some of the cabins could use new outside hooks, and the chalet needs a replacement lightbulb."

"I'll help," Dawn smiled affably, smirking at Matt, who had stopped by the door. "You fellas go have your ride. Us girls will go another time."

"You can't leave here without going riding at least once, Cassie," Doris said. "It wouldn't be right not to have the full ranch experience, bruised backside and all, honey."

Cassie smiled. "Another day, then." Secretly, she had no intentions of ever going horseback riding.

Dallas had to touch Hunter in order to lift him off of his lap. Setting him on the floor, he wiped his palms nervously on the thighs of his jeans and studied the child, who looked wisely back up at him and studied him right back. "Does he have jeans?" Dallas asked Cassie without looking away from Hunter. "He ought to wear jeans out on the trail. And boots. There's likely to be a few stray branches up there."

"He has both," Cassie offered. "Just look in his bag. Get Ry up. Here, give this to him." She handed him the second half of her bagel, which annoyed Dallas because the peanut butter had been put on when it was hot and was dripping, along with the sticky strawberry jam, over the sides. Switching the bagel to his other hand, Dallas licked his fingers and frowned. Cassie treated him to a sweet kiss on the cheek. "Have fun, fellas. Watch out for bears."

Matt laughed at Dallas and reached down to swing Hunter up into his arms as they all left the house. It felt good to hoist the little fellow up and hold him close to his chest. Matt could feel his small heart beating. It was a joy to see the light come back into Hunter's eyes, which brought Josh to mind; Josh, who lived for the freedom of the open trail, whether on the back of a horse, or on the classic Harley the actor kept spit-shined all year round.

"I can't believe I agreed to this," the ladies heard Matt saying to Dallas as the guys jogged down the few outdoor stairs. "Your sister's a handful."

"For a man usually so calm under pressure, I can't believe you let her get to you!"

Inside, Dawn was in hysterics.

Cassie rolled her eyes. "You and Matt are like school kids."

Doris set a glass in the dishwasher. "Dawn, there will be no more flirting with that man. You are a married woman and the handsome fellow you love to tease is a married man."

"That doesn't seem to stop most people, Mama," Dawn said with a wry twist of her lips and a careless shake of her head. "I don't know how your generation did it, but mine seems pretty messed up."

Outside, they heard Dawn's three kids greeting the men and horsing around. At the table, Jade whined for more juice, which Doris immediately retrieved from the refrigerator and poured into her glass.

"Your generation needs a solid kick in the butt," answered Doris as she poured. "You've had too much freedom."

"But aren't you a woman of the hippie generation?" Cassie asked. "Free love, wasn't it, back then?" She gave Doris a pointed look.

"Not once I met Boone," Doris replied. "True love is forever love, girls. I think you both know that." She looked at Dawn. "What Johnny did that one time was just a man thinking with his balls. He loves you. Don't go messing that up."

"Oh, Mama, give me a break. I'm just playing with Matt because he's such an easy target. Johnny's long been forgiven and I love him to pieces. You know I do." With a happy hop in her step, Dawn bounced over to her mother and brushed her lips against her cheek.

Cassie had to bite her bottom lip in order to keep her smile from bursting too widely across her face. She pinked up when the two women looked her way. "My man writes love songs for me. I'm jelly in his fingers."

"I bet." Dawn crossed her arms and gave Cassie a saucy look. "I mean, he may be my brother, but I'm not blind."

"Um, yeah," Cassie giggled, reddening. "I mean, right?"

The laughter emanating from the house was sheer bliss. Outside, Dallas slapped Matt on the arm and grinned. "Happy women," he said. "That just makes the world go easier. We might get ourselves some raspberry pie tonight."

Uncharacteristically, Matt snorted, which made Dallas chuckle for its unusual inelegance. "*You* might," Matt bit off. "I rarely get raspberry pie any more. My wife's too busy chasing Vivien Leigh's shadow around." He gave Hunter a bounce to adjust him in his arms. "This shoot of Shanda's in the States is hard on a man's ego."

"Well, my friend," Dallas gloated, his face alight with mocking humour. "In honour of your, shall we say 'predicament,' Cassie and I will try to be quiet. But I can't promise you. I can make my wife pretty happy."

"Too much information," Matt said bleakly, covering Hunter's small ear with one hand. "Keep your bedroom prowess to yourself, Dallas. You don't want your fans to think you're actually who they think you are."

"As long as my wife is happy, that's all that matters to me. A happy wife equals a happy marriage. Don't worry, old man. Shanda's doing what she wants to be doing. She's a satisfied woman. Next time you see her, she'll be all over you."

The thought of seeing Shanda soon, perhaps on a quick weekend break, made Matt smile. *I'll introduce her to Hunter,* he thought. *Maybe, just maybe, I'll get my raspberry pie and then some.*

They were almost at the corral. He lowered his lips to Hunter's cheek and whispered. "Look," he said, "Starbuck's waiting for us. He's coming over to say hello."

The graceful palomino was ambling over. Matt was fairly certain the horse was smiling.

"Well, I'll be," Dallas said, stretching out an arm to lean against the top rail of the fence.

Hunter wriggled down from Matt's arms. The guys watched as the big horse nudged its velvety nose into the little boy's outstretched hand in greeting.

Hunter lit up, and contentedly slipped his other hand into Matt's big paw. "Stawbuck," he said. "My Daddy's howse." He didn't notice when Dallas ran a set of fingers over his mouth and turned away.

Solemnly, Matt touched his friend's back. Aloud he said, "A sunny blue sky, a mountain trail, a happy kid, and raspberry pie at the end, Dal. Today let's just take what we're given in the little bits and pieces we're given it, buddy."

Dallas nodded with a sniff. "Aw'right," he agreed, and turned to go rouse up Ry and toss on some boots. He took a bite of the peanut butter bagel and chewed as he walked and talked. "Tell that damn horse it'll be me on its back, not Dale or Hunter. No shenanigans like throwing off its rider allowed."

"Not a promise I can make," Matt said quietly to the hot, fresh Alberta air as Dallas strode away. "Hunter," he said to the child whose hand firmly grasped his, "the world will always be an unpredictable, wild place. We don't know what it'll bring from one day to the next. But I'll tell you this—no matter what happens, there will always be a horse to ride on a sunny day, or a fresh wind whispering through verdant green leaves, or a good song on the radio to sing along to, or a soft rain to nourish the earth. We have to take what little rewards we are given, and rise up and make the best of things. Okay?"

Hunter looked up at him with reverent respect. "Waspbewwy pie," he said. And smiled.

Matt swore he saw light there, in the dark eyes that were usually filled with never-ending pools of sadness. He ruffled Hunter's hair. "You got it, kid," he agreed. "Somewhere, someday, one of our rewards, if we are lucky, might just be raspberry pie."

Bending, he lifted Hunter back up. "Now, tell Starbuck you will see him in a few minutes. One thing I've learned about trail riding. You can piss on the trail if you really want to, but you might be staring into the eyes of a bear. Or a cougar. Me, I'd prefer to stay on my horse as long as I can. Let's do ourselves a favour and hit the john before we hit the trail."

They followed Dallas back towards the little circle of cabins. Behind them, Starbuck raised his mighty head, and watched them go.

Chapter Eighteen

*W*ith Johnny's help, Boone had the horses saddled by the time Matt and Dallas made their way back over with a sleepy Ry and a jubilant Hunter. Ruby was in the house now with Jade and their moms. Cooper and Colt, on the other hand, were hanging over the top rail of the fence and begging to go along.

"Not this time," Johnny told them. "You two will help around the ranch today. They're never too young to pitch in," he said to Matt, who smiled, his heart leaping with the knowledge that he would soon be with Josh and Jessie's kids, who he'd practically helped raise over the years.

Within the half hour they were on the trail, Boone in the lead with Hunter on the saddle in front of him, Ry second, Dallas following Ry, and Matt taking up the rear. For the most part the horses were gentle and experienced; they were older horses lacking in the youthful spirit that would make them dangerous on the trail. The only mount that was a wild card was Boone's, which Matt thought was risky given that Boone had little Hunter in the saddle with him. Dallas took notice that the horse, a frisky chestnut aptly named Spark, crow-hopped and kicked when Boone first mounted, but he didn't think much of it. His memories of riding with his father at that age were always tainted with fear. Boone's sense of what was dangerous was ranch-raised and ranch-tolerant.

"There ain't no time on a ranch for fear," Boone told his kids when Dallas, Dale, and Dawn were small. "You need to have a healthy respect for large animals. But there ain't no room for outright fear. Toughen up."

Either Hunter was too young to know any better, or he subscribed to the same ranch credo as Boone. The little boy seemed to enjoy the challenge of riding the spunky horse, which pleased Boone, who allowed himself a growing pride in Dale's son and a minuscule hope that somewhere along the line perhaps Hunter would be a natural for the rodeo circuit. Hunter held onto the saddle horn, occasionally gave the cracked leather reins a reverential touch, and smiled to beat the band, wider and wider the further they got from the ranch.

The first part of the trail led the small group through the meadow bordering the corral on the far side. It was a well-marked, easy to follow path, already pock-marked with the hooves of heavy horses. Once they passed through the tall grass, they entered a sleepy woods. The hot day was stifling; horseflies bothered the animals, landing on their necks and haunches with regular alacrity. Coarse tails flashed at the pesky winged critters, sometimes dislodging them, sometimes not. The horses didn't break stride. They were accustomed to being annoyed by bugs and such. Most of their riders were not. Matt was the most bothered, and he wondered why anyone would want to be out on horseback on a sweaty, hot, scorcher of a day, making their way through overheated woods.

He soon figured it out. When they broke through the trees, Boone led them to the upper part of J.I.'s companion river, the Panther. The cool water was knee deep here; the big animals lazily picked their way through until Boone encouraged them to emerge back up onto the marked trail and into the woods again. The ride had a curative quality. Peaceful and serene, it was a far cry from the harried pace of civilization, from the busyness of cities and the frenzied life of five-day-a-week nine to five jobs, from frenetic freeways and the painful volume of crowded city cafes and restaurants. Out here, reins casually dangling from one hand, a man could settle comfortably back into his saddle, relax his legs, and move with the easy rhythm of his horse. If he wanted to, he could raise the other hand in the air and let it waft through the many green leaves that drifted by in waves.

There was something sacred out here—a spiritual, mystical, quietude. Even knowing that dangerous predators like bears, wolves, and cougars shared the woods didn't dampen the serenity that settled in and enveloped Matt on his ride.

Dallas' horse farted, amusing Matt and breaking him out of his reverie. There were other sounds filtering around him too, once he relaxed enough to tune in. The whisper of wind in the trees he'd told Hunter about back at the corral, birds that called to one another in songs that were surely all about peace, the occasional nonchalant swish of a tail, a far off whinny from a horse left behind at the ranch, an answering call from Ry's mare on the trail.

And…Hunter.

Humming, again.

Dallas' old tune.

The one Dallas said he didn't sing anymore because he was sick of it, which Matt knew was an outright lie. The fans would never let him off the stage without playing what was now deemed a country music classic, a Dallas White special.

Before long, the small procession came around a long curve and made its way towards the gravel road. A short walk along the road first, then they crossed and started through a section of low brush. Overhead, Matt took note that the sky was clouding over. Patches of blue were still evident but a hazy greyness was settling over all. It had the welcome effect of cooling things down. Reaching up, Matt pulled the front brim of his new cowboy hat down over his eyes. He chuckled at what Jessie would think of him out here acting all cowboy-like, right down to the boots that Matt had pulled on again despite his new raw blisters (he'd raided the first-aid kit in the men's washroom for Band-Aids). A quick guilt assaulted him for letting his thoughts wander to Jessie instead of to his wife, Shanda. He was just so tied up in Jessie, so imbued in her, and had been for so many years, that she was just always there. This meditative ride on horseback was granting him time to pause, to think, to reflect. Closing his eyes, Matt mouthed a silent 'sorry' to Shanda and filed away a reminder to call her when they got back, before he dove into work mode.

Shanda. She was a quandary, sometimes. There was a time when they had separated, early on in their short marriage. Jessie was the root of that, but it was all sorted now, partially by Matt taking steady work with Dallas these last few years. He still worked directly with Jessie, just not as often, although he actively helped Charles and the other members of the Keating security team with the overall planning. Shanda was okay with that. As far as Matt knew, she was faithful to him. When they managed to find time to be together, they were happy. The two were close friends which made things go easier since they were good company for each other. Fine wines, delectable dinners, and a handsome man at Shanda's side at awards and industry events evened out the known reality that Matt would always carry a longing to be with Jessie. Jessie was happy; that was the other part of the equation. Her marriage to Josh was hard-earned. Their family had gone through hell. Jessie's contentment these days was paramount in Matt's self-worth. He gleaned a lot of pride in knowing that his actions over the years, although sometimes wrong, had paid off and gifted Jessie the happiness he felt she truly deserved.

Shanda rarely complained. Matt was grateful. Sighing, he shifted his butt in the saddle and grinned at the echo of Dawn's words earlier, teasing him about getting his precious butt bruised.

Boone, on Spark, gave the chestnut his head so the animal could start to pick its way up the mountain. Matt was rather disconcerted when he spotted deep claw marks about six feet high on the sides of trees. *Bears,* he thought, and was glad Doris had reminded him one night by a campfire that bears weren't generally a concern until evening, and even then, only when a rider got between a momma bear and her cubs.

The notion circled Matt around to Cassie. *I suppose it's good she didn't come on the ride. Furrows left by claws would have given her a fright.* The other side of the thought took him back to the kitchen at breakfast. Dallas had clearly frozen when Cassie dropped Hunter in his lap, and he had stilled entirely when she asked him to offer comfort to the child.

Dallas, in Matt's experience, was a solid man. Sure, he had his moments on tour when he made it clear that he enjoyed his success, like when people catered to him or sought him out for autographs. Truth be told, he was a stand-up guy whose ego was really not all that swollen, considering how inflated Matt knew it could be in light of his longevity at the top of the country music charts.

This bear thing, though. Never get between a momma bear and her cub. Is Hunter becoming Cassie's cub? It's Cassie and me who are seeing to the child.

Ry and Jade are treating him like a little brother. It's only Dallas and Dallas'
immediate family who are unresponsive, who are wary. For reasons I completely
understand.

Dallas is retreating from Cassie, where Hunter is concerned—it's more like
she is putting Dale's son between herself and Dallas. I better stay out of their way.

A voice from the lead horse drifted back to the rear of the small column.
It was Boone. He was talking to Hunter, and sometimes looking back to
speak to Ry as well. He was teaching, Matt discerned. Telling the kids about
the flora and fauna they were passing through, about the wildlife peppering
the mountains, about herbs along the trail that one could safely consume if
they so chose. About the benefits of breathing in crisp, fresh mountain air,
even in the winter.

Especially in the winter.

He loves this, Matt mused, enjoying the gentle, easy swaying of the horse
beneath him. *Boone loves the solitude. Likely he needs it, now more than ever.*
No wonder he and Dallas are so often at odds. Dallas craves it too, but he seeks
a different kind of solitude. His solitude lies in song, in music, and he can find it
on the stage in front of thirty thousand people. He wondered how Dallas was
responding to this ride through nature, and whether his thoughts were taking
him to some place quiet and reflective, or to someplace agitated and fretful.

Matt didn't have long to wait to find out.

They'd been going uphill for quite some time when Boone reined up and
brought Spark around to face the little group of horseback trekkers. Matt
was glad for the break.

"I'm glad we stopped," he said to Dallas after he dismounted.

"Your knees?" Dallas asked with interest, bending over with a stretch
and a yawn.

"No, my horse. I wouldn't be surprised if this poor girl lays down and goes
to sleep. She huffed and puffed the entire uphill ride. I was starting to worry."

Dallas laughed and straightened so he could bend slightly backwards.
He stretched his arms up into the air while Matt tied his mount's reins to a
tree and wandered up to Boone to lift Hunter down. "Dad did say they need
some exercise," Dallas called after him. "Jesus, my old bones are practically
creaking. And I didn't do any of the work."

"Molly's tougher than me, I'll give her that," Matt admitted, setting Hunter on the ground and pulling off his helmet.

"Aren't they all? Females, I mean?"

"Hilarious, Dal. I don't know if I'd make it up this mountain as quick as she did, that's all I'm saying. How far are we from the top, Boone?"

Boone gave Spark's reins a good yank to be sure they were well tied, although he gave the horse a second look when its ears pricked up and it whinnied. "We're only going up as far as a clear-cut. Even you city boys ought to appreciate the view." He winked at Ry, who seemed not to want to get off of his horse. Spark whinnied again. "Spark, what are you seeing out there?" Turning to the fellas, he said, "We often see elk out this way. Spark's catching a scent."

"Wish I'd brought my phone so I could take some pics in case we see some." Grinning back at Boone, Ry finally gave in and hopped off his horse.

The guys were enjoying a few minutes of lighthearted camaraderie when another of the horses whinnied and did a little dance. Taking a good look around, Matt tensed. He recalled a time when Josh got badly hurt while out on a ride not far from the Sawyer family's Alberta ranch. The memory drew up all kinds of unwelcome emotions, which Matt hastily swallowed down since some of them had to do with serious deep-seated fear. Something flickered in an opening just beyond the trees ahead of him. The tall, dry grass of a meadow beckoned. He caught movement not far behind a grouping of wild shrubs clustered in the meadow about a hundred feet away. Open-mouthed and pointing, he started to step over the exposed roots and deep hoof indents in the trail, suddenly so focused on what he saw and on moving forward quietly that he forgot to wince at the blisters hurting his feet.

"Wild horses," he announced in a hushed, respectful tone. "About six, I think. They're really something."

All four heads whipped around to follow Matt's gaze. Nobody said a word.

There were six, two young colts and four full-grown mares and mustangs. Behind Matt, the domesticated horses were growing more antsy, perhaps with the memory of a freedom they never experienced yet somehow knew to yearn for.

The leader of the wild herd, the alpha male, seemed unaffected by their presence. He was grand, that horse, a magnificent creature who, when he raised his head to peer at the grouping in the trees, stood so proudly and with such almighty reign over his kingdom that the men's knees buckled. The guys were so caught up in the unexpected vision that they remained still as statues, afraid to breathe for fear that the rising and falling of their chests would send the majestic animals on their way.

Even Boone was stationary and noiseless. Boone, who'd come across wild horses a hundred times, was so knocked over by the loss of Dale again—because Dale was all about the wild horses—that he was rendered mute from a sudden, relentless, tidal wave of grief.

Matt and Dallas should have known better than to lose themselves in the magic. They should have known to keep track of Hunter, but they got caught up in the windswept grass, the mountain vista, the welcome isolation, and the mystical aura of the wild, regal creatures.

They didn't notice Hunter take a circuitous route around them, around their own tame beasts, and steal softly out between the trees. They didn't see him bend down so low that he was almost invisible in the tall grass. They didn't catch him creeping up to the stand of brush that stood between them and the wild animals.

Until Hunter was amongst the herd.

Ry cried out. The three men all whipped around, ready to rescue Ry from whatever it was that scared him. Eyes wide, Ry echoed Matt's earlier movement, and pointed. His fingers were shaking.

"Jesus Christ," Boone said when he finally spoke, not loudly, but with the dignity and reverence the horses and Hunter's affinity with them deserved. He took a single step forward.

Heart quickening, Matt started to move. He only made it a few feet. A faint voice emanated from somewhere deep in his soul. Listening to its steady thrum, which was growing more and more coherent by the second, Matt crouched, and took a knee.

Dallas remained standing, just behind and beside Matt. The sight before him was not new. Hunter and Dale suddenly got all mixed up in his mind, and in Boone's mind too. They watched Hunter wade softly through the tall grass; watched him part it with his small, confident hands. Before them,

Hunter stood tall, moved gracefully between the horses, turned once, lifted his face towards the sky, and lay down on his back.

The mustang tossed its head in welcome, or perhaps in salute, its mane flying free against the backdrop of what the guys were surprised to see was now an astonishingly indigo blue sky. The grey clouds were gone, although nobody had fully noticed their retreat.

The six horses stood in an unplanned, unofficial honour guard around the small boy who'd lain down amongst them. Encircling Hunter, they provided a protective border, separating him from a world he didn't understand but that he knew hurt; from a world that had become frightening and lonely.

The men and Ry could barely see Hunter. Only a dark image was visible—his jeans, his shirt.

"Dale used to do this," Dallas managed, the voice that gave magic to millions through song quivering in awestruck wonder. "Do you remember, Dad? When he was a teenager, he communicated with them. He used to say they spoke to him. And you thought I was a dreamer, that I had my head in the clouds."

"Son, watching your brother lie down amongst wild horses was real. It was a real thing that I could see with my own eyes. Watching you float around lost in thought and skipping out on chores was not."

"This, Dad," Dallas tried to explain, stepping forward ahead of Matt so that he was a few steps ahead of Boone as well, "this child, in this place, after all that's happened, is just as real as Dale ever was. What he's doing is just as real as what Dale did. And you know what I think, Dad?" Swiveling slowly around to face his father, Dallas said, "Now that I've had some distance from you, now that I'm a man who knows how to put his thoughts into words, I have something to say. And I want you to listen." He took a breath and contemplated his father closely to see if Boone was paying attention. His father was staring at him with a confused longing in his eyes. It unnerved Dallas, and made his breath come quickly and unevenly. He swallowed back the open, vulnerable fear that came with looking his father in his eyes and having his father stare right back at him, and spoke his mind. "I think the wind is the bass line," he said. "The tall grass is the melody. The horses are the rhythm. The birds are the lyrics."

"This…" Turning back to the horses, Dallas swept his arm slowly over the extraordinary beauty that literally lay in front of him. "All of this, it's like a song. It's how I learned music, Dad. Thank you for raising me the way you did. Thank you for giving me a soundtrack for my music."

Boone cleared his throat. He pawed at the ground. "It doesn't make sense to me, Dallas. I don't see how what you do can in any way compare to a hard day's work. I don't mean to be disrespectful. It's just how I feel."

"You don't get how incredible music is, Dad? Is that it?" Dallas was facing his father again. Something about this place, about what Hunter and the horses brought to this place, about their elevated foothold on a mountain with the ranch and the world far below, was opening a hole for father and son to climb through. Something about where they were standing was making it safe to converse with a raw, open honesty.

"This kid," Dallas went on. "You, watching him. I know you get how amazing this all is because you got it when Dale did it. And let me tell you something. This kind of beauty—the wind blowing through the long grass like that, the echo of it in the horses' manes, a child lying amongst it all…" He had to stop and swallow three times before he could continue. The mist clouding his eyes was making it hard to see his dad. Dallas struggled to say what it was that all these years he could not seem to make his father understand. "It is truly like a song. Lyrics and melody and instruments, they all come together with nature in a place like this, and create this incredible tapestry. Tell me you see this, Dad. Tell me you get it and that you see how amazing it all is, and how it's reflected in my music. All these years, Dad, I took what was given to me. I took it and I molded it and I created—I still create—something beautiful from it. The same damn way you're taking that green sunuvabitch horse of yours and molding it into an animal you can safely take up here. You ride it up here and you sit on its back and you admire the goddamn beauty of all of this and the peace it brings you, the same way I mold what I see and hear into songs that bring me beauty and peace."

"There's a difference, son."

"I don't see how, Dad."

"You create your songs in order to please others."

"Do you think so, Dad? Do you really think that's what it's all been about?"

"Hasn't it been? So you can rake in millions?"

Dallas shook his head. "I'm wasting my breath here." He turned back to the protective posse surrounding Hunter. "He'll never get it."

The horses seemed to agree. The mustang at the forefront looked right at Dallas and gave a whinny that Dallas decided was a sympathetic battle cry. As one, the herd turned.

After they galloped away, tails and manes flying, Hunter sat up and wiped his eyes. He was crying when Matt, who was the only adult to go for him although Ry was close behind, crouched down and met his eyes. "Hunter," Matt said softly, "that was really something. That's quite a gift you have there, little guy. How'd you learn to do that?"

"Daddy," Hunter whispered. A new tear trailed down his cheek. He swiped at it with a tightly closed fist. "I miss my daddy."

Matt's heart almost crunched to a halt. "I know, Hunter. I know you do."

Ry stooped down next to Matt. "Hunter, I miss my dad too. I don't really remember him, actually."

Hunter's eyes flicked beyond Ry to Dallas. They asked a silent question.

"Dallas is not my real dad," Ry told him. "But you should know that he makes a real good substitute once you get to know him."

Matt smiled, and lifted Hunter up. "Ouch," he said to the boys when his knees cracked. "If Dallas writes a new song about this experience, I wonder if he'll put my aching knees in it."

They started walking back through the long grass to where Dallas and Boone stood in mute discord.

"Probably," Ry teased. "They can be the cymbal cracks." He mimed slamming drumsticks down on cymbals.

"Pictures," Hunter cut in, ignoring the friendly repartee. Lowering his eyes, he used a finger to draw a picture on Matt's chest.

"Pictures?" Matt asked him. "Of the horses? I'm sure we can find you some. Leave it with me, Hunter." If pictures of the horses comforted Hunter, Matt would climb over Mount Vesuvius to get him some. The child had just given them all an extraordinary gift. He deserved extraordinary measures in return.

Twenty minutes later on the way back down the mountain, they were riding beside a pristine, sparkling lake when Matt said to Dallas, "I have to tell you, Dallas, your dad's a tough old bear. I'm sorry that he's so hard on you."

Dallas was quiet for a minute before he answered his friend. "Today wasn't all bad, Matt."

"Okay." Matt pondered that. "How so, Dal?" In his heart, he felt Boone was only worth defending for his honesty. What Boone said to Dallas, his only remaining son, was not worth defending at all.

Dallas smiled, and started to rein up ahead of Matt. He took off galloping. "He called me son," he called back. "I'll take it."

With a grin, Matt watched him try to catch up to Boone and Hunter, and Ry. "Well, you forgiving bastard," he grinned at Dallas, "you'll take your nuggets where you can get them, won't you?"

Leaning forward, he gave the horse a little cluck and a gentle nudge with his sore heels. "Good for you, buddy," he added as he followed, "good for you."

Doris, Dawn, and Cassie had a delicious lunch ready and waiting for the guys when they returned. Johnny and his kids were already fed—Shane and Cormac were around as well, so they took over the equine duties while the hungry trail riders went up to the bungalow for nourishment.

Jenny was in the kitchen when they appeared, washing dishes with her back to everyone.

Cassie asked how the ride was. Excited and awed, Ry told her about Hunter lying down amongst the horses.

Jenny stopped washing and cocked her head to listen, her dishcloth limp and forgotten in the soapy water.

Doris slid a plate of sourdough biscuits in front of Boone and studied him. Her husband's eyes were on Hunter, who was sitting next to Matt, propped up on cushions.

An uncomfortable silence overtook the room.

Matt broke it. "Hunter would like some pictures of the horses," he said as he forked up his summer salad of greens and vegetables. "Maybe we can go to the Internet later and round some up."

Hunter stared at him and shook his head.

He's afraid to talk about the pictures in front of the others, Matt considered. "No?" he asked his young friend out loud, slightly confused.

He was partially right, but this was too important for Hunter to let go of. "My daddy," Hunter said with conviction. "HIS pictures."

Nobody breathed.

Jenny whipped around and stared at him.

It was Doris who got the answer they were all seeking. "Your daddy took pictures of the horses?"

Nervous with everyone looking at him, Hunter bowed his head but managed a few nods. Slipping off his chair, inadvertently throwing two cushions to the floor in his wake, he trotted into the dark living room. He came back holding a heavy photo album. His lips were set and firm.

He thrust the book into Doris' hands. "My daddy," he said, pointing. "His pictures."

"Dale kept photo albums of pictures he took of the horses?" Dallas asked the room in general.

"Apparently," Dawn said dryly. "If you can believe a four year old."

Doris grabbed a pot from the drying rack and gave it a vicious scrub. "Will wonders never cease?"

"No," Dallas said, thinking about watching Hunter lying amongst the horses today, and the warm sound of his father calling him 'son.' "No, they won't."

He grinned up at his dad before slathering one of his mother's homemade still-warm-from-the-oven biscuits with strawberry-rhubarb jam. "No," he said again, as the jam dripped over the side. No paparazzo were watching him here. Bending forward with a sideways grin, he clumsily licked the yummy jam off of the biscuit's side. "They won't."

Chapter Nineteen

*T*hat evening, Ry took his guitar out of his case and carefully carried it out to the front deck of the small chalet. Not far ahead, the adults were arranging white plastic chairs around a nascent campfire, dropping into the chairs with the kind of grateful fatigue that follows a hard day's work. Jade was asleep in the chalet; Hunter had lain down in a hammock Dallas had installed on the deck earlier in the week. The little boy's even breaths told Ry that he was off in dreamland.

"I don't know if I should play," Ry said to Shane, who was just approaching. He gestured to the curled-up body in the hammock. "I might wake him up."

"So what if you do? He can go inside." Shane grabbed a deep wooden Adirondack chair and pulled it over so it was closer to Ry who, guitar slung over his shoulders, was leaning casually back against the deck rail. Shane's chair screeched across the wooden floor. Both boys jerked around to see if Hunter moved. The child didn't blink and his chest maintained an easy up and down rhythm. "I think you're good," Shane declared, easing back into his seat to watch Ry tune. "He's off in la la land."

Ry watched Hunter for a minute before he plucked at the first string and gave a gentle twist to its tuning peg. He went on to tune all six strings before Shane spoke again.

"Do you practice every day?"

Brushing his fingers down the strings, Ry shrugged. "I try to. I don't always get to."

"Do you want to?"

"Yep." After a moment he said, "Don't you? With rodeo training?"

"Nope. Not every day, anyway. Sometimes I just wanna play video games."

"You won't get better if you don't practice." Ry started to play an easy ballad, an Alan Jackson tune from the nineties. Half expecting his mother to holler at him to keep it down for Hunter's sake, he played at a low volume. None of the adults said a word. Without looking up from the strumming hand, Ry let out a slow breath. "If it was Jade out here sleeping, I'd be ordered elsewhere."

Pondering the bit about practicing, Shane said, "Well, like how good do you have to be?"

"At guitar?" Ry asked, looking over at Shane. "Or at rodeo?"

"At anything," Shane decided.

"As good as you want to be, I guess."

"You're already good. We watched you at Dallas' show in Vancouver."

Ry stopped playing with a discordant strum. He wrinkled his brow. "Wasn't that the day your dad, um, died?"

"Cormac and me watched it. We streamed it on the iPad in the barn."

"The Internet sucks out here."

"We're used to seeing parts of stuff." Shane ran a finger along the painted wood of the chair's arm. A chip flaked off. Shane studied the spot of bare wood that was left. "We saw most of the song you played."

Ry didn't answer. Humming quietly because he couldn't remember the Alan Jackson song's lyrics, he started on the song again and focused on making up runs to give it some ornamentation.

"You must want to be really good."

A few expert runs later, which Ry repeated until he got them right, Ry responded with, "I just want to be able to play whatever I want."

"Country's easy, Grampie says. He says it's the easiest kind of music to play."

"Dallas says he doesn't really get it."

"My dad thinks Dallas is really good. Uh, my dad thought he was, I mean."

"He is." Positioning the guitar more securely against his body, Ry strummed a popular bluegrass tune, Wayfaring Stranger. "Shane, look," he said. "I can play this with three chords. Or," he started to add a few new chords,

"I can pretty it up by adding more. If I want to play it the way I hear it in my head, which is the way I think it should be played, I can throw in some finger-picking and a few runs and really have some fun with it." He looked up and smiled. The overhead light and the simple bliss of playing music gave his pale eyes a contented, warm glow. "You see?"

"Dallas teach you that?"

"He got me started. The rest I've been figuring out on my own."

"I don't know what me and Cormac are gonna do now that my dad's gone. We got no one to help us now. I guess that'll be the end of the rodeo for us."

Ry strummed quietly.

Shane had picked up the paint chip; he turned it over and over, studying it as if it might contain secrets.

"Shane, I'm real sorry about your dad." Ry said it without looking up from the guitar.

"Mom said your dad died when you were two."

"Something like that. I don't really remember him."

"Does it still suck? I'm wondering how long..." Shane's words faded out.

"I've got Dal now, so that helps."

"Mom says that Dal's a shitty dad."

"Why?" Ry stopped playing and stared at Shane.

"Because all he cares about is being a star and all the money he makes. Is it true that he collects sports cars?"

"And airplanes," Ry mumbled in uncertain agreement.

"Airplanes."

"Yeah." Perking up, Ry said, "Dal's great, Shane. You ought to tell your mother that. My mom's crazy about him."

"Cause she's married to a star. She gets to spend all his money."

Speechless, Ry turned back to his guitar. Fuming, he played a whole song at a higher volume and a fast tempo without even looking at Shane. When he strummed the last chord, he said, "Dal doesn't cheat on my mom. Tell your mom she's picking on the wrong brother."

Bristling, Shane stopped fidgeting with the paint chip.

"He's nice to me and Jade."

"He's not nice to Hunter. And he better never be."

"He's not NOT nice to Hunter. Matt says that Dallas just doesn't know what to think of him yet."

"If it was up to Mom, she'd take him to some foster home and drop him off and leave him there."

"He's your little brother."

"Cormac's my little brother. Hunter's my dad's bastard."

"Do you even know what that word means?"

"I know it don't mean anything good."

At this, Ry set the guitar down and leaned it up against the rail. "Dallas would kill me for setting my guitar down like this," he muttered inwardly. Glancing back over his shoulder, he saw that Dallas, at the fire, had his back to him. He exhaled and turned back to Shane. Out loud he said, "Like it or not, Hunter is your kid brother. Half brother. Same as Jade's my half sister. No matter what happens to Hunter or where he goes, he's got your dad's blood in him. I don't have a brother. I'd kill to have a brother. You got two. You always got someone to play video games with."

Shane wriggled back in the low chair. He took a good, hard look at the sleeping boy in the hammock. "More like ride horses with."

"Like your dad."

"It kind of pisses me off that Hunter's already good at that stuff. How much practicing could he have done? He's only a little kid!"

"It's a gift, Shane. Hunter has a gift."

"Well, why don't I have it? It don't seem fair."

"You got some of it. You're great with horses! Besides, Hunter's gift is rare. I overheard Johnny telling Dawn that it's a Cree thing, being able to lay down with wild horses and stuff. Hunter's mom's Cree."

"It just seems like he got to spend a lot of time with my dad. That's all. It pisses me off. Me and Cormac always got left behind."

"With your mom."

"Yeah, and she's always mad. It's not fair."

"She does seem pretty mad. I guess I don't blame her."

"Brother or not, I don't think I'm gonna be seeing a lot of Hunter. I think he's on his way out, Ry."

"Maybe." In his heart, Ry knew that Shane's words rang true. As if to cement that fact, the volume of the people at the campfire increased. Both kids looked over—Dallas and Cassie had left the fire and were standing behind the chairs in a small grove of tall lodgepole pine. Ry could see Matt watching them. Matt was still seated at the fire, but he was leaning over his knees, forearms resting on his thighs, hands clasped. His head was twisted to the right, eyes locked on Dallas and Cassie.

The argument got louder.

Shane sighed and let his paint chip fall between his fingers. It landed on the ground and lay there, used and then quickly forgotten. "Here we go again," he grouched. "Maybe you guys should all just go. Then things would go back to normal around here. Sort of," he added, catching Ry's concerned eye.

Cassie's voice rose above the light breeze and made its way to the chalet. "You're being stubborn, Dal!"

"He's not my responsibility. He's Dale's mistake, not mine."

"The child needs a home."

"You've gotten too attached to him, Cas."

"Hunter is an easy child to grow attached to!" Cassie rocked back on a heel and crossed her arms. "Oh, I see. That's what you're afraid of, getting attached to him. The great Dallas White with his fear of attachment always lurking one step behind."

"Look, Hunter brings back memories I don't care to dredge up. In fact, this whole last while has dredged up too many damn things, things that I thought I let go of a long time ago."

"Like what your dad thinks of your music—"

"Not just my music, Cassie!" Dallas interjected loudly. "Don't you get it? My music is me." In a softer voice he added, "My music—is me. You of all people ought to know that."

"So you and your dad have problems, who doesn't have problems with their father? Or mother? Get over it, Dal. You're a grown man, let it go. Let the past go."

"So you want me to take in a child who, every time I look at him, brings up a past I'd much rather forget."

"Let the bad stuff go, Dallas."

"That's the thing, Cassie. It's not just the bad stuff. There was a hell of a lot of good stuff back then. Me and Dale, we were best friends. We lived out of each other's pockets. Then it turned out he was living a lie all these years. It's like from the time of the stampede, the night I introduced him to Maria, he changed. He changed in ways that I don't understand."

"Then you took off for Toronto and didn't take the time to understand."

"And left us to pick up the pieces." Boone stepped out of the fire's glow and stood with his feet apart, bracing himself against the ground like a man digging in for a fight.

Dallas' shoulders drooped. The comment rang true.

Boone added, "You abandoned your brother, Dallas. He needed you back then. All those years while you were off being a performing monkey, Dale needed you. And now look." Gulping, Boone had to choke back his emotion; either that or he would have collapsed at the weight of the last few weeks, of the last many years.

"Thanks, Dad. Thanks for that cozy reminder."

From the chalet verandah, Ry had been watching with his back twisted around; now he turned all the way around and sucked in a breath. He'd never seen his mother and Dallas fight this way before.

Shane hoisted himself up and joined him at the rail. "They're fighting over Hunter. Over what to do with him."

"I think Dallas is ready to leave. He doesn't want to take on another kid."

"Imagine what it would be like to think nobody wants you."

"Funny thing about that is that I kind of can."

Ry didn't have time to elaborate on the lonely years with a depressed mother, the years after his father died—the hard time before Dallas came into their lives in a magical Prince Edward Island campground.

Boone dug in a little further. "There were things that happened with Dale that you don't know about, Dallas."

Whipping around to him, Dallas shouted, "Like what? Like him stealing my girlfriend right out from under my nose?"

"Is that what this is about?" Cassie said over the crackling of the big fire Johnny was tossing splits onto—his way of staying busy and trying to appear unconcerned.

Ry could almost see the gears turning in his mother's mind.

"Is that why you left Alberta?" she asked. "Because your brother stole your girlfriend out from under you?"

Boone sniggered. "Who'd choose a scarecrow-skinny dreamer over a champion bronc buster? I never did understand what it is women see in singers. Seems like a pretty weak way to make a living, if you ask me. Every night, standin' up in front of half-naked girls pickin' out the ones you want to take home to play with."

Ignoring him, Dallas said, "I left Alberta because I wanted to see if I could make it in the music business, Cassie. I left because Dale and me grew apart."

"And Maria had something to do with that."

Dallas got quiet. "I won't lie to you. She had something to do with it. When she got him, she changed him. I didn't recognize the brother I had grown up with anymore. But that was a long time ago."

"So now that old anger's come back."

"You don't know me as well as you think you do, Cas."

"Oh yes I do. I know you well enough to know that you think you can run away from here and push these people—your family, your brother—out of your brain. You can get back on stage and pretend if you want to that Dale is still here, that he's the same old brother you grew up with, the one who protected you when you got bullied by the kids at school. Or," she gave Boone a pointed look, "by your father."

"That's not what I—"

"Even worse," she went on, and Ry and Shane had to strain to hear because she lowered her voice in an attempt to keep herself under control, "you can choose to ignore the fact that Dale got to have a child with her. It didn't happen right away because he had a family with Jenny, but eventually he and Maria met up again and lo and behold, they had a baby. A baby that maybe you wished you had with her back in the day. One that, now, you wish was yours."

Unbelievably, Dallas was blinking back tears. "I got my family, Cassie. It took a while, but I got it. You and Jade and Ry are all I need. I don't need a physical reminder around of something I used to long for."

At the fire, seated stiffly on a mold-stained chair, Jenny was paralyzed. For the most part, the argument was loud and boisterous. It was bringing to the surface a lot of very personal hurts and shortcomings. Dallas seemed to forget she was there, and that her sons were within hearing distance.

Cassie pushed one button too many. "You and Matt found her, didn't you? Maria? Maybe you want to pick up where Dale left off."

"Where Dale left off? Where Dale...left off?"

Matt leaned further into his thighs before saying a silent prayer and standing. Wheeling slowly around, he faced Dallas. His eyes were fierce; they had a message for Dallas—*Don't.*

Dallas saw the look; distracted, he'd turned when Matt stood. He chose to ignore it.

One peek at Cassie, then he planted his feet and faced his father. At his sides, his fingers curled into fists. Raising his chin so that the moon's glow and the campfire light combined to create an eerie prescience that danced across his pale eyes, he spat, "That's the thing. Dale didn't really leave off, not back then, anyway."

Jenny held her breath. She couldn't look at her youngest son, Cormac, who knew enough around adults to keep his curious mouth shut. Cormac's scared eyes darted from one incensed, emotional speaker to the other.

"Dad," Dallas continued, "I know you loved him more. And I know you wanted the best for him, for Dale. That's why you forbade him to see Maria, which, I have to admit, seemed like really great revenge for me at the time. You wouldn't let him get into a serious relationship with her because she was Cree. Indian, as you put it, which, by the way, is a term no longer used. I'm sure it seemed like the right thing to do at the time, Dad, but this is the thing. When you love someone—and I mean truly love someone, with every ounce of your being, with every fibre of your soul—you're not gonna stop seeing that person just because your father told you to. Especially when you're what, nineteen?"

Dallas stopped to catch his breath. Close by, the fire crackled a warning as a split fell sideways, sending sparks and ashes sizzling into the air to fizzle out in the blackness. Below the darkened cliff, the shallow riverbed managed an echo when some unseen creature unseated a rock that splashed loudly into the running water. If it were any other night, someone would have gotten up to look. Tonight, the only person to turn a head was Johnny, who pulled out a flashlight and aimed it loosely in the direction of the river and then, seeing no large animal of concern, flicked it off and went back to monitoring the angry men before him, who he was half afraid would come to fisticuffs before the night was out.

Dallas dove in deeper. "So, Dad, I repeat—this is the thing. Dale did not end the relationship with Maria. He kept it up. He kept it up when he started seeing Jenny, through the birth of their children, through all the years Shane and Cormac played hockey and trained for the rodeo. Through all the years he was your shadow on the ranch, and through all the years he sat at your table at Christmas, or on your birthday, or on Mom's birthday, or on the birthdays of his kids, or on Jenny's."

An audible gasp came from the direction of the fire. Doris. Putting a shaking palm in front of her face, she started to weep.

Jenny rose.

Dallas looked over. A slow nausea worked its way up his belly and stopped in his throat. In his peripheral vision he saw Cassie's shoulders sink, but that wasn't what scared him the most. What truly frightened Dallas, slowing his adrenaline and bringing him back to earth, was the disappointment on Matt's face, showing itself in darkened eyes lined with tired, sad wrinkles, and in lips set in a firm, straight line.

"I'm s-sorry, Jenny," Dallas stammered. "Matt and I found that out the day we went to Calgary. Dale and Maria never gave each other up. I don't know why they only had one child near the end, and I sure as hell don't know why Dale killed himself, especially knowing just how much they loved each other, unless things were starting to go sour for them. The only thing I know for certain is that the reason they stayed together in secret was because our father, the great Boone here, forbade them to be together in the first place."

Jenny threw out two short sentences, both to Cormac. "Get your brother. We're leaving."

Cormac was sitting in a foldable lawn chair. When he stood, it creaked. "My iPad's in the house," he muttered.

"Leave it."

"No."

"I said leave it. Let's go." She gave him a shove. Tired, disillusioned, confused, he staggered towards the truck, a chunk of his childhood left behind in front of a crackling fire that was meant to bring the family together, but which quite soundly tore them apart.

"I'm sorry." The apology was from Dallas. With a half-hearted wave, he let the small family start to disappear from sight so they could go process their harsh new reality alone.

Dallas forced himself to look back over at Cassie. "I'm not without a soul, or without mercy and understanding," he said, unsuccessfully trying to keep his voice steady. "Obviously Dale didn't want this kid or he wouldn't have left him here on the planet alone. Maria doesn't want him either. Maybe he brought them bad luck. Maybe Hunter was the thing that finally tore Dale and Maria apart."

On the deck, the hammock squeaked on its rope when Shane went by it and gave it a shove. Everyone turned. Hunter was sitting up, clinging to the ropes the hammock was suspended from, ears tuned in to the adults at the fire. The haunted look on his face almost brought Matt to his knees. He'd seen that look before, on a sad, scared young singer back in Vancouver many years ago, and on her face many times since.

It screamed trauma. It screamed lonely.

"Oh, J-Jesus, Dallas." Faltering, Cassie took a step backwards. Her eyes filled. The moonlight above turned them a liquid jade olive-green and danced over them like fireflies as Cassie computed what just happened at what was supposed to be a relaxing evening sitting by the fire. "I hope you're proud of yourself. Your petty jealousy and your me-me-me ego just destroyed your brother's wife and will no doubt have a hand in your nephews' ability to process the death of a dad they loved and whom they need to grieve. And that child," she pointed at Hunter, whose cheeks glistened in the soft verandah light, "will one day be an adult. You've just put a huge nail in his coffin. Why do I suddenly feel like I don't know you at all?"

She headed to the chalet and brushed past Ry, almost knocking his guitar over. Grabbing it, Ry coloured instantly. Cassie disappeared inside.

Swiping a hand under one eye, Dallas paced in a circle before he looked back over a shoulder and hollered at Ry. "Put that goddamn guitar away properly, Ry, before I take it away altogether." Slamming a fist against a tree, he winced before giving his father one last hard look and continuing his pacing.

Matt's swift footsteps got Dallas' attention. In just a few quick motions, Matt bounded up the few steps to the cabin, passed a surprised Ry, and scooped up Hunter. He turned to Dallas. "I'm getting a jump start on the drive down to Josh and Jessie's ranch. I'm taking Hunter with me. The Sawyer kids will love him."

"Now?" Dawn hollered. "Matt, it's almost eleven. It's not the right time to be driving through the mountains, the predators will be out. You'll have deer and wild horses to contend with, bounding onto the road. Wait til morning. Please."

Shoving open the door of the cabin without the courtesy of knocking, Matt called out, "Cassie, pack up Hunter's things."

Ry jumped in before someone else had a chance. "The Sawyer kids? Let me go with you, Matt. Please? I can help watch Hunter." He lowered his voice so that just Matt could hear. "I think my mom and Dallas need some time alone."

"Well, I'm not taking Jade."

A wide smile spread across Ry's face. "Thank God."

"Ask your mother. And pack in a hurry. We're leaving in half an hour." With that, Matt hopped down the steps and started towards his own tiny cabin. Cassie popped her head out of the door. "If Ry's going, I'm going," she pouted. "It would do Dallas good to spend some time alone with his daughter."

Before Matt could open his mouth to protest, Dallas called out, "You think I'd let you go somewhere alone with him? Do you know about the arrangement he has with Jessie Wheeler?"

"Jesus," Matt growled, pivoting around so he could point an accusing finger at Dallas. Hugging Hunter to him, he said gruffly, "Is that what you think of me? Is that what kind of man you think I am? Do you understand anything at all about love, Dallas?" He strode a few steps before stopping and turning again. "I guess not, otherwise you would never go there. And you'd understand just how precious this child in my arms is." He moved on. Over his shoulder he said, "I know you're confused and angry, Dallas, so I'm going to let that one go."

"Matt," Dallas called, as Matt's footsteps receded into the night, "There is no room in my life for a child of the wild. For a child who needs to do what my brother did because it's the only way he'll ever find peace, it's the only way Dale ever found peace, right Dad? Living with horses, lying amongst wild ones, living secretly on the brink of society with an exotic Cree woman, and with animals nobody else can ever get close to! I live in the fast lane—I gave up an idyllic mountain life a long time ago—it's like it never happened."

He spun around to his father. "Dad, it's like it never happened. Dale stayed out here, he found a way to be calm and wild and free that worked for him, and I moved on and I found what worked for me. He calmed his spirit amongst the horses, I calm mine with music. The impasse between us was big then and it's even bigger now. There's no room in my life for a kid who needs the same damn thing his father does. Jesus—did. I meant to say *did*."

A loud holler came from the distance, from the direction of Matt's cabin. "There are many ways to find joy, Dallas. To find peace. These boys need it, Hunter and Ry, and for the next few days they're going to get it. I wish I could take Cormac and Shane with me too but I have a feeling Jenny won't be speaking to me or to anyone close to you for the next while. In the meantime, can I give you some advice? Listen closely—the rest of you, your entire family, need to get over yourselves. Think about Jenny and her boys and this new pain Dallas just unleashed on them. I know you're grieving, and I'm real sorry about that, but damn it, people, get past yourselves. Goddamnit."

It was a quiet group around the fire twenty minutes later when Matt spun dirt under the rented SUV's tires and turned its nose to the road with both Ry and Hunter along for the ride. Cassie rejoined the family at the fire and laid a hand on her husband's knee. They sat for another hour sipping on beer and listening to the subdued beating of their lonely hearts.

Later, in bed, Cassie told Dallas she was surprised he didn't storm off, that it had taken courage to stay at the fire with his father close by. Outside their small window, the crickets chirped in relief at the renewed semblance of peace.

"Matt doesn't lose his cool very often, Cassie," Dallas admitted. "When he does, I listen."

"He was right to say what he did," she responded, drawing the back of a finger over his cheek. "And to take the boys. Families are never easy to navigate, Dal. I think yours has been in trouble for a while now. Your father moving everyone out here to the depths of nowhere was likely the catalyst that set Dale off on his final path. Maybe the distance from Maria and Hunter was too far, if he needed her. Them."

A sad smile played over Dallas' lips. "Matt may never work with me again. Hell, he'll probably never even speak to me again. I guess I deserve that." He rolled over and turned his back to his wife. "I'm just going to lie awake all night and go over and over and over all the things I've done wrong over the last forty-some years."

Cassie leaned over him. She ran her fingers over his lips, the top and then the bottom.

He clasped her fingers in his and pressed them to his cheek, and inhaled before saying, "You should be really pissed at me right now."

"I am. Dawn is more pissed. You sent her crush away." Wriggling in close to his back, she added, "I happen to love you, and part of loving you is understanding what hurts. It's clear to me, Dal, that you and Dale—and your dad—had a complicated relationship."

"The more I think about it, Cassie, the more I think something happened in Calgary that night, the night I did the talent show there and met Maria for the first time in the service station on the way home."

"Like what? What do you think happened?"

"I don't know. My dad's not far off about me—I am a dreamer, and I certainly was that night. I was this country hick farm kid who'd just won this big contest and I had a beautiful girl on my arm. We'd had this crazy instant connection and messed around in my truck and then gone back into the city to party. I was full of myself. Full of the irrepressible hope of youth, of the incorruptible dream. I thought I had the world by the tail. The more I think about it, the more I think I was too into myself to realize that something was off about Dale that night."

Cassie ran that over and over in her mind. After a bit, she said, "You've told me that your dad found you in Calgary, that he drove you home. I thought it was odd that Boone would be in the city in a country and western bar with your brother, at least then when Dale was so young and probably full of piss and vinegar during Stampede Week."

"I thought so too, that night, but I got so pissed about the way Dad treated me and then having to go home that I guess it wasn't on my radar right away. In later years, when I took the time to reflect on it, I admit it did strike me as odd. Dad was never one to spend time in the city, and he sure as hell was not the kind of man to hang out in bars. Especially in the middle of the night."

"Maybe you should ask him if something happened that night."

Dallas got quiet. "Maybe I don't want to know."

"I think if you and your dad tried to talk to each other, I mean really talk, you'd find a balance somewhere, Dal."

"That's because you're the kindest, sweetest person on the planet, Cassie. You want everyone to get along."

"I want my husband to be happy, that's all. A happy husband makes a happy wife and together they make for happy children."

"I know how you can make your husband happy, Cassie."

Giggling, Cassie reached down his body and tucked her hand inside his boxers. Starting to knead and play, she said, "Is this what you had in mind?" With Ry, Jade, and Hunter all in close quarters, lovemaking had been sporadic at best since they came to J.I. and what cuddles they did share were not in the least very athletic or inspired. "The boys are gone, Matt's cabin is empty, and Jade sleeps like a rock. I can make noise."

"Well then, wife, make it," Dallas begged. "My eyes are rolling back in my head." Easing over on his back, he brushed his lips softly over hers. "I'm so sorry, Cassie. I was a real asshole tonight."

"You were," she agreed with a pout. "Make it up to me."

He started to move down her body.

She shivered with anticipation. "My darling man," she breathed. "I love you."

Dallas smiled, and loved her back.

Chapter Twenty

Matt wasn't surprised to see an older green dirt-spattered Range Rover at Josh and Jessie's low one story rancher when he cruised through the property's privacy gate and up the long driveway. He braked to a stop next to the well-travelled vehicle, which was parked in front of the barn. As he opened the door and forced his body upright, he reveled in the peace of the early morning. Dawn was just breaking; the new sun was bathing the earth with an earnest early morning orange-pink glow.

Standing outside his rental with the driver's door open, he stretched his arms up to the sky, almost bending over backwards to try to inject some energy into his tired body. He'd gotten so sleepy on the drive down that once Hunter and Ry dozed off he pulled over for a nap. It went against Matt's usual mode of operations to stop and sleep out in the open like that, but traffic in the backwater boonies of Alberta was a rare thing during the day and almost non-existent at night. He'd parked the SUV in as secluded a spot as he could find, in a dry field behind a clump of trees. Just closing his eyes was a relief. It took seconds for Matt to fall off into a welcome but fitful sleep for a few hours.

Fifteen minutes ago, he'd been glad to spot the turnoff to Josh and Jessie's place. The older Matt got, the more he had to accept that he didn't have the stamina to burn the candle at both ends as much as he used to. Driving when he was tired, especially with two precious kids in the car, was as hazardous as driving under the influence. Cruising into the clearing a few moments ago had given Matt further reason to exhale. There was something steadying about the weathered shingles of Josh and Jessie's low rancher when it came into view.

Less satisfying was laying his eyes on the barn. A few years ago, the Sawyer family suffered through a terrifying barn fire and had to rebuild. It was jarring to see and smell the new construction afterwards and be reminded of the dark days that led and followed the fire. At least the elements were helping to age and weather the place now—howling winds, a baking sun, and harsh mountain thunderstorms had eroded the newish shingles to a darker, more seasoned grey.

Matt's jaw cracked when he lowered his arms and punctuated his big stretch with a few blinks and a yawn. The yawn ended with a happy, satisfied smile. Rubbing a palm over the rough new whiskers on the tender part of his crackling jaw, Matt wandered into the clearing and scrutinized the area. Unfamiliar horses, a palomino and a chestnut, along with a caramel and white paint pony, were lolling around the corral to the left of the barn, grazing on scattered tufts of tough grass that had somehow survived the scorching summer heat. Matt wrinkled his eyebrows at the sight of them. His smile did an about face. These weren't the usual horses he recalled from the old days at the ranch. These new animals seemed none-too-threatening as they munched away, occasionally swatting at annoying horseflies with swishes of coarse tails, yet their presence in Josh's corral was jarring. Like the barn, they represented a pretty tough patch in the collective history of Matt and the Sawyers, which led to the distance Matt felt he had to keep from the family these days.

He scratched at his jaw, thinking about the times when he knew every detail that ever changed in Josh's and Jessie's lives. These days, he was lucky if Charles and Ulysses remembered to tell him when the Sawyer kids were starting school.

Some memories will never die, Matt thought, a cold sweat beading across his forehead. Inside his stomach, a knot was forming, twisting and tightening like a roller-coaster ready for a rider. In this case the rider was dread. Matt reached deep inside and tried to yank it away; revolted, he tried to pull up some of the good stuff so it could wipe out the bad. He would never forget the horror associated with the darker times when there was room for nothing in his brain but trying to keep the Sawyer family safe. Clinging to Jessie, and she to him, had led to an inevitable long-distance battle. The loneliness of living apart from the Sawyers back then was gut-wrenching.

He whispered a silent prayer that Dallas and his family would never have to experience such terror.

I have my reasons for loving Jessie, for needing her, he thought, surprised at the quick jolt of anger towards Dallas that zipped up his body. Trying to shake it off, remembering Dallas' cruel snipe about being alone with Cassie, Matt raised a chin proudly and said to himself, "I'm not that kind of man."

Still, even as he said it, shame filled his heart. He'd first taken Jessie to his bed when both were alone and disconnected. It hadn't been easy to push Josh aside, to push Jessie's love for him aside. "We're connected," Matt told the air around him now. "Me and Jessie. We're deeply connected. We need each other."

The palomino raised its head and gave Matt a woeful stare that Matt interpreted as judgmental.

I used to be an honourable man, he berated himself. His heart ached; he slumped and let the hand rubbing his jaw fall limply to his side. He just felt old. Fatigue from the drive had settled into his weary bones, keeping him from rebounding from the self-deprecating thoughts haunting him. He shook his head but the cobwebs stayed put. Turning to the right, he stared again at the slowly greying barn. *Some things are just not black and white,* he mulled. *Some things are only meant for those caught within the torment to understand. Josh understands. He gets it. He's okay with where things landed.*

Isn't he?

Josh was in an untenable situation. If he wanted to keep Jessie, he had to end her anguish, hence his decision to step aside and give Matt and Jessie the freedom to connect sexually if they needed to. If anyone understood how deep Matt's blood ran in Jessie's veins and vice versa, it was Josh. Yet, not surprisingly, there was a distance between Josh and Matt now. It stemmed from Josh's weakness—addictions, the weakness that stalked him—and from Matt's loss of personal honour. The distance was necessary, it was real, and it was regrettable, but it gave all of them the grace and the space to be in each other's company without overt tension.

And for what? Matt considered, thinking of the friendship with Josh that he once took for granted, that he now missed. Stepping back to the SUV, he leaned an elbow on the top of the door. Raising his right hand again, he absently rubbed his bottom lip with a thumb and two fingers. *Jessie and I have only been together a couple of times in the last few years. Was it worth it? Has all of this been worth it? The hell Dale must have gone through to be with Maria…was it worth it?*

For me and Jessie, we had that one rare time when we were in Europe for a series of shows, when distance gave us a kind of illusive permission and a night of dinner and dancing in the company of royalty made us feel invulnerable. That night was unreal, her laying back on the bed like that in a gorgeous, silky dress, eyes half-lidded with desire and her breath coming in quick, ragged gasps… slowly spreading her legs to invite me in, teasing me with her fingers first, already wet with desire and want, and holy god I went there, undoing my belt with shaking hands on my way over to her because I wanted her so badly, and for so long.

And that other time, when Josh was in the States on a shoot, it was the only other time but it was equally surreal. Jessie and me drank too much one night at my place; we drank and we laughed and she wriggled in under my arm on my couch that faces the full window wall. Outside, the twinkling lights of the ships on English Bay beguiled us. They were echoes of the stars—I remember it was a clear night, it was like the clouds disappeared, like they went into hiding just for us, and the stars melted into the water, and the water melted into the stars, all of it velvety black except for those mysterious pinpricks of light, which seemed like secrets leading this way and that to other dimensions, maybe.

We drank exquisite wine at dinner earlier that night at Charles and Dee's, that expensive 2008 Chateau Lafite Rothschild that Jessie likes, Charles is putty in her hands and he got it out of his wine cellar just for her. Jessie and me carried the party over to my place since the kids were asleep at Charles and Dee's and so Jessie I had a rare evening alone. Eventually we lost the honour fight, how could we not? She smelled so sweet, her hair like lavender as always, and her lips tasted like cedar and blackberries from the wine.

I craved her the way a good man craves forgiveness after he's gone bad, I needed her the way a dying man needs grace. She opened up for me like a prized English rose in fresh bloom; I dove in and took her like a warrior.

She screamed when she came that night. Again and again, Jessie being who Jessie is, raw and real, every bit of her out there for the world to see, not a stitch of her held back.

Like when she sings. She lets it all go. She lets her soul go free.

I think I cried. I was drunk, I know I was drunk. So once I got my breath, I think I might have cried, for love of her.

For love of having her, that singular, rare night.

It was the last time we were together that way.

Letting go of the car door, Matt turned around in a small, anxious circle. The lovemaking that night at his place was uninhibited and surreal. It was love meets history meets need.

Meets wine, he laughed wryly.

I'll see her soon. But I can't...

Touch.

The truth derailed him. He climbed back into the vehicle and raked a quaking hand through his hair, took a peek in the rearview mirror at the still-sleeping kids in the back.

Matt knew Josh thought of himself as weak. But in Matt's books, Josh was a hero. A fighter. He went down, but he fought his way back up. All along, the reasons for much of Josh's and Jessie's troubles stemmed from Josh. They were rooted in his difficult childhood and the loss of a loving mother when Josh needed her most. Josh went under, Matt was there to help. The family went under, and Matt was the rock that held them together, sometimes from a great distance but always focused on their safety and on Jessie's ability to survive, to be a good mother to her children.

In the end, the precious Sawyer family got past the troubles. The fallout? It was the never ending fear that Josh could go under again. Drugs, alcohol. A disease, they say. *Well,* Matt thought, going back to the dark days as he stared at the barn, *Josh is doing well, Jessie and I have not been together in over a year, my wife reluctantly understands and I rarely see her anyway, and here I am at a ranch I wish to hell I owned, with two children that don't belong to me, and a good buddy that's messed up and hurting on my mind. I'm lonely as hell.*

And I'm going to see Jessie tonight.

A tiny smile flitted over his lips, sending light catapulting into his eyes.

Sure, Josh was an understanding kind of guy. It had to grate on him, though, when Matt and Jessie were in each other's space, it just had to. *Seeing us together is a reflection of Josh's weakness, of where he failed—failed her, their children, but most of all himself.* One look in those haunted, hurt chocolate brown eyes and Matt's knees always crumbled in shame. Still—one look in Jessie's deeply loving, kind eyes, and Matt was metaphorically on his knees on the ground, arms around her waist, face buried in her body as her fingers stroked his hair. While all the while through her lips were murmured soft songs of love.

Sometimes it's enough just to hold her, he told himself, steeling his heart for the pain. *It has to be. Sometimes it's enough just to see her happy, to see Josh and the kids happy. Safe. The Sawyer family is safe. I'm the man who watches from the perimeter. I'm the man who glues everyone back together, not the one who tears them apart.*

I can get through this.

Dale didn't. But I can.

A spring door creaked open behind him, and slammed. Matt's gaze flicked to his rearview mirror. He was surprised, when he saw his reflection, to find his eyes moist. He swiped the dampness away and smiled wearily when he spotted Jessie's Aunt Evelyn bounding towards his rental, brown leather boots untied and flowery top swinging.

"Hellooo," she called as she approached. "The fun begins! Welcome, Matt!"

Matt pushed his door open further and eased himself upright for the second time with a yawn and a catlike stretch. "Hello, Evelyn," he said kindly. He pointed at the horses and pony in the corral to the barn's left. "You and Gary have been busy. I don't recognize these horses."

"Gary and Josh did a buying trip this spring. Thought you knew…"

"Oh," Matt said, recalling way back in the reaches of his memory that Charles had indeed said something about that during one of their long distance Skype meetings a few months back. "Ulysses would have handled that one. I've been on tour with Dallas White."

"So I heard." She glanced into the back seat of the SUV. "You've brought company."

"I did," Matt said. Striding around the hood to the passenger side, he opened Ry's door and nudged him awake. "This is Dallas' boy, Ry," he said by way of easy explanation since Ry was not Dallas' biological son. Ry blinked sleepily up at Matt, who smiled down at him. "There's a comfy bed inside," Matt said, "if you can make the walk to the house."

It was early morning in this neck of the woods, for adults as well as for sleepy kids. Ry and Hunter would likely doze a few more hours, Matt figured.

"And this one," Evelyn said, a sad frown colouring her otherwise cheerful features, "is the little fella that's all over the news." She was looking through the back driver's side window at Hunter.

"Dallas' brother's son," Matt said quickly before Evelyn had a chance to say something like 'surprise son,' which Matt did not particularly want Hunter to hear. He went around the back of the vehicle and pulled open the door. Bending, he lifted the little boy out of the car. A pitiful, sleepy groan reached Evelyn's and Matt's ears. Hunter snuggled closely into the muscled body of the man he trusted above all, and buried his face in Matt's warm neck. One deep inhale, and he was breathing evenly again.

Grinning at Evelyn, Matt stood a little taller. This child fit. He couldn't wait to introduce him to Jessie. *And to Shanda,* he remembered, feeling a little emotionally healthier at the thought. Filing away a mental note to call Shanda and invite her to the ranch, he said to Evelyn, "I'll set us up in rooms in the new wing. These two need a few more zzzzs."

"So do you, I think," Evelyn remarked, concerned. "Those dark shadows under your eyes have rings around them. And there are rings around the rings. Your body is sending you a message, Matt. It's been a rough time up at Dallas', huh?"

"I'll be fine," Matt said with a defensive frown and what he hoped would pass as an indifferent shoulder shrug. Evelyn laughed and rolled her eyes when a yawn followed the statement. "I'll catch up tonight. For now I need quiet time to get some work done. Charles tells me that Josh and Jessie are rolling in this evening."

"A lot of the security work is done," Evelyn said brightly, adding a casual wave meant to take in the area. "Ulysses has been and gone and the Calgary firm is all set up. The message I got was that all you need to do is a simple walk around, for the most part. Then relax." She smiled, and turned her head to scan the gorgeous mountain vista beyond the rancher's low rooftop.

Matt felt compelled to follow her gaze. His eyes softened. The rising sun was mirrored in the jagged rocks of the mountain summits. Liquescent pearl-pink honey dripped lovingly over the tops.

"Jessie's orders," he heard Evelyn say in a firm voice, drawing Matt away from a sight he never tired of seeing.

"Jessie's?" he asked, startled.

Evelyn did a turnabout and started walking up to the house. Matt followed, his heart and brain in disarray. He knew Ulysses and Charles were on top of things. It felt weird, though. *This new reality,* he sighed. *Me being at a distance…it sucks.* The notion was traitorous as far as Dallas and Cassie and the kids were concerned. If Matt had his choice, he would go back to Jessie full time, although it would open up a whole new kind of hurt. The passing of the years haunted him. Maybe if things had never gotten so crazy, he would still be married to Julie, his daughter would still be in his life, and he and Josh and Jessie would be working together in harmony. Like in the old days.

And holding Jessie really would be enough.

Evelyn held the screen door open so Matt could usher Ry through the doorway and step through himself with light Hunter in his arms. At the back right of the open concept one story rancher, Matt slipped through a doorway to a newly built guest wing designed to house the numerous security and visitors the Sawyers always had around. Before he closed the door behind him, he snuck a peek across the rancher's floor to the master bedroom, which was tucked innocuously behind the kitchen on the opposite side of the house.

Matt closed his newly moist eyes and buried his nose in Hunter's long hair. Murmuring quietly, he stroked Hunter's back. A rush of love swept through Matt, and it was everything he had in him to let go of the little boy in his arms, and lay him down.

Chapter Twenty-one

*I*t was Boone's bullying that finally got Cassie on horseback.

"You're worse than Dallas," the older man declared one morning at breakfast. "You're letting your fear get in the way. Think of Ry, he's not scared. He's soaking up life on the ranch."

A droll eye-glaze was Cassie's way of preventing herself from lashing out with some kind of sardonic verbal response. She noticed that Boone did not mention Hunter's eagerness to ride, and his special affinity with horses. Tossing her ponytail, she curled a corner of her lips downwards. "Your first guests are arriving this evening, Boone. I need to be here to help Doris and Dawn."

Boone threw his hands up in the air in annoyance. "If your husband hadn't pissed off Jenny last night, there'd be lots of hands on deck! As it is, we'll be lucky if we ever see her or our grand-boys again."

Doris was nipping around the floor with a broom. She irked her husband by poking it at his slippered feet. Grumbling, Boone moved one foot back and then the other. He took the opportunity to get back at her when she bent to get at the far reaches under his chair. Winking at Cassie, he gave his wife's hefty bottom a healthy pinch.

Doris yelped and let go of the broom long enough to swat his arm. She slipped into the conversation. "Cassie, we're more than ready for tonight's guests. I'm taking Dallas' father's side on this. He's got some old nags out there on the downside of living. They're well broke and very gentle. You'll be safe as long as you get on the trail by four."

"Why four?" Cassie asked, giggling at the mischievous schoolboy grin on

Boone's face when he reached for his wife's butt again. Doris ducked aside and took her broom elsewhere.

"Because that's when the predators come out," Dawn announced, sweeping into the kitchen with her usual self-assurance and grabbing an apple from a bowl in the centre of the table. Taking a big bite, she leaned back, crossed her ankles, and spoke while she chewed. "Bears, wolves, cougars. It's best not to be on the trail in the evening."

Cassie gulped. "That settles it, then. I'm staying where shelter is a thirty-second run away at most. Speaking of which, I'm going to start doing my midnight peeing in a bottle. No more treks to the public bathroom in the middle of the night for this girl."

"I knew you were a princess," Dawn laughed. Sobering, she swallowed her apple bits, gnawed off another chunk, and stared at a cracked fingernail while she delivered news she wasn't sure Cassie would take well to hearing. "So FYI, just a few weeks ago a young ATV rider got mauled by a bear. Not by a grizzly, either. Just by a plain old run-of-the-mill black bear. Just east of here."

Doris gave her daughter a warning look and jumped back into the conversation. "Now that's a rare occurrence, Cassie, don't let that frighten you. That youngster got between the sow and her cubs. You don't want to get between a mama and her babies."

Boone harrumphed. "Learned that one too many times," he grumbled, crossing his arms and giving Doris a pointed look. "Got my ass swatted with that very broom right there for doin' it, too."

"Dad," Dawn jumped in, communicating a half-assed complaint in a light, singsongy way. "You're making Mom look bad! You're gonna hurt her feelings."

"Not possible," retorted Boone with a sly grin. "My wife's a rancher's wife. She's tough as nails. Only thing hurts her feelings is when I don't compliment her cookin.' Learned that one the hard way too." Grinning sheepishly at Cassie, he pointed to his backside. "The hairbrush that time," he mouthed.

"Oh boy," Cassie mouthed right back at him. "Thanks for the warning."

In the end, Boone's strong nature won the day. Cassie reluctantly agreed to go for a ride.

"He seemed to really want to show me the view from up the mountain," she explained to Dallas fifteen minutes later, relieved that Dallas had agreed to go on the trail ride too. "He said something about being able to take a really good look at J.I. Mountain from up there." Shyly, she added, "Your father said that J.I. was really special to Dale, that it was your brother's favourite place on the planet for its remoteness and stark beauty. How could I turn a view of that down?"

"I'm not sure anything we thought about Dale was accurate," Dallas rebutted. They were making the bed in the chalet. He swept a corner up to the top left and helped Cassie, on the opposite side, fold it down. "My dad's a bully no matter how you interpret him, Cassie. Sometimes he's frank and obnoxious, and other times he's a passive aggressive old bastard. If you're not comfortable riding, you damn well shouldn't go."

Cassie turned around and sat on the bed with her back to Dallas. "Maybe," she answered softly, unaware that she was nervously wringing her hands, "I need something to talk to Ry about. He'd be proud of me if he knew I faced my fear and got on a horse. Besides," she brightened, twisting around to catch her husband's eye, "it wouldn't be my first ride ever. I rode at my grandmother's when I was a child. It won't be so bad. You know me, I'm a sucker for adventure and beauty."

"Are you," Dallas questioned rhetorically, sitting down next to his wife and taking her hands in his to still their nervous motion. "You're wringing your hands, Cassie. I know you, and I can tell you're not wholly comfortable with this."

"Maybe it's you who isn't comfortable," she pouted, yanking her hands from his grasp and forcing them into stillness on her lap. "The idea of two hours on the trail with your dad likely terrifies you, without Matt and the kids around as buffers. Maybe that's why Boone wants to go—so he can spend some time with you before we leave."

"I don't recall him inviting me," Dallas grumped. "The invite came from you."

"Well, he invited me. And he knows you'll go where I go. That was likely his whole plan all along."

"Oh, I will, will I? Go where you go?"

"Yes. I'll prove it!" Sitting by Dallas on the bed, she pulled her sundress up to reveal a petite yoga-toned thigh. "Follow my lead, husband?" she asked, eyes flashing with delight.

He pulled her to him, and stuck his face in her belly for a tickle. Cassie's high-pitched laugh had the others wondering what the two of them were up to. Squealing, she had to turn away and shove her face in the pillow. It was either that or let Dawn hear her cries of ecstasy, in which case Dawn would clue in that the couple in the rustic chalet were sneaking in some morning glee. And that, Cassie figured, would give Dallas' baby sister ammunition to torment the two of them for the rest of their visit.

She gave up on the pillow a few minutes later. And caring about what Dawn thought? By the time Dallas moved south down Cassie's belly, Dawn's merciless teasing was the last thing on her mind.

They had to make the bed a second time that morning, and shyly duck their heads when they tiptoed across to the showers for another spritz.

Dawn, bucket and cleaners in hand, passed Cassie on the way. To her credit, she kept her mouth shut. After she passed Cassie, though, she broke out into a smile and started whistling. She didn't break stride.

Cassie was wringing her hands even more when she approached Dallas later that afternoon. "He was hanging signs. He was hanging signs all day, and now he's sitting on a picnic table by the stable fiddling with a bridle, putting a new buckle on it or something. It's twenty after four, Dallas. He says another twenty minutes!"

Feet resting on a tree stump, Dallas was lazing casually on a white chair on the bank overlooking the riverbed with Jade snuggled up in his arms. She was sound asleep. Dallas used one arm to cradle her and the other to raise a cold beer to his lips. "That's my dad," he replied, unconcerned. "Always on his own time."

"So he's not worried about bears and the like?" Cassie hopped from one foot to the other. "Cause after what Dawn said, I sure the hell am!"

"Aw, Cas, bears won't bother you as long as you don't bother them. They'll hear us coming a mile away and will stay away. The last thing they want is to get in a human's face. They don't want anything to do with us, trust me." He grinned up at her. "Scaredy cat."

She would have screamed in frustration, except the idea of abruptly waking Jade up and having to dance around the sour mood of a tired three year old made her nauseous. Still, Cassie wanted to wipe the all-knowing smirk off of her husband's pretty-boy face.

"You probably saw lots of bears and cougars on the trail," she fumed, righting a chair and plopping carelessly down into it. "S'probably why you left the west in the first place!" She grabbed his beer and took a nice, long drink.

The little trio got on the trail at 5:23 that afternoon.

The plan was to follow the same route the men took a few days earlier when Ry and Hunter were along for the ride. Boone was in his glory. He would lead the way on his newest horse, Aviator, an unsettled buckskin gelding he wanted to break for the rest of the busy tourist trail ride season.

Aviator had Cassie ready to dismount and bolt before they even started off. The big horse crow-hopped and bucked before Boone even got a foot in the stirrup, before Johnny got its lead untied. *Jesus*, she cursed uncharacteristically to herself, clinging to the reins the way Johnny showed her when he helped her take the saddle. *The damn haunches on that thing! The horse is all muscle. Look at its hind legs! Aviator likes to fly, huh?*

Cringing, Cassie eased her left foot out of the stirrup and moved it backwards when Boone's horse danced just a little too close to her leg for comfort. Glancing over a shoulder at Dallas, she flipped her frown right side up in an attempt to act tough. *Scaredy cat my ass,* she breathed inwardly. *I'll show him, the righteous bastard.*

Raising her chin proudly, she tucked her horse, a pretty bay called Lady, ('a lady for a lady,' Johnny'd said with that cute dimply smile of his) behind Boone's and headed out just ahead of Dallas who was on a lazy horse called Snip.

It took a good twenty minutes for Cassie to relax. By the time they got to the riverbed part of the trail, she was settled enough to at least admire the serene natural beauty of the area. It helped that both Boone and Dallas were calm. "They've done this a thousand times," she said to herself. "If there was anything to be afraid of, they wouldn't be taking me out here in the first place."

When they crossed the road and the meadow and entered the woods at the bottom of the mountain, Cassie blanched at the sight of the lower halves of many of the trees as did Matt before her, on his ride. The bark was torn off and deep gouges rutted the interiors.

Are those from bear claws?

She wanted to ask Boone or Dallas about the trees, but Boone had gotten a fair distance ahead of her on Aviator, and Dallas was preoccupied, humming some random tune as he bounced along behind her on the leisurely moving Snip. *Maybe it's something new he is putting together,* Cassie considered, which made her reluctant to disturb him. He seemed to be enjoying the tranquil, peaceful ride. *No point in raising a false alarm,* she rallied. *The men aren't worried so I won't worry either. I'm fine.* In her head all the way up the mountain, a constant conscious refrain ebbed and flowed. *It's mind over matter. I just need to stay calm.*

It morphed into *They're probably watching us. The bears, the...predators. They're part of nature. We're part of nature too! We're just doing our own thing, minding our own business. Think about this logically, Cassie. Why would bears or cougars want to mess up a perfectly fine day of hanging out in the mountains?*

Oh, to eat, she answered herself, accompanying the logical realization with a little whine. *Oh God, please don't let them like the taste of humans.*

As the men had on their earlier ride, they stopped a few times on their way up the mountain. The trail was steep in places—well marked, but steep. The horses needed breaks to catch their breath. Boone turned his mount around every time they stopped. Facing Cassie and Dallas, he relaxed in his saddle and chatted easily about the forest around them, about the trees, about his mountain home. He was a different man out here in the woods, in his realm. There was no edge to his voice out here, no underlying tension.

I guess he's in his comfort zone.

Humbled, Cassie pushed her fears aside long enough to sit back on the stiff leather and simply respect how hard Boone and Dallas were trying to get along. They were being civil, and were having what seemed to be an easy back and forth yak about their surroundings, which was neutral territory for a father and son trying to forge a connection, she supposed. Occasionally Cassie thought she saw dampness settle across Boone's eyes—inklings of sorrow, maybe, or regret, she wasn't sure, because Boone turned away every time his voice got thick, and when he looked back, his eyes were dry.

Dallas saw it too, Cassie was certain he did. He tried to half-smile back at his father every time Boone ducked his head and inhaled.

What's this sorrow about, Cassie wondered. *Is Boone sad because Dallas will never replace Dale? Is he sorry that he and Dallas lost a lot of years?* Cassie figured she would never really know the truth behind the mist of hurt in Boone's eyes. He seemed resigned to it. Every time he reined up and swung Aviator around—the buckskin horse bucking and crow-hopping and scaring the bejeesus out of Cassie—he raised his head and carried on his way.

The meadow where Hunter lay amongst the horses was sacred, judging by the way Boone whispered to Cassie while she dismounted. She handed him Lady's reins and strode forward with her phone in hand to take a closer look and maybe snap a photo. There were no wild horses around today, but to her surprise a lone elk was there, standing at ease and feasting on something Cassie couldn't see.

Just beyond the edge of trees that skirted the meadow, she got past her fear a little more, and remarked silently at the serenity of the place—at the sheer pristine, untouched glory of this mountain haven. It was no surprise that Dale loved it here.

Cassie was just surprised that Dallas didn't. His comments when they talked about his home were usually always centred around his mother, around her home baking, around meals they shared. Around his brother, some, and his sister a little more, but more in a longing kind of way for the family lives they led. Dallas carried an ache for those old days. Cassie was certain that kind of home life was a path he didn't regret not taking, it was just that a part of him missed it—the simplicity, the coziness, the easy familiarity of rural living amongst people he knew and loved.

Cassie managed to get a photo of the lone elk before it dashed off across the meadow. Excited, buoyed by the freedom and majesty it represented, she almost forgot to worry about bears when she got back aboard Lady. Boone's horse was pissing her off enough, anyway, occupying most of the room in her head for fear.

Boone himself was clearly annoyed. He gave the animal a good kick and reined it around in two tight circles before he started back up the trail. "Don't let elk fool you," he said at the same time to Cassie while she gripped her reins and tensely recovered from the nervous pacing and sidestepping of Boone's frustrated horse. "You don't hear a lot about elk and the damage they can do because bears and cougars get all the fuss. Keep this in mind, though—elk can be dangerous. This one's gone back to his herd now. An elk will charge you if you get too close."

"Good time to tell me," Cassie muttered to herself. Dallas had pulled ahead of her on the trail. Growling at him for leaving her behind, she chided herself for having princess syndrome and wanting all of his attention. Stubbornly she bit her bottom lip and fixed her gaze on his sexy body as he swayed hypnotically in time with his horse's languorous walk. Sighing, she let her eyes drift up his back to the layers of careless, wind-blown blond hair cascading loosely out from underneath his cowboy hat. Deciding she liked the view, Cassie eased back in the saddle and smiled wickedly at the fresh memory of the morning's erotic, spontaneous cuddle.

Super proud of herself for settling into the ride, Cassie let one hand fall to the side and handled the reins alone with the other. Letting her thighs and knees relax, her mind wandered to Jade back at the ranch in Dawn and Doris' care, hopefully rested and good-tempered, and of Ry at Josh and Jessie's ranch. She hoped Ry would get a chance to ride with Josh and Jessie and their kids. She'd met the famous couple a few times now. A few years had passed since she met and married Dallas. It boggled her mind that she was traveling in the circles of the rich and famous. An easy smile flowed across her lips and gave a sweet blush to her cheeks when she considered her first husband, Eddie, and what he would think of her life now.

"You'd toss your head back and laugh," she decided with a sincere from-the-heart giggle. "You'd be amused as heck." An eagle dipped overhead; it soared almost directly in front of and above Cassie at the very moment Eddie crossed her mind. She wondered if the old wives' tales were true, if souls really could come back as birds such as eagles and drop in once in a while to say a mystical hello.

Lady's rhythmic pace was mesmerizing. The slow and steady clop-clop of the horse's hooves as it picked its way over the trail had a soporific effect.

"I get why people like this," Cassie yawned. Content with her husband's comforting presence just up the trail, she was about ready to doze off back at the far end of the pack, relieved and almost truly joyful at the light banter drifting back to her. Boone and Dallas were chatting up a storm 'Boone and Dallas style,' which meant opinionated verbal sparring now that their confidence in each other was up. The occasional phrase floated back to Cassie, who giggled. It seemed they were arguing about the vegetation alongside the trail and the habits of the birds and animals that fed on it.

"At least they're getting along," Cassie confided in Lady, bending forward over the horse's neck to give her a grateful scratch. "True story. My husband is having what I would consider a reasonable dialogue with his judgmental, angry, sad father. We must do more of these nature walks, Lady. Turns out they're healing after all." *Hunter gets it,* she mused. *The child is four years old, but he gets it.* She sent a silent prayer up to Heaven on the wings of the Eddie-eagle floating above that Hunter would never lose his love of horses, nor the ability to find peace amongst them.

A raindrop spattered on her arm. Moments later, another. Cassie was so intent on the woods around her and on the dull thuds of Lady's hooves on the trail that she hadn't pondered the sky at all. Now, she looked up and made a visor above her eyes with one palm. There were a few grey clouds hovering overhead, but nothing that screamed ominous thunderhead or lightning. Blue sky peeked out from the west.

"Good enough," she breathed, and gave Lady a gentle nudge with the heels of her boots, accompanying the movement with an encouraging, "tut-tut." They were falling behind Dallas and his dad on the last leg of the uphill climb. "We're okay," Cassie said loudly to Lady, her new best friend on this lonely sojourn. "It's just that I don't want to get too far behind. You understand, right? We've been out here for about two hours already, I know you're tired, sweet girl, but we've got a little ways left on this uphill grind and then I think it'll be all downhill from there. Let's quicken up our pace and catch up, okay girl?"

An anxious glance behind her, and Cassie tried nudging the horse again. This time, Lady trotted until Snip's rump was close enough to bite. Bouncing along, Cassie grabbed the saddle horn and giggled the whole way. "Owwwww," she moaned.

Twisting around in his saddle, Dallas was all light and joy. "My pretty society girl gonna have a sore butt tonight?" he teased. "A little black and blue action going on, huh, Cas? I might have to have me a look-see later."

"Keep your look-sees to the trail," Cassie tittered, blushing. "Don't get us lost up here, sexy man. Don't lose sight of your dad and that insane horse of his." Boone was disappearing over the top of the ridge, into an area that Cassie soon discovered was a clear-cut plateau. Littered with stumps of tree carcasses bleached by the sun, it was a stark contrast to the lush emerald fairy-tale magic of the wooded area, which was bursting with life and was a protective animal habitat. Awed and overcome by the desolate feel to the plateau, Cassie's voice got quiet, fading almost into nothing when she spoke again. "They're an art gallery, these mountains. They change; around every corner is a whole new vista."

The horses picked their way carefully across the rocky plateau. Jiggling in her saddle to arrange the new bruises on her backside into more tenable places, Cassie was astonished to reach the ridge at the far side and spy, far below, a magnificent, sparkling lake. Hugged by sumptuous treed slopes all around, it was a lush valley oasis worthy of kings and queens.

Sucking in a breath, Cassie breathed, "Oh! How beautiful!" Reining up next to Dallas and Snip, she was moved to tears to see sheer love and peace on his handsome face. Boone, too, was alight, secretly thrilled at Cassie's reaction, and pacified and humbled by Dallas' obvious delight.

"Surprised you can see anything under all that hair," Boone remarked to Dallas, who took the joke the way it was meant to be received, with good humour and a fun snipe back.

"Surprised you don't freeze in the winter with none. Don't your ears get cold?"

Recoiling, Boone grabbed his cowboy hat and raised it. "I got hair!"

"Like, three," Dallas joked. "Good thing they're on top."

"I don't have to take this," Boone chuckled, throwing a leg over the back of his fidgety horse to dismount. "Cassie, get out that fancy shmancy camera phone thing of yours. Let me get some pictures of you two lovebirds."

"I'd love that," Cassie agreed, unzipping the side pocket of the windbreaker she'd worn on the ride in anticipation of a cool mountain evening.

She pulled her phone out and handed it to her father-in-law. "It's perfect. The lake looks like it has fireflies dancing all over it, the way it's sparkling in the sunlight like that."

The sky was still partially grey overhead, with little pockets of golden evening sunshine poking through the clouds here and there. It was picture postcard perfect; the rain had stayed away on a whisper and a prayer as if the universe was telling the trio to believe that the bad times would pass, and good times would come.

Best part? Cassie figured there was no way to go up from here, which meant they'd soon be heading back down, to a late but hot supper.

Striding over the uneven ground, Boone made his way back about twenty feet, in the direction from which they'd come. Standing with his feet apart, he raised the phone and took a number of pictures.

Happy with his efforts, he walked back to Cassie with one arm outstretched, her phone clutched in his fingers. She was laughing. One arm was bent low over her horse's neck. Lady, enjoying a respite from the tiresome uphill trudge, had her head down and was snacking on the bits of grass poking through here and there.

"It's hard to keep her from eating," Cassie told Boone, "although I don't blame her. My stomach's growling too. But it's hard to have to lean over her! I think I need longer reins. Don't happen to have any in your back pocket, do you Boone?"

"It *is* getting late," Boone agreed in his signature gentle cowboy tone. "And no to the reins. Sorry. Short ones are meant to keep her from eating." Putting his hands on his hips, he looked over the pretty lake. "I suppose it's time to head back. Although I hate to leave this view." Smiling up at Cassie, he said, "We've got the back of 'er broken. Don't you worry, we'll be home before you know it. You're doing great, city girl."

Instantly, Cassie felt bad. The men were bonding up here, letting their old grievances go, it seemed. *Or maybe I am just being naive. Maybe once we dismount in the real world back at J.I. it'll be all fisticuffs and harsh words.* "No," she said out loud to Boone's back as he headed ahead to where he'd left his horse. "Let's not hurry. It's exquisite up here. Really, really special. Extraordinary, even."

Dallas piped up, his voice reverential and cautious. "Dad, you said we'd be able to see J.I. Mountain from up here. Can you point it out to us?"

Boone stopped walking. It took him a moment to find his voice. This was emotion overload for him, a man accustomed to puttering away inside a normal life. It was a big chance to take, bringing Dallas up to this place where Boone had often ridden alongside Dale in peace. Then there was the knowledge that the son Boone thought he knew best was a man he never really knew at all. Add to that the reality that a child with some of Dale's features and most certainly his ability to lie amongst wild horses existed, and needed a home none of the family felt emotionally equipped to offer. On top of it all, Boone had alienated Dallas, the one son he had left, by virtue of criticizing a thing that was sacred to him—the music that fed his soul.

After a moment, Boone wiped a wrist across his moist eyes, extended an arm, and pointed. "There," he said. "That mountain that you can just make out in the distance in the gap between those other two mountains, that's J.I."

"Oh," Cassie exclaimed. "It actually has a J and an I on it…are they trees?"

"They're trees," Boone confirmed with a choke. He put his hands back on his hips and took a good, long look.

"Did someone clear-cut around them or something to make them look that way?"

"Nope. They just grew that way, the locals out here think." He was staring at his oldest son's favourite mountain, accosted by grief as hazy as the heavy air between the mountain gap. His shoulders sank and curved over, but he remained standing, his back about three-quarters to Cassie and Dallas so they could just make out one side of his face.

"That's really something, Boone. Isn't it, Dallas?"

"You said it, Cas." Dallas was in his own place now too, lost in childhood memories of a brother who once watched over him—a brother he would have liked to have along for the ride all these years, yet who Dallas for the most part lost touch with as his career escalated.

"Regret," he said softly now, almost under his breath. "I regret it, not staying in touch. Not finding out what changed you, brother, what made you retreat. I should have tried harder. I shouldn't have let you go."

Boone heard him anyway. Coming alive, he stopped staring and headed for Aviator. "No point in harbouring regrets, Dallas," he said abruptly. "I just don't see how looking backwards can serve any of us now."

It wasn't really a spiritual thing to say, but in some ways Boone was communicating a wise way of looking at things, especially since the words were uttered from between his lips in this beautiful, ethereal place. It was not normally a Boone-like thing to think in any kind of positive way, or to deliver any kind of hopeful message, and that made his words all the more incredible. It seemed like the White patriarch was at least thinking about moving forward, about climbing out of the mire of loss and grief.

Dallas nodded his agreement, and tightened his grip on the reins.

Cassie was smiling when Dallas' father swung his leg over the saddle to start them on the journey home.

Chapter Twenty-two

*L*ater, Dallas would tell Cassie that the girth on Boone's saddle slipped. Boone had tightened it when they stopped to look at the elk, as is common practice on long rides, but perhaps it needed another quick tighten. At any rate, the disgruntled horse did its usual crow-hopping, bucking thing. Boone's foot hadn't gotten all the way over the big horse to the stirrup yet. In horror Cassie watched, in what seemed like slow motion, Dallas' father get bucked off, fly through the air, and disappear from sight on the downhill edge of the plateau.

The horse bucked a few more times, its great hooves slashing through the air and landing on…Boone? His chest, his legs, his head?

Aviator, pleased with himself for losing the annoying thing on its back, finally adjusted his footing in the pockmarked clearing and found an undisturbed place to stand, facing its prone rider.

The horse stayed there.

On the gentle bay, Cassie, stricken with terror, sucked in a breath. Next to her, Dallas' fingers went white on his reins. He straightened, and froze. Both Cassie and Dallas trained their eyes on the sky above where Boone fell, waiting for him to stand up and brush the dirt off his jeans with an embarrassed grin.

He didn't. Seconds passed, and then a minute.

Cassie screamed. "Dallas! Do something!"

The eagle circled above, and watched the eerie tableau with curious eyes. Boone's big horse jerked its head and snuffed what seemed like a greeting.

Dallas didn't answer Cassie. Nor did he look at her. Slipping out of the saddle, he handed his wife his horse's rope lead and started a slow trek over to the area where his father lay. Lady took advantage of the extended rest and decided to eat. Now Cassie had another grazing horse next to her, its lead clutched in her shaking right hand, while Lady yanked her head stubbornly, leaving Cassie practically chest down over the horse's neck.

It was a minor inconvenience, considering.

Oh, God, she sobbed to herself, fingers whitening. Her stomach clenched; tasting bile, she thought she might throw up. The sight of those huge hooves slicing through the air, coming down to land on something unseen, more than sickened her. It was an exercise in control just watching Dallas' tense back as he trod carefully over the rough ground towards the big horse that scared Cassie even when Boone was seemingly in control of it.

Time slowed to a crawl; what would Dallas see when he got to his father? Unbidden, images of wartime soldiers lying crooked, their arms and legs at odd angles, their heads smashed by bullets, blood and brains leaching into the soil, filtered through the jumbled terror in Cassie's mind. Reasonably, she knew that a horse would not step on its owner if it could help it. But she was a lover of history, of westerns. She was a watcher of television news. Cassie had seen images of badly damaged bodies on screens and in print. She had no interest in having to look upon one now in this majestic mountain clearing as the sun was lowering in the sky, and as unseen predators wandered the forest.

Nor could she imagine the grief Dallas' family would have to face if they lost another loved one so soon.

Holding her breath, she cursed at the annoying horse beneath her just as Dallas approached Boone and stood profile to Cassie, staring down, his back to the frightening horse that bucked his father off in the first place. A gust of wind came up and blew Dallas' long hair into his eyes. He raised his cowboy hat, swiped his hair backwards, and replaced the hat. Positioning both hands on his hips, he took in a long breath, looked off at the retreating eagle, and stared back down at his father. He didn't cringe, or turn away to puke. Cassie took that as a good sign.

Lifting his right foot, Dallas toed his dad with his boot, first once, then again. Cassie couldn't see Boone but it was obvious that Dallas was trying to nudge the man into wakefulness. Leaning over Lady's neck, trying to keep her sobs inward, she watched as Dallas said something, and then repeated it.

No visible movement came from where Boone lay. Insufferably, his horse watched, clearly the victor in the day's quest for domination.

Snip decided he wanted to munch on a patch of grass to his right. Lady decided a thatch on her left looked more appealing. Cassie groaned when it became clear she'd have to annoy at least one of the horses by yanking it in a different direction than it wanted to go, all from an uncomfortable, compromised position bending over Lady's neck.

"Damn it," she cursed, and gave Snip's lead a pull. The horse snapped its head sideways. The green rope flew out of Cassie's sweaty, shaking fingers. "Oh, shit!" she cried as the end of it hit the ground and lay there in a snake-like coil. Snip went back to eating, just out of Cassie's reach. "Oh for fuck's sake," she moaned, glancing up over Lady's thick mane to Dallas, who was just standing there staring down. *What's he looking at? What horror is he seeing?* Minutes were slipping by and now there was a whole new, albeit hopefully minor, predicament. *How the hell am I going to get Dallas' horse's lead back?* Angry at herself for dropping it in the first place, Cassie considered how stupid she would look in the eyes of an experienced rider. He or she would just hop off a horse, grab the lead, and hop back on. The notion was almost unfathomable to Cassie—what if she couldn't get back on? What if both horses decided to continue to go different ways? Plus the horses looked a lot bigger from the ground…

They seemed much more manageable from Lady's back. "At least from up here you can't step on me," Cassie said to Lady's twitching ears. She looked over at Dallas. He was oblivious. He had his own much more pressing problems at the moment. "All right, toughen up," she boosted herself. "Get it together. Solve this problem." Ready to vomit at the unknown that still lay ahead as far as Boone's condition was concerned, Cassie pulled Lady's head up and tried to turn her towards Snip, who was wandering away, the loose lead dangling behind him. "You damn well better not trip over that thing and break a leg," Cassie hollered after him. Immensely pleased with herself when Lady got the message and, with a snort, took a few important steps towards Snip, Cassie leaned out over the saddle and grabbed the stray lead rope. Hauling it up between her fingers, she forced out a small, scared smile. "And thank you, Yoga," she breathed, wrapping the rope around her fingers while hoping, at the same time, that the horse wouldn't suddenly spook and take off.

It was an excruciating long twenty minutes before there was movement at Dallas' feet. Cassie was too terrified to ask about Boone. Finally, Dallas extended an arm downwards and bent to help his father up.

"Oh, thank God," Cassie exclaimed to her horsey charges. There was no visible blood on the man. His head wasn't squashed or bleeding. Boone was talking. Like a sweet summer rain, relief washed over Cassie.

Another ten minutes ticked by. In that time, Cassie's left arm and her lower back started to ache from the constant strain of trying to keep Lady happy and from wandering off. Her right arm was stretched to its limit, holding Snip's reins like a tightrope between the two large animals. The sun was sinking further and further; Cassie's ears were tuned to the perimeter of the woods. She could imagine sets of yellow eyes staring out. She and the two men were sitting ducks on the clear-cut plateau as far as she was concerned, soon to join the ranks of the scattered, bleached detritus scattered about that in reality was tree stumps and branches, but this evening looked like bones to Cassie's nervous, darting eyes.

Dallas managed to get Boone over to the finicky buckskin, managed to convince him to cling to Aviator's saddle, to hang on to the buckle. Boone leaned his whole body against the horse.

Dallas twisted around, fixed Cassie in a concerned, frowning gaze, and strode over the rough ground to her side. "He's got a concussion," he proclaimed, a darkness Cassie didn't like setting deep into his eyes. "Can you get cell service up here? We need help."

"Oh, fuck," Cassie exhaled. She knew damn well there was no cell service up here. Regardless, hoping against hope, she handed Dallas Snip's lead and reached for her phone in the pocket of her windbreaker. "Nine-one-one," she whispered as she dialed, trying to hang onto the phone and Lady's reins at the same time. "Please work." *A helicopter,* she thought. *We can airlift him out of here.*

The sky was darkening. *But we will still have to get down this damn mountain with these horses! Which took two-and-a-half hours to climb!* Tears pricked at the corners of Cassie's eyes. Sneaking a peek at her husband gave her cause to strive for calm. Dallas' lips were turned down at the corners. The earnest, serious set to his jaw and the deep worry in his eyes motivated Cassie to suck up her fear and think the situation through.

She held the phone up to Dallas and shook her head. "No luck," she told him.

"All right," he said, handing her back Snip's lead. "The old man doesn't know if we're going up the mountain or down. He hurt his leg, too, and his arm. I don't know if he can ride."

"He doesn't know which way we're going?"

Dallas avoided looking at Cassie. Placing a thumb and finger thoughtfully to his lips, he looked over at Boone, who was managing to stay upright. He shook his head.

"He doesn't know the way back? Dallas?"

A heavy sigh was Dallas' only answer. Turning back to Cassie, he set his lips in a firm, straight line, and said nothing. His eyes pierced her with their need for her to admit the only possible way out of this predicament. No way was he going to tell her what to do—the decision that needed to be made was hers to decide.

And she was thinking it through. Out loud.

"Dallas! Jesus! Do you mean to tell me we are stuck here with a hurt, lost guide? It's almost night time, for God's sake! The predators!" *The recent bear attack…oh, Jesus. Two-and-a-half hours to get up here…*

Unbidden, a sob snuck out.

"Well, fuck it!" she cried. "One of us has to go down this mountain to get help. There's no fucking way I'm spending the night up here!"

She pictured yellow eyes staring at her, at them, and big cougar paws treading so softly in the dark that neither she nor Dallas would hear the big cats, or see them coming…

Leaning sideways away from Dallas, Cassie retched.

When she came back up, swallowing back her fear, she heard an unfamiliar voice say, "I'll go." It was her own voice, narrow and high-pitched. "I can't stay with that horse. I'm scared to death of it."

Dallas pointed in Boone's direction. "The road is that way," he told her, his voice urgent and demanding. "Just head towards the road."

It was an obvious place to start. Boone was their guide; he'd been leading the way. Below, the lake sparkled like a ring set with diamonds in the golden magic hour light. Trees as far as Cassie could see buffeted back and forth softly in the evening breeze. Ahead and below, a worn trail beckoned.

"Just follow the trail," she told herself. "It's got to lead back to the ranch." Giving Lady a gentle kick, at the same time she pulled up the horse's head and begged her to lead the way. A last look back at Dallas, and she was on her way down the mountain alone, trying to urge Lady to move at a brisk pace while trying not to think of what perils lay ahead, and of how long it would take to find a safe haven out here on a lone mountain in such rugged, isolated country.

She took one last twist around to look at Dallas. He was watching her, hands on his hips, frowning, unmoving.

Cassie forced her gaze ahead. Determined, she gave Lady a harder kick, and headed for the trees.

Chapter Twenty-three

*W*atching her go, two things crossed Dallas' mind. One, horses always head back to their barns. And two, Cassie might be petite and feminine on the outside, but she was a tough cookie on the inside. Children depended on her. Jade was likely, at this moment, giving her grandmother a run for her money. The odds were that Cassie would simply follow the trail and find her way home. Still, Dallas had to stifle his nerves when he lost sight of Cassie as she made her way into the trees. Raising a hand to his nose, he gave it an anxious tweak before turning around to deal with his father.

"Dad," he said when he approached Boone from where he'd been watching Cassie at the crest of the hill. "Do you think you can ride?" A slow ride down the mountain would be better than a long wait at the plateau.

Boone answered by bending over and tossing his cookies at his feet. When he was able to stand up a little straighter, he gripped the saddle and said with a quizzical look, "Are we going up or are we going down?"

It was about the twentieth time he'd said that in the last ten minutes.

"We're fucked," Dallas muttered under his breath. "It's gonna be a long, cold night."

Two of his friends had suffered brain injuries in the last ten years. One was still recovering from a brain bleed that would have killed him if his teenage daughter hadn't found him sleeping in the garden and called an ambulance. The other friend was still seeing a range of medical specialists in a quest to get 'her head back,' as she said. Studying his dad as the man struggled to stay upright, Dallas fought his own growing nausea. *Dale's gone*, he thought. *Dad, I know you and I seem to live on different planets, but*

I gotta tell you—I want you in my life. Mom needs you. Dawn needs you. Jenny needs you. The kids...

Hunter sprang to mind. Hunter, who Boone seemed to be starting to warm to the more he recognized Dale via the child's affinity with horses, like in the mystical way Hunter could lie down amongst the wild ones without fear, with a kind of spiritual grace. Boone needed Dale's child so he could keep some kind of connection to Dale, so he could keep their bond alive and vibrant. Hunter was a direct conduit to Boone's oldest son. He was an extension of him; it was like there was a crackling telephone line hanging between their two different worlds.

Hunter could use Boone in his life. The man had an ornery, crusty side to him, all right. Yet he also had an accumulated wisdom, especially in the ways of Alberta ranch country. Hunter was wired for open meadows; he was meant to be surrounded by majestic, snow-capped mountains. The boy would need a man to show him the ways of the mountains, to teach him to rope and ride, to speak to him of his father, to give him memories to hold dear for the tough, lonely days ahead.

Not once did Dallas consider that he, too, needed his father. He wanted him, but he didn't consider that he needed him. The thought was there as a niggling, annoying bug, buried somewhere behind his liver. If it were given lease to appear, if Dallas set it free up on the jagged clear-cut, he might throw up next to the man whose approval he sought all these years. Boone was a hard case. Dallas was determined to make a graceful exit away from J.I. and its strange rustic newness. J.I. wasn't his childhood home, which in some ways was a blessing since Dallas couldn't walk around corners and be forced to face visual memories of his mixed-up childhood. In other ways, it was a curse. Dallas often found himself clinging to a past he barely remembered, and which some days he chose to forget.

Facing his sick and injured father now, he found the past hurtling towards him with the great daring and speed of a grizzly. Like a massive heaving ball of sinew and bone, it almost knocked him down with the force of what was, and of what could be.

If.

With a reluctant sniff and a nervous swipe of a palm over the stubble on his cheek, Dallas faced his father. "Well, Dad," he said. "It'd be a helluva lot easier to force you up on that horse if you were just hungover like Dale and me were the morning after we lit up the Innisfail Rodeo barn dance back when we were in high school. At dawn, remember? You made us saddle up and ride the fences the whole live long day, puking our guts out for most of it."

Reaching for his father's arm, he eased Boone away from his death grip on the saddle. "My wife's gone down that mountain alone, Dad. My wife, whose only experience riding horses was at her grandmother's as a child. She's alone and she's scared, and who knows when she'll reach the bottom to send us help. It could be midnight. So by God, you need to suck it up and get on that ornery horse you so stubbornly decided needed a trek up the mountain today."

Leveraging a hand under his dad's boot, Dallas gave his father a boost up. It took three tries and one more attack of nausea before Boone was seated on the hard leather. Clutching the saddle horn, he tried to focus on his son. "Are we going up or are we going down?" he asked.

"Jesus H. Christ," Dallas swore, and gave the horse's bridle a pull. "Back to the barn, ye stupid mighty beast," he demanded. "Damn it, Dad, stay in the saddle. Please. I'll be right behind you."

An easy vault got him into his own saddle. Giving Snip a cluck and a kick wasn't necessary. Dallas' mount was as anxious as Boone's horse to end the long tiring ride and get to the barn to feast on some oats. The horse started out at a quick pace right away, nose to tail.

Boone's face had taken on a sickly green pallor. His shoulders were hunched. He was bent over the saddle horn like a greenhorn. Years of riding were paying off, though. Despite the aches, his body's muscle memory held him in good stead. He had sense enough to stop wondering which direction they were supposed to be going in, and to let his horse lead the way.

"Go easy, Cassie," Dallas whispered. "If Dad can stay in the saddle, we'll soon catch up to you."

He closed his eyes and said a silent prayer as the gorgeous watery vista below disappeared when they entered the oblique darkness of the stark, mysterious trees.

At the lake, the pounding in Cassie's chest got heavier, louder, and faster. "It's a relief to get this far," she said to Lady, who twitched her soft ears in response. "I just didn't think we'd have so many trails to choose from once we got here." Sure enough, the downward trail Cassie had been following branched out into three more at the far north side of the lake. She had a feeling all three would eventually take her to the road. The darkening sky, however, and the significant distance between all of the properties in this remote part of Alberta, were cause for serious contemplation when faced with the three trails. Make the wrong choice, and Cassie and Lady could be wandering the mountain for hours.

Choking back a sob, Cassie pulled the reins to stop Lady, and took a scan of the area. "God, it's beautiful here," she said to the horse, the only companion she knew of in the immediate vicinity. "I mean, it's really stunning, Lady." Inhaling the fresh mountain air, she wished circumstances were different so that she could enjoy the view with her husband at her side and with much less thrumming in her chest. Before her was a pristine lake surrounded on three sides by trees, coniferous and deciduous, like white birch and black spruce. Low shrubs bordered the trees, maybe dogwood or buffalo berry, Cassie considered. Beneath and alongside those, colourful wildflowers grew in abundance. As Cassie watched, a whisper of wind blew through a nearby cluster of trees, turning their leaves over into a silvery white in the fading light. Stones around the lake almost glowed. The lake itself was no longer a cluster of fireflies and diamonds this close up. Now the water was rippled and alive, speaking to Cassie via light gusts that stirred its voice with whispers of peace and harmony.

"I love how quiet it is out here," Cassie murmured back to it. Tilting her head, she listened for a few minutes. "It's different kinds of sounds," she said, bending over to give Lady's neck a scratch, reminded that she was actually on horseback when Lady snuffled and bent to graze. "It's wind and it's birds. Out here has its own kind of noise. No noisy coffee shops. No traffic, no loud voices telling me what to do. No children crying," she sniffled, wondering if Jade was doing okay back at the ranch, "and no judgmental, bickering fathers." The thought of Boone brought her out of her peaceful place. She sighed. "We'd better keep going, Lady. No time to waste." *That family has already lost someone they love. We can't let them lose Boone too.*

The lake granted her one more gift. Birds, small ones. She had no idea what kind they were but there were dozens, swooping down from the trees to skim the lake's diamond surface as one. Cassie glimpsed them from the corner of her eye at first. When she craned her neck for a better look beside and behind her, the birds banked into a turn that took them back the way they'd come. They were grey-backed, the colour of sealskin. Their white bellies became more pronounced on the turn when they caught the sinking sun's last breath, which turned their undersides all a divine silvery-gold. Cassie's breath caught. From her angle at the top end of the lake, she was gifted a rare and special air show the likes most never get to see. In the wilderness, nature was the key player. These birds, like the Canadian Snowbirds or U.S. Blue Angels aerobatic teams, were flying in synchronicity. Unlike the highly maneuverable airplanes, their movements weren't choreographed, and it amazed Cassie that a grouping of birds this big could do this—could fly as one, mere inches apart. Could rise as one, dive as one, and make sweeping, graceful curves as one, all in a wave-like pattern skimming just above the lake's surface.

"Magical," she sighed, momentarily forgetting the frightening predicament that she, Dallas, and Boone were in. The tiny birds took one more broad flight, in Cassie's direction this time, which included one last curve to the left—bellies up in a final golden-white salute—and flew off to skim the treetops, their gift to a lonely horse and its scared rider final and complete.

Yanking Lady's head up with a sad smile, thinking that she may never witness such wonder again, Cassie got started back on her way. For a moment, she almost let the horse lead but Lady seemed to want to go straight, which was more of a level trail than the one the furthest to the left, which had enough of a slope in the direction of the road to give Cassie the notion that it might get them to the roadside the quickest. "Go, Lady," she urged, her pulse quickening at the idea of having to go back into a treed trail again, with dark, shadowy corners and invisible leafy bits.

Two more sobs, and she shook her head and raised her chin. "No time for that," she said loudly, hoping her voice would scare away any potential predators. "Must be strong." Thinking of Dallas helped. Sometimes it was hard to be his gal. He was an active man, for the most part—ambitious and successful—and part of that formula was eating well and staying fit, which meant serious workouts at the gym and a relatively healthy eating plan to go along with that. The summer they met was an anomaly for him, Cassie had discovered—he ate steak, burgers, greasy sausages. It was always chicken or tofu for her. "And too much ice cream," she grimaced, remembering, trying to focus her mind on good things and not on the blackness behind every tree. "Although we shared many gorgeous sunset beach walks."

The beach…thinking of that now…lacy wavelets, warm, soothing sand between her toes, the dozens of sand castles she, Dallas, and Ry built over the summer…brought full-on tears.

She gave her head a shake, clicked urgently, and urged Lady into a trot. Laughing through her tears, Cassie grabbed the saddle horn. "I'll be black and blue tomorrow thanks to you, Mizz Horse!" *Just better be from the saddle,* she thought, decidedly choosing not to peer into the shadows for fear of what she might see.

Down the trail a ways, she groaned. A fallen tree with a girth the size of a tractor tire lay smack in the middle of the trail. Around it was dense bush. Branches jutted out from the tree in uneven smatterings, their sharp pointed ends significant deterrents to a tired horse and its frustrated, anxious rider.

"All right," she said out loud, her voice thin and afraid, the earlier frightened confidence that she showed in Dallas' presence dissolving into piles of mush. "We go around, you and me. Which means you have to go where I tell you." Miraculously, Lady responded to the pressure on the reins, and between her slow, patient movements, and Cassie's desperate ripping off of branches, they blazed a trail. The only downside was the realization that they had to be the first to go that way. So now…

"Lady, should we go back up? Maybe we should go back up. This can't be right."

They were beyond the felled tree. A bend in the trail ahead seemed worth exploring. Most important of all, the path still led downwards. "It's gotta come out somewhere," Cassie sobbed. By now, they'd been on the trail for over an hour. The sky above was a deep, dark, indigo blue—twilight. "I just want to go home," Cassie cried, urging Lady to a quicker pace, which at first the horse seemed happy to agree to, sensing barn and shelter somewhere ahead. "Lady, please just get us home."

Another fifteen minutes passed. A tiny part of Cassie was enjoying the ride despite the overwhelming fear. Sitting tall in the saddle, she allowed a miniature bit of pride to sneak into her heart. "Look at me, Ry," she announced. "Your mother is on a horse on her way down a mountain. Alone. Cassie to the rescue!" Humming her way through the trees, she tried to keep Lady going at a brisk pace. The horse started a new dance—sidestepping, tossing her tail, flattening her ears back. "What's up, Lady?" Cassie asked, leaning forward to encourage the horse along.

Her eyes landed on a pile of fresh dirt upon which a large rock lay, obviously recently overturned. "I am not going to try to compute just who or what turned that over. Oh God, I think I'm going to throw up."

Cassie was at the point where every ear twitch from Lady was a sign of hidden danger. Every flick of the gentle horse's tail was surely acknowledgement of a cougar or a coyote in the woods, or perhaps a…

Bear.

"Oh, fuck." Cassie yanked hard on the reins. Lady stopped, then sideways hop-stepped backwards and came to a standstill three-quarters on to a small brown blob fifty feet down the trail. Squinting in the semi-darkness, Cassie thought at first that it was a stump or perhaps a shrub, that maybe the trail swung around a corner down there. "Dallas," she sobbed when the image moved and came into focus. "It's a bear. Can you believe this? It's a goddamned bear."

There was nothing Dallas could do to save her. Even if he were around, he didn't have a gun with him. To Cassie's knowledge, neither did Boone, although she'd watched him haul a knife out of a leather sheath attached to the saddle. He'd used it to cut some branches away from a narrow spot on the uphill trail.

Lady was vehemently protesting the presence of the bear. She started backing up, and trying to turn around. "Don't you fucking throw me," Cassie wailed, changing her tone to more of a demand than a frightened whine the second time she voiced the demand. "If I'm going to die today, so be it. Just don't let it be from being clawed to death by a bear all by my lonesome. You and me are in this together, horse! I get clawed, you get clawed. Not you alone, and not me alone. We're a team!"

It was impossible to judge the size of the bear from this distance and in what little stilted light remained. A fragile moment hung between the horse and rider, and the bear. Like a moonbeam shining between them, the moment lay still and quiet and glittering and gold all at once, slowing time down to nothing and bringing Cassie's heart and mind almost to a standstill. Containing nothing and everything at once, it hung suspended, awash with the faintest blue, giving it a vitality that glowed in the increasing moonlight, and that seemed, for a suspended second, to gift Cassie—and the horse, which magically stopped trying to back off and run—renewal and hope.

Hope for what? Cassie wondered in that surreal, heart-stopping moment as she sat still as a statue on the quieted horse's back, locked in a supernatural visual embrace with a wild bear. Dallas came to mind. Dallas, with his little-boy hurt, trying so hard to be tough around a father that still had the power to destroy him. Dallas, lost in childhood memories of a brother who once protected him. Dallas, who always ducked his head to hide behind his long blond hair when it all got to be too much, who went on long walks alone and who resisted getting too close to Jade and Ry, who kept his relationships simple and uncomplicated.

Dallas, completely thrown by an unknown child, uncertain what path to take, ready to run back on to the stage so he could hide behind his guitar and leave the hard memories—including a frightened child—behind.

The bear stood up on its haunches. It wasn't tall, but even if it had been a grizzly, neither Cassie nor the horse would have run. Like the circling eagle earlier, it had a message, and that message was delivered in the twilight blue.

For the first time since hearing of Dale's death, Cassie pictured her husband at peace. Hunter was in his arms.

She smiled. The bear yawled its recognition of her acceptance, and trundled off into the woods.

At once, the moonbeam moment dissolved. Like the tiniest of fireflies, its particles retreated into nothingness. The spell broke; the jarring snap of a branch under Lady's right hind foot brought recognition and awareness back like the rush of a swollen river in spring.

"What the hell was that?" A hushed reverence made Cassie's words barely audible to Lady, who seemed to suddenly awaken as well and start to back up again. "Okay," Cassie said softly, giving the horse her rein to move in whatever direction she wanted, "we'll go back."

Back up the trail they went, in a kind of peaceful stupor this time, and Cassie wondered if this was how soldiers about to die felt, as if they were victims of circumstances beyond their control so they might as well make the best of it, and find purpose wherever they could. In her case, nature was either playing tricks on her shattered, fearful mind, or was gifting her beautiful possibilities through visions.

"I'll take the visions," she said, urging Lady back uphill around the fallen tree. "No magic mushrooms needed, thank you very much." It was humbling. Smiling, she raised her chin to the first star of the night, and relaxed in the saddle as her trusted horse picked its way back towards the lake. "What will be will be."

Chapter Twenty-four

*D*allas got Boone back to J.I. just as Doris was ready to send Johnny and Dawn out on the trail in search of them.

She came running. Johnny and Dawn and their youngsters, with Jade lagging behind them, had already emerged from the barn. The tired trail horses whinnied greetings to the horses in the barn and paddock. Relieved, Johnny took Boone's reins.

Dallas slid down off Snip's back and handed the reins to his sister. "Dad got hurt," he told her quietly so his mother wouldn't freak out. "He's concussed and banged up."

Wide-eyed, Dawn got serious for once and stuttered back a response. "Where's Cassie?"

Dallas was on his way over to Boone's horse, to help Johnny ease the older man down out of his saddle. He flipped back around and covered the few short paces back to Dawn in a hurry, just as Jade grabbed his leg and started in on a subdued whine-cry. Eyes on Dawn, Dallas touched his daughter's silky blonde locks with a mixture of love and trepidation. "She's not back?"

Swallowing a lump of fear, Dawn shook her head. "No. Should she be?"

"She started out ahead of us, to go for help in case the old man couldn't make the ride down. She should be back by now." Striding over to Boone, Dallas grabbed one arm while Johnny grabbed the other. Boone made it to the ground and immediately bent over, hands on his thighs, and puked at Dallas' feet.

Doris took her husband's arm and pelted instructions. "Johnny, look after these horses. Dawn, take the children to the chalet and tuck them in for the night. Dallas, come with your father and me, I want to know what happened out there."

Balking, Dallas let Boone limp out of his grip on his way to the bungalow. "It's getting late, Mom," he said, backing up and snatching Snip's lead out of Johnny's hand. "I'll explain later. For now, all you need to know is that Dad got bucked off and landed on his head. He didn't know if he was going up or down." Reaching for Snip's saddle horn, he pulled himself back up into the saddle.

"Where do you think you're going?" his mother asked, voice shaking, vaulting back around to watch him.

"My wife is still out there. Mom, it's just about full-on dark."

A distant whinny got his attention. It was followed shortly by a toss of Snip's head and a whinny back.

"That's Lady," Johnny determined. "She's close, Dallas. Lady knows her way to the barn." He nodded at Boone, who was leaning over his thighs, groaning. "Cassie's a smart lady, she'll make her way back here. Give her a few minutes. Right now I think your mom and dad need your help."

Grumbling, Dallas knew Johnny was right. Doris was having trouble getting her husband through the clearing to the bungalow. Rubbing a nervous finger under his nose, Dallas was shocked at how small they both looked, his mom and dad, bunched together like that, one sick, the other worried. His parents had been married a long time, pretty much right out of high school. They raised three kids and had just buried one. Sickened, Dallas slipped back down off Snip's back and moved on shaking, tired legs towards them.

"I think Dad should go get checked out," he said, taking his father's left arm, surprised at how thick and scared his voice sounded. "Just in case, Mom, okay?"

"Your father's an old rodeo cowboy," Doris rebutted. "He's had concussions before, Dallas." She caught her son's eye. An unsettled anxiety flitted across her own, a weak and useless mask for the strength she was trying to portray in words.

"And there's our answer," Dawn said. Bending, she scooped Jade up and away from Dallas, which started Jade into a much louder wail and a round of serious flailing. Dawn had to raise her voice to speak again. "He's had multiple concussions. Dallas, drive them in to Sundre."

"I'm not goin' to Sundre," Boone protested between retches. "I'll be fine by mornin.'"

"I wish Matt was here," Dallas muttered under his breath. To Jade he said, "Honey, Grampie needs Daddy right now. Go with Aunt Dawn."

"I want Mommy!"

"I know, sweetheart. Mommy will be home any second, riding in like a trooper on her big horse. Just another few minutes." *I hope,* he added inwardly, sucking back the lump of fear that was making his chest heavy and stiff. *God, please let Cassie be okay.*

He whispered a silent prayer to be a better husband to Cassie, to stop pushing her and Ry and Jade away, to be more attentive and less of a wet blanket. Grasping his father's arm, he looked sideways over at his mother. "To the truck," he declared. "Driving always seems longer at night, Mom, and I expect we'll be stopping a few times along the way."

"Your father will be fine, Dallas," Doris insisted. "Let's just sit awhile before we decide to go gallivanting down these isolated roads in the middle of the night."

Dawn was still within earshot. "It's not the middle of the night yet, Mom. Better to get on the road now."

A silent protest passed over Dallas' face. Ashamed, he stared at his feet.

His mother read his mind. "We'll wait on Cassie before we decide if we're going anywhere."

"I just—Mom, she's not a rider. I need to go in search of her. Then I'll take Dad to the hospital, all right?"

Doris assented with a shrug. "That's fine, Dallas. Just remember that your father is not the tough young scallywag he used to be, that's all."

"Make up your mind, Mom." That, too, was muttered inwardly, although Doris got the gist of what Dallas was saying. She forgave him on the basis of worry.

With a raised hand, Dallas beckoned to the young security stationed at the main gate. A uniformed white guy in his twenties galloped over. "Kevin,

I'll likely be heading into Sundre shortly," Dallas explained. "My dad needs to get checked out at the hospital. Can you let your boss and whoever is stationed on the grounds inside know? And call Matt. Also, Cassie's still out on horseback. Keep an eye out for her, okay? I'm hoping she'll come trotting down the road any minute now."

"Will do, Sir." Kevin started to walk away. Over his shoulder he said, "One of us ought to go with you."

"Nobody's going to trouble us overnight in Sundre, Kevin. You're needed here."

As am I, Dallas thought wildly, hanging onto his weakened father's arm and staring out at the darkened road just beyond the gate and parking lot. *You picked a good time to leave us, Matt. And Dale,* he added with a wry twist of his lips. *Assholes, the two of you.*

Dallas was accustomed to being waited on. He was used to being served, and being heeded. Here at home? He was used to his father telling him what to do, belittling him and making him feel useless. This new position of having to take charge was baffling. He had a mind of his own, all right, usually facing off with Matt or Phil or one of his band members, and sometimes Cassie. In those cases, Dallas generally came out on top or at least got some kind of recompense for his trouble. Isolated out here in the mountains with nobody telling him what to do with the exception of his mother and Dawn, whose opinions Dallas respected but didn't necessarily adhere to, he was a fly in a pond of lily pads, waiting for a frog to pounce.

They were at the bottom of the steps now. One last wistful, worried look towards the road, and Dallas helped hoist his father to the top.

"Ah ha! A cabin!" Sure enough, not far down over the new trail Cassie had chosen at the lake was a cabin, likely a hunter's cabin, she thought. Giving Lady a nudge to move her closer quicker, Cassie strained to see signs of occupation, like smoke from a fire, or an ATV parked nearby.

"Nada," she sighed, leaning back in the saddle. The place was pitch dark. No welcoming lights shone through the small rectangular shelter's rustic windows. It looked as if the place hadn't been lived in for a while. A pile of chopped wood splits that appeared to have once been piled high with precision was now a toppling wasteland of moist, cobwebbed wood.

"Lovely." Pushing on, Cassie put invisible blinders by her eyes to block out her peripheral vision, said a murmured, dejected prayer, and shifted her butt in the saddle for another downward, treed stretch of trail.

Then, straight ahead, she saw a break in the trail. Passing through shadowy, low brush, she heaved a tremendous sigh of relief when the dusty road appeared in front of her. Letting her hands relax on the reins, she laid her forearms on her thighs and closed her eyes. When she opened them, she realized she had yet another decision on her hands.

She and Dallas, with Ry and Jade, and Matt at the helm, had turned up this road on their way to J.I. There were few occupied properties. Looking right and then left, Cassie could only see a long unpaved moonlit gravel road. No vehicles, no signs, no telltale markings to show her the way.

"Oh my God," she moaned. "Lady, if we go the wrong way, we could be out here all night. And then some." She wondered how Boone was doing. Was Dallas holding up okay? Where were they?

A white butterfly floated lazily by to the left, its erratic flight quite beautiful in the white light of the moon. Angling her head to look up, Cassie was relieved to see open, cloudless sky. The earlier threat of rain had given way to clear skies that now housed an enlightening, sparkling sky. The pristine beauty reminded Cassie of the surprise flight of the enchanting little birds back at the lake. Her eyes darted down and to the left. The butterfly was there, barely visible in the dim light.

"We'll go left," she whispered to Lady, who whinnied and protested the decision by taking two steps backwards. Tired, legs aching, Cassie sob-talked to her four-legged friend. "Listen to me," she begged. "I am a big believer in signs, and after seeing that incredible aerial display of those pretty little birds, I believe that lovely, flimsy white butterfly is definitely a sign. We're going left."

The entire fifteen minutes they were on the road was marked by an agonizing, tear-filled, self-deprecating rant. "We'll get hit by a truck that won't see us. A cougar will be around that next corner. Lady will stumble in a hole and I'll fall off. We'll have to ride all night. Lady will get hungry and start trying to buck me off. We should have gone the other way. We should have turned right."

Just as the sob-talking was morphing into outright wailing—*Jade comes by her wailing honestly,* Cassie thought with a half-assed choke-laugh—a sign appeared. A real one this time. An actual wooden sign.

'Bear Creek Lodge,' it announced in glittery gold letters against a forest green backdrop.

"Oh my God. Oh my God Oh my God Oh my God!" Without hesitation, Cassie gave Lady a few significant heel kicks. Leaning forward, she clicked at the horse until Lady was going at a full trot. Holding her breath, Cassie sobbed a few more times when she spotted vehicles parked in front of a large, wood-stained building that Cassie assumed was likely the property's main office. The Oh my Gods became Thank Gods. "Thank God Thank God Thank God!"

Bouncing ungainly into the parking lot, Cassie looked around for signs of people. Nobody appeared. Raising her chin, she hollered, "I need help! Somebody please help me! Please!"

Still no one. Slipping down off the saddle, Cassie was surprised at how big Lady was when she faced her nose to nose. She gulped, and pulled the reins over the horse's head, and almost buckled into full out crying when Lady dug in her heels and raised her head to protest being yanked in a direction she clearly didn't want to go.

"For God's sake, horse!" Cassie cried. "What's the issue here?"

Beyond Lady's glistening bay back, Cassie spotted a fence post. A good pull on the reins got Lady close enough to tie off the reins. By then Cassie could hear footsteps, running towards her, she hoped. When she turned around, she almost sank to the ground and kissed it at the sight of a young fellow in jeans and a flaring, plaid shirt.

"I was out on a trail ride with my husband and our guide got hurt," she sobbed, weary of the whole adventure and ready to collapse into bed with her husband curled around her body, and her body curled around her daughter. At the same time, she imagined the reaction she'd get from Ry when she told him. Would he laugh and downplay the whole thing or would he be proud?

The young fellow took charge. Shortly, Cassie found herself in a brand

SUSAN RODGERS

spanking new Ford truck seated in the front passenger seat next to a man about her age who turned out to be the property's owner.

"If we have to, we'll take my helicopter up and do an overhead scan for them," he said. "What's your husband's name?"

Sitting back, Cassie closed her eyes. "Dallas," she sighed, which came as no surprise to the owner of Bear Creek Lodge. "Dallas White. His father, Boone, was our guide."

The man cleared his throat. "I thought so. There aren't too many neighbours out this way. I'm sorry for his—and your—loss, Cassie. I knew Dale. We sat on the board of the Wild Horse Association together."

"Oh," she said, not quite ready to digest any more information on this crazy evening. "That's good. I'm glad."

"Look, Dale was a pretty capable guy. I'm sure your husband has everything well in hand." The guy cleared his throat again, and steered the big truck out onto the sparse road. The young fella who'd met Cassie listened closely in the back seat, at the same time peeling his eyes for signs of the wayward trail riders, and his ears for sounds.

"Before this trip," Cassie said, "Dallas hadn't been on a horse in years. Let's face it, he's gone a little soft since his childhood on a ranch."

"Still," the guy said, at a loss to add anything else. He sighed and rifled his fingers through spiked black hair in need of a trim. He was picturing his cherished idyllic mountain isolation overrun, if this news broke and Bear Creek was deluged by more crazy obsessed country music fans. Already, the loss of Dale and Dallas' known presence down the road was causing issues. At the same time, bookings were up at the lodge.

He looked over at Cassie. "We'll go to J.I. first. If we don't find them there, we'll get the heli out."

"Works for me," she agreed, melting into the comfortable seat. "Thank you."

Humbled at just how far J.I. was down the road, Cassie stayed silent for the remainder of the drive. When they pulled into J.I. and Kevin at Security came running over, she almost collapsed in his arms at the welcome news that Dallas and Boone were back, and that Boone seemed to be functional, at least.

234

Dallas heard the truck pull in. He jogged down the bungalow's steps and strode over to his wife, his expression serious, eyes misty with concern.

Facing him with damp eyes of her own, Cassie reached out and took his hands. He was trembling. "Dallas," she said, intent on making him understand. "I just rode down a mountain alone, on a horse, in the dark. I saw things, I…" Halting, she caught her breath and searched for strength before she continued. "Baby, I realized something when I was out there, and it has to do with fear."

Nodding, Dallas gulped and switched his stance. He listened closely.

"The thing about fear is that it can be consuming. We can give in to it, or we can grab it by the balls and face it head on. Dallas, I know how scared you are about Hunter, about taking a child that comes with so much confusion and hurt into your life, into your heart. But baby, the thing you need to realize is that Hunter is scared too. But he comes with gifts, Dallas, he comes with so many incredible, beautiful gifts. And so, sweet man, do you."

"I love you," Dallas choked. Taking his wife in his arms, he pressed her small body close to him and whispered, "You must have been so scared out there, Cassie."

"I was," she murmured into his hair, wrapping a few strands around her finger and breathing him in. "And I got through it one step at a time, Dal." Leaning back, she smiled through her tears. "And so, my darling man, will you. With Hunter. He belongs with you, babe. With us."

"Matt…" Doubt clouded Dallas' pale eyes, turning them a soft, scared grey.

"He's a grown man, Dallas, a man with integrity and compassion. He knows what the right thing to do here is. I know you care about him. He'll be okay. You'll see."

"He's grown very attached to that little guy."

"I know, Dallas. I know." Smiling sadly, Cassie leaned in for a kiss. After, she said with an attempt at lightness, "And I've grown attached to my horse. Go rescue her, will you, Dal? I need to go see my daughter."

Dallas smiled, and watched Cassie walk away before he turned to the man who brought her home. The guy was chatting with Johnny, who'd appeared from the direction of the barn pulling a horse trailer behind his truck. "I hear we have a horse to rescue," he said.

"We could always keep her and charge admission to see her," the guy said with a grin, extending a hand for an introduction. "Paul Lewis of Bear Creek," he said. "Great to meet you, Dallas. My wife will be jealous as hell. Dale spoke highly of you."

"Dale, huh? Did you know him well?" Dallas started towards Johnny's truck.

"Not so much," Paul answered. "He kept to himself, your brother did. Sure cared about those horses, though. Had a real gift with them. Took some really incredible photos."

"Photos." Dallas had forgotten about the photos Hunter had mentioned one day at lunch. "I'd sure like to see some of them."

"There are some on our website. The others, well I expect...I expect Maria has them."

Dallas stopped short just as he was about to pull open Johnny's passenger side truck door. "Let me get this straight. You didn't know my brother well, but you knew about Maria?"

Paul shrugged. "He brought her with us a few times to study the herds. I didn't know that Dale, uh..." He cleared his throat and toed the gravel for a moment before looking back up. "I didn't know they were a couple until I saw them one day, close, you know? Wasn't my business. At first I just thought they were friends because of the horses." He saw a way out and went for it, his voice taking on an air of confidence as he waded away from the dangerous territory involving Dale and Maria. "Speaking of which, let's go rescue yours. I understand you've got a long drive ahead to get your dad checked out."

"I do," Dallas said, ducking into Johnny's truck. *Lots of time to think.* He pictured the isolated road to Sundre.

Settling back against the truck seat, he exhaled, closed his eyes, and let Johnny do the driving.

Chapter Twenty-five

*M*att was beat by the time his ear picked up the sound of a deep chug chug. It was a bike, a big one, getting louder by the second on its way up the long lane towards Josh and Jessie's ranch. A relieved, easy smile brightened up Matt's eyes and lightened the heavy load of worry he dragged around with him on days like this when his favourite girl was on the road.

The Sawyers were arriving in two bits. Josh wanted his Harley at his fingertips in Alberta—the massive bike gifted him freedom. Cruising winding mountain roads, slowing to admire the ghostly greyish green of glacier-fed lakes, was time Josh could take to exhale, to breathe. Matt hadn't wasted his breath on an argument when Josh insisted on driving the Harley from Vancouver to the Alberta ranch near Canmore. *Let the guy live his life*, he'd figured, even if it meant Jessie would be riding in the open air behind her husband the entire drive. Hell, Josh deserved the good life; he sure as heck had earned it. He wasn't the kind of guy to go rogue when his wife was snuggled up behind him on a long highway drive. He and Jessie would cherish every second they were alone together today. It was Matt and Charles and Deirdre who feared the Harley.

Good thing Charles and Dee have the kids today, Matt considered, wandering outside to stand at nervous attention to wait for the Harley. The busy youngsters would keep the older couple's worried minds and hearts occupied. Dan, the kids' usual assigned security, would bring Emily-Grace, David, Dylan, and Micah to Alberta the next morning via Charles' private jet.

Kids…Matt dropped a nervous hand to his thigh and absently rubbed a tight muscle that had started bothering him after a late afternoon run. He studied Ry and Hunter while, in the distance, the big bike gradually grew louder as it chugged its way closer. The boys were in the corral with Gary, seemingly getting a spontaneous lesson on equine hoof care since Gary had a hoof in one hand and with his free hand was pointing something out— accumulated hard-packed dirt, maybe, Matt speculated, or a pebble—within the hoof. Ry was bent over the hoof, seemingly captivated, Hunter less so. For a four year old, Hunter had a wise, stoic kind of patience, but today had been a long day and judging by the way he was teetering behind Gary and Ry, he was plain worn out.

Matt had spent most of the day working. He and Charles Skyped for a while, then Matt got on the phone with the bosses at the trusted Calgary security firm. Afterwards he did a lengthy detailed walkthrough with the ground security assigned to the ranch. The Sawyer family would be content to keep most of their stay contained, but high profile friends were expected for visits and those visits needed to be managed, from the arrivals at Calgary International Airport to scheduled departures a few days later.

Evelyn had flitted around here and there all day, which Matt appreciated because she saw to the boys' meals and water breaks, and more than once today she'd slipped a mug of coffee and a warm, fresh muffin across the old thick pine harvest dining room table to Matt, where he'd set up camp. She made up the beds and hummed while she prepped lasagnas for the freezer, she cut out and baked oversized doughy cinnamon buns, spit-shined the bathrooms with environmentally friendly 'green' cleaner, and pushed the vacuum around when Matt wasn't Skyping or on the phone. Evelyn's husband, Gary, rolled up his sleeves and focused on the outside work. He tidied up the barn, weeded the vegetable and herb gardens, powered a weed trimmer around the house, and at one point Matt glanced out of the window and saw him crouched on the barn's roof tarring down replacement shingles in place of some that had blown away over the winter.

Which mostly left Ry and Hunter the freedom to explore on their own.

"You stay where at least one of us can see you," Matt had ordered them early on in the day, and since he was an intimidating kind of guy who was meant to be listened to when he spoke, the boys humbly listened, although

Matt needn't have said a word. For the first few hours, Hunter kept his unexpected guardian in sight at all times.

Now, thinking back while waiting for Josh and Jessie to pull up on the Harley, Matt put his hands on his hips, spread his feet a hip's width apart, and let his lips curl downwards. He was remembering checking on Hunter in the back bedroom a few hours after arriving at the ranch in the morning, in the back wing that was so new a whiff of curing paint accosted Matt's nostrils when he walked down the hallway. The smell had surprised him since he hadn't noticed it earlier. *Too tired to notice when we first got here,* he thought. He'd been thinking about that, about how damn exhausted he was, like done-in-body-and-soul-exhausted, when he'd raised a hand to push on the door to the boys' bedroom.

Awake, sitting up, Hunter was leaning side-on against the wall, both small fists curled tightly against his mouth, clinging to his bedraggled homemade pony. Large wet tears were trickling down already glistening trails on both cheeks. His wide eyes stared fretfully at Matt's booted feet when Matt pushed the door all the way open.

Scanning the small room, Matt let his eyes adjust to the dim light. He could make out Ry comfortably curled up on the twin bed just opposite Hunter, dozing peacefully. Tiptoeing into the room, he reached for Hunter and was surprised when the little fellow shrank away from him and resisted being picked up.

Lowering his arms, Matt's heart twisted painfully when he took a closer look at the clouds of sorrow in Hunter's eyes. "What is it, little guy?" he asked him in a whisper.

Hunter sighed, a long, deep sigh that Matt decided came from the depths of his soul, it was so profound. A damp, sweet odour tickled Matt's nose. It wasn't pleasant.

"Ah. It's okay," Matt assured him, quick to realize why Hunter was in retreat mode. "It happens, Hunter. Little kids wet the bed all the time."

Hunter still wouldn't meet his eye. He scrunched his lithe body up into a tight ball.

Jessie, Matt realized with a start, watching him. *He reminds me of Jessie. When I first met her, she had that same haunted look. Loneliness. It's profound loneliness.* Matt knew loneliness. It was what drew he and Jessie together all those years ago, and what finally took them over the edge the night they first acted on their feelings for each other.

"Other kids are coming here tomorrow," Matt tried. Just to get the words out, he had to suck back a tremendous lump that was clogging his throat. Still, the entreaty came out raspy. Hunter's pain was Matt's own, today. Somewhere along the way over the last little while, the boy's hurts had encompassed Matt. Like a bubble the hurts expanded until Matt was inside them with Hunter, sharing his broken heart, living in his sorrow.

Like a parent, Matt thought.

The notion wasn't new but by the end of the hustling, busy day it had grown more profound, long after Matt had grasped Hunter's thin biceps, lifted him, and carried his weeping body to the bathroom, ran a soothing bath, went back and stripped the bed, and carried the sheets to the washing machine. Long after he'd watched the clean sheets dry on the clothesline in the light breeze after Evelyn hung them out. Long after Matt took his laptop into Josh and Jessie's cozy sunroom that afternoon so he could look through the windows and keep an eye on Hunter outside.

All day the idea of being a parent to a wounded, hurt child followed Matt, the same way Hunter followed Ry around like a lost puppy.

They'll miss each other.

Matt didn't consider that someday he might be the one to have to miss Hunter. Hell, missing Jessie was enough. He and she had earned their way fully into each other's souls. Ripping her away from him wasn't like tearing a bandage off an old wound, it was like annihilating him entirely. Having to let Jessie go had torn Matt up the way an IED rips a soldier into shreds.

He wouldn't let that happen with Hunter.

Some time in the middle of the day, Matt had picked up his phone and called Shanda. He asked her to take some time off and come to the ranch for a few days, and was surprised by the warmth that gushed through his veins when she agreed. It was a warmth that, in a marriage ruled by long-term absences, Matt hadn't felt in a long time.

Maybe Hunter is the key to bringing Shanda and me closer, he thought. *The key to encourage her to cut her schedule down so we can spend more time together.*

Maybe Hunter would be the key to easing the constant ache that plagued Matt night and day—the one named Jessie. The one whose arrival was imminent.

Thinking about Jessie now, Matt smiled. From the corral, Hunter looked over, and Matt waved. He thought he detected a tiny hint of a return smile, but he wasn't sure. He did notice a yawn, though, a big one, and determined that once he greeted Josh and Jessie, he'd have to hunker down and get the little fellow to bed. It was late evening, which added to the relief that the big bike was drawing closer. The Harley was worry enough—the idea of Josh having to steer it through moose and deer infested highways in the dark would almost put Matt, and Charles and Dee too, he figured, in the crazy house.

Matt could have put Hunter to bed earlier—Evelyn had strongly hinted at it twice before outright suggesting it. She had offered to tuck Hunter in herself, but Hunter wouldn't go with her, which instilled in Matt a kind of warped, humble sense of pride. There were a few reasons why the little guy was still up. One, Dawn had called from J.I. to tell Matt about the trail riding accident, which totally threw Matt for a loop. Kevin, on security there, called right after her. Dallas was on the road now with his parents, taking them to the hospital in Sundre. The whole thing meant that Matt had a ton of unplanned calls to make, to Sundre police first to get manpower to the hospital to eyeball the family and potentially keep any overzealous fans away. Another call was to the hospital itself to prepare the local medical staff, who informed Matt that most likely Boone would be transported to a larger hospital in Red Deer for scans and treatment. Which meant more calls to Red Deer, and to the Calgary security firm to apprise them so they could get security on site.

By the time the calls were made and Matt let his knotted gut uncoil at the certainty that Dallas' world was again under some modicum of control, Josh and Jessie had texted that they'd reached nearby Canmore, and Matt was so tired that he thought if he tucked Hunter in he might doze off right next to him, and if he did that, he wouldn't see Jessie til morning. The idea of wrapping a safe, protective arm around Hunter was actually appealing on a lot of levels, and Matt's heart softened at the idea of holding a small child's hand on a regular basis again, of giving comfort to help a child ease into sleep. Ry could lie down with Hunter, but he wouldn't be going to bed for a while yet—Cassie's boy was way too wound up to sleep. He was patient and easy-going with Hunter, but right now he was more concerned with learning as much as he could about horses, which seemed to bore Hunter. Matt wondered if Dale's son had some innate sense of how to care for horses already, some 'past life' wisdom, maybe, that he carried with him from a former life as a wrangler, cowboy, or Indigenous warrior.

Chuckling at what he considered was a far-fetched idea of living many lives, Matt eased his tired body into a tree-shaded deep yellow Adirondack chair that faced the corral across the dirt clearing. He shoved a wrinkled shirt sleeve up past an elbow, then did the same with the sleeve on the other arm. They were repeated nervous movements. Seeing Jessie always did that to Matt these days, made him nervous, that is, after any kind of separation.

The shirt was yellow plaid. Matt wore it on purpose, to throw her. Some of the teasing he took at J.I. was legit—he had always been the kind of man who put a great deal of care and concern into his wardrobe. And money. Very good salaries via Charles Keating's and Dallas White's payrolls meant lots of money to play with. The western shirt was a ploy. It wasn't about taste. Pricey enough at one of the Innisfail rodeo's merch booths, it was a soft cotton with pearl snaps, reminding Matt of one Josh used to wear a lot in the old days. Jessie would love it. She'd laugh at Matt and run her hand along his arm, maybe twist the sleeve between her fingers to feel the softness of it. Of him. If Matt were lucky, maybe she would even rest a hand on his waist, hook a thumb over his belt. Let her fingers dangle there.

He shivered. He couldn't help himself.

Matt was wearing the shirt tucked into the waist of his jeans. A large engraved silver belt buckle Dallas had loaned him a few days ago (with much teasing, yet a firm *you need this if you want to play cowboy*) tied the ranch look together. Matt had pulled the denim hems of his stiff jeans down over the new cowboy boots he was finally starting to break in, although he'd 'borrowed' a half dozen Band-Aids from the Sawyer kids' bathroom first-aid kit to keep the raw blisters covered. Snorting out a half-laugh, Matt shoved the heel of one of the boots into a patch of dirt beneath the grass at his feet, and toed some loose dirt up over the other boot. He used the first boot's sole to rub the Alberta dirt in.

"Got to make them look worn," he said with a grin just as the Harley's headlight finally crested the last rounded turn in the long lane. It almost took Matt by surprise when the magnificent road-weary bike itself became suddenly visible with a mighty roar as it eased around the turn, its two riders laughing over some private joke as Josh piloted his way alongside the corral before planting the cherished Harley next to Matt's SUV in front of the barn.

Gary had both kids by their elbows by then. The horses had gotten jumpy the closer the thunderous bike got to them. Looking over, Matt caught himself wondering whether the animals were nervous or whether they knew the sound of Josh's bike and just couldn't wait to see him again. Josh, like Dale and Hunter, had a deep love of horses that seemed to come from some aged wisdom. *Or more likely from the pain of loneliness,* Matt decided, watching Josh and Jessie swing their legs over the Harley and haul off their black half-helmets, and lean in to share a sweet kiss and some tender words that made Matt smile because he knew their love was hard earned.

Josh waved to Gary and grinned at the boys and horses in his corral before turning to tend to the helmets and to the creaking, tired bike. Jessie, shaking out her hair, seemingly relieved to be free of the helmet, wandered over to meet Gary at the corral fence to give him a big hug. She spoke to Ry and Hunter and rifled guitar-callused fingers through the limp curls in her hair before turning at the sound of the springed screen door that slammed when Evelyn practically skipped through it.

Her pale eyes flicked over to Matt in the chair; the clearing was well lit in the increasing twilight but he was in dusky shadow underneath the large tree so she hadn't noticed him there at first. Her wide smile was manna, to Matt. It was heaven, that beautiful smile, meant just for him—meant to communicate in silent acknowledgement that she, too, was happy that they would be in each other's company again just for a little while.

Jessie hugged her Aunt Evelyn before letting go so Evelyn could skip over to say hi to Josh, whom Gary and the kids were also approaching so they could admire the bug and dirt spattered bike and fire questions at him about the long drive from Vancouver.

Matt was alight when Jessie reached him. She extended a hand down to the chair to give him an upward yank so they could stand nose to nose.

"Love the hair," he murmured, unable to resist running his fingers through her auburn-tinted curls. "Windblown much?"

"Omigod. I love the bike but all day on it is overkill, Matt. Give me my Mustang with room to stretch out and nap once in a while!"

"With a pack of smokes stashed underneath the driver's seat."

"Hell, yeah. I mean, how'm I supposed to hide smokes on Josh's Harley? He'd freak."

"Not about you smoking. I can just imagine his reaction if you got ashes anywhere near that thing. Did he stop every fifty miles to shine it up?"

Throwing her head back for a hearty laugh, Jessie swatted her best buddy and grabbed his sleeve. Bending forward, she kissed him smack on the lips, which was far more than Matt had dared hope for.

His eyes grew serious. Placing his palms on her cheeks, he smiled affectionately and slowly shook his head. "Glad you made it safe and sound, Jessie. You better call Charles and Dee right this second. I'm sure they're worried sick." His voice was soft and loving. He didn't let go of her.

"In a minute." Her tone matched his. Laying a hand over his on her face, she rocked over on one heel, tilted her head in a cocky way, ran her eyes over his body, and said, "You've gone cowboy on me."

A twinkle danced through Matt's eyes, sending shockwaves of love rocketing around Jessie's heart. Her smile grew wider when he said, "Dallas' family has no mercy."

"Uh-huh. Good thing. You look adorable, my sweet Matt. I love you to the ends of the earth and back, in cashmere or in denim. You know that, right?"

"I know." This time his voice was gruff. There were days when Matt wondered why he had ever let Jessie go when he'd had the chance to keep her. The thought was never long to disappear into a cloud of fairy dust. The answer was always crystal clear—because ultimately Jessie loved Josh more. She had from the day she first laid eyes on him, and she always would. Final.

A long, slow sigh escaped from between Matt's lips. Closing his eyes, he pushed back the wistful sadness that always accosted him when he let himself sink that far, back into the old longing, and he pressed her body hard to his. "Sweetheart," he whispered, knowing she also still had moments of struggle where he was concerned, "I'm glad you're here. I can't wait to see the kids tomorrow."

A moment passed before Jessie could bring herself to speak. When she did, her eyes were misty but lit up by an inner light that Matt had not always had the pleasure of seeing. Beyond her, he caught sight of Josh watching them. Raising his hand, Matt waved. Josh was a stand-up guy. He knew damn well how deep Matt and Jessie ran in each other's veins. Hell, his life flowed along better when Jessie and Matt were able to share in each other's lives, on whatever level it took. Exhilarated from the freedom of the Harley ride and from the lingering smell of the wind in his messy, layered hair, Josh grinned and waved back.

"Speaking of kids," Jessie smiled, taking a step back from Matt and twisting half around to face Josh and the others at the Harley. She unzipped her heavy fitted leather biker jacket and took Matt's hand in hers. "You have Ry with you. And that adorable little guy standing apart from everyone else, the one yawning and practically falling over, has got to be Dallas' brother's child. The one that's all over the news."

"Hunter," Matt managed, fighting the ache in his chest and running a thumb tenderly over Jessie's fingers. He cleared his throat and shifted his stance. "His name is Hunter."

"Hunter," she repeated, testing out the name and taking a good long look at Matt's newest little friend. "He's a beautiful child. He has Indigenous blood in him."

"His mother is Cree."

She turned back and gave him a solemn look. "How are they all doing? Dallas' family?"

Matt shook his head.

"That good, huh?"

"It was suicide, Jessie. Nobody knows what to think or how to feel. They're all just ticking time bombs going through the motions. Dallas wants to get the hell outta Dodge, to try to outrun the pain, but he's scared shitless to leave his family right now. His mother gravitates between working non-stop or staring aimlessly at her shoes trying to figure out how to tie them, and his father's so angry and confused he lashes out. Mostly at Dallas."

"God, I can't imagine how any of them are coping. Poor Dallas."

"One breath at a time, Jess. That's how."

For a few seconds, their eyes locked and stayed locked. Jessie blinked sadly and then looked away. Neither needed to say out loud just how familiar they were with coping at a level where each single breath was a major victory.

Jessie cleared her throat. "What about this little boy, Matt? I'm surprised to see him here with you."

Gesturing to the kids, Matt bit the corner of his lip before speaking. "Those boys have been living under a very dark cloud, Jessie. I figured they could stand some joy."

Mustering up some spirit, Jessie stood a little taller. Her eyes shimmered. "Well, they'll get it here. Our kids are wired. You know how much they all love this place. Charles and Dee won't get any of them to sleep tonight." Tapping Matt's arm, she added, "Jacob and Kayla are flying in tomorrow too, with little Lily."

"Great. We'll have ourselves a party."

"All those little kids will drive you nuts, old man. You know how they feed on each other. It'll be chaos."

"Shanda's flying in tomorrow too, Jessie."

Eyebrows arching into question marks, Jessie found herself at a loss for words. Josh and Shanda were close, and had worked together on a number of television and film projects. It was no secret that Shanda held a torch for Josh, and that the two were drawn even closer together because of Matt and Jessie's history. Despite a lot of tension, mostly on Shanda's part, they had all managed to maintain some kind of strained friendship. Not without angst, and not without occasional harsh words, but for the most part they managed to stay civil when in each other's company.

"I'm surprised," Jessie said finally. "She's on a shoot, right?"

"She is. She's able to get away for a few days."

"To come here."

"Yep. Here." Matt licked his lips nervously and looked over at Hunter. He sighed, just a little one, but it was there. And it was wistful. It was followed by a tiny up-curve of his lips and a sweet paternal light in his eyes.

Jessie followed his glance. "Oh. I see." Her heart sank. At the same time, her eyes widened and her breath caught.

"Nothing to see," Matt smiled, lifting her hand so he could brush his lips over her fingers. "Apart from a lonely little boy who needs a family, that is." Letting Jessie's hand fall away, he moved past her and started to walk towards the tired child in his care, deciding now that Jessie had seen Hunter, and Matt had seen Jessie, that he ought to put his own wants aside and tuck Hunter in for the night.

His heart was racing. "Damn, that girl can read my mind," he said to the cool evening air as he strode towards the small group huddled around Josh's bike. "She knows. Why am I not surprised?"

"Nothing to see, huh?" Jessie murmured softly to his back. "I beg to differ. Oh, Matt." She knew pain. She understood the level of loss decimating Dallas' family right now. Yet Jessie also understood what it meant to start to thaw out, to wake up and act when the more raw-edged pain eventually shifted into something more bearable, into a more even-keeled level of pain that brought with it the ability to reason and to function. And the ability to let love in again. Matt was always the saviour—in her life, in Josh's life, in the kids' lives, in Shanda's life. In Charles' and Dee's lives. Jacob and Kayla relied on him to pull it all together when things went haywire. They all did. And he always came through for them.

Even when it meant Matt would end up suffering, he never failed to step up and do the right thing.

Watching him, Jessie took a tentative step towards the others. "They'll want him. When they can think again, when they can let themselves feel again, they'll want that little boy. He's their blood. He belongs to them. Oh, Matt."

Near the bike, Hunter practically fell into Matt's safe, loving arms. Lifting him, Matt held him close and rubbed his back. Melting fully into the body of the only person he really trusted, Hunter buried his face in the hollow of Matt's warm neck and strong shoulder, and closed his eyes.

There was laughter amongst the small group, lots of good-humoured joking coming from the happy people standing around the Harley, including from Josh, which meant the world to Jessie, who for far too long had seen her husband struggle. Without meaning to, she telegraphed to Josh, with sinking shoulders and sorrowful eyes, this new concern for Matt, instantly biting her lip with regret when Josh caught the fear and his eyes darkened.

"What?" he mouthed.

"Later," she whispered behind Matt's back, knowing that Josh would understand her meaning even if he couldn't hear the words. Walking up to Matt, she touched Hunter's dark hair with the fingers of her right hand, and forced a smile when Matt sensed her presence and looked sideways in her direction for approval. "He's really special, huh Matt?" she said.

"You have no idea," he replied, his words thick and dusky with fatigue and emotion.

"I can't wait to hear all about him, Matt. Really."

Evelyn butted in. "Put that worn out child to bed, Matt, before I take him out of your arms and do it myself."

"She's the bossy type," Jessie giggled, letting her fingers drop from Hunter's head to cover Matt's hand on the little boy's back. "But she makes yummy chocolate chip muffins, so we let the bossy part go." She gave Matt's thumb a light rub with hers, and fought the urge to wrap her arms around both him and Hunter, as if by doing so she could somehow protect them both.

"Had some," Matt said, losing himself in her worried gaze. "I beat you to it. The muffins. I got the fresh-out-of-the-oven ones."

"Aren't you the lucky one?" Jessie murmured to him.

The downturn of her lips telegraphed that she thought he was anything but lucky.

Forcing his gaze away from the woman Matt wished to hell he could haul off to bed with him, he rallied by inhaling in a stuttery kind of way, and bent to land a kiss on her cheek that he hoped didn't linger too long in Josh's presence. "Goodnight, sweetheart," he breathed. "Sweet dreams, girl." Standing tall, he hugged Hunter close. The child made a good wall against the world. "Goodnight, everyone," he called out in a voice that came out just a little too forced, and a little too peppy. "See you in the morning to welcome the chaos." Tousling Ry's blond surfer locks, he added, "Come on, kid. Bedtime for you too. Tomorrow will be a busy day."

"Just one sec," Ry begged. He turned to Josh. "D'you think I could have a ride on the Harley tomorrow?"

Josh's shoulders straightened proudly. Shoving his hands into the pockets of his comfortably faded jeans, he grinned. "Now there's a kid I can respect. And he likes country music too. Sure, Ry."

"He's just buttering you up so he can date your daughter," Jessie laughed when Ry had sauntered off out of earshot with Matt and Hunter. With longing, she watched the little made-up family go, and at the same time had to fight back a tidal wave of love for a man that always put others before himself.

Hooking an arm through Evelyn's, she forced a smile and turned her back to Matt, praying that this time he wouldn't get hurt in the process.

Matt spoke to Ry when they were almost at the screen door. "I think you might not want to tell your mother if you take a ride on that bike."

"Are you kidding?" Ry said, almost jumping up and down with glee at the idea of sitting on the Harley with all its power and might beneath him just like some kind of modern day horse. "I'll be behind Josh Sawyer. That ought to be enough to win my mom over. She's a big fan. She's crazy about him."

"Aren't they all," Matt muttered under his breath.

Matt stopped the spring door from closing by putting his body between the door and the doorway when Ry hopped up over the step ahead of him, went in, and rather thoughtlessly let the door go. Using his hip, Matt nudged the screen door open wider since he needed both arms to fully support and protect Hunter, and he stepped into the sanctuary of Josh and Jessie's ranch house.

After turning for one last lingering look to Jessie, who glanced up in time to catch his eye and wave a solemn goodnight from inside the warm cozy yellow glow of the barn's outside light, Matt quietly let the door close, and surrendered to the day.

Chapter Twenty-six

They got more than they bargained for the next day. Dallas and Cassie showed up. With feisty Jade.

"The more the merrier," Josh said, throwing up his arms in feigned defeat when Matt told him mid-afternoon that Dallas had texted. Supposedly Boone was doing fine, and so Dallas and Cassie decided they'd like to come down. It was a gorgeous day in the foothills and the place had a party atmosphere about it. A grand campfire was planned for later. "Just tell him to bring his guitar to balance things out so I don't have to listen to Jacob's pouty tunes all night. We'll make it a country night instead. That'll put Jacob in his place."

With a mischievous gleam in his deep brown eyes, Josh handed Matt a shovel. "Now get to work, Matt. Those fancy new cowboy boots of yours were made for a reason. Unlike the rest of your Yuppie threads, those boots have a practical purpose."

A wry grin accompanied Matt's acceptance of the shovel. Part of Dallas' text communicated that Boone had been sent home around three in the morning with an order of complete bed rest. "Dallas' dad's a tough old coot, though," Matt had said to Josh when he approached him in the barn a few minutes earlier and filled him in. "If I know him, he's not resting. He's mucking stalls despite having a son-in-law there to help. But he's likely ornery as hell. Hence Dallas needing some space, I figure."

"Shit doesn't shovel itself, Matt. A crusty cowboy like Dallas' father likely works sunup to sundown twenty-four seven every day of the year, sick, hurt, or not. He's got quite a few horses, doesn't he?"

"A couple dozen," Matt informed Josh. Bending over the shovel, he got his back into cleaning out a stall, to Josh's great amusement. "Stop it," Matt ordered him. "I see you laughing over there. You're enjoying this far too much, Josh."

Josh would have been in hysterics except that Hunter was at Matt's side, leaning against a stall door. The quiet little boy with the solemn eyes had a similar effect on Josh that he had on Matt. The sad look screamed *Jessie*. In one way, it gave both men hope for Hunter. Jessie had come a long way since her twenties, when she wore that desolate look far too often. In later troubled times, the look had come back. Josh and Matt hoped to never see that kind of trauma on Jessie's pretty face again.

The reminder lowered Josh's spirit.

Setting down the rake he was using in the stall next to the one Matt was working in, Josh wandered over to Hunter and crouched down to look him in the eye. Sobering, Matt leaned on his shovel's handle and watched.

"Hunter, did Evelyn show you and Ry the new kittens yesterday?"

Other than a twisting of his fingers by his belly, Hunter didn't respond to Josh. He'd peed the bed again last night. This big man in front of him was between him and Matt right now, and that scared him. The guy had kind eyes, and Hunter had watched Josh's four children falling all over him, and Matt seemed to like him, but still...

At least he was a horse guy. That was the main reason Hunter didn't walk right around Josh to Matt, although he did look up over the guy's long chestnut hair to meet Matt's soft, gentle, loving eyes.

A quiet smile from Matt preceded the words he spoke on Hunter's behalf. "Ry didn't say anything about any kittens."

"Micah found them this morning, up at the storage barn," Josh said, studying Hunter. "You met Micah, right Hunter? He's my youngest. He's about your age, actually."

No answer. Just a blink.

"Evelyn was too busy filling your freezer and cleaning your house to take the boys on a hunt for kittens," Matt teased.

"Loser," Josh grinned. "In all honesty, I doubt she knows they exist. Nature has a way of taking care of itself when it comes to barn cats."

Outside, the other kids were chasing each other around the clearing. The place was a regular circus. The volume level wouldn't be going down when Jade arrived later. Her strong vocals were already raising eyebrows amongst Dallas' artist management friends.

"It's too crazy out there for you, isn't it, Hunter?" Josh tried. He leaned towards Hunter and spoke in a whisper. "Can I tell you a secret? That's why me and Matt are in here too. And that's why I have horses and a big bike."

Hunter raised his head. His eyes widened.

"The bike or the horses?" Josh asked, tilting his head curiously. "Which got your interest?"

"The horses," Matt said from above, switching the shovel handle to his left hand. As a parent, he'd be out of his element there. A serious look passed over his face. He started to shovel manure into the large wheelbarrow he and Josh were sharing.

Josh was not out of his element. He was deep into it. "Ah ha," he said, reaching for Hunter's small hand, which Matt was surprised to see the little boy took. "My son Dylan is the rider in the family. Should we see if he wants to go for a ride?" Catching Matt's nervous eye, Josh added, "We'll just go around the corral, Matt. We'll keep it contained for today, okay?"

Uncertain, Matt nodded and tossed a heaping shovelful of horse poop and straw into the barrow. "I'll help," he announced.

"Wow," Josh said to Matt as he led Hunter towards the barn's opening. "Alberta's done some job on you. Are you riding these days too?" Thinking about the arrangement he and Matt shared with Jessie—although rarely were she and Matt together, and Josh kind of thought maybe things had eased off between them, at least he hoped so—Josh coloured. If the whole thing hadn't caused so much pain between them back in the day, he would have added, *I meant horses. Not my wife, right?*

The earnest way Matt swallowed and stared at Hunter settled Josh a bit. He narrowed his eyes. He was starting to get the picture of why Jessie seemed so concerned about Matt last night. He pushed it away and called out to Dylan.

Soon, the horses and pony were saddled and the kids were taking turns riding. Josh kept the pony around for his smaller children. Diego was a soft-eyed caramel and white paint. He was good-natured and responsive. Before long, Hunter was on his back for the fourth time in less than an hour.

Josh was handing the little guy the reins again just as Jessie approached from behind. It only took Hunter a second to urge Diego on his umpteenth walk around the corral, following Dylan on one of Josh's horses. Jessie came to a stop between Josh and Matt, and tucked an arm through Matt's elbow. "He's a natural," she said. To nobody's surprise, she turned to Matt and said outright, "You're thinking of taking him in. I'm not surprised. He's crazy about you."

Josh leaned away from her, against the split rail fence. He was in his happy place out here under the big sky. He tried not to let Jessie's closeness to Matt phase him. "We could take him in," he said, and gave Jessie a big smile meant just for her. "We always said we'd have five. The kid fits right in around here."

A pink blush crept high over her cheeks. "We're working on that number five, Josh. We'll get there."

Matt turned his head away.

Jessie refocused. "Josh, I think Matt is seriously thinking about taking Hunter in." Letting her hand slip down to Matt's, she wound her fingers through his and spoke directly to him. "You are, aren't you, Matt? That's why you invited Shanda up here, right? To see if she would be interested in adopting Hunter?"

Out of the corner of her eye she saw Josh shake his head in warning. Jessie had a habit of sticking her nose in where it didn't belong. Clearly Matt's tense body language was telegraphing a defensive caution.

Ignoring her husband, Jessie forged carefully ahead. "Matt, baby, I just don't know if you're seeing the whole picture here. I'm worried."

Matt snapped to attention. Facing the kids on the horses, he cut in with, "The picture I've seen is a family torn apart by tragedy, and then suddenly handed a bastard child none of them care to acknowledge even exists." He glared at Jessie, which threw her. She and her beloved Matt had their history of down and dirty fights, but rarely did he fire angry looks in her direction.

She cringed. "Matt, honey, I just don't want to see you get hurt."

Yanking his hand out of her grip, Matt pounced. "Why not, you've made a history of it."

"Ouch," she said softly, crestfallen. "Was that for my benefit or for Josh's, Matt?"

"Look," he said, capturing her in his gaze and holding it while Josh looked on, lips pressed together in an effort to stay quiet but eyes locked on his wife's in warning, "somebody's got to step up and help this child. Cassie's grown attached to him but Dallas is so lost in the past and in his father's judgment that he doesn't know if he's coming or going. Shanda used to talk about adopting. Hunter and I get each other. I think we can do this. I think we're the right people to do this."

"He needs other kids, Matt. He seems like the kind of kid who needs horses. That's not you. You're a city boy. Cowboy boots and pearl buttons on a plaid shirt aren't gonna change that."

"He needs love. That's what he needs." Blood was starting to pound in Matt's ears. It was a big ole caution sign demanding he take it easy, to be careful not to say something he'd later regret. "It worked with you, all those years ago."

Jessie's gaze flicked over to her husband for a second. Sighing, she let her shoulders relax and took Matt's hand again, glad that he let her hold it and rub her fingers over his. "I didn't belong to anybody," she said softly. "And I was twenty when you and I met. Twenty-seven when I met Josh. Hunter is only four. He needs a different kind of love, Matt. Besides, he's already got a family."

"Jessie…" Matt considered what to say. "You and Josh, you've got everything I've always wanted. I had a family, and I lost it. Over you, I might add."

She recoiled.

Josh sighed and rubbed a worried thumb and forefinger over his lips before settling on watching the kids. Dylan was in the lead, with Hunter on the paint following capably along right behind him.

Matt went on. "I humoured Shanda at first when she started talking about adopting. I'm not stupid, I know I'm supposed to be slowing down now, not starting up again. But I have news for you. I've still got a lot of love left in these old bones and in this broken heart of mine. Hunter needs me, and I need him."

Silent, Jessie blinked away tears before laying her other hand over Matt's and rubbing his fingers between all of hers. "I know, baby," she said, as Josh listened, although he had one elbow up on the fence now and was leaning even further away from them. "Don't you think I know how much love you have in your heart? More than anyone," she thrust a pointy finger into her chest, "I know."

For a few minutes, none of them could get past their emotions enough to trust themselves to speak. In the distance, the steady clop-clop-clop of the horse and pony making their slow, plodding ways around the perimeter of the corral, and the background screaming and happy yelling of the other kids at play, were welcome distractions.

Finally, Jessie took a breath and said, "Why do you think Dallas and Cassie are coming here today, Matt?"

He withdrew his hand again and started towards Hunter on Diego. The pony had ground to a halt and was trying to graze, and Hunter wasn't quite strong enough to pull up his head. Calling back over his shoulder, Matt said, "Space. Dallas needs his space. He needs a break from his ornery, grieving father." He also figured Cassie likely wanted Ry back in her fold. It had crossed his mind that the trail riding accident had spurred the couple into leaving J.I. for good, that they were on their way to the airport and were just stopping at Josh and Jessie's to pick up Ry. Matt would get the scoop when they arrived. He was fairly certain they weren't coming for Hunter. Dallas had quite clearly voiced his intentions as far as Dale's son was concerned. It pissed him off that Jessie was sticking her nose in his business. As connected as they were, and as concerned as he knew she was, she had her own family to worry about—a family he once felt a part of and that now felt like distant relatives.

Stopping mid-stride, Matt swung around and gave Jessie a hard look. "Why would you not want this for me? Why would you, of all people, not want to see me happy?"

A slow tremble started in Jessie's legs. Lifting her right hand, she knuckled her fingers and ground them against the outside corner of her right eye. A tiny diamond of a tear snuck out of the left eye. "Of course I want to see you happy, Matt," she said. "You know I do. I just see you getting close to this child and it scares me, that's all. A child is a lot to lose, honey. That kind of love…it's a lot to lose."

Matt had to force his next words out from between clenched teeth. "You don't have to tell me about losing love, Jessie. I'm the master." Swinging back around, he made his way to Hunter's side.

"Oh, fuck," Jessie groaned, toeing herself around on one boot to face her husband, who was watching her quizzically, eyes uncertain. Josh never quite knew how to deal with the deep feelings between Jessie and Matt. Watching Matt bare it all the way he just did was excruciating, and there were many times that Josh did not feel that he—himself—should have emerged the victor as far as Jessie was concerned.

Jessie cut into his dark thoughts. "When Shanda bails to go back to work, whose gonna pick up the pieces, Josh?"

"He could be right, though," Josh said with a heavy shrug. "Maybe Dallas' whole family is too torn up to take this love child on."

"Course they are, right now, Josh. Give them a few months. Or a year. Give them just enough time to break Matt's heart."

Josh looked over at Matt and Hunter. For the first time since he'd met Hunter the night before, he saw the child smile. It wasn't a big smile, and it wasn't wide. But it was meant just for Matt.

"I think it's too late for that," Josh said. "I think Matt's heart has long been broken. And I think it's beyond ever getting fixed."

Giving himself a shove away from the fence, he pressed his lips to Jessie's forehead, and strode off across the corral to help with the kids.

Chapter Twenty-seven

"There," Emily-Grace huffed, dropping a box of chocolate-covered Celebration cookies on a plastic table by the fire her father was stoking to blissful campfire perfection. "Now if David would just put his electronics away and hunt up the marshmallow roasting sticks like Momma asked him to, we could make S'mores."

"Ask Jacob to sharpen up some new sticks," Josh said amicably. "And bring out that old guitar Momma lets you play out here by the fire. See if she'll tune it up for you."

"I'm switching that around, Daddy," Emily-Grace said, marching back up to the house. "Momma can sharpen the sticks, and Jacob can help with the guitar. It likely needs new strings, since it's been sitting here unused for like, forever."

Josh watched his daughter skip into the house. Lordy, between Jessie's feelings for Matt and Emily-Grace's constant longing to be in Jacob's company, it was damn hard to feel good about oneself. Grabbing a new split, he threw it end over end into the fire.

Dallas wandered up with a small cooler. Dropping into a canvas lawn chair, he unzipped the padded bag and reached inside for a bottle of beer, which he drew out and extended towards Josh.

"Nope," Josh said, raising a palm. "Thanks anyway. I'm good."

"Not drinking tonight?"

"Not drinking any night. I almost lost my family over drinking. More than once, actually," Josh mumbled, not really caring to relive those tough days, in his head or otherwise. Cornering right, he asked how Dallas was handling the day's noise.

257

"Noise I can handle," Dallas returned politely. "Kid chaos is another story. Why do little kids think they have to scream all the time?"

"Because their parents let them," Josh chuckled, leveraging himself up to a standing position by putting his hands on his thighs and giving himself an upwards push. "I know, because I'm one of those parents."

"If you don't mind my saying so," Dallas said, "your kids seem pretty well behaved, Josh. Excited, maybe, but polite and respectful, with their sirs and ma'ams and setting the table and all that stuff."

"The sirs and ma'ams are from Jessie's time in the deep south years ago, from when she lived in Charleston. Apparently it's a very polite city. By the way, I'll say the same about Ry," Josh responded kindly. "He's a very well-mannered kid."

"You forgot to add 'especially when he's following Emily-Grace around like a doe-eyed deer.' Then he's got manners upon manners." The bottle was still in Dallas' hand. He gave its cap a twist and took a long, luxurious drink, which Josh found himself having to look away from. In his life, such pleasant cool luxuries on hot days were a thing of the past. "Were we like that when we were boys?"

"Hell, I'm still like that. Head over heels. And yeah, Ry does seem to be sweet on my daughter," Josh said, trying to steer his thoughts away from the beer Dallas was obviously enjoying, judging by the way he was relaxing deeper into his lawn chair and licking every drop of moisture from his lips.

"Get out the shotgun." Dallas grinned and raised the bottle.

"She's oblivious."

"Good thing."

"Hunter doesn't have much to say."

Dallas took another long swig before responding. Since arriving a few hours earlier, he was keeping his distance from the little guy, just standing back and observing. "Hunter was starting to relax a little back at my dad's spread. I messed up and set him back, I think. I'm sure Matt told you."

"Matt didn't say much," Josh answered honestly. He lowered his voice respectfully. "Look, I can't imagine it's been easy, Dallas."

"I think for some people this kind of thing would be easier than it is for others."

Josh poked at the fire with a long, thick stick until the silence got to be overwhelming. He looked over at Dallas to see him hanging onto the beer with both hands, just staring at it. Dallas glanced up from the label and peered helplessly over the rim at Josh. He was like a lost puppy with those wide, damp eyes of his, begging someone to show him the way back home.

Josh's shoulders sank. The guy was gutted. "Take it one day at a time, Dal," he encouraged quietly. "Hell, take it one breath at a time, if that's what you need to do to get through this."

"You've had your dark days too, hey Josh." It was a statement, not a question. The whole world was privy to the nefarious things that almost broke the Sawyers.

"Did Matt fill you in?"

Shrugging, Dallas answered, "Some. Some I read." Squinting into the orange-pink glow of the descending sun, he hesitated. "Josh," he said after a bit, "this parenting thing. Does it get easier?"

"Are you asking about Jade?" Josh questioned carefully, poking at the fire with the long stick and watching the sparks fly. "Or Hunter? Because you and Ry seem good."

A quick intake of breath was Dallas' reaction to Josh bringing up Hunter as if the boy was his. "Ry and I connect over music. It helps." Dallas paused. "It may not seem like it, but Cassie has Jade under control. The little princess is just wired, being here with all the other kids."

"So Hunter, then."

Dallas sucked on a lip. Lifted the bottle to his lips. "Hell, yeah," he breathed, and tipped his head back for a drink.

"Every kid is different, Dal."

"Hunter's got issues. He'll always have issues. His father killed, uh," Dallas looked away, regained control, and choked out, "his father took his own life. How does a kid get past that? How does an adoptive parent raise a kid that fragile and expect him to come out whole?"

Josh swiped a nervous hand under his nose and gave a little snort. On one hand, he was pissed that Dallas was even asking, because Matt wanted Hunter, and Matt knew the answer.

Love. Period.

On the other hand, Josh really felt for the man's vulnerability. Dallas, in the greater scheme of things, had not been married long. Ry was not his biological son—he'd come into Dallas' life at age eight, already half-grown. Jade was three. She was growing up in the weird, wild world of fame and money, with unequalled luxuries and notorious pitfalls. Josh knew firsthand what the glass-house life of a singer of Dallas' level of fame was like, because Jessie lived that life, and Josh was a part of that experience. Plus Josh was a star in his own right, under the public microscope far more often than he'd like to be. As much as he and Jessie fought against it, their lives were filled with long or at least regular periods of distance from each other, and their children were growing up with a skewed sense of what most people would consider normal. Throw a damaged child into that mix? How could you possibly expect to succeed as a parent?

A sizzling mixture of flames and blistered bits of wood spewed into the air at Josh's next hard jab at the burning splits in the fire pit. Undulating waves of sparks and ash filtered down around him. "So you're taking him, then," he determined, unable to look away from the hypnotic, captivating, glowing, breathing orange embers beneath the flames. The embers were magnets, they were life. Undeniably, they had a power that was drawing Josh to them, that was compelling him to journey through fire, to venture beyond the spitting, troubled flames to get to their core.

Josh understood then the power of damaged people like Jessie and Hunter. They drew in wounded hearts the very way the embers were drawing Josh in now, with 'come-hither' bottomless, lonely eyes, and souls that would bleed forever.

To get to their hearts, you had to walk through fire.

"I don't know," Dallas retorted darkly. "I don't know if I can be the father Hunter needs. Dale…"

"Was a God?"

Dallas met Josh's eyes. "Aren't all dead men?"

"Jesus, Dallas. Harsh."

Shifting in his chair so that he was leaning forward, Dallas let out a breath. "Something broke in Dale a long time ago. When we were just out of high school. We kind of lost each other after that. So I don't know the answer to

260

the God thing except to say that it sure seems that way. In my rearview mirror, you know what I'm saying? And to my dad."

"Dads have a way of making us kids look bad against our siblings. I wouldn't take it personally."

Dallas grunted. "You don't know my dad."

"No, but I do know a dad who's got that down pat. Anyways, if I were you I'd be looking a little closer at hand for your competition. For someone to compare yourself to."

"Oh? Who?" Dallas sat back. "Oh," he said. Josh knew the second the light switched on in his mind's eye. "Matt. Of course."

"He's a helluva man, Dallas. That kid adores him. *My* kids adore him. My wife would walk over hot coals for him. She'd swim through fire if he asked her to."

"You're not helping here, Sawyer."

"Two things," Josh said, lifting his free hand and holding up two fingers. "Let's get real here, Dallas. One, stop right now with the comparisons to others, living or dead. All that will do is sink you into a hole of self-pity so deep it'd take Godzilla to pull you out. Two, I don't know you all that well but based on what my wife says about working with you, and based on the kind of guy you seem to be, I think you're likely a helluva lot better parent than you give yourself credit for. Ry worships you. Jade craves your attention, that's part of the reason she's a ball of fire—she's after your time. Dallas, the best gift you can give yourself is time with your family. It comes back to you in spades. Make time to be with Cassie and the kids, and spend time with your father. Get to know each other as adults. If it feels like Hunter is meant to be with you, then act on it."

"And Matt?" It was a pointed question. The way Dallas said it, with his chin in the air and the beer held almost too steady in his hand, his eyes unwavering and definitely challenging Josh, judging by the way they were narrowed...well, Josh had the uncomfortable feeling that Matt had divulged way too much to Dallas about his relationship with Jessie, and about Josh and Jessie's past heartaches. A lot of the old agony had made it to the mainstream media, but not all of it, not the...lingering mutual arrangement. Maybe Dallas had seen Matt and Jessie together at some show in some city somewhere. It was entirely possible. They likely all got together in restaurants for meals, or in hotel rooms for post-show drinks. For years, Jessie and Matt travelled together on her gigs. In the old days, they were inseparable.

Josh wondered how much Dallas knew. He almost groaned out loud. "Matt is complicated, Dal. He is everything to my wife and kids. His wife is a good friend of mine. If it weren't for Matt…Jesus. I wouldn't be sitting here across from you right now. I'd probably be dead. I owe him everything I have. My family—"

"No," Dallas cut in, a tainted note of sarcasm sneaking into his voice. "Stop with the false hero worship, Josh. If you cared about Matt the way you say you do, you wouldn't be sitting here telling me to take a child he clearly loves out from under him. Your stripes are showing, Sawyer. Don't put on a show of caring about Matt. What you're telling me to do doesn't sound like much of a bromance to me."

"You don't know—"

Dallas air-palmed him. "I do know, Josh. I know that you step aside and let your wife sleep with him when she wants to."

Okay, so he does know. Matt, you bastard. "Like they've been together maybe twice at most in the last three or four years, and it's not your business, Dallas. We have our reasons, reasons that would have destroyed most people. We found a way to carry on, a way that works for us." His tone changed, it got higher. "Don't make me hate you, I like your music. I need your music." The attempt at jocularity fell flat.

Dallas' eyes were moist. "I don't get how a woman like Jessie can love two men, how she can bounce back and forth between them without considering how much damage she's doing to both of them. I don't get my brother's deception. It doesn't work. Loving two people, sharing that love in both the emotional and the physical sense, I don't see how it can work! Someone always gets hurt. I've seen the pain in Matt's eyes when he talks about your wife. I see how much it kills him not to have her by his side every day the way you do. And you can't tell me it doesn't drive you insane knowing how she feels about him. How can you even stand to have him around? How can Shanda put up with that?"

Josh took a few steps backwards to grab some more splits from a nearby pile. He let Dallas throw knives. It seemed the guy needed to. Josh and Matt were friends—strained friends at times, but still friends. What Dallas was saying rang true, but Josh had made his peace with how they'd decided to carry on at least as much as he could, and he knew Matt had as well, as best he could. Their hardest days were old news.

"Jenny," Dallas said, effusive now, desperate to make Josh see, "is…was, I guess…Dale's wife. She is red-haired and freckled and a real dynamo, a good mom and the perfect sun-up-to-sun-down hard working rancher's wife. They have two sons, Shane and Cormac, something like twelve and, uh, I dunno, maybe eight or nine. You'd like those kids, they're naturals with horses and will probably both follow their father to the pro rodeo. You tell me she isn't reeling right now, Josh, after losing her husband the worst way possible, then having a kid she didn't know existed thrust upon her, and now," Dallas was reeling, himself, thinking about what he'd said in Jenny's presence a few short nights ago, "now she knows that Dale was with this other woman, Hunter's mother, the entire time he was with her. With Jenny. Before, and during. How's Jenny supposed to live with that?"

"I guess that's up to her, Dallas. This is something she's got to sort through on her own."

"She might not make it."

Josh blinked. "Maybe not." He curled his fingers into tight, hard fists. "Not everyone does."

"So here's my question. How did you? How—*do*—you? I mean, how do you stand it? Knowing how your wife feels about another man?"

Josh had to decide whether to pitch a split of wood at Dallas or clench his fists harder to control his temper. After a bit he said evenly, "How well do you know Matt, Dallas?"

Dallas gave him a blank stare.

"I'd guess not well at all," Josh determined. "Or you wouldn't be asking me that question."

"No, I wanna know. How does a man or woman ever come to terms with their partner loving someone else? Let's put the burger on the grill here—*sleeping* with someone else."

Josh pointed at the object of their conversation. Matt was just coming out of the barn with Hunter tagging along next to him. Josh's two youngest, Dylan and Micah, were alongside, skipping and chattering. Matt's hands were stuffed in his pockets, but he was glowing. "That man is extraordinary," Josh said quietly. "I love him almost as much as Jessie does. He *is* a hero to me. So I do what it takes to keep him in our lives. You would do well to do the same."

Holding up the beer bottle, Dallas tipped it back and drained it. His eyes were locked on Josh, and stayed there. "Would I."

"Don't be an asshole, Dallas. Matt and me are not the ones you should be angry at." Josh swallowed. It was a hot day. That beer sure looked cold and refreshing. He watched as Dallas wiped his hands on the condensation on the bottle and rubbed his wet palms on his sweaty forehead. "Talk to Matt about all this stuff," Josh said. "Ask him how he makes it through each day."

"I did. I know how. He hurts. That's how."

Slayed by that, Josh licked a lip and blinked away the truth.

"But maybe he deserves to hurt," Dallas tossed in angrily, digging for another beer and then holding it up like a trophy while he unscrewed the cap, which he tossed into the fire. "Matt has admitted to sleeping with another man's wife. He admits he's in love with her." His eyes landed back on Josh. They were intense, angry. "He ought to hurt."

"Well," Josh considered thoughtfully, holding Dallas' gaze and wishing he could help the man sort through the pain of his loss. "Love can cause the worst kind of pain. But it can also bring the greatest joy." He took a breath. "Look, Dallas, it sounds like maybe your brother did what he had to do to get through, you know? Like Matt, he had some joy, by the sounds of things. But he also hurt too, is what I mean," he explained plainly, with reverence. "It doesn't mean he deserved to, and neither does Matt or Jessie. It's just that love sometimes comes with a price, and in Dale's case Jenny and the two boys and Hunter are paying it too. Love ain't easy. People can get hurt. Your brother hurt."

It wasn't like Dallas hadn't considered that. *Jesus, my brother killed himself,* he said to himself. *Of course he was in pain!* It was just that nobody had really said it out loud. Dallas had to look away from Josh and blink back a whole slew of sudden tears. It'd have to take a helluva lotta pain for a man to take his own life. *I should have been there. All these years I should have been someone Dale could talk to, instead of someone who hid behind music pretending everything in my life was magic. Damn it, I miss him. I…failed him.*

He drained the new bottle in one long succession of swallows.

"Look, Dallas," Josh said, noticing out of the corner of his eye that Kayla and Jacob were on their way over from the storage barn with more lawn chairs, "don't make this something that it isn't. Don't invent stories and try to understand what may never become clear. The world is bigger than us. The reasons why people do the things they do, make the choices they do, belong to a force bigger than us, you know? Dale and Matt are two different people, making choices that for whatever reason make, or made, sense to them. Don't punish Matt—or Jessie—for something Dale did that you may never understand."

He wiped shaky fingers over his lips. God forbid if Matt ever got to that dark place Dale had seen no choice but to go to. God forbid if he…

Jessie would never get over it. Heck, Josh doubted he or his kids would ever get over it.

"Dallas," he tried again since Dallas seemed to be struggling, "if you and Cassie decide to take Hunter, take him for the right reasons. Let go of all that anger towards your brother, and that you're slinging at yourself, and raise Hunter up right, the way he deserves to be raised, with love and compassion. The world is going to be hard enough on him, as you said earlier. Okay?"

Kayla was getting closer—her bubbly voice was almost singing, she was so happy to be here at the ranch with her much-loved husband and little girl, and with her big brother and his family.

"Okay?" Josh said again, adamantly this time, kicking a wood split in Dallas' general direction to get his attention. "And for Jesus' sake don't bury your shit in drink. That's a long and lonely dark road, my friend."

Dropping his empty bottle to the grass at his feet, where it clinked in greeting when it touched the earlier bottle, Dallas looked across the fire at Josh. "You're a better man than I am, Sawyer," he said with conviction. "The forgiveness thing's a tough row to hoe. Especially when it's yourself that needs it the most."

"One breath at a time," Josh said, and gave the fire a big poke. "One goddamned breath at a time, Dallas."

Chapter Twenty-eight

*K*ayla and Jacob showed up with lawn chairs in carry bags slung over their shoulders. Ry, thrilled at the opportunity to pick Jacob's brain since Jacob was a talented guitarist, showed up right after them with one more, and set it right next to Jacob. Before long, strips of glowing pink sunset melded into a full-on inky dark night with a canvas of twinkling stars above, and the whole gang was seated happily, for the most part, around the fire.

Once S'mores were inhaled and little kids started yawning, Jacob stood and grabbed a guitar from a hard case behind his chair. "Who's up for a tune or two?" he called to the assembly.

The kids' effusive cheer left no room for conjecture. Kayla reached behind her chair and grabbed a worn knapsack full of noisemakers—tambourines and shakers and other assorted hand instruments. Soon the place was rip-roaring with a singsong that fans of Dallas, Jacob, and Jessie would have paid top dollar to see, starting with some fun, easy bluegrass before diving into a few of the kids' favourite tunes. Once the music started, Dallas lightened up enough to join in. The songs he led the others with, on his own guitar, were top hits over his long career.

"Don't you get sick of playing those old tunes?" Evelyn asked him in her forthright manner. "Your fans likely never let you off the stage without playing them, Dallas."

Jessie snickered, she couldn't help herself. She and Jacob connected across the fire and had a good laugh. They had lots of those kinds of tunes in their combined repertoire.

A down strum on Dallas' guitar accompanied by a genuine smile was the answer Dallas gave Evelyn. His dimples were easy to spot in the soft glow of the crackling fire. Watching him, Cassie wanted to lean sideways and plant a few sweet kisses. She could tell his mood was a little better now than when she first joined the fire, despite the ongoing quick, nervous glances she noticed he kept sending in Matt's direction, and the way Matt was responding by wrapping his strong arms tighter around Hunter.

Hunter was on Matt's lap, snuggled in to the chest of the one man he felt was safe enough to trust. No smiles were forthcoming from either. Both were so silent at the fire that when everyone else was singing, they almost forgot the two were even there. Dallas rarely spoke, either. His communicating was done through song.

Matt's and Dallas' separate thoughts were like water droplets dancing on a sizzling griddle, jumbled and confused, bouncing around unable to land. Like a hawk, Jessie watched the unspoken tension travel awkwardly back and forth between them, on an invisible heated wire that seemed about ready to snap. She helped Josh navigate the S'mores with the kids, clueing in when he burned three marshmallows in succession that he was distracted and was spending most of the evening at the fire tentatively watching the interplay between Dallas and Matt too. She wondered what her husband and her country singer buddy had talked about when the two of them were alone by the fire earlier.

Jessie was pulled out of her curious reflection when Emily-Grace and Ry, with a wink and some fancy finger-picking from Jacob (Jessie rolled her eyes at him and mouthed *Show-off*), launched into a fun tune that Dallas strummed along to in a lazy kind of way. Jessie wasn't playing guitar. By the time the S'mores had gotten eaten, Micah was snuggled into her lap, snoring softly. With a grateful, loving smile, she adjusted his small body and then let her gaze drift across the fire over to Hunter and up to Matt. She realized with a start that Matt was smiling down at Hunter in the same soft loving way she'd just looked at Micah. Absently tucking a light blanket around Micah, she spied on Matt; watched him tenderly murmur to Hunter who, Jessie noticed, had a finger under Matt's T-shirt sleeve and was twisting it around and around in an adorable little-boy way. Their eyes were locked on each other. *It's trust*, Jessie thought with a start. *And love. Real, true, love.*

Next to Matt, Shanda was oblivious, caught up in the singing led by Kayla and the kids.

Oh, God, Jessie thought, glancing over to Dallas. It was obvious by the way Dallas suddenly stopped strumming that he was also conflicted by the genuine adoration he saw pass between Matt and Hunter.

Shifting her butt in the lawn chair, which made Micah protest with a moan in his sleep, Jessie went back to Matt and Hunter. Matt sensed her watching him, and looked over. Between them, sparks from the fire Josh kept regularly stoked breezed up into the air, their orange-red glows eventually snuffed out with tiny last-breath *pffftts.* The rising sparks and accompanying ashes were creating a screen of sorts between Jessie and Matt—a wall, not made of bricks and mortar, but every bit as difficult to traverse. Once in a while a slow, sluggish breeze stirred up energy and gave a huff and a blow, which forced the campfire smoke in new directions. It made Jessie's eyes water when it headed her way, or water more; truth be told, they were swimming anyway from the second she saw the tenderness pass between Matt, a man she deeply loved, and Hunter, a child she instinctively sensed Matt felt could somehow save some broken part of himself.

Surely not his marriage, she wondered, sneaking a peek at his wife. *Surely that's not what he feels he needs to save. Shanda's crazy in love with Matt.* Jessie took a scan of the lovely Shanda, with her perfect blonde Marilyn Monroe curls and slim, childless physique. Not to mention a set of luscious cherry-red lips. *Very kissable,* Josh had once teased Jessie, since he'd had to kiss Shanda many times on various sets. *She tastes like strawberries,* he'd said, and Jessie had lapsed into a sulk, wondering if Josh said it to hurt her, to add to the guilt that plagued her about Matt, or to test her, to see if she would take the bait and push Josh into revealing whether he and Shanda had ever hooked up, maybe out of revenge. As far as she knew, Shanda was faithful to Matt and Josh was faithful to her. Yet who could blame either for stepping out?

It's so damn complicated, she thought, studying Matt, watching the flames bestow a warm, mystical glow upon his face, creating shadows and mystery that surprised her, since she thought she knew him so well. *Relationships, marriage, love…children who land in the middle for no damn reason other than fate…it's all so damn complicated.*

Does Matt think he can save his marriage by adopting a child? Really? Or does he just need someone close to him that he can love full time, since Shanda is rarely around? Is he that lonely?

Matt bit a lip when he saw Jessie so closely focus in on him and Hunter. Earlier in the day he'd switched the hot cowboy boots and jeans for leather flip-flops and plaid shorts. His hair was perfectly gelled—in the old days, Jessie used to call him Spike for the little bits that he gelled straight up. These days he was wearing his hair longer, telegraphing a trendy big city vibe. He knew he looked good in a tanned and fit kind of way. It was fun to see Shanda's eyes light up when one of the Calgary security team folks dropped her off to him at the ranch earlier.

Jessie wasn't looking at him now with love and lust, though. *Well, maybe love,* Matt considered, a little put off by the compassion and sorrow she was clearly transmitting through the wall of sparks. She looked about ready to cry.

I'll show her, Matt said staunchly to himself, running his fingers through Hunter's dark hair. *I can do this. I can love this kid.*

Then he looked to Jessie's left—at Dallas.

Dallas had a guitar on his lap but he wasn't strumming it, even though his strumming hand was positioned oddly over the strings so that it was kind of floating there, forgotten. Dallas' eyes were fixed solidly on little Hunter. And in them was a kind of longing, the kind a parent has for a child.

It startled Matt to see the look. He'd convinced himself that Dallas was too lost in grief to even consider taking Hunter in. Maybe it was the geographical distance between Dallas and his father tonight that was giving him strength. Maybe it was the power of the music, the cozy campfire, the comfortable friends, the security of the isolated ranch. Hell, Matt had no clue. All he knew was that something had changed. The sheer longing in Dallas' eyes frightened him.

Matt snuggled Hunter in a little closer, and turned his face away from Jessie for the remainder of the night.

Chapter Twenty-nine

S tanding next to Josh at the kitchen counter the next morning, Jessie was drying the last few breakfast dishes Josh had washed when Dallas sauntered into the kitchen and plucked an apple out of a pottery bowl in the middle of the island. Cassie, seated at a stool her husband ended up next to, fingertips red and juicy from hulling strawberries, smiled up at him. He bent over and gifted his wife with a sweet little kiss, right smack dab on the top of her elegant blonde head.

"Good morning, beautiful," he murmured. Taking a bite of the apple, he crunched his way over to the big window bordering the kitchen and the sun porch.

Shanda, in the living room bent over emails on her laptop, watched Dallas scan the yard outside. She noticed that he stopped chewing when his eyes landed on the corral.

Outside, with his back to the house, Matt was leaning on the top rail of the corral's fence. One foot up on the bottom rail, elbows jutting out to the sides on the top rail, he was cheering on the kids, most of whom were lined up awaiting pony and horse rides that Gary and Evelyn were capably organizing. Jacob was with Matt at the fence, staying out of the way of the organized chaos, cheering from the sidelines.

Shanda stretched up for a better look at the action in the corral. She smiled. It looked like Hunter was pretty much anchored on Diego, but happy to share the pony's warm back. While Shanda looked on, both little girls under Kayla's charge—Jade and Lily—were giddily plopped on behind him by Kayla for a turn around the corral. Shanda was relieved to see Kayla start to walk alongside the popular pony and his three young riders, and even more relieved when Jacob bent and climbed through the fence to walk on the other side, one arm supporting his daughter behind Jade, who Kayla was adeptly closely guarding.

Dallas seemed pretty relaxed about it all. He was just standing by the window, absently holding his apple up in the air. Deciding he was just curious about all the cool happenings in the corral, Shanda went back to checking email.

At the island, Cassie had pinked up after her husband's show of affection. Averting her eyes from the others, she went back to her strawberries.

"None of that," Josh teased, referencing the kiss. "It makes the rest of us guys look bad."

"I'll take what I can get," Cassie returned with a smile. "There hasn't been enough of it lately. He tends to shut himself in with his first love."

Jessie hung a frying pan from a hook overhead. "Guitar?"

"Yeppers. That's the little love-stealer." Cassie pushed the overflowing bowl across the counter so Josh could take it and give the succulent strawberries a light rinse. "I suppose I should be glad he's got a place to hide."

"Music's about as safe as it comes," Josh said, recalling last night's angsty fireside chat with Dallas. "Secretly, I'm glad he's writing. I'm a big fan."

Jessie rolled her eyes. "He's a bigger fan of Dallas' music than of mine. Can you believe it? Country. Groan. My husband is a traitor." Looking beyond Cassie, she picked out Matt by the corral. Her eyes flicked to Dallas' muscled back at the big window, and she wondered why he was staring out at the action in the corral and holding his apple suspended in the air as if he'd forgotten about it.

Every pore on her skin suddenly sizzled. The way Dallas had looked so longingly at Matt and Hunter last night at the campfire was weighing on her mind and suddenly came into sharp focus. "Jesus," she cursed, and threw the dishtowel on the island.

It broke Dallas out of his reverie. Scratching at a mosquito bite by the armband tattoo just beneath his T-shirt sleeve, he turned around and wandered back over to his wife. He laid a hand on Cassie's arm.

Thrown by Jessie's quick, aggressive movement with the towel and the hard way she was staring at Dallas now, Cassie sputtered, "We were just talking about music. I was about to ask Jessie what it's like up there on stage for her. Do you sometimes forget that you're in front of an audience, Jessie? I know Dallas does. He just disappears, he says."

"I wish he'd disappear," Jessie muttered, catching Dallas' eye and locking on.

Seeing his wife's eyes narrow dangerously, Josh stomped lightly on Jessie's toes. He gave her a warning look.

Cassie caught it. "Is this about Hunter?" she treaded in softly.

In the living room, Shanda's fingers froze over the laptop keys.

Dallas took his hand away from Cassie and set his half-eaten apple on the counter. He wiped both palms on the thighs of his jeans. One hand and then the other crept up to the edge of the kitchen island. His biceps tensed, which always gave the armband tattoo a sexy vibe at his concerts, but which now only served to put Josh on high alert. Gripping tightly, Dallas exhaled and let his weight shift mostly to his hands. Staring Jessie down, who thrust a hand onto a hip in anger, he growled. "Something you want to say to me, Jessie?"

Aware that she was the focus of everyone's attention, Jessie sucked on her bottom lip and looked over at her husband.

Josh shook his head from side to side. "Not our business, Jessie," he warned, his voice low and cautious.

"The hell it isn't," Jessie declared. Grabbing the dish towel, she twisted it up and gave it a sharp crack against her thigh for courage. "Dallas," she started, "if you want Hunter, take him now. Please. Because the longer Matt has him, the harder it's gonna be for him to let go."

"Am I...that transparent?" Dallas stammered.

Shanda bristled. If anyone should be standing up for Matt, it should be her. Yet a tiny bit of relief washed over her at the thought of Dallas taking Hunter. Cassie might be second to a guitar, but Shanda was already second to a real live human, a popular superstar, in fact, that was standing just a few dozen feet away defending Shanda's husband. She had a strong feeling Hunter would put her two people behind.

Jessie pointed at Matt, outside. "If you take Hunter, that man out there will instantly understand because he is a good, honourable man who always puts others before himself. In his heart, he knows where Hunter belongs. It just kills me that he never gets what he wants." One last toss of the towel, this time so it landed right in front of Dallas, and Jessie choked, "You're gonna break his heart." A quick exit to the left saved her from breaking down in front of her guests.

Crossing her arms over her chest, Jessie went into the sun porch and leaned against the far window. Josh apologized to Dallas and Cassie and followed his wife. Landing next to her, he took up a post facing the corral and laid an understanding palm against her lower back.

In the kitchen, Dallas let go of the island and took Cassie's small fingers in his. "It's big, Cassie," he said quietly. "If we do this, we're taking on a troubled child. It won't be an easy ride."

"I'm prepared," she whispered back to him. "Dallas, I know loss. When I lost Eddie, I wanted to die too. Do you know what saved me?"

Shifting his weight from one foot to the other, Dallas waited.

"You did, baby," she said, and smiled sadly. "Hunter needs you as much as I did. As much as I do."

Closing his eyes, Dallas leaned his forehead against his wife's petite head. "We might lose Matt," he admitted. "I trust him, Cassie. With you, with the kids, with my own life. All these years, he's the best chief of security I've ever had."

"He's become a good friend to you. I see that, with him."

"He'll hate me. He picked up the pieces and held us all together, and now I'm going to screw him over."

"No," Cassie maintained, giving Dallas' hands a squeeze. "Hunter was never Matt's in the first place, Dal. He was just a soft place for Hunter to land for a little while."

"And Hunter was his, I think."

"Maybe. I suppose so. I'm truly sorry about that, but Dallas…"

"Mmmm?"

"Hunter's place is with us. Go get our little boy."

Dallas smiled. When he left Cassie's side, his eyes met Shanda's. It gave him a start. She was a beautiful woman, even with her hair back in a messy headband, and with jeans on that had holes in the knees. Her eyes were soft and misty.

Sitting back, she closed her laptop and gave Dallas a tiny—almost imperceptible—nod.

The living room window was as large as the ones in the sunporch. Standing so she could see better, Shanda watched Dallas make his way over to her husband at the corral fence.

Sensing more than hearing someone come up behind him, Matt half-turned and saw Dallas. Something about the slow way Dallas was moving, the damp sheen in his eyes, the way he was nervously picking at his lips with a thumb and forefinger and running his fingers through his long hair many times in quick succession before landing at the rail fence next to Matt, put Matt on the defensive right away.

Intuitively, Matt knew what was coming. It was just that his heart and brain refused to accept it. He braced himself.

It was a while before Dallas spoke. He could feel the eyes of everyone in the house boring holes into his back. Jessie's judging eyes were gunshots. Cassie's were the opposite. Her eyes were bright and warm, they were deep set emeralds filled with hope and longing and love for her husband and for the made-up family they were raising together. Cassie's love for Dallas gave him the strength to say what needed to be said.

Matt was staring straight ahead. Dallas doubted he could even see the kids or the horses anymore. They were likely obscured by some big cloud. Likely all he was seeing was a heavy grey mist.

There didn't seem to be much point in dragging out the inevitable. "I need to take him, Matt. Damn it all. He's my brother's kid."

After a few bitter swallows and a lowered nod later, Matt muttered, "A'right." The mist Dallas suspected he was seeing grew dark and ominous.

Dallas thudded a palm on the rail as if now everything was settled and therefore perfect. "Good, then," he said in an inward breath so that the words came out thin and muffled and damp. "Come back up to J.I. for a few days, okay? I think that'd make it easier for, uh, for Hunter."

Striding away backwards, Dallas gave Matt a hard clap on the shoulder before flipping around and heading over to the corral gate. Swinging it open, he went in and stood alone between Matt at the fence and the happy gathering of kids, adults, and horses inside. His shoulders lowered with one great exhale, and he smiled at the little boy that was about to become his son.

Inside the house, Josh gave Jessie's back a little rub. "It's the right thing to do, Jess."

"I know. Just rip off the Band-Aid and get 'er done, right?" Jessie's next few inhales were juddery and rough. Touching Josh's hand lightly, she spun to the left and headed for the living room.

The screen door slammed. Big Dan came in. The tension in the house was thick as mud. Sensing it, he stopped not far from Shanda, whose gaze was on her husband's back, and he hovered uncertainly.

Jessie passed him on her way from the sun porch. "You up for a run, Dan? Cause I sure as hell could use one."

"Any time, Jessie," he answered, surprised that she asked him since Matt was around, and Matt was usually her first choice for a running partner.

"Gimme five," she managed, and went into her bedroom behind the kitchen. Closing the door, she leaned back against it and allowed herself the liberty of a few strangled sobs before pulling on shorts and a running tank and joining Dan for a vigorous run.

Josh was watching Shanda. "I'm sorry," he said.

With a sad smile, she moved from where she was standing by the couch and whispered a quiet, "Thank you," as she passed by him. Pushing open the screen door, she grabbed it before it could slam, and eased it closed. Coming up behind Matt, she headed for a post at the rail on the opposite side of where Dallas had stood.

Matt was in that awkward place where he was aware that he was the object of everyone's pity, but he didn't want to move because it would draw more attention to himself. Besides, he was struggling to keep it together. *So stupid*, he was saying inwardly, over and over. *I'm so stupid. A failure. I can't keep anyone I love in my life.*

When Shanda sauntered up next to him, all perky and blonde and serious and sweet, he was relieved that it was her and not Jessie. Jessie would have pulled him into her arms to offer comfort, and because her arms always felt the safest, all of his broken bits would have landed at her feet in large, wet puddles. Which was absolutely not the kind of public display of his failure to love that he wanted right now.

Despite being married, he and Shanda spent most of their time apart. Which relegated Shanda to the 'good friend' club more often than the 'intimate partner' club. Now, she kept a little bit of distance between them. And so did he.

Still, her presence was a comfort. Matt was useless at hiding the gulping, choking sobs he wanted so badly to bury. He made sure to stare straight ahead, to try to keep Shanda from seeing just how badly this hurt.

She understood anyway, and told him so in two simple, succinct words. "I know." It almost broke her to see her strong man so emotional. Bending so that she could lay her chin on his jutted-out elbow, followed by a turn of her head to lay her cheek against his hand, she murmured, "Jessie says you never get what you want."

It was revelatory, to hear that from Shanda. It sounded wistful, coming from her. Beneath her, almost, to admit that although she, Shanda, belonged to him by virtue of the bonds of marriage, she knew in her heart that she did not belong to his soul.

Not the way Jessie did. No one ever could.

He tried to make her feel better, and somehow it eased his own pain as well. "Sometimes I do," he said softly, his pale grey eyes floating and more earnest than Shanda had ever seen them. Laying the left side of his face on his forearm on the fence, he forced out a small smile.

"I'm glad," she said, and closed the distance between them with one small step so she could steal a soft, tender kiss.

Chapter Thirty

Jessie and Dan jogged back to the low ranch house just as a big grey cloud overhead cracked open and started to pelt rain down upon the people below. It was a warm day overall so she and Dan didn't care about getting wet, but apparently everyone else did, because the whole kit 'n caboodle were inside looking for things to do.

Emily-Grace and Ry were head to head in one corner, she cross-legged with a guitar in her arms, and him lying on his belly. Ry had a notebook sprawled open in front of him and a pen in his hand; a pen that right now was stuck in his mouth being heartlessly chewed.

The little girls were colouring at the coffee table, being quite capably annoyed by the little boys, or by most of them, anyway. Hunter, not used to the commotion and hopelessly cowed by it, was off in the far corner by the door to the new wing, scrunched up in a ball, a silent observer.

Most of the adults were gathered around the kitchen island rustling up mid-morning coffee and tea. A scrumptious aroma floated through the house—new freshly made cinnamon buns, bursting with goodness, made with pride from an old biscuit recipe Evelyn had garnered from her ninety-six-year-old grandmother, that the grandmother had inherited from *her* mother. Evelyn was just pulling a tray bursting with the soft, golden buns out of the oven.

Looking around for Matt, Jessie's shoulders sank when she didn't see him. Josh wandered over and followed her to the bedroom, closing the door behind him as she started to strip off her wet, sweaty clothes for a shower. "Matt and Shanda went for a drive," he said.

"Oh. Okay. Good, I guess." Stepping out of her shorts, Jessie let them fall to the floor.

Josh smiled. "Too bad our house is full of people at the moment."

She gave him a crooked 'screw-you' grin. "That's all your gender ever thinks about, isn't it?"

"Twenty-four seven," he laughed. Sobering, he added, "Dallas and Cassie are all packed up, Jessie. They're just having a cup of coffee before they hit the road."

"Oh. Oh!" Off came the running tank and then the sticky sports bra, slowly and with a grimace. "Are they leaving without giving Matt a chance to say goodbye to Hunter?"

"Unless Matt gets back before they go." Josh sighed, and picked up his wife's damp clothing. He dropped them into the laundry hamper in the corner. "Maybe that's the point," he suggested carefully, before focusing his intent liquid brown eyes back on her pale baby blues. "No drama."

"Good luck with that," Jessie growled. "Did you see Hunter out there amongst the chaos? He's hiding in a corner. The only person likely capable of urging him out of it is Matt. It sure as hell ain't likely to be Dallas."

"Cassie's gained his trust. Hunter will go with her, and with Ry."

"I like how you didn't add Jade in there."

"I think Hunter's scared of her."

"Aren't we all? She's a busy one."

Striding towards the bathroom, Jessie asked Josh to pour her a coffee and save her one of Evelyn's famous cinnamon buns. "I'll just be a few minutes," she said, before slipping under the soothing, refreshing water.

Ten minutes later, Josh was starting to wonder where his wife had disappeared to. Giving himself a little push away from the counter he was leaning against, he moved out into the living room to eyeball their bedroom door. It was open.

He took a good, long look around the living room. The kids were all happily engaged; some were now in their parents' arms munching on the cinnamon buns and lapping up glasses of homemade lemonade. Hunter wasn't there; Hunter was...

"Ah," thought Josh, spying Jessie in the corner with Hunter. "Figures." He took up a post against the far wall, and watched.

Jessie had wandered over to Hunter when she left the bedroom after her shower. A child as lonely as he was called to her, spoke to the inner child inside of herself, the one instantly decimated upon her father's sudden death when she was twelve. The one that squeaked out of existence entirely when her stepfather molested her. Now, she was sitting on her haunches, cross-legged, four feet away from Hunter. Across from the solemn, quiet boy, whose eyes were now buried in hers. The other adults had given up trying to reach him. Hunter was adept at pushing them away, with sad little mewls or with flailing arms and legs. The only adult he wanted, and trusted, was Matt, and Matt was nowhere in sight. In Hunter's mind, Matt had abandoned him. Hunter kept looking for him, kept wringing his fingers and wishing he would appear.

Jessie guessed that on the first try. Which was why Hunter was silently appealing to her now.

As Josh watched, and then the other adults too as they slowly clued in to what was happening, Jessie inched closer to Hunter. Shortly, she was seated next to him, her back against the wall and her knees drawn up to her chest, arms wrapped around them.

She didn't have to say a word. The pain in Hunter's eyes was reflected in hers. She was someone Hunter knew Matt cared about. Within minutes, Hunter scrunched his small body up next to her, and wrapped his arms around hers. Laying his head against her shoulder, he closed his eyes and let out a long, deep sigh.

Jessie turned her head away from her friends' stares. Some pain was meant to be kept private. She raked her fingers gently through Hunter's black hair, and sang him a song her children cherished and begged her to sing every night at bedtime.

Eventually, the others went back to their coffee. All except Dallas, that is, who stood transfixed.

"Just sing to him," Cassie whispered to Dallas when he confessed, by the big truck they'd borrowed from Johnny for the drive, that he was afraid Hunter would throw a fit and not get in the car seat they'd borrowed from Josh and Jessie, an old one Dylan had outgrown.

"I'm not soft like her," Dallas said, tossing a bag of cinnamon rolls into the glove compartment. "Jessie has this tender side that little kids get. Probably because she's a bit like a little kid herself. You try singing to him."

"He'll be fine. Let's go get the kids moving and load them in."

A vehicle was inching its way up the driveway, its tires making small swooshes in the new puddles as it passed through them. The drying raindrops on the car's windshield became miniature rainbows as the bright sun peeked out from behind passing clouds and lit them with a prism'd grace.

Dallas shut the truck's passenger side door just as Matt swung the rented SUV into the clearing and braked to a stop in front of the barn.

"Well, that's that," Dallas grumbled. "Now we'll never get Hunter near the truck."

He was wrong. Ry was the secret force that at least got Hunter close to the truck. He did it with music, deftly bringing Dallas into the equation by using one of Dallas' songs, the favourite that Hunter had once sung along to because he knew it, because his father had played Dallas' CDs over and over, according to Boone and Doris. Ry blue-toothed his iPhone and played the song in the truck, cranking up the volume so that Hunter wouldn't mistake it.

Still, Hunter hesitated by the truck's door and wouldn't let Ry lift him up. Dallas wanted to try but he was too afraid of losing face in front of Matt, who was watching from the safety of the SUV. Seeing Matt hiding in the shadow of the barn aching to say goodbye to Hunter without everyone watching, Cassie took Dallas by the hand and led him inside the house to say 'so long' to Evelyn and Gary and the others, who all discreetly gave them hugs and made promises of future get-togethers at a better time.

Outside, Matt strolled over to Hunter and crouched down in front of him while Ry and Shanda—and Jessie, at the screen door—looked on, expressions serious and hopeful that this would not be too traumatic of a break for the hurting man and lonesome child in their midst.

"I'll be along in a day or so," Matt told Hunter. "In the meantime, let Ry here be your buddy, okay? Ry will help you."

"I want to stay wif you." The boy-sized hands started their wringing again.

"I wish you could," Matt said, taking both small sets of fingers in his so he could stop their anxious movements. "I would like you to stay but this is the thing, Hunter. You're gonna be a part of Ry and Jade's family."

"Stay wif you."

"I'll see you in a few days. I swear."

In the end it was Matt who lifted Hunter into the car seat, which was one of the hardest things Matt ever had to do in his entire life.

Hunter was too tired to fight. It worried Matt to know that; he'd seen that look of sheer mental exhaustion and defeat on Jessie's face many times. There were tears, though, on Hunter's pale cheeks, and that meant something, Matt decided. It meant he was thawing out. He was relieved to see Ry take the little guy's hand in his, and start to sing.

Cassie gave Matt's hand a squeeze before she climbed up into the truck. She didn't say a word, and neither did he, although he closed her door gently behind her when she was comfortably seated.

He turned to Dallas, who stood with his hands on his hips and faced him, a piece of Timothy grass between his lips, plucked from the country flower garden behind the campfire pit.

"He's been wetting the bad, Dal," Matt said, already feeling this sudden strain in their friendship pulling at his heart. "Go easy on him."

"Are you coming up?" Dallas asked a little too quickly. He raised a hand and twisted the timothy grass between his lips. His eyes were pensive. Guarded.

"Not right away," Matt answered. "Calgary's got your security under control."

"Uh huh." Dallas didn't move.

It was just the two of them now. Cassie's window was shut, and Shanda was with Jessie at the screen door.

Dallas thrust out a white flag. "There will always be room for you in our family, Matt."

The gentleman in Matt responded, "I appreciate that."

One solid handshake from Dallas' end secured the invitation. "I'll see you," he said, stepping forward to round the truck and hop in. The door slammed with a final nail in Matt's good, kind heart.

Jessie stepped up behind him and wrapped her arms around his waist.

"I guess that's that," Matt said, letting her hold him together.

Dallas put the big truck in gear, and drove little Hunter away.

Chapter Thirty-one

*I*t wasn't until late morning three days later when Matt finally landed back at J.I. to check in with Dallas' family.

Shanda rode shotgun on the way up, curling adorably up into a ball to sleep while Matt piloted the big SUV on the narrow gravel mountain road that would deliver them to the ranch. During the drive, Matt found himself wanting to pull over to watch her sleep. Over the last few days he'd decided that distance between he and Shanda was the biggest threat to their marriage, and not Jessie, who had floated through his heart during so many lonely nights over the past few years.

The Sawyer home was a joyful place these days, which hadn't always been the case. Living in that kind of light healed a lot of Matt's old hurts and soothed the loss of Hunter, especially last night when Micah climbed into Matt's lap, stuck a thumb in his mouth, and drifted off to dream about teddy bears and lion cubs. Micah's warm body was a reminder that Matt would always belong to a family, albeit not in the traditional sense. Micah was named in honour of Matt's grandfather. He was the closest to a son Matt now accepted he would likely ever have, and he was Jessie's child. Something about that was divine and beautiful—Matt just had to remember to see it that way.

Glass half full, he'd whispered to himself while running his fingers through Micah's soft little boy hair, which Micah wore longish like his father, and like his older brother, David.

Jessie had wandered into the room from the kitchen, sat her bum down on the arm of the couch Matt was lounging on at the time, and laid her hand over Matt's.

The smile in her eyes was all love and concern for her old friend and occasional lover. *Micah knows you're hurting,* she told Matt. *He knows you need him.*

Matt and Micah had a special connection, partly due to Matt's steady presence in Micah's life during the little guy's first few months of life. What they rarely had these days was coveted quiet time together. That hour last night with Micah in his arms, filling the hole left by Hunter, was sheer bliss.

Matt shifted his memory to this morning, to the wistful look in Jessie's eyes when she said goodbye. Tightening his hands on the wheel, Matt stiffened and shifted his butt in the seat. *Wistful contentment.* It was like wistful contentment—contentment with her life the way she was living it now, Matt supposed, mixed with a healthy dose of longing and love for him. No longer did he spy the old pain, the old anger and confusion over his hard choice to bring her back to Josh—to her husband, whom Matt knew she would always love with the same desperation Matt loved her—a few years earlier.

"I'm already missing you," she'd whispered in his ear when she hugged him, her breath warm on his skin, her fingers gently rubbing the back of his neck, her eyelashes like butterflies fluttering against his ear and sending shockwaves of desire catapulting through his body.

He didn't want to let go. Ever.

It wasn't a lie, her telling him that she would miss him. Matt knew she would; they both suffered through soul crushing agony every time they parted, because of the heartrending pull towards each other that Matt could only compare to being inside an elastic band. They were at opposite ends, so it felt like when they were physically separated, the band stretched, sometimes so far that Matt was scared it would tear at its farthest reach. The pull was less acute for Jessie than for Matt these days. Once upon a time it was the other way around, and it left her angry at him for a long time. The repercussions of the day Matt walked away from her still hovered. Still hurt.

Some of those lasting effects were good ones—these last few days were proof of that. Jessie and Josh were good, they were always touching each other and whispering little secrets in each other's ears, sharing special smiles that Matt enviously thought would likely play out in their bedroom later. Their children were happy, the younger two spending the long summer days

following Gary or their father around the ranch in search of all of its mysteries—kittens, herbs in the garden, the welcome soft nose of Diego the pony.

The older two were close—their free time was mostly spent huddled in a
corner working on songs they'd started writing with Ry during his visit, and
texting Ry, and sending him video clips. Sometimes, Matt was secretly tickled to watch Jessie and Emily-Grace bake together—cookies, cinnamon rolls,
or more creative delectables Emily-Grace found online and wanted to try.
She was going through a phase of microwaving desserts in mugs, like apple
crumble, which Matt and Josh gamely scarfed down, to Emily-Grace's delight.
Sometimes David joined his mother and sister, he loved to cook and bake; other
times he traipsed off after his father to do some work around the ranch—simple
jobs like painting or firming up the fence around the corral. Yesterday morning when Matt and Jessie got back from a run, they'd found David and Josh,
along with Emily-Grace, hunkered up on low wooden stools by Josh's Harley.

Hey, they asked, Josh told Jessie, who stood at the open door of the storage garage with her legs apart and arms crossed. *They told me it's research
for a song.*

Learning how a Harley runs is research?

Now, navigating a slow turn on the dusty road, Matt smiled, recalling
Jessie's worried pout at the time.

Josh had just shrugged.

Emily-Grace piped up—*Momma, if you want the song to have depth, you
need to dive deep into its layers.*

Superstar Jessie Wheeler's daughter, a pre-teen, telling her mother that
songs need layers? *Jessie doesn't need to go looking for layers,* Matt thought.
She's lived them. As is Dallas now, he considered, slowing to take the vehicle
over a pronged cattle gate in the road. The SUV bumped lightly along. Dallas'
newly accumulated layers were like the rock formations Matt spied along the
road, up the steadily climbing sides of the near distant, sloping mountains.

Just don't get any crazy ideas about riding that thing. That's what Jessie'd
said yesterday to her kids, by Josh's beloved big bike.

Matt said it again now, in his head, jolting upright at the sudden pain that
almost choked him with worry at the memory of hearing Jessie say it. He
remembered seeing the same fear crisscross Jessie's eyes then. It showed itself

too in the way she tightened her arms across her chest, and in the way she swallowed back fear of a new, unspeakable horror. She and Josh had shared a look of worry and dread, that they quickly guarded and hid from their children. It was replaced by a bond of strength, a unity that went deeper than any layers Emily-Grace could ever possibly discover for her songwriting. Whatever new typhoons life chose to flood them with in the future, Josh and Jessie would wade through together.

On the road now, Matt's fingers loosened on the wheel. The corners of his lips turned up, just slightly, accompanied by a tiny twinkle in his eyes. Gratitude. He was glad Jessie was happy, was grateful that Josh was staying clean and that the old terrors that stalked them were done and gone. For them, and for their children, and for Charles and Dee and for all of their friends, for their fans, for everyone who wanted nothing more than to see joy in Josh and Jessie's eyes, Matt was thankful.

Depressing the gas, Matt picked up speed as the road in front of him straightened. At his side, Shanda stirred, so he peeked over at her, lifted one hand off of the wheel, and laid it over her arm, which was warm from the sun and the heat of the day. They were driving without air conditioning, leaving the windows open about halfway for this slower, relaxed part of their drive. The breeze was welcome, a bridge between an insulated modern life and the gifts of nature.

Somewhere up ahead, life was gonna get tough again. Determined, Matt decided that if he was going to go through any more crazy shit in this humble lifetime, he didn't want to go through it alone.

"I'm glad you're here," he murmured to Shanda, and was surprised when she responded.

"Me too." Her words were slow and thick, dulled with the need to sleep, but they were sincere.

Bending to brush his lips against his wife's forehead, Matt smiled, and drove on.

At J.I., they found the extended family coping with Hunter in their midst as best they could. Doris and Boone were not heartless; it helped that Hunter's love for horses drew the still stiff and sore Boone naturally to his side. Doris' love for her lost son brought a need to her soul—a need to study Hunter, to look for physical similarities at first, in his eyes, in the way he walked with a gentle gait, and then in the serious way he sat back and contemplated what was going on around him or focused his dark eyes on the clouds passing overhead, or on the tops of the trees when the wind whistled through them.

Jenny wasn't around. Her kids weren't around. *That is not a surprise*, Matt thought, thinking about the night Dallas lost it and he, Matt, scooped Hunter and Ry up for the drive to Josh and Jessie's place. He didn't ask about Dale's widow. Dawn and Doris talked openly about Jenny, and Matt was quick to learn that they had plans to bring her and the two boys back into the fold when Jenny seemed ready.

Dawn and Johnny were busy busy busy with the day-to-day operations of the ranch, Johnny in the barn and doing general maintenance, and Dawn with the cleaning, and helping with the cooking and baking. Their three youngsters trotted alongside where possible, and took off when they could, glad to have Hunter and Ry back for company so they could go looking for stone treasures in the riverbed or invent role-playing games they could play around the hay. Jade wasn't quite so welcome, with her high-pitched screams and occasional temper tantrums, but she won them over with her cute ways when she was rested and happy, and so her presence eventually evened out.

Cassie and her three charges had settled back in, although Cassie told Matt on his first day back that it likely wouldn't be for too long. Dallas was yanging for work, bugging Phil to get him back on the summer festival circuit.

"Not that he told me," she said wryly to Matt an hour or so after he and Shanda arrived. "I overheard him on the phone, talking to Phil." She went back to kneading bread dough in the small bungalow's kitchen, stopping to brush a dusting of flour off of Jade's rosy cheek as Matt watched and munched on an apple beside her.

Making a mental note to give Phil a call later to see whether he planned to move ahead with rescheduling Dallas into the shows, Matt summoned up some courage and asked, "How're things with Hunter?" He stared at the apple while waiting for a response, surprised that his usually affirmative voice had come out squeaky and uncertain.

If she noticed, at least Cassie had the compassion not to flinch. "Hunter himself, or Dallas with Hunter? Which?"

"Both." Twisting the apple around as if he were scanning for worm holes, Matt tilted his head to listen.

"Hunter latched onto Ry. Ry's a saint with him—very patient, which I think is easy for Ry because Hunter barely speaks. Ry tucks him in, gets him dressed, sings him songs, keeps him company. The songs calm Hunter; the music seems to be very soothing to him. Dallas says Dale didn't take up guitar, so we figure there was likely always a radio or music on in Hunter's environment somewhere. Unless Maria played, but it's definitely Dallas' music that Hunter reacts to mostly." She paused in her kneading, and stared at her daughter's small fingers, buried in the dough. "Sometimes Hunter cries. Silently," she added, glancing over at Matt, whose gut twisted at the memory of Jessie doing the same during the hard times. "Just tears. No sounds."

"Does he still wet the bed?"

"Every night, Matt." Sighing, Cassie pulled a small chunk of bread dough out of Jade's fingers, since it was on its way to the little girl's tiny pink mouth. "It's okay, we're dealing with it. And by that I mean Ry and me are dealing with it. Dallas just…well, you know Dallas. He's not really the hard core parent type."

Which pissed Matt off to hear. With a grunt, he took a big bite of his apple and left Cassie humming, with Jade at her side helping to knead the dough. He'd only had a cursory chat with security when he arrived. So, grumbling, he went looking for the young guy stationed by the road. Matt was relieved to discover that things were settling down at the ranch in terms of curious fans on the prowl for a glimpse of their favourite country singer.

Afterwards, on his way up to the small camp store where Shanda had earlier told him she was going in search of souvenir postcards to send to some acting buddies, he ran into Dallas. They did an awkward dance when Matt lowered his head and went around him. Dallas stood back and watched him go.

Three days later, Matt drove Shanda to the airport in Calgary. He let her go with promises to fly down to her shoot that weekend for an extended visit before he flew back to Vancouver to check in with Charles. The whole drive back he'd thought about his calls with Phil over the last few days. It made Matt even more pissed at Dallas to know that he was already ready to run, to hide back out on the road behind his music.

"With his family, or without?" Matt had asked Phil politely.

"Without," Phil told him.

Picturing Cassie's reaction to that, Matt had sucked in a breath.

Phil's explanation eased Matt's mind a little, but not nearly enough. "Dallas says the boys want to be near the horses, and that Cassie's tired of life on the road with a three year old. And," Phil added, "now there's this new child to consider…" He drifted off.

Matt could hear, on the other end of the phone, one of Dallas' recent hit singles playing, a song about mothers and daughters that rocketed up the charts practically before it was even released. He kneaded his forehead and paced back and forth—at the time, he was standing on the edge of the river-bank. Dallas needed a good kick in the head, as far as Matt was concerned. In the singer's heart, Dallas seemed to know he needed to take Hunter in, or at least on a soul level he knew that. Or maybe it was just Dallas' guilty conscience that spoke to him, that made him take Hunter.

It would be easy to leave the tough stuff to Cassie and Ry, and to the extended White family. Where would this kind of distancing behaviour leave Hunter as he grew older? In the boy's uncertain teen years, for instance? And where, Matt wondered with a groan, would it leave Dallas and Cassie? In his experience, distance in a marriage spelled only one thing—doom. *Hell, I'm still trying to make it work,* Matt thought, thinking of the usual geographical chasm between him and Shanda.

He'd decided then and there to consider telling Phil to find someone else to run Dallas' security for the upcoming shows, if they happened. And maybe for the rest of Dallas' shows, too, and for Dallas' family's security. Hell, it hurt too much to be around Hunter anyway, at least for the time being. It was a mistake getting too close to Dallas, becoming friends with him. Matt should have remained aloof and distant. He'd made the same damn mistake with Jessie and Josh. Caring too much for the people he watched over just left him hurt.

Now it was time for Matt to leave as well. He had avoided Dallas the whole final stay at J.I. Hunter was tougher to avoid but Matt had made a point of, at least for the most part, keeping his distance from the child so Hunter would bond with the family that would, for better or for worse, be his caregivers. *I've got to give Dallas a chance*, Matt had figured the first day back.

Now it was clear that Dallas was dropping the ball. Cassie seemed patient about it. At least around the others she was putting on a good face.

Matt wasn't that patient. He was pissed. In silence, he seethed.

He swept Hunter up in his arms before he planned to climb into his SUV to drive away from J.I., away from the grieving, healing family Matt had come to respect and cherish.

"You be good," he choked into Hunter's coarse black hair. "You remember Jessie, at the other ranch where Micah and Dylan live? She says music helps her, and I see that it helps you too. Stick around Ry, and when you're bigger maybe you can learn to play guitar too, little guy."

He set Hunter down and crouched to peer into his eyes. Matt's own eyes were so moist he could barely see. Losing this child once was hard enough. Time number two was excruciating. "You'll always be in my heart, Hunter," he managed. "You're the strongest kid I know."

Hunter pointed to his chest, which he puffed up proudly. At the same time, his small lips curved downwards. "I go wif you," he said, in an echo of the scene at Josh and Jessie's ranch.

"Can't." *I can't stand this. Too many goodbyes in my life…*

A foot stomp on the hard-baked earth preceded Hunter's repeated words, "I go wif you."

A long inhale calmed Matt's frazzled nerves enough to grant him a voice, even though it was soaked and came out coarse. "I'm sorry, Hunter. Ry and Jade need you to stay here and keep them company. Besides, I don't have horses. You need horses in your life, and I'm pretty sure they need you too." The last part hurt to say because Matt had no clue what Dallas' plans were. Dallas' main household was in Toronto. The family also spent time in Halifax at Cassie's heritage home, and in the summer months when they could sneak away, it was usually to a summer home in beautiful Darnley, Prince Edward Island, with its gorgeous sunsets and pristine white sand beaches. None of those places had horses.

In the end, fists clenched at his sides and his mouth set in a firm, straight line, Matt had to turn and stride away from Hunter. He couldn't bear to look back. Good thing, too, because it would have torn a whole new jagged hole in his heart to see the four year old struggling to stay composed in front of a group of people that, to him, still felt like strangers.

At his SUV, Matt leaned against the door, arms raised, nose pressed to the window, his body shaking. It was another sweltering summer day. He was dressed for the city, not for the ranch, and his black dress pants and white button down shirt just felt wrong out here under the big sky. Sweat dripped into his eyes and rolled down his cheeks, or was that dampness he was feeling just brand new tears, echoing his frustration and this new deep-seated loneliness Matt was having a damn hard time shaking off?

"Fuck!" he cursed, slamming a palm against the window before whipping around to lean back against the SUV to take a final look at the rustic, beat down place he'd grown to love.

Something was in his way. Someone…

When Matt's vision cleared and his stomach stopped heaving, his pale, angry, hurt eyes landed on Dallas.

Dallas was there, thumbs poked into the pockets of faded jeans that had holes in the knees and strategically faded thighs. A tight-fitting light green T-shirt from one of his shows was loosely tucked into the jeans just beyond a wide leather belt with a bright silver buckle. As Matt watched, Dallas lifted a brown cowboy hat he was wearing to keep his long blond hair out of his eyes. He swept the hair back, and replaced the hat at a jaunty angle that partly hid his eyes. Shuffling his dusty brown boots so that his weight was on his right leg, he raised his chin and arrogantly faced the man responsible for his life, and for the lives of his family.

"What the hell's your problem?" He shifted his weight to the other foot and stuck the thumb of the hand that had moved the hat back into the pocket of his jeans. His heart was pounding so hard it felt like it might leap right out of his chest. Matt was the one real friend he'd ever had, not counting the brother Dallas grew up with. And Matt was about to climb into his car and motor off down the narrow mountain road, leaving nothing in his wake but dust and heartache. "You really gonna leave things between us like this?"

Shoving his body away from the hot black vehicle, Matt settled across from Dallas, planted his feet securely apart, and pulled at the chest of his shirt—the heat was making the expensive fabric stick to him. He stuck a hand in his pants pocket, nervously rubbed a forefinger back and forth under his nose, and waited, eyes locked on Dallas.

"Look," Dallas said, "I get that you're angry about Hunter. I'm real sorry about that, but…" His shoulders moved up and down in what Matt perceived as a half-assed shrug. "The kid belongs here."

Digesting that, Matt had to work to keep his blood pressure from shooting up so high that he was afraid he'd lose his shit altogether. The family wasn't close by, but they'd hear him yell, and he didn't want a public breakdown to be their last impression of him.

Raking fingers through his hair, unable to stand completely still, he fired his first bullet. "You know what your problem is, Dallas?"

"No," Dallas snapped, "but I have a feeling you're gonna tell me."

"You're damn right I am." Taking a step towards his friend, Matt struggled to keep his voice even. It came out brusque and trembling anyway. "The only thing you really open up to is your music. Cassie had a shot with you but I see the cracks, Dallas. They're getting wider. Jade will grow up one of those kids desperate for her father's attention because you keep pushing her back to Cassie when she comes to you, and Ry is pretty capable on the guitar now so you're leaving him more and more to figure things out on his own and he's confused as hell. Hunter's going to bail when he's fifteen or sixteen in search of his mother's roots in the city because you aren't capable of letting down your walls enough to let him in. He'll end up addicted to crystal meth or whatever the hell despicable, evil drug will be around to lure the broken kids in by then, and he'll die alone in some dark alley."

"Jesus, is that what you think of me? That's the kind of father you think I'll end up being?"

"No, Dal. That's the kind of father I think you already are. Your kids are just too young to mirror you back to yourself just yet."

"Look who's talking, the father of the year!"

Circling around, Matt took six vigorous, angry strides before he faced Dallas again. "I don't need my mistakes rubbed into open wounds, Dallas. I do that well enough on my own."

"Fine, you already screwed up. Your fuck-ups don't give you the right to make assumptions about me as a father."

"So prove me wrong. Show me, the big screw-up, how it's supposed to be done. Go on, I dare you. Call Phil before he books those shows for you, and start helping Cassie with the kids. All of them, in case there's any confusion as to exactly which kids I'm talking about."

Dallas got quiet. Under the brim of his hat his eyes were in shadow, lending mystery to what he might be thinking.

Matt decided he'd had enough drama, enough self-story guesswork as to why Dallas made the choices he did, about why he was creating distance between himself and the people who needed him. Tossing a metaphorical hat in the ring, Matt flipped around and reached for the SUV's handle.

Dallas' voice chased him. It emerged high, and sounded strange. Freezing, his hand stiff and cumbersome on the handle, Matt took in what Dallas said.

"I don't know how. I don't know how to be that kind of man, Matt."

Matt let his hand fall from the handle. He stared at it, let it dangle uselessly before he caught Dallas' reflection in the car window and turned back around.

Encouraged, embarrassed, Dallas tried to find the words to help make his buddy understand how hard this was, how hard all of it was. "Look, I know I bailed, Matt. All those years ago, I mean. I bailed on the family I grew up in. I bailed on Dale, but most importantly I bailed on myself." His voice got quiet, so quiet that Matt had to bend an ear to listen. "I missed so much chasing dreams, didn't I? And so did you…and they weren't even your dreams."

"Yeah. They were. They just weren't the same kind of dreams."

"Jessie, huh? Practically your whole adult life has been sacrificed for her, to keeping her safe." Deciding he was stepping on thin ice when Matt seemed to grow distant by ducking his head and staring at his feet, Dallas circled back around. "I don't think Jessie ever chased dreams, did she? This life— fame, stardom—it just landed in her lap. She didn't choose it. It chose her."

Taking in a long, slow breath, Matt looked back up and said, "It took her a long time to stop fighting it, if you want the truth. She's got it figured out now. She and Josh found a balance that works for them."

"I don't think it was ever about balance for me, Matt, not before Cassie and Ry, at least." Diving in, Dallas toed a hole in the dirt as the memories came tumbling back. "The scales were always tipped so far in one direction that there was no jumping off or the whole thing would have crashed. Once the pendulum started swinging, there was no middle ground and there sure as hell was no going back." Waving an arm back at the bungalow behind him, he caught Matt's somber eye. "I called my mother once a month, I saw my family once in a blue moon at a show, or I popped in if I was in the area, that was all. Why in God's name did I ever think that was enough? All I have now is years of wasted time."

"I don't think your fans would think it was wasted time, Dallas."

"Damn it, Matt." Desperate to make Matt understand, Dallas took a sideways, unbalanced step, and wiped sweaty palms up and down his thighs. "I'll never see my brother again. I'll never be able to ask what happened that changed him. Or why he lied for so many years, to Jenny, or to our mom and dad." Facing Matt again he said, "I'm so goddamned disconnected from the people that matter, even from Cassie, who just smiles and pretends that everything's okay even though I know inside she's lonely as hell. I don't know how to fix it. All I know is music, recording, being on tour."

"So do something about it. Don't let it continue."

"How? I can't stand myself. I'm here, but I'm not here. Since high school it's been this way with my parents, and then with Dawn and Dale and their families. With Dale doing what he did, it's gotten worse. I see it starting to happen with Cassie too. I smile, I talk, I laugh, but it doesn't feel like me. It's like I'm in a bubble, separate from everyone else. I deserve this disconnection, Matt. I bailed, so I got punished by not really knowing them anymore. And you," he paused and took in a breath, "I needed you to carry the ball for me and then what did I do? I screwed you over and now I'm losing you too." He paused, letting his next words take their time and emerge quietly. "Aren't I, Matt?"

Matt wanted to breathe but his lungs wouldn't cooperate. *I'm drowning,* he whispered to himself. Going to see Shanda on set suddenly felt like such a sham. It was like Dallas just told it all like it was, like the way Matt himself had existed since finally acting on his feelings for Jessie when they were in Brussels so long ago, the night he first kissed her. *Shocked her,* he remembered, his eyes tearing up at the soaring, yet agonizing, memory.

He wondered if everyone in the whole entire world felt the same way—ultimately apart and alone.

"My brother," Dallas was saying when Matt's ears stopped ringing and he tuned back in, "my own brother, the guy who watched over me and protected me when I was a kid, killed himself, Matt." Dallas' voice got weird again, all high-pitched and thin. "I wasn't there to protect him. So he decided..." Gulping between words, Dallas managed to get out the hardest thing he had to reconcile with himself about being the brother that bailed. "He decided...that being dead was better than being alive. My brother took his own life. Why, Matt? Why would he want that? Why would Dale rather be dead?"

Disconnection, Matt thought. *That's why.* The truth slayed him but he kept it together for Dallas' sake. Out loud he said, "We're not always meant to know the reasons, Dallas. Only Dale knows why."

Dallas threw his arms up into the air. "Well, I don't know how to do it right. I don't know how to be here for the people I love so it never happens again."

"Let your walls down, Dallas. Let them in. That's how." *Can I do the same? I don't know if I can do the same.* Matt had to turn his head away and swallow back years of ache that were quickly catching up to him, suffocating him.

"I worry about you," Dallas said, clueing in. "You're not happy. You're living a shadow life, Matt, you're every bit as much an imposter as Dale was. You'll never have what you really, truly want; you'll never be truly happy. How do I know you won't—"

"I suppose you don't," Matt cut in. Stubbornly, he put his hands on his hips and frowned hard at Dallas. Despite his own personal struggles, he needed to throw his friend a bone. "Look, Dal, I learned a long time ago that living in fear for others' safety only churns up endless anxiety. I can assure you, however, that I can't imagine being anywhere where Jessie isn't, meaning I don't want to exist in a different dimension than she's in, so I won't go there, okay? I won't—do what Dale did. I promise you."

Forcing back the harrowing truth bumps slowly crawling up his spine, Dallas nodded. He wanted to reach out and pull his good friend close, or drop to his knees and sob out a bunch of thank yous. Instead, partly to preserve his dignity and to keep from falling completely apart, he took another tack and went to another arena that terrified him. "And what if Maria shows up? What if she comes back for Hunter? How do you get close to people when you know how much it will hurt to lose them?"

"Back to Jessie again, are we?"

Matt's sarcasm raised Dallas' courage a bit farther. He forced a weak half-smile.

"You take what you can get," Matt answered softly. "You take the precious moments when they come. You live in the present."

"Staring at her from across a campfire once in a blue moon? That's enough for you?"

Dallas' earnest gaze unnerved Matt. He shrugged, trying to make light of what he really felt, which was fueling the desire to jump into the SUV and roar away, and pull into a meadow somewhere down the road where he could just let it all out in a downpour of pain and tears. "I sometimes get to hold her for a few precious moments."

Guffawing, Dallas laughed—a mean, cocky laugh. "Is that enough? Come on, Matt, really. Is that enough?"

"No. No, Dallas, it's not enough. But most times it has to be."

Sobering, Dallas let the spiteful light in his eyes fade. "I want it back, Matt," he said simply. "My time with my brother. I want it back."

"I know."

A silent acknowledgement passed between them. It wasn't coming back, that precious time, for either of them. Dallas would never see Dale again— not in this lifetime, anyway. And Matt would never have Jessie to himself again.

Dallas struggled. "What do we do?"

"We honour the time we had. You honour Dale, your family."

"How?"

"Let his child into your heart for as long as you get to have him. You'll be rewarded beyond your wildest dreams, Dal. Children have a way of helping us see the world in a whole new, beautiful way. As for your dad—let him in too. Start new with the man he is now, with the man you've become. He's not so tough now, right? After what happened on the mountain, the concussion?"

Taking in the advice of his friend, Dallas nodded.

"Suddenly he's vulnerable," Matt went on. "He needs Hunter as much as you do. Hunter is a gift, not a burden. Turn your heart inside out so you can see him that way. It will help your father see him that way too."

"Will you be okay?" *Please tell me you'll be okay.*

"I'll put my record on a new loop, Dallas. Shanda and I are good together. We just need to spend some time in each other's company."

Hesitating, Dallas asked, "Does she take away the ache?"

"For Jessie?" Matt chuckled. "Hell, no. But she helps dull it down."

"Then I'm glad you have Shanda, Matt."

"That makes two of us."

"Hey, Matt, I need…Look, I know this is selfish of me, and that I'm a coward, but I need you to help me with one last thing. As my friend, not my security. Please."

Pausing, Matt cocked his head. "All right," he said coolly. "I'm listening."

Dallas inhaled. "I need to go see the old lady one last time. Ethel. I need to see my brother's photographs of the wild horses. He had my music. I need the thing that mattered the most to him. Apart from Hunter and Maria, and Jenny and the boys, I mean."

"Okay. All right. When?"

"Tomorrow, if she's around. I'm sorry, I know you want to see Shanda."

"I understand. She will too."

"Thank you."

Matt leaned back against the SUV, tucked his hands into his pants pockets, and smiled. "Great. Can I put my shorts on now?"

"Nope. Jeans."

Pushing his body away from the SUV, Matt started to walk next to Dallas, who raised a hand and clapped it on Matt's shoulder. "No. Too damn hot. Why jeans?"

"Well, I think we should get the boys and Cassie and go for a ride. Your legs will get all cut up if you wear shorts."

"Hunter will be confused as hell as to why I'm still here, since I already said goodbye."

"Hunter will be thrilled. He'll get used to seeing you show up in his life. At least—I hope he will." Looking sideways at Matt, Dallas added, "He will, right Matt? You're not quitting me, are you?"

"I thought about it."

"I know you did."

"I might still be thinking about it."

"I wish you wouldn't."

"You were being an asshole. I can't stand by and watch you throw away everything I've ever wanted. You've got a beautiful family, Dallas. Be there for them. Don't mess it up."

"I'll try, Matt. At the same time, give Shanda a solid chance, okay? Let Jessie go."

"Shanda knows the score. She loves me for who I am, and that's always meant loving Jessie."

"Doesn't mean she's really okay with it, in her heart."

"How about we make a pact to never talk about my relationship with Jessie ever again?"

"How about we make a pact that we can talk about Jessie if you ever need a shoulder, okay Matt?" Grinning, Dallas pointed ahead of them.

Hunter had spotted Matt, and was walking over. When he got closer, he broke into a run, and a wide, joyous smile that lit up his entire small face brought heaps of sunshine to his eyes. A few feet away, he leapt up and into Matt's arms.

Laughing, Matt hugged him tight before pushing the hair back from Hunter's cheeks and peering into his happy eyes. "Now that just made me feel more loved than I think I've ever felt in my lifetime."

Dallas stood apart from them, and watched as the two beheld each other with mutual respect and love. "Am I wrong to take him, Matt?" he asked.

"Nah," Matt said. "You're every bit right, Dallas. But I'd like to be around some, if that's okay. I think Hunter and I need each other as much as you and Hunter do. Eh, little guy?"

Hunter rewarded him by flinging both arms around Matt's neck and sighing with pleasure. He smiled happily over at Dallas.

With a chuckle, Dallas placed a hand on Hunter's back and gave him a little rub. "I guess we're co-parenting you, kid," he said. "And how about we start with a trail ride? Can you and me ride Starbuck together? Your dad's horse?"

Neither man thought it was possible for Hunter to light up more, but he did, although he quickly asked if Matt was coming on the trail ride too.

"You bet," Matt grinned, chastising himself for immediately thinking that Jessie would love to be out on the trail with them, and that she would get a kick out of watching her usually impeccably dressed security ride a horse in cowboy boots and jeans. A red blush washed across his cheeks, and he shook his head and reframed Jessie—with Shanda. "I have to update Shanda," he said to Dallas. "Meet you at the barn in ten." Leaning towards Dallas, he handed Hunter over with a smile. "Go find Ry," he ordered, "then get some jeans and boots on, Hunter. Maybe we'll see some wild horses along the trail."

Dallas adjusted Hunter in his arms. Walking away, happily jostling the little boy in his arms as he moved over the patchy grass, he started whistling. Listening, Matt laughed. Hunter was whistling too—he knew the song inside and out.

"They'll be fine," he considered with a smile. "I think they'll be just fine."

Chapter Thirty-two

Matt and Dallas were at Ethel's doorstep by nine the next morning. She opened the door before they made it to the top step. It was raining, a soft, misty rain that was sure to promise rainbows when the sun snuck out between clouds later in the day. On this visit, the men didn't bother looking for a face peeking out from behind a curtain next door. They'd already learned for certain that Maria no longer lived there.

"More questions, have you?" Ethel asked, extending an arm and stepping aside to invite them in. "Otherwise I wouldn't think two handsome men the likes of you would bother coming to my humble domicile a second time."

Dallas gave Matt a knowing look. Matt ducked his head and tried to hide a bashful smile.

"I saw that," she huffed. "So you have an agenda. Surprise, surprise. Sit, I'll put on some tea."

When she joined them in her tiny living room, Dallas had a framed photo in his hand—the exquisite shot of the wild black horse staring into the camera, hiding behind a long ebony forelock, that the men saw on their first visit. "Is this one of Dale's photographs?" he asked, handing it across the small space to his hostess.

"It is," she answered honestly, a tinge of sadness colouring her response. "Your brother was a very talented photographer."

"He left a lot of photos, I think," Dallas tried, testing the waters.

"He did." Looking up, Ethel handed the framed photo back to Dallas. "That one is, uh, was Maria's favourite."

The slip-up didn't go unnoticed. Dallas' gentle smile flipped over. "Where's Maria?" he inquired gently.

"How's Hunter?" Ethel concentrated on sipping her tea. She was pale, and her hands were shaking so much that the tea spilled over the rim, landing on the saucer in little puddles.

Matt glanced sideways at Dallas before jumping into the conversation. Dallas seemed preoccupied—too mystified—to respond. Matt cleared his throat before speaking. "Hunter is doing very well," he said with confidence. "Boone, his grandfather, is teaching him some of the finer points of riding, although Hunter's a natural anyway and doesn't need a lot of help. He's learning alongside Ry, Dallas and Cassie's older son. He seems happy."

"G-good. I'm glad. That's good to hear."

"You can report that to Maria," Dallas murmured carefully, leaning forward to set his teacup on the coffee table. "Maria must be anxiously awaiting news of her son."

"What is it you want to know?" Ethel asked, shaking her head as if to summon up courage. "Just ask, gentlemen."

"I want to know if I'm falling in love with a child who might be removed from my care at any moment," Dallas said, knifing a hand through his hair. "I want to know if Maria has any intention of taking Hunter back, maybe when things get better for her."

"She'd love to take him back," Ethel said.

Dallas' shoulders crumpled. Matt straightened, more alert than concerned, at this point.

"But she can't." The addendum was spoken in a lowered, sorrowful tone.

Reaching out to touch Ethel's gnarled fingers when she set her cup down, Matt encouraged her to go on. "Please explain," he said.

She sighed. "Maria won't appreciate this, but I don't know if my elegant company will ever warrant a third visit from you two dashing fellows, so here I go. I'm diving in. You deserve to know the truth," she added, specifically focusing on Dallas, who crunched on a bottom lip and tried to stop nervously rubbing his palms against his jeans. "As I told you before, Dale and Maria had a very special love. But one night they had a terrible fight, and Dale stormed out." She paused. "What you need to know about that fight was that Maria engineered it in order to cover up a truth she didn't want Dale to know."

Looking over at her, forcing himself to remain silent and not interrupt, Dallas held his breath. *What truth?*

Their hostess continued. "Afterwards, Maria split and left me with formal interim custody of Hunter, since no father was listed on his birth certificate. After a week or so, Dale started coming around again. He was shocked to see that Maria was gone, but I think in his heart he believed she would come back. One night I went into Hunter's bedroom and found Dale holding him, all scrunched up into a ball with Hunter in his big, strong arms, crying. This formidable, kind man—weeping like a child, saying over and over that Hunter would have to be strong for a while. It threw me. I backed out of the room, unseen, I hope. Not that it matters now, I suppose. It's just that Maria was your brother's rock, Dallas. There were reasons for that, which I'll explain later. Dale couldn't cope without Maria, without knowing where she was and if she was okay. And even more so, he never understood why she left him and Hunter in the first place. He thought everything was okay, that they were doing great. You see, Maria was the only person who ever truly knew your brother, with whom he could be truly authentic. He could be himself around her."

"Ouch. Jesus."

Capturing Dallas in her gaze, Ethel continued, almost forgetting that Matt was in the room. She was sharing information Dallas needed to know. Matt was of no consequence, apart from being a trusted friend to Dallas.

"I knew he was in trouble, that something was seriously wrong, but what could I do besides try to talk him into carrying on? A month later, the news broke that your brother took his own life. I cannot tell you how sorry I was to hear that. Dale was a good and trusted friend, and a loving father to Hunter. He was in pain, Dallas, and nothing I could say or do had the power to heal pain that big."

"He loved her that much."

"Honey, he did, but it wasn't just that."

"Our father? The bullying? I thought Dad was okay with Dale. Or was it because of Jenny and the boys? The guilt?"

Ethel shook her head. Matt and Dallas shared a quizzical look.

"It was a lot of things, but it all stemmed from a very bad day a long time ago. A day Dale was never really able to put behind him."

"What? When?"

"After high school. Something happened to your brother at Stampede in Calgary. It's just…I'm not the one to tell you, Dallas. This is a truth that belongs to Maria and Dale, and it's theirs to tell, if they choose."

"Well, Dale can't." Dallas swallowed. "So I guess what you are saying is that I'll have to get this out of Maria, if I can find her."

Ethel blinked back at him. Her expression was a tiny bit cat-that-swallowed-the-canary, and a lot just simple grief.

"Oh," Dallas said, reacting with a quick rise of his shoulders. "Oh. You do know where Maria is. Why am I not surprised?"

"Let me tell you a little more, son."

"I'm listening."

"I'd been talking to a kind woman at child protective services since the night I found Dale crying in Hunter's room. I guess you can say I had a feeling that Dale wasn't going to be able to pull it together, to cope without Maria. Although I thought he would just go back to his family. I didn't think…well, how could I know?"

She took a breath, a moment to consider the trauma of the past while, before she continued.

"I had a few meetings with the government lady, Sally is her name. I knew she would try to place Hunter with family if she could, and Maria had been certain to get a paternity test done before she, um, before she left. So when I heard about Dale, I called Sally and begged her to drive Hunter out to his grandparents. I told her I couldn't deal with the loss of Dale, that I had no clue where Maria had gone. It wasn't all a lie. My grief that day was overwhelming. Well, Sally came right over. She wanted to put Hunter in temporary foster care but I begged her not to. I knew you'd come, Dallas, but I had no idea how long you would stay. I needed Hunter to be on your family's radar right from the get go. For Maria, you know? And for Dale? All along Maria was really hoping you would take her son in, Dallas. She remembered how kind you were to her the night you met, and afterwards as well when she dated you, before she went to Dale."

"Before she dropped me like a steaming cow turd, you mean, so she could go screw my brother."

"Not bitter, are we, Dallas?" Matt joked lightly, attempting to toss some brevity into the dark shroud holding the room hostage. "I mean, it's only been what, twenty-five years or so?"

"More like twenty-seven," Dallas grumbled, and sighed. Raising his head, he gave Ethel a wave so she'd go on.

"I'm a pensioner," she explained. "Without Dale, without some income to help me with Hunter, I just couldn't imagine raising him. Not knowing that…" She gave Dallas a good going over, head to toe and back again.

"Not knowing that I'm around and can easily afford him," he finished.

"And Maria and Dale always spoke so highly of you. The media speaks well of you. Other celebrities speak well of you. Your wife is just lovely, a simple east coast girl. I'm from the east coast, and I know you've grown to love it there, in Nova Scotia and in Prince Edward Island. You were the right person to raise Hunter, and if you wouldn't take him, we hoped your parents or your sister would. After all, Hunter is like his father. The boy needs wide open spaces. He needs nature. Dale's family owned a ranch, with horses. We didn't want him going to live with inner city foster families. I know some of those adults in those families are beautiful people, but that's how Maria grew up, and for whatever reason, that life damaged her." She paused. "And there was one other reason you were the one we were hoping would take Hunter."

"Why?"

"Your music, honey." Ethel let that sink in before adding, "Dale loved your music. Maria still loves it—she has your albums on repeat. She said anyone who writes the kind of beautiful songs you write has got to be the kind of person a sad child like little Hunter needs."

Dallas had to clear his throat three times before he could continue. "There's one thing I don't get," he choked out.

"I think I know where you're going," Ethel responded, picking up her tea-cup for another sip. Matt noticed that her hands were a little less shaky this time. "You think you understand why Maria left your brother, but you want to know why she left her son. You want to know what kind of mother abandons her only child."

"Did Dale cheat on her or something? Not counting his wife," Dallas said soundly, with emphasis on the word 'wife.' "I can see her being depressed, I guess, and walking away for a breather."

"Hoping, you mean," the old lady said with a hint of a tease. "All those years and you'd still like to see Maria dump Dale, wouldn't you?"

Her teasing fell flat. Dallas grumped back, "They coulda stayed together forever if it meant I'd have had another chance to talk to my brother, to make things right between us."

"Of course. I'm sorry, Dallas."

"Continue, please," he said with a flourish of his hand. His tea sat on the coffee table, lukewarm and cooling. "I want to know what kind of mother abandons her only son." He stared at the teacup's rim, and waited for this big piece of the puzzle to click into place.

"If it wasn't an affair, then what do you suppose it was? You're a smart man, figure it out, honey."

Before Dallas could snap some snotty answer back to her, Matt jumped in. He was trained to observe—this woman's eyes were floating. She was struggling to stay composed, judging by the way she lifted the teacup partially to her lips and then set it down again, two, no three times, now. "You can't say the word," Matt said softly, gently, compassionately. "Maria is sick. Cancer, I suppose. That's usually the word nobody ever wants to say out loud."

"Sick?" Dallas questioned, surprised. "Okay, I suppose, but I have to add that even though I didn't spend a lot of time with my brother in the last number of years, I would still think he'd be there for her, for a woman he loves."

"Precisely. Ah. I knew you had some brains in that artist's mind of yours." Ethel winked.

Dallas growled.

Like a schoolboy, Matt raised a hand. Expectantly, Dallas and the old lady looked at him. "He had Jenny and the boys to consider. Maria knew he'd choose her over them, maybe because Jenny is strong and capable, and Maria knew he would feel they would be okay without him, for temporary absences, maybe. Maria saw it another way. By rushing to her side and ignoring the needs of Jenny, she thought Dale would be putting his marriage at risk, he'd risk losing his and Jenny's sons. Maria didn't want that to happen, especially thinking that Dale might soon be without her anyway."

"She thought he would find his way. Maybe not in a romantic true love scenario with Jenny, but at least as far as dependability and responsibility go. What Maria didn't count on was how lost Dale was without her. She was his anchor. She knew he suffered terrible bouts of despair throughout his life, but she never thought he would take his own life."

Abruptly Dallas stood, surprising his elderly hostess, who spilled her tea. While Dallas paced by the door, Matt bent forward over his knees to take Ethel's teacup from her and set it on the coffee table. He grabbed a napkin from next to an untouched cookie tray and mopped up the small puddles the spilled tea left on the end table next to Ethel's chair.

Spinning around, Dallas faced his hostess, a woman who apparently knew Dale better than most, likely even better than Boone and Doris, the men's parents, did. Certainly better than his wife did. "How could I not know this about my own brother? How could I not know all of these secrets about him? Why didn't I make it my business to know?"

Ethel hushed him with a wave and a *pshaw*. "You were like a distant relative, Dallas. Bigger than life. You were not the brother Dale grew up with."

"I shared chores with Dale. We fought over the good shovel in the barn. I was responsible for him falling out of the goddamned hayloft and breaking his arm. We shared my dad's shit, the constant pressure to become the kind of tough men Boone expected to have around the ranch. Why did Dale not think he could reach out to me?" Dallas' temple was pounding. A white rage was eating its way up his spine, clawing at his heart. The closest thing to him was a blue bag half full of cans waiting for recycling pickup that Ethel had set by the entrance to her small kitchen. One mighty kick and he sent it skittering across the linoleum floor in a cacophony of jingles and jangles. It landed in a huddle next to a weathered mustard yellow stove.

"Dallas," Matt cautioned, jumping up. "Easy."

"Easy?! Are you for real right now, Matt? Nothing about this is easy! All this time I've been thinking I left Dale behind, but I think what I've come to realize is that he left me behind!" He stared Ethel down. "I want to know why."

Ethel ignored Dallas' angry treatment of her tidy recycling and focused on his confusion. "Your brother," she said with sympathy, "was always sad for you, Dallas. Did you know that?"

"What? That's crazy! I have a great job, way too much money, a garage filled with sports cars, bikes, airplanes…why would Dale be sad for me?" Dallas knew why, though. In his heart he knew exactly why, and it hurt to acknowledge the truth. It was a truth that started to sink in the summer he met Cassie on a gorgeous Prince Edward Island beach; it was a truth that sank its fangs in deeper over the last few weeks while Dallas was hanging out at his father's ranch.

Matt was certainly aware. The fast-paced celebrity lifestyle had been his playground too for much of his adult life, thanks to his work with Jessie, Josh, Jacob, and Dallas. He was hyper aware. Stardom had its rewards, but it also had its pitfalls. *Just ask Jessie and Josh,* he said to himself as Ethel opened her mouth to speak.

"Dale was sad that you chose such a big life. He always thought you were terribly lonely, at least after the initial thrill of fame and money wore off. He said he could see it in your eyes, in the way you sang. Loneliness. Sadness."

Speechless, Dallas dropped slowly back down onto the couch. He couldn't bring himself to look at Matt. His temple wasn't throbbing at high speed anymore. In its wake was a slower pounding, more of a regular low-level thrum. "It's not like that so much anymore," he admitted, digging his fingernails into his knees so he'd have something to focus on. "Not since Cassie and Ry came into my life." Forcing a smile, he added, "And after my good buddy here, Matt, showed up. I'm better now."

"Dale thought you need nature in your life. He thought you were in that place where, because you didn't spend time in nature, you didn't realize what you were missing."

Visions of the mountains passed through a slideshow in Dallas' mind— craggy, majestic, shadowed, mysterious. Filled to overflowing with all manner of unseen life. A spectacular east coast sunset drifted through his eyes; Matt and Ethel could almost see it there, laid out in Dallas' mind in multi-hued shades of pinks and oranges—opalescent, shimmering, spreading across the horizon like a new life in bloom.

"He was right," Dallas said, adding the images of Hunter communing with the wild horses to his list of nature's sheer perfection. "But again— I'm better now. I suppose I can thank Dale for that, in some kind of weird, warped way. For bringing me back home."

"He'd like that. Your brother would be glad."

Rising, Ethel accepted Matt's help when he leapt forward to assist. She pointed to the bookshelf. "Can you grab that photo album for me, handsome young man? The one with the decorative calligraphy on the spine."

A quick blush crossed Matt's cheeks. He grinned at Dallas before retrieving the album in question.

With a chuckle, Dallas rolled his eyes at Matt. "I've got to find me another security chief. I'm getting a little tired of all the women fawning over the one I have." He winked at Ethel and said, "He's so shy, isn't he? Look at him. You made him blush!"

"Stop," Matt insisted. "Go back to nursing your tea, old man."

Ethel was having a laugh at their expense. With the newly acquired album in her lap, she settled deeper into her comfortable chair. After opening the album, she lifted it by the edges and held it up with the insides facing the men.

The photographs Matt and Dallas saw carefully pasted into it were stunning. And there were pages and pages of photos, all of wild horses—horses running free, manes and tails flying, horses standing still as they fed on long Alberta grass, horses staring stoically at the camera. Old horses, young horses, muscular horses, thin horses, bays, buckskins, paints, white horses, black horses. Interspersed with the images, words were written here and there, carefully decorating the pages with elegant black calligraphy scrollwork—names, seasons, places, dates. The album was a record of lives well lived, of two people whose greatest joy once upon a time was roaming Alberta's great mountain meadows in search of equine spirits that ran free. The horses galloping across the pages, and the ones standing proudly at attention, were like mirrors for humanity. They were a touchstone between this world and the next. They were bliss and pain and freedom and spirit, they were soulful, spiteful, wistful, and strong, all photographed by Dale—and some by Maria, the guys were told by Ethel—and all contained in meticulously decorated albums like the one Ethel was holding between her sore arthritic fingers.

"Take this one," she told Dallas, holding the album out to him. "And when I pass on, come and get the others. For now," she added with certainty, "I hope you understand that I need these too."

And there, in the blink of an eye, Dallas saw Dale as clearly as he ever saw him, reflected in the eyes of an aging woman who knew him well—who loved him, who loved a woman he loved, and who loved a son he sired.

"Thank you," Dallas whispered, and Ethel smiled.

"Dallas," she said tenderly, "you are so, so welcome."

Chapter Thirty-three

"Maria should have asked for help," Dallas said to Matt three hours later. "I met her before Dale did. We're not strangers." In consternation, he rubbed his jaw so hard he winced. "She can't be here. No way can she be living here."

The guys were sitting in the SUV, parked at the end of a short, sparse mountain laneway that reeked of poverty. The laneway was bare and pot-holed, carved out between a stand of white spruce, underneath which rusted farm implements spit long wild grass out of broken blades and empty wheel wells. A tipped-over toilet, once white but now pockmarked with what Dallas and Matt hoped was just mud, sat smack dab in the centre of what likely passed as a rough front lawn; at least a half dozen jagged tree trunks made the area look as if someone had once tried to clear it.

The positioning of the toilet made Matt think it was once used as a lawn chair. Now its lid lay askew, sideways and wanting, likely coming loose after the toilet was shoved over by a bear in search of berries, he thought. More than a few abandoned beer cans scattered around the toilet completed the picture. If the guys' reason for being here was less sobering, he would have smiled at the idea of a bear sitting in pure contentment on the toilet with a beer held high in one paw. He sure as hell doubted any bear would have found berries underneath the decrepit thing.

"At least the view in the other direction is spectacular," Matt said to Dallas. "I'd sit on a toilet to drink too if I got to look at the mountains all day."

Oddly, yellow blooms peeked through the toilet basin's gaping hole. "Wildflowers," said Matt to his serious, dumbfounded friend. "They're growing up through the toilet." He jabbed Dallas in the thigh with a pointy finger, which he then lifted to guide Dallas' eyesight. "Check it out."

"How is it possible, Matt?" Dallas asked, dazed at the sight before him. "How can beauty exist here? How is it that nature can co-exist with such neglect?" He let his eyes drift upwards beyond the toilet. His vision was consumed by what appeared to be a dejected one-room shack, complete with a sagging, swaybacked roof.

"Maybe nature's trying to swallow it up," Matt replied calmly, with his usual wisdom. "It's trying to claim back the mountain, Dal. Maybe that's how the good and the bad can co-exist." He gestured to the toilet and its perky yellow wildflowers. "Nature's winning. Look, see?"

Dallas spoke in a monotone. He had one hand on the car's handle but seemed hesitant to push it down and shove the door open. "Ethel said Maria was living in a hunting cabin in the woods. I don't think hunters would spend a single night here. Bears'd break in and hunt *them*."

Matt laid a hand on his door handle. "Let's go in," he said, steeling up the usual authority that motivated Dallas during shows.

"Yes, sir," Dallas agreed, slipping out of the vehicle and opening the back door to grab the bags of groceries and supplies Ethel had asked them to pick up for Maria. "Indeed. Let's see Maria for ourselves, and find out what magic she held over my brother for all those years. If she's even here. There's no car."

Protectively, Matt tucked his vehicle's keys into a jeans pocket. He didn't bother voicing his thoughts. What would be the point of saying anything to Dallas about the likelihood of Maria being well enough to drive a car? From Ethel's expression and tone, Matt wondered if they would even find her alive. Maria...Hunter's mother.

Unlike Ethel, Maria wasn't waiting for them at the door. Matt knocked three times before finally turning the knob and giving the door a push.

It took a while for the men's eyes to adjust to the dim light. A south-facing window let in some light; however, dark cotton curtains and the grey, rainy day filtered most of it out.

They heard Maria before they spotted her.

"Are you here to finish me off?" Her voice was thin and strained. She had to take a breath before she could continue. "Because if you are, I hope you do it quickly. I've suffered enough. I'm tired. I want to go."

A shiver ran up Matt's spine. The hairs on his arms stood up. Maria's words brought him back to a very dark time, a time when Josh once delivered a similar message. Pushing that awful memory away, Matt glanced over at Dallas, whose earlier saucy comment about Maria's magic had come and gone—the singer was now rendered silent. There was no magic here, in this godawful place. Whatever magic this woman once held seemed to have long since fled. Maybe it had departed to some far away enchanted cosmos with Dale, the man she loved for so long. Maybe it got sucked out with a whoosh the last time she laid eyes on her mysterious, solemn child. The air was still, and thick. The aura in the space was as weak and drained as the disembodied voice.

Dallas' eyes were focused on something. Matt followed his lead. He spied a single cot in the far northeast corner, back against the wall. On it was Maria, buried in a threadbare quilt she had drawn up over her fragile body. Dallas was unable to speak, or move, beyond a stilted shudder of revulsion. He stood just inside the doorway and stared at the birdlike body under the quilt, and tried to force his brain to work, to reconcile the bare crumbs of Maria that were left with the powerful presence that had shared his brother's heart and soul for so many years.

Her body had almost nothing left to give. Yet Maria still had power. Maria—had answers. Only she could grant Dallas peace. Only Maria could help him understand.

Matt, leaving Dallas to pull himself together, stepped over the wooden floor towards a simple wooden table surrounded by four unmatched wooden chairs. The table was littered with medicines, dirty plates, sticky unwashed glasses, musty books, and magazines. Trying not to look too closely for fear of what he might see, Matt reached for a chair. He dragged it loudly over the floor, lifted it, and set it down about three feet from the bed.

"I wouldn't get too close," Maria managed dryly. "Unless you have a bandana." She raised a bony finger and pointed it at her nose. "Smells like roses in here."

A *screek* behind Matt signaled that Dallas was on the move, finally. Matt heard more than saw Dallas set a chair down more behind him than beside him. Cementing his presence there in the semi-darkness, Dallas coughed.

Maria forced a laugh. "Told you. Stinks in here. Like death. Makes a person not want to breathe at all."

Matt pinched his nostrils and forced himself to take short, even breaths until he adjusted to the stink. Maria lived in it, yet she appeared to know exactly what her visitors must be thinking, how appalled they must be to have to take breaths inside her putrid environment. The air was foul, rancid. Her body was ravaged by disease; if the smell didn't give it away, the thin, paper weight of her bones sure did.

Matt reached for the switch on a bedside lamp. At his movement, Maria flinched. The earnestness in her weak voice stopped Matt from turning the lamp on. "I'd prefer you leave it off," she said. "I didn't do…my makeup… this morning."

"All right," he agreed, folding his hands on his lap so as not to frighten her again, since she'd jumped when he reached for the light. "Maria," he said, noting that she didn't appear surprised that he knew her name, "my name is Matt Kelly. My friend here is—"

"Dallas," she whispered, her woeful, sharp eyes seeking out, in the shadows, the brother of the man she loved.

Matt twisted around to look at Dallas, who was cowering almost behind him. The vague light from the single front window backlit Dallas so that he was almost haloed. His layered hair and muscled chest and forearms were unmistakable to any Dallas White fan.

"Hello, Maria," Dallas croaked. "It's been a long time." Matt recoiled at the bitterness he detected in his friend's famous voice.

"Too long," she breathed with a wistful smile. "You've been busy."

Dallas didn't answer. He couldn't. Seeing Maria this way, so sick, so alone, on the fringe of society, was devastating. She was a living, breathing example of everything Dallas felt he'd done wrong by Dale. Gasping at the insanity of it all, he stared at the dusty bare floorboards and let Matt do the talking.

"Maria," Matt said, "we want you to know that Hunter is well."

It was Maria's turn to look away, to avert her eyes. She raised a weak fist to wipe away a tear, but couldn't quite make it all the way to her cheek. Matt did the honour with a corner of the quilt, although he smiled just a little first and asked her permission. She allowed him.

"Is he happy?" Maria asked, looking back over at Matt before letting her gaze drift to Dallas.

Matt decided honesty was key. There was no point in lying—Maria knew her son. "Not yet," he said with cautious sincerity. "He's coming along, though. A little at a time. The horses help. Dallas' son Ry helps."

"Are you going to take care of him?" The question was directed at Dallas.

He looked up. "Yes," he told her. "I will. I am." Nodding at Matt, he added, "This guy's helping Cassie and me. Hunter and Matt have some special connection I'm not privy to."

"Not yet." Matt tried to grin. "It's just a lonely thing," he disclosed to Maria. "Hunter and me were lonely. We're both good now." Looking back at Dallas, he said, "That's not a club you need to belong to, Dal. Trust me."

"I know about loneliness," Maria said. "I didn't for a long time, though. I thought that part of me was done and gone. But I know all about it again now."

Matt cleared his throat before responding. "We're very sorry about Dale," he said.

"Dale." Saying his name out loud felt so odd after all this time. "I doubt if you understand about me and Dale." Again, Maria set her watery, limpid eyes on Dallas.

"We think we do, to a point," Matt offered, since Dallas' mouth was working but no words were coming out. "Maybe you can help fill in the blanks."

"Something happened," Dallas blurted out. "The old woman, Ethel, your neighbour and friend, she confirmed what I always thought. Something happened that changed my brother. That made him distance himself from me. I want...I need...to know."

Maria studied him before responding. "Dallas...I doubt you can handle it."

"The thing is, Maria, I can't handle *not* knowing. Please."

A long silence filled the dark cabin. Outside, the wind was picking up. Branches from a tree that Matt idly thought ought to be trimmed scratched eerily at a corner of the cabin. Somewhere off in the distance a wolf called a warning to its pack.

Inside, nobody spoke until Maria took a rattly breath and started them down a rough road. It wasn't an easy tale to tell; for someone as sick as she, it was downright draining. Maria had to pace herself, to gauge when to speak and when to breathe, although Matt wondered whether some of her pauses were more about watching Dallas for signs of breakdown than they were about helping herself.

"It happened the night you and I met, Dallas. While you and I were fucking in your truck, Dale was...getting the shit kicked out of him by some... bastard...renegade American cowboys. It's why your father was in the city with Dale that night. Someone...found your brother and brought him to the bar to...to... clean him up. It was a friend of your father's, so...he called Boone to come get Dale."

Dallas tried to shrug, but his bulging, tense biceps and forearms gave away his inner fear. He knew damn well the worst was yet to come. Wishful thinking on his part hoped that Maria was done talking. "So Dale got beat up. What the hell, we got beat up all the time, me for being a wussy singer, and my brother for protecting me."

A new silence overtook the room. Matt clued in first, and intentionally stared at his fingers. He later swore to himself that he heard the very moment when Dallas' brain clicked into place.

Dallas shuffled his butt in his chair first. "Okay, so it was worse than that. That's what you're telling me by your unwillingness to say more at all, and the only thing I know that could be worse is—"

Somewhere in the cabin, a wee rustling signalled the presence of a rodent— a mouse, or perhaps a rat.

Matt shivered.

Maria waited.

"Was my brother raped?" Dallas murmured into the darkness. Bile rose in his stomach. He gagged. When Maria nodded, Dallas got up. He made it outside the door before he puked. Oddly, he hoped the fresh rain would wash his vomited lunch off of the muddy wooden step that led up to the cabin's only door.

Inside, Matt touched Maria's wispy, bony hand. "May I?" he asked. She nodded again, so he wrapped his warm fingers around her cold ones. "Maria,

I wondered if that might be the case. I suspect that your pain and Dale's pain brought the two of you together. I'm guessing that's what was up between the two of you all these years, because I know two other people who were drawn together by past hurts, and who can't stand to be apart. And if that's the thing with you and Dale, then I want you to know that I am truly, truly sorry. For both of you."

"It's worse than that, Matt."

"What?" Matt glanced over his shoulder. Dallas was out of earshot, retching just outside the door. Matt turned back to Maria. "Tell me," he demanded, his voice hoarse.

She studied him before she spoke. "The cowboys that hurt Dale were really after Dallas. They'd seen him sing at the bar earlier…and they wanted him. Dale was at the show, standing at the back…cheering Dallas on. Since it was one of Dallas' first big shows, Dale didn't want him to know he was there. He thought he'd…make him nervous. He just planned to meet him after the show, outside. He'd hitchhiked…into the city and was just going to go home with Dallas afterwards."

She had to take a longer break to catch her breath. Matt waited, warming her cold fingers in his warmer ones.

"When Dale got to the side door to wait for Dallas," Maria said finally, "he got into a tussling match with the guys after…overhearing their plans to sweet talk Dallas into going drinking with them. They were going to take him…down by the river to some remote park and jump him. You have to understand…Dallas was always a good-looking guy. And on stage he's always been larger than life, right from the start. He puts people under a spell. His music puts folks under a spell. People…want him. Women, of course. Some men too."

"So Dale tried to, what, bargain with them? With drunk cowboys?"

"He told them Dallas had already left by the front door. That he was Dallas' brother, and that they had planned to meet somewhere else after the show…at another bar a few streets away. He said he was just going back into the club to grab something Dallas forgot…a jacket or something."

"He lured them somewhere else so Dallas could get away."

"They parked outside the other bar and sat Dale down between them, as

315

collateral, I guess. And an hour or so later when Dallas still hadn't shown up…because by then he was with me…"

"They took Dale to the park and beat the shit out of him instead."

"And they raped him. Both cowboys did."

"In those days a tough young ranch-raised fella like Dale would never go to the hospital or to the police. He'd never report it."

"God, no. It was bad enough when he was found, and his father was told… about what happened, not by Dale, but by the guy Boone knew, the guy who found Dale. In Dale's defense, out of sheer terror of what his father would think of him, I think, he told his father…that he was trying to lure the bastards away from Dallas. Dale told me Boone…has held it against Dallas ever since. Boone apparently said that it should have been Dallas. That he was… the weak brother. The runt of the litter." She paused and looked straight at Matt. "Dallas wouldn't have survived it. Maybe he's tougher now, but back then he was a naive, innocent dreamer, believe me. Dale…was the tough guy. It just took a while to wear him…all the way down. It destroyed him in the end. I always knew it would."

Dallas made his way back into the cabin and stopped by the door, leaned back against the wall, and bent over as if he couldn't find the energy to stand up straight. He started to listen again to Maria, who picked him out in the shadowed space and spoke directly to him, while Matt hung his head and tried to digest what he'd just been told.

"He was so ashamed," Maria explained with as much fervor as she could muster. "Dale couldn't face himself, much less anyone else, Dallas. He just… geared up every day and went to work, and did…what was expected of him. Buried his pain and humiliation in physically hard work, and transferred it… to the injuries he got by being bucked off broncs. Stayed low key as much as he could. Your father kept him close by, encouraged Dale to…buy into the ranch. Boone's way of protecting him, I think."

"Jenny?" Matt asked into the quiet. In the distance, the rodent skittered across the floor. In another time or place, Matt would have lifted his feet. Here in this dank, sparse cabin, during this dark telling, having a mouse or rat run over his feet or even up his leg somehow seemed apropos. He doubted he would even flinch.

"Dale married her because his father wouldn't allow him to be with me, because I am Cree. Dale's parents…were always after him to find a nice white girl and settle down. Dallas was gone by then, and Dale…had no fight left in him, you see?"

"He had some fight," Dallas said weakly from where the wall was holding him up. "He stayed with you. That was a helluva risk to take, once he got married, I mean."

"Dale stayed with me because he needed a place to land, a place to fall. You see what happened…when your brother no longer had a safe place." A sob snuck out; it sounded like it came from a newborn calf more than from a living, breathing human. "I thought Hunter would be enough to keep Dale going once I was out of the picture. I was wrong."

"That's a lot to lay on a child," Matt said. He looked at Dallas. "Don't ever let Hunter get wind of that, Dal."

"Hunter is like a spirit child," Maria wept. "He can lie down amongst wild horses. Like his father."

"We know." Dallas approached his vacated chair, his boots hard and unrelenting on the wooden floor. Weary, he flipped the chair around and straddled it, laying his arms, elbows out, over the top rail. "We've seen him do it. It scared the shit out of us at first."

"He's a very special child," Matt offered kindly. "Hunter has a gift."

"My son has a lot of gifts." Maria shivered.

Letting go of Maria's hands, Matt grasped the quilt and pulled it up over her body. Once again, he wiped delicately at her tears with a corner. "You need proper care, Maria," he said. "You need to be somewhere warm and safe, with twenty-four hour care. With proper nutrition."

"Someone looks in on me here," she replied. "I'm not entirely alone. I can't eat, anyway. I just vomit food back up." She smiled, a crooked, fatigued smile. "No more movie popcorn…for this girl. That's the food I miss the most. That and coffee."

Matt paused and looked around. Other than the table, chairs, bed, and bedside table, the place was empty, with the exception of a small fireplace. "Is there even running water in here?"

"No. Nor is there heat. I can't get up…to light the fire anymore."

"Were you planning to just wither away out here? Go to sleep and not wake up?"

"Dale did. He just went to sleep."

"Dale was in agony," Dallas returned quickly, ignoring Matt's instantly raised head and wide, cautious eyes. "Damn it, Maria, you should have told him you were sick."

"I didn't want it to affect his family."

"It did anyway, Maria. It's a mess. Jenny and her two boys will never recover."

"It was never my intention…to hurt anyone."

Matt was a little more gentle. "Is that why you won't let Hunter see you? He could use some closure. He wets the bed just about every night."

Maria sighed and looked away.

Dallas leapt back into the fray. His mind was in overdrive; he was still trying to go back to the night he first introduced Dale and Maria. That night was one of the reasons he decided to leave Alberta, to vacate the ranch and drive away in search of a singing career. "Did Dad know the truth of what happened to Dale? Or did he just think he got beat up? Because if good ole Boone thought Dale just got beat up, I can't see him driving to Calgary to get him. He would have expected Dale to tough it out on his own."

Matt stared at the floor. What Maria had just told him about Dale trying to protect Dallas was a secret Matt wished to hell he'd never been told.

Maria avoided Matt's eyes and gave Dallas a half-truth. "Boone knew but Dale said that other than the first night, he never spoke about it. It was a shameful, disgusting thing. Your father…told Dale when he first got to him…that he always thought it might someday happen to you. Because of your music."

"All right." Dallas knocked over the chair when he got up this time. Maria and Matt stayed silent while he went outside and vomited again. When he waded back in, hunched over and sick, Matt stood to lift the overturned chair and put it back to rights.

Dallas eased his nauseous body down into it. "Look, Maria," he said in earnest as Matt listened. "We're not prepared to leave you here. We'll find you hospice care in the mountains, somewhere with a view of wild horses, maybe. Somewhere equipped to ease your passage into the next life."

Proud, Maria raised her chin. "I made sure I was never a burden to your brother. He came and went as he pleased." Her eyes were moist. "I am nobody's burden."

"You helped my brother," Dallas said, appealing to her to let him try to make things right. "Let me help you."

"Just go," she begged. "I'll slip off into the night. I'm not afraid."

"You will be a burden to your son his entire life, Maria," Dallas said, "if you don't let him see you one last time to say goodbye. Do you want him to see you here, like this?"

"Don't you dare. Hunter is too little...too special..."

"We'll be back tomorrow," Matt said, standing. "If the person checking in on you is important to you," he noted medicinal herbs on the table, and wondered if Maria's caregiver might be a healer from the Cree nation, "then he or she can come with you. We'll have a place ready for you, Maria. We'll be back at noon. In the meantime, we brought some things for you."

A slow, quiet turn, and Matt went to the door to pick up the bags he and Dallas had brought at Ethel's request. Together, the guys unpacked them—things they doubted Maria would ever touch. Things she and Ethel and Dale and Hunter may have once enjoyed—ginger ale, dark chocolate, hard candies, pink peppermints.

Dallas dropped a stack of gossip rags on her lap. "Just so you know," he said with a hopeless attempt at a smile, "none of it's true. Except the part about how great a lover I am."

"Ha," Maria laughed. It was faint, but rose and fell in a tiny wave like a small bird's song. "Well, I hope you got better. I'll at least give you the benefit of time, Dallas."

"I was skinny back then. That's so not fair."

She sobered, yet allowed the corners of her lips to stay lifted. A glow from somewhere deep within almost reached her eyes. "You were passionate and sweet, my darling Dallas," Maria said. "A rare, gentle soul in a rough, untamed land. You did the right thing to go when you did. You should know," she caressed his fingers, and lifted them for a kiss—he had to help her with the lifting part—"that your brother loved you very, very much. He was so proud, Dallas. Dale was your biggest fan. And not just of your music, honey. Of you."

Overcome, Dallas bent and brushed his lips along Maria's pale cheek.

Matt watched them for a moment before he stepped quietly to the door and went outside. Hands in his pockets and tears in his eyes, he moved down the walk and stood facing the SUV. Before him, the mountains loomed, their natural beauty a wonder to behold. "I don't get it," he said to the magnificent sky, to the clouds, to the birds, to the rain that wet his jacket, that dotted his cheeks. "How are we letting this happen? How can we, in our modern, civilized world, allow so many of our people to suffer in poverty, many of them alone?"

The answer was not forthcoming. Nearby, the yellow flowers growing inside the broken toilet were drooping. They were heavy with rain. When Matt looked over at them, he swore they were weeping.

Inside, Dallas brushed his thumb over Maria's fingers. "So soft," he murmured quietly. "Your fingers are so soft. I remember that about you."

"I'm not sorry about it all, Dallas. Leaving you for him, I mean. He needed me. You just... needed your music."

"I thought he was so tough back then. All his life, I thought Dale was so damn tough."

"Life has a way of turning things inside out. Doesn't it, Dallas?"

"Sounds like a song." He smiled.

"Maybe it should be."

"Maybe it will be."

Bending over, Dallas pressed his lips to Maria's forehead. "I need to do right by Dale," he said. "I need to do right by Hunter. You will have everything you need to bring you comfort this next while, Maria. I wish you would have asked a long time ago."

"Jenny will hate you. She may never speak to you again if she finds out you are taking care of me."

"Dale married Jenny, Maria. He thought she was worth loving, too. She will come around when the pain is less acute. When she begins to understand."

"Maybe."

Backing away, Dallas held Maria's soft gaze until he could no longer make her out in the semi-darkness. Pivoting around on a heel, he put his head down and strode through the doorway. He was careful to close the door quietly behind him.

He found Matt still standing in front of the car, staring up at the mountain tops, at the sky.

Dallas stood there too, and took it all in. "A speck of dust," he said. "We're all just specks of dust."

After a while, Matt moved to one side of the SUV. Dallas went to the other.

They got in, and drove away in reverent, humble silence.

Chapter Thirty-four

Boone was picking at a stirrup buckle when Dallas sauntered by, whistling some new melody he was trying to work out. Cassie was at his side, rocking new western wear—jeans, classy embroidered cowboy boots, and a pale green tank top.

"I don't think this is a whistling kind of day, Dallas," Boone reprimanded sharply.

Grinding to a halt, Dallas twisted around to look behind him. He gave his father a quizzical look.

Cassie ran a finger over the long braid she'd fixed that morning, that fell part way down the middle of her back, and sent her husband a look of warning.

"I think if there was ever a day to whistle, this'd be it," Dallas said to his dad, before taking Cassie's fingers in his and continuing on his way.

He stopped next to a saddled horse tied to the side of a long metal horse trailer. Pointing to a white horse next to it, he said to Cassie, "Johnny says you're to take Allie. She's gentle; she'll give you an easy ride."

"And she's not scared of water, right? On Heartland, there was this horse that was scared of water, and—"

"She's not scared of water." Grinning, Dallas pulled his petite wife close for a hug.

"Dawn said we will have to cross the river about thirteen times on this ride. I can't be on a horse that's jumpy around water."

With two fingers, Dallas gently lifted Cassie's chin so she would meet his eye. He frowned. "It's more the bears, wolves, and cougars that you need to concern yourself with."

Pouting, Cassie dipped her nose into his chest. Her words came out muffled. "Thanks for the reminder." Hands on Dallas' elbows, she looked up. "God, your father says it's about two-and-a-half hours in, and the same back. Plus we're having a cookout somewhere along the route. What if we're the ones to get eaten?"

Adopting a sympathetic stance, Dallas played equalizer. "Cassie, sweetheart, at least a dozen of us are going on this ride, if you include the wagon riders. We'll be making far too much noise for any wildlife to be peeking their noses out at us."

"I hope so. I already saw a bear this summer, and I'm not keen to see another."

"You said it was cute."

"Um-hum, yes, well it was from a distance. True. I didn't get close enough to look for blemishes on its fur or poop stuck to its bum or anything like that."

Throwing back his head, Dallas laughed outright. "And you call yourself a cowgirl."

"No, actually. No. No, I don't." To make the point super clear, Cassie stomped her foot, which made Dallas' smile all the broader.

"You're gonna be if we buy a ranch out here, Cas."

"Nope. I'll stay in the kitchen and bake bread. Our boys can be the cowboys."

"Our boys." Dallas lit up. "I like the sound of that. What about Jade?"

"She'll scare the horses away."

The sound of Dallas' joy echoed throughout the windswept meadow alongside the remote mountain road where horse trailers, pickups, and an old west-style covered wagon were parked. If the earlier whistling annoyed Boone, the laughter should have thrown him around the bend, but it didn't.

Over Dallas' shoulder, Cassie snuck a look at Boone. To her surprise, the older man was whistling.

He waved at Cassie. "Hop on," he called. "Time to go. Tell that long-haired hippy husband of yours to find his flower child and mount up."

Cassie scrunched up her shoulders and gave Dallas' wide leather belt a yank to bring him closer for a kiss. "Did I ever tell you that I actually really like your father?"

"That makes one of us." Laying his hands on his wife's hips, Dallas searched Cassie's lips with the tip of his tongue. "Ummm," he breathed as his groin started to tingle. "How about we take our horses and ride off in the opposite direction of everyone else? Find us a little hidey-hole by the creek and have some play time?"

"Later, cowboy. Priorities."

"Ah. Dale. Yes, he's worth the wait, Cassie."

"He is. Indeed. Oh, there're Hunter and Ry."

The boys were on either side of Matt and Shanda, giving the impression of a sweet little family. Matt's ear was bent to Ry, no doubt taking in the latest news on the most recent long-distance songwriting with Emily-Grace and David. Next to Shanda, Hunter was skipping happily, his hand tucked securely into hers.

"I think they're going to have to buy a ranch very close to us," Cassie mused.

"If Matt buys a ranch, it'll be near Canmore where Josh and Jessie live."

"Maybe not," Cassie considered. "Children trump lovers, wouldn't you think?"

"Nobody trumps *my* lover."

Cassie squealed with delight when Dallas growled and put pressure on her lower back to press her body tighter into his. "Okay, about that hidey-hole near the creek…"

"It'll wait," Dallas decided with a lopsided grin, unable to suppress the sheer joy of being in the beautiful mountain-hugged valley with an incredible woman at his side, about to ride deep into the wilderness to J.I. Mountain, so named for the way two sets of trees grew up its side, one forming a J and the other forming an I. According to Maria, J.I. was Dale's favourite Alberta sanctuary, far from civilization and its perils. At J.I., Dale and Maria could ride underneath expansive skies unseen by any human eye for hours, their hearts beating in unity as they guided their horses through narrow mountain trails and peaceful, wildflower meadows. When Hunter was old enough to sit on a horse he went along too, according to Maria—even as a toddler he went, sitting proudly atop Starbuck with his daddy.

Dallas added a post-script to his earlier pronouncement that adult playtime could wait. It was accompanied by a quick yank on Cassie's belt. "Although I'm not sure if I can."

Pushing his hand away, Cassie pressed her lips to his and treated him to a *just-you-wait* giggle. There were definite bonuses to spending time out here in Alberta together—a more relaxed lifestyle, being one, especially after the hurry-up-and-move stress of the last tour when everybody wanted a piece of Dallas. Usually Cassie and the kids were the last in line to get one. Every second having Dallas 'almost' to herself was cherished.

Cassie wrinkled her nose and started to back away. Johnny was beckoning her by Allie, the gentle white horse she would ride today. "Just one thing I've been wondering," she said to Dallas over her shoulder as she turned and headed over to Johnny.

"Mmm?" Dallas said, admiring her toned Yoga butt as she walked away.

"Where'm I supposed to pee?"

Johnny was quick on the uptake. "Wherever a snake isn't. That's where." He patted Allie's saddle, signaling Cassie to mount up.

She stopped in her tracks and looked back at Dallas. The look she gave him would have been menacing if it weren't for the sheer delight in her eyes that she couldn't possibly disguise. He was so much more relaxed these days. Meeting Maria had its pitfalls—Dallas had a lot to work through. Yet Maria's disclosures also brought forth an advent of peace, a seed of hope. A starting place from which Dallas could stop asking questions, and begin to heal.

He raised his hands in a truce-like gesture. "I wasn't gonna mention the snakes! You can blame Johnny for that!"

Cassie pointed to her chest. "You weren't gonna mention them because you know you won't get me on my back in some meadow if I'm thinking about snakes. You know what you are? You're sneaky, Dallas! That's what you are! Sneaky!"

Their joyous sparring caught on. What might have been a long sorrow-filled ride instead became what Dale would have wanted—an awe-inspiring, breathtakingly beautiful, mountain outing.

It had started by vehicle—the group had to trailer the horses to a place where they could enter the river and follow it along until they reached J.I. Once there, they would dismount to select a clearing or treed area of the mountain where they thought Dale might have especially enjoyed taking his horse, where he and Maria may have picnicked, and likely even made love a time or two. Hunter seemed thrilled to be here in this familiar area; perhaps he would know the exact right place they needed to be.

The adventure was a quest, of sorts—a quest to set all of them free.

A quest to set Dale and Maria free.

Today Dallas and his extended family—including Jenny and the boys, and of course Dallas' buddy Matt and his wife, Shanda—were taking Dale's and Maria's ashes to J.I., to spread them in a sacred place that meant so much to both.

Until last night, Jenny had no intention of bringing her boys and coming along. Dallas had shown up at her door after supper. They'd gone out onto her back deck to talk.

Leaning forward against the rail, Dallas started them off. He told her what he knew about the assault on Dale in Calgary all those years ago, and how Maria's similar pain united the two. How Dale was more complicated than he, Dallas, ever understood. Yet how when they talked the few times they got together over the years, the first words out of Dale's mouth were always about his boys, Shane and Cormac, about how they were already winning at rodeo in the summertime, or getting 'Player of the Game' at hockey in the winter.

"He talked about you too, Jenny," Dallas said. The sun was setting over the mountains that enveloped them—Jenny and Dale had bought a simple place not far from J.I. Outfitters. Awed by the spectacle, humbled by the treasured gift of a sunny day and blue skies so they could be treated to the magic of a sunset in the first place, Dallas nodded at the perfectly round ball of golden orange just about to duck down behind the mountains in front of them. "It doesn't last," he mused. "Perfection, I mean. It comes and it goes in the blink of an eye. Just like life."

Jenny stepped up to the rail and stood stock still next to Dallas. Somber, she let the sunset mirror itself in her eyes.

Dallas went on. "I know that you and Dale shared a lot of perfect moments, Jenny," he said. "He and I did too, as kids. I believe there was a reason he chose not to share his pain with us."

"Why?" she asked, begging for an answer that would help her heal, that would help her forgive a travesty that big. "Why would my husband not feel like he could share his pain with me?"

"Because," Dallas answered evenly, as the sun dipped behind the mountain and was lost from sight. "What we had was too good to be marred. Dale was always my protector. He was yours and Shane's and Cormac's too. He was too good of a man to scar what we had, to bring us down into the things that hurt him so badly. Maria lived that pain long before she met Dale. He went to her the same way I go to music."

"He had the horses, the wild ones. He didn't need to bury his wounded heart in Maria!"

"Jenny, Maria gave Dale the gift of the wild horses. It was her way of showing him that he could be free."

She was quiet for a few moments before she responded. Then Jenny said, "I don't know if all of this will ever really make sense to me, Dallas. It's too much."

"Right now it is," he agreed. "But sweetheart, one day the skies will clear for you. You'll see my brother as he was meant to be, as he tried to be—a good husband, a good father. You'll understand Maria's place in his life, and that she wasn't just a lover, to him. She was a lifeline."

"I wish he would have let me be his lifeline."

"I think, Jenny, in a lot of ways, you were."

Standing more upright, Dallas wrapped an arm around his sister-in-law. Together, they watched the sun backlight the mountains on its way down.

"It looks like they're on fire," she whispered under the comfort of Dale's brother's strong arm.

"Someday," Dallas tried, "it'll look more like a halo."

"Promise?"

"I promise." He kissed her cheek, made his way down the steps, and left Jenny alone, bathed in the wild orange light of a descending sun.

It was the going down of a day, and the rising of a new hope.

Today, Jenny was coming along on the ride to say goodbye to a man she was only just beginning to understand.

Maria had passed away five days earlier, after just more than a week at the hospice retreat Dallas set up for her a half hour down the road from J.I.

Hunter got to see her one last time. Snuggled under her arm, he sang his father's favourite Dallas White tune while they leafed through his parents' cherished photos of the wild horses.

"There were sketches at the end," Dallas said to Matt when they dismounted by the river to stretch their legs about halfway to J.I. Mountain. "Three of them, tucked underneath some of the last photos. Hidden, as if Dale didn't want anyone to see such intimate portraits. Hunter pulled them out to show me the night he saw his mother, when I was tucking him into bed."

"Drawings?" Matt asked, tossing a polished stone into the riverbed. It made a little splash. "Of what?"

"One of the horses. All three sketches were of the same horse, from different angles. Front, side, three-quarter. The black one, I think. Dale had sketched some areas of the horse multiple times. I mean, you could tell he was fascinated by, well, the mane blowing in the wind, the round curves of its haunches, its graceful neck, as if he couldn't let the beauty go and by drawing and redrawing the horse he could memorize every curve of its neck or length of its mane or expression in its eyes. Haunting. This was an artistic side that Dale didn't dare show anyone but that Maria must have embraced. Jenny was a working wife—she would have had no time for the arts, just like Dad."

"So Dale had a creative side. Like his brother." Matt bent to pick up another stone. Grinning, he handed it to Dallas. "Go on," he said, "make a splash."

Dallas stood there holding the stone in his hand for an extended minute. Turning it over, he rubbed it with his thumb. It was warm, heated throughout from the sun. "Why is it," he posed quietly to his good and trusted friend, "that we don't really get to know people until they're gone?"

"Because that's when we take the time to get to know them," Matt offered. "We need the connection. We crave it. So we hang out with their stuff. With their letters and their drawings and their cheque stubs."

"And their playlist," Dallas decided. A mighty arm heave later, and the stone landed smack in the middle of the riverbed. "There," he said, "I made a splash. I wonder if Dale ever stood here and tossed stones too."

"I have a feeling he did," Matt said. "I have a feeling your brother did a lot of cool stuff in his lifetime. A lot of the kind of stuff you need to do, Dal. Out here in nature."

Dallas bent and picked up one last stone. This one, he tucked carefully into a pocket. This was one river he wanted to remember forever.

After a minute, Matt gave Dallas' elbow a tap. "Come on," he said, starting to walk away. "The others are mounting up. Let's go set your brother free."

Hunter knew exactly where to go. The sacred meadow was obvious to everyone the second they saw it. Standing in its centre, surrounded by a growing circle of Dale's family, Hunter spun around and around, slowly, his face raised to the heavens.

"I've never seen him so happy," Dallas murmured to Matt as they stepped through the long grass towards the little boy who had become so central to their lives. "I've never seen such pure joy on a child's face. I wish he could be that happy forever."

"Not likely," Boone said, coming up on Dallas' left. "Nobody gets a gift that great. Life gets in the way. Except maybe for people like you, big famous stars with so much money they could buy a whole country. Dreamers like you get off better than the rest of us. You're not rooted in reality."

Bristling, Dallas was shocked at how his father's words, in this incredible place, still had the power to wound him so deeply.

Matt crunched on his bottom lip. He was about ready to deck Boone. The older man was pretty much healed up from the riding accident—he'd be a worthy opponent in a fight. Anything to keep him from relentlessly picking on the only son he had left.

Cassie was on Boone's left. Firing up her nerves, she acted via the pleasant relationship she'd established with Dallas' father. She called up all the petite little blonde blood she had in her body to help her hunker up the courage to speak her mind 'kindly' in defense of her husband. "Um, Boone?"

Boone looked over and down at her. In her tank top and jeans, she was anything but the beauty queen the gossip magazines liked to show off.

"Dallas' world *is* reality," she said. "Sometimes it's hard, and sometimes it hurts. Do you remember the headlines about me, when I met him? About my first husband, Eddie? All the controversy about how Eddie died, as if all of that played into who I was and whether I was good for Dallas? And before that, Dallas had to publicly endure headlines about Deborah, and he had to somehow process the media gossip about why she hurt him the way she did. He lives with untruths, he has very little privacy, and he has to watch his family suffer under unfair scrutiny too. Dallas lives in reality, it's just that his reality is different from yours, that's all."

The mini-outburst quieted Boone. Almost under his breath, he said to Cassie without looking at her, "I owe you an apology, young lady. I had forgotten about the hell you went through over the passing of your first husband."

"Dallas went through it too," she replied succinctly, with a stubborn chin-thrust forward. "And so did Ry."

"It must have been a very bad time for you, losing your man that way."

They were about to spread Dale's ashes to the wind, and Maria's, too. Loss was on their minds.

"I had to face a lot of fears," Cassie admitted, as Dallas and Matt listened. "I was so scared. Kind of like how I felt during that ride down the mountain the day you got hurt. You know something, Boone?"

A low grunt was his response.

Smiling, Cassie went on. At least he wasn't walking away. At least the ornery Alberta cowboy seemed prepared to hear what Cassie had to say. "Sometimes moving ahead means facing fears. Sometimes the only way to go forward is to wade through all the muck and the grime and put your head down and just do it. I learned that I could move on. I didn't do it alone, I had your beautiful son to help me. To show me the way."

Dallas let a small smile flicker over his lips. He walked behind his father, took Cassie's left fingers in his right hand, and gave her a little squeeze.

"What if I'm too old to move forward, Cassie?" Boone asked in a subdued voice, afraid to look at her or at Dallas. "What if at this point in my life I can only look backwards?"

"Boone," she said insistently. "If you choose—let me repeat that, choose—to spend all of your time looking backwards, then all you will accomplish is replaying the old songs over and over again. And don't you get tired of listening to the same old songs?" Hooking her right arm around his elbow, she added, "Our friend Matt here apparently told my husband that he is putting his record on a new loop. He's trying to let the past go—not all of it, but some." Smiling past Boone at Matt, she blushed. "Sorry," she said, "but my husband and I actually talk sometimes. I was worried about you. I asked."

"No worries," Matt laughed, waving her away. "My life is an open book."

Dallas chuckled. "You can say that again."

"And on that note…" Shaking his head, Matt picked his way over to the wagon to help Doris and Jade dismount. Dawn and Jenny were gathered there too, each with an urn in their arms.

Boone picked up on what Cassie said. However, his words were directed at Dallas, who he didn't look at until the end of what he had to say. "I've been hard on you, haven't I, son?"

Cassie let her fingers slip out of Dallas'. With a sad smile at her man, she took two steps backwards and stepped lightly over to the group at the wagon.

Dallas tried to make a shrug look casual. "We're just different people, Dad. That's all."

"Still…"

"Dad, it's okay. I've been out here for a while and we haven't killed each other yet."

"You've been a big help around the ranch, Dallas."

"Doing what? Enlisting my marketing team to help get some clients out for trail rides? That wasn't so hard."

"You think I didn't see you polishing tack with the kids?"

"I draw the line at mucking shit out of stalls. But I can lift me a mean bale of straw." Taking the joke a step further, Dallas raised his arms and flexed his biceps. "Thank God for the gym. Right, Dad?"

"Dale'd whip your ass in an arm wrestle, Dallas."

"He mighta. He used to." Dallas sobered. "I guess he won't anymore."

"It's all right, son. We'll get through this."

"Yep, Dad, we will. We are."

Boone frowned. He was watching the younger kids running around the meadow, laughing, wild and free, pretending to be wild horses.

"What, Dad?" Dallas asked, tensing, ready for another battle.

"I am getting used to the idea of you feeling you need to go to a gym to muscle up, son, but looking at Dale's boy running out there with his long hair blowing in the wind, I have to say that I don't think I'll ever get used to men wanting to look like girls. You ought to cut your hair. And Hunter's, too." He started to move away, and looked back at Dallas with a smile. "So we can see your eyes," he said. "Stop hiding, son."

"Ah," Dallas grinned once his father was out of earshot. "That's the passive aggressive bastard I've come to know and love."

A short time later, the family formed a rough circle in the meadow. Doris led them in prayer before Dallas went to the wagon and retrieved guitars for himself and for Ry. The song they chose to sing was Hunter's—and Dale's—favourite, a song about a simple, straightforward kind of love.

The wind that day was gentle, but it was blowing the tall grass around. Everyone backed off when Dallas, with Hunter at his side, carried Maria's urn twenty paces to the north, and let her go. The breeze picked her up and carried her away, returning her to the meadow she and Dale loved. Returning her to the earth, to the universe.

Dale was next. There was no debating who would set him free. Jenny had his urn held firmly in her arms. Halfway out to where she planned to let him go, though, she turned fully around and held the urn out to her boys.

Cormac shook his head. Shane sauntered casually over and took the urn.

Then he faced Hunter, and held out a hand.

"I don't know if you're old enough to really understand all of this," he said. "It's just that, well, Hunter—you and me and Cormac are brothers." He looked at Cormac. "C'mon, kid. Let's do this."

Cormac was crying. He understood far too well what was happening. Hunter took his hand before going to Shane and taking his.

The three boys stood together, their backs to everyone else, with Hunter in the middle. Shane handed the urn to Hunter. It was heavy; both Shane and Cormac took hold of it too. With a yell, Hunter signalled Shane and Cormac to help raise it. Soon, their father was returned to the mountain that gave him peace.

When they were done, Dale's three sons turned and faced the others. Jenny was the first to approach. She took Cormac in her arms while Doris wrapped Shane in hers.

That left Hunter. Panting from the exertion, eyes wide, he waited.

Cassie was holding Dallas' hand, with Jade at her left and Ry on Jade's left. She thought about going to Hunter, but at the last second took a step back. Glancing over at Matt, she wondered if he would go to the child, but he was standing behind Shanda, his arms securely wrapped around her shoulders, his face buried in her neck. She was smiling through a rainbow of tears.

Dallas got the message. He handed Cassie his guitar and walked forward without hesitation.

Hunter met him halfway, and let Dallas—his father's brother—lift him, hold him, and bury wet cheeks in his coarse, black hair.

Overhead, a bald eagle circled, soared downwards, and dipped a wing in salute.

To the west, a wild black horse watched with solemn reverence through the strands of a long, coarse forelock. Momentarily it raised its head and whinnied, before it swept around in a lingering, wide turn, and galloped away.

Chapter Thirty-five

"*Y*ou ready for this?"

"Nope. It'll be a tough one."

Jessie and Jacob were standing in the wings at stage right, waiting for the Calgary country station's morning show host to take the microphone and introduce them. It was concert time—they had agreed to appear in a special, spontaneous show.

"Do you think he'll get through it okay?" Jessie gave her arms and legs a shake to loosen up.

Jacob eyed Dallas to try to get a read on how he was doing. The country singer was waiting across from them, at stage left. Matt was standing to Dallas' right. The men weren't talking. Both were fixated on the last minute touches a few of the stage crew were making to the back line musicians' gear. "The show or just the one song?" Jacob asked.

"Both."

"He's tough. He'll get through most of the show okay. I don't know about the one song."

They were talking about a song Dallas wrote to honour his brother, and to honour everyone who ever lost someone they loved to suicide. Jessie and Jacob had rehearsed the song with Dallas for the first time earlier that day. It would make a thunderous impact when he sang it in front of an audience tonight for the first time, and Jessie and Jacob fully expected it would race to number one on both the adult contemporary and the country music charts. A haunting ballad, it started with a single loud strum that would instantly command attention.

"I don't know if *I'll* get through the song," Jessie grumbled, gazing across the stage at Matt. She stopped moving, and squinted so she could see him better under the dim pre-show stage lights.

He picked up her vibe, and looked up. Catching his eye, Jessie smiled a greeting. Matt shoved his hands in his pockets and simply watched her. She thought she saw him sigh.

She frowned.

Jacob noticed. "Are you ever going to take Matt back full time?"

"That's a loaded question."

"You know what I mean."

"I'd like to. Charles says Matt's thinking about it. But he and Dallas have this bromance thing going on now. It's heavy. I think I now rank below Dallas in the greater scheme of things."

"Not a chance. Matt's only with Dallas to protect his own broken heart."

"Life is short, Jacob. Tonight's show is grinding that message in rather deeply."

"Meaning?"

"Meaning I miss Matt. I miss my buddy."

"You'll get over it. Time and distance, girl."

"That how it works?"

A sardonic chuckle accompanied Jacob's next words. "Hell, no. I wish. There's no getting over that kind of pain. Thank God for music." The announcer strode onto the stage. The house went to full dark. Jacob grinned. "Lights out, my favourite high. Here we go. Good show, Jess."

"You too, Jacob. See you on the flip side."

Waiting for the morning show host to finish his welcome spiel and say her name, Jessie took another long look at her old security. Matt was alone now. Dallas was behind him, stretching out a hand to take his guitar from a guitar tech. "Feels weird to see you on the other side," she murmured. "You're always over here."

She and Jacob had security with them—a woman from the Calgary company Matt always contracted when the Sawyers were in residence at their Alberta ranch. Yuka was a good-natured no-nonsense Japanese gal Charles and Matt trusted. She was nice enough, and smart enough to keep her distance from her two charges, but she was a stranger.

Jessie sighed and watched Matt straighten when the announcer hollered, "Please give a warm welcome to Alberta's own Dallas White, here to help raise awareness and funds for suicide prevention, accompanied by two friends y'all will know, Jacob Ryan and Jessie Wheeler!"

Ducking her head shyly, Jessie said, "Thank you," to her usual guitar tech, who handed over her well-worn Gibson J-45, freshly tuned and yanging to be played. Stepping out onto the stage, Jessie raised a hand to the delighted crowd, who were already on their feet, and took up her spot behind the closest microphone. Dallas stopped in the centre; he and Jacob high-fived each other when they passed so Jacob could position himself at the mic on stage left.

The show was divided into parts. The three sang a few tunes together at first, then Jessie and Jacob retreated back to the shelter of the wings on stage right to give Dallas the stage for a few numbers of his own. Afterwards, Dallas returned the favour and gave Jessie and Jacob the spotlight while he watched from the wings with Matt, a tumbler of whiskey in one hand and a damp bandana he was using to mop up the sweat on his brow in the other. They finished the first half with a ballad meant to stir up heartstrings to encourage donations from around the world, since the concert was being live-streamed.

After the short intermission to catch their breath, the stars would repeat the format, with the exception of the ending, which Dallas was determined to mark with an uplifting tune.

Halfway through the break, Matt wandered into Jessie's dressing room. He was munching on a bag of trail mix. She was alone and was texting Josh out in the audience.

"Hey, you," Jessie said when she saw him come in. Putting down her phone, she settled back against the make-up counter to sip a honey-lemon tea Deirdre had started her on a few years back to help protect her vocal chords.

"Hey back." Matt took up a space opposite her, against a wall, next to a large planter of fresh flowers the country station had sent along to brighten up the dressing room. "Got a twang in your voice yet?"

She blushed, and checked out her booted toes. "Dallas' music is pretty crossover, Matt. Thankfully it's not twangy country."

"Josh must be sitting pretty high, watching you sing in a country show."

Reaching behind, Jessie lifted her phone and held it high. "You don't want to know what he just texted. He'll never let me live this one down." She set the phone down again. Sobering, she wrapped her fingers around her warm mug and said, "How's Dallas holding up?"

Matt dropped his fingers back into the trail mix for another handful. "He's okay."

"It's a tough night for him. He was really quiet at rehearsal and sound check."

"His family is here. All of them, kids included. He'll hold up all right. He won't lose it in front of his father."

"That's too bad."

"Meaning?"

"Meaning he should be able to lose it in front of his father. I don't get this thing about boys needing to be strong all the time. It's not a thing anymore in our increasingly gender-neutral world."

"We all lose it at times, Jessie. If you think we don't, then I suppose we're all just good actors."

Jessie was lifting her mug for another drink, but she stopped with it halfway to her mouth. From behind the rim she took a good long look at her friend.

"Stop staring at me," Matt ordered.

"I'm trying to figure out if you're okay or not."

"We're at a suicide prevention show. You're overthinking whatever it is you think you're seeing." Uncomfortable with her scrutiny, Matt adjusted his dark blazer over the grey dress shirt he'd put on to stay discreet backstage.

"You're forgetting how well I know you."

"All right, then. You want to know what I'm thinking? I'm thinking about Dale and Maria. About their secret life. Where it led them in the end. How much it hurt everyone around them."

Alarms went off. "They're not us, Matt. Besides, you and I haven't been alone together in a very long time."

"I had a long talk with Charles today."

"Thought that was yesterday."

He hesitated. "We had another long talk today."

She clued in. "Ah. I see. It's official, then."

He raised his eyebrows and dropped the trail mix he was about to pop into his mouth, back into the bag. Waited.

Jessie set her mug down and rubbed her warm palms together. "When we work together, it's too damn easy to hook up. Is that it? And even though Josh is neutral about us, and Shanda's sort of half accepted it, it's just better if we don't."

Matt swallowed, and shifted his weight to his other foot. He held her gaze.

"All right, then. Today's talk with Charles—you're not coming back to work with me full time. I told Jacob I didn't think you would. You in love with Dallas now, Matt?"

"Don't get bitchy." Matt tossed his trail mix bag over to Jessie. She threw it on the counter behind her. It slid to a stop next to the mirror. "He's going through a rough time. He needs me."

"Bullshit. It's because he has Hunter."

"And? So?"

"You want Hunter. Something about that child is compelling to you. You want to be around him."

"It hurts less, Jessie. I like Dallas, I like Cassie. Ry's a great kid. Jade's—well, she's three. Hunter—yeah. Dallas needs a little help navigating the whole parenting waters. Hunter and I get each other."

"So you're the one to help him navigate, is that it?"

"I did okay with your kids."

"Dallas isn't likely to abandon ship the way my husband once did."

A long pause in the conversation gave both Matt and Jessie the time they needed to compose themselves.

"Fuck, Matt. You're choosing country music! Give me a break," Jessie finally said. Her eyes were damp. "I miss the classy Vancouver guy I used to know."

Matt ignored the jibes, which were indirectly aimed at Dallas' country-music loving soul. Matt was feeling super protective of Dallas these days. "Speaking of your husband," he said, steering them down another, albeit no less rocky, path, "this concert can't be easy on you. Suicide prevention and all."

"He's here. He's on the planet, he's at this show. I expect it's Josh who is not finding the subject matter all that easy on the heart."

"Why'd he come?"

"To prove that people in a shit ton of pain can get past it, I suppose. To help me through it. To help me sing that song with Dallas that's gonna have everyone flopping on the floor like dying fish in puddles of their own tears."

"Jessie…"

"Oh, fuck, Matt. Take a fucking hike. Go live your life with Dallas. Just…"

"What, sweetheart?"

She gave him a sorrowful warning look—when Matt called her 'sweetheart,' it was pretty much the most tender word in the English language. Hearing that word slip between his lips, aimed at her, made Jessie want to cross the room in one fell swoop and bury her face in the deeply loved hollow between his neck and shoulder. She had to dig her fingernails into the back of a hand to avoid acting on the feeling.

She cleared her throat. "Matt, just…" Tossing her hair and shifting her weight, she fixed him solidly in her gaze and spoke with passion. "Just don't forget about me, okay, baby? I mean…Josh…"

"Josh will be okay, Jessie. He's doing great." Crossing the floor, Matt took Jessie in his arms and crushed her body to his. Whispering in her ear, he said, "I will always be your soft place to land, sweetheart. You are not alone. You will never be alone again. Not so long as I share this earth with you, and not in the sweet hereafter, either."

"Thank God for my blessed Matt," Jessie murmured in his ear. "Thank God for you."

A shuffle at the door drew them apart. Jessie swiped at a tear, and smiled at the intruder. "Hey, Dallas," she said with a light wave.

"I echo your sentiment about this guy," Dallas said, taking a few heavy, downcast steps into the room. "He's a wise voice in a crazy mixed-up world." His eyes were dull and sad. Tonight's concert was taking its toll. He was downing another tumbler of whisky.

Jessie decided to give him something to smile about. "Take care of him for me?" It was also a genuine plea. Jessie was clutching Matt's hand. She couldn't bring herself to let go.

A slow half-smile started across Dallas' lips. Eyes suddenly alight, shoulders straightening, he looked at Matt. "You're staying on with me?"

It took Matt a few seconds to form an answer. He and Dallas were suddenly grinning at each other like long-lost brothers about to head off on a fishing trip. "What choice do I have? Hunter doesn't stand a chance alone with you."

Laughing at that, Dallas wiped a hand under his nose and then shoved a thumb and forefinger into the outer corners of his eyes so they'd squish the happy tears that were threatening to leak down his cheeks. To Jessie, he said in a serious voice, "I get it. Just so you know…I get it now. You and this guy."

"Different people, different needs," she whispered. "Jesus, Dallas. Fucking don't get into any real shit, okay?" She grabbed the tumbler from his hand and shoved it onto the counter next to the bag of trail mix. "Matt deserves to live a quiet, semi-retired life with you." She threw up her hands. "What am I saying—you sing country. Him working for you is like taking him out to graze. Country, shmuntry."

A knock at the door summoning them back to the stage cut the conversation short, although Dallas nodded a quiet assent and left the dressing room without looking back at the not-quite-empty glass of whisky. Matt delivered Jessie to stage right before planning to follow Dallas around to the other side. He let her go with a slow, sad smile. "We're leaving right after the show, Jessie," he told her. "No lingering tonight. Dallas has to be in New York for an early morning interview."

Instantly, she deflated further. "Cut my heart into a few thousand more pieces, why don't you? Not even staying for one beer, Matt?"

"One beer will lead to five. Plus Dallas…" He raised a shoulder towards Dallas' disappearing back. "Tonight's not a good night to put more booze in his hands. I'd rather keep it out of reach and out of sight."

"Party pooper." She forced a smile. "You're gonna take good care of him for his sweet little family, aren't you, Matt? You're an earthbound angel, darling man. You're the real, absolutely perfect, deal."

"You know better than that, sweetheart. No man is perfect. Especially not me."

"Close, though," she murmured in his ear, breathing in his musky male goodness before she let him go.

They separated with wistful sighs. Close by, Jacob rolled his eyes and stuck his tongue out at Jessie. When Matt strode around to meet up with Dallas at stage left, Jacob was quick to lift a protective arm, however, so Jessie could slide cozily underneath for a comforting squeeze.

The stage manager was left with the shakes. "Ten seconds," he growled, trying to cover his anxiety with a fake, plastered-on smile.

"Ten seconds it is," Jessie answered back, as Matt's strong back disappeared from view. "Ten—precious—seconds."

After one final hug from Jacob, Jessie turned to the guitar tech who was holding her Gibson out to her, grabbed the cherished instrument by the neck, and swung it over her shoulders.

Chapter Thirty-Six

*T*he downward strum that started them off on the ballad Dallas wrote for Dale cut Dallas' heart right in two. Something about being on the stage was usually cathartic and healing for him, with his penchant for hiding behind his music. Tonight nothing was hidden. Tonight was all about being real.

The rest of the show had gone okay—he got through it. He expected his assembled family was getting through the whole thing as best they could too. Sure, the subject matter was tough—suicide and mental health in general were frightening topics that hit far too many families right in the gut. The songs Dallas—and Jessie and Jacob—had chosen to play were a good mix, some fast-paced and upbeat, others more serious and meant for quiet reflection.

This song—the ballad for Dale—was a bullet to the heart.

Dallas stepped out of the shadows on that first earnest down-strum. Jessie and Jacob had just finished an upbeat tune. The applause was loud, enthusiastic. The clapping crested over a wave and was on the downswing itself when the spotlight operator stilled his golden beam so Dallas could step into the light. Four main chords to establish the melody and a new one on the bridge—C, G, E minor, D, B minor. A song about loss, about the great mysteries of life, in four-four time. Dallas' voice as steady as he could keep it, Jessie and Jacob providing support with the harmonies.

Angelic, breathtaking.

Heartbreaking.

Dallas lost it during the bridge. Looking sideways over at him, Jessie could see he was in trouble before Dallas himself knew it. His eyes gave him away—moist, wide, staring. Skirting him with her own eyes, she signalled to Jacob on the other side of Dallas via a serious nod, so he'd know to help pick up the pieces.

Their quick thinking and expert musicianship got Dallas to a point where he could breathe again. He came back to them with a drop of his head and a half-step forward, shook his head as if he were chasing away a ghost, and finished the song.

In the audience, his father hung his head too, and let out a few great gulping sobs before fixing Dallas in his vision again. Doris took his hand and helped him through it. When the tribute song was over, Dallas, Jessie, and Jacob stood silent and let the audience rise to express the mixed bag of emotions the beautiful, heartfelt tribute brought to the core. Dallas put his hand over his heart and whispered a solemn *thank you* to his brother. In the wings, Matt bowed his head. His lips moved. Jessie looked back at him and almost cried when she realized he was praying.

When the last bit of applause faded out, Dallas stepped forward again and led everyone in a happy, rousing tune to finish off the night—it was the song Dallas sang on J.I. Mountain with Ry.

Clinging to his wife's hand in the third row, Boone eased himself upright and said to whoever would listen, "That's my son. That's my son."

A woman behind him leaned forward and laid a hand on his shoulder. "I'm so very sorry," she said, and it took the tough Alberta cowboy a full minute tumbling it over in his head to realize why she'd said it. He had to sit down again. He had to cry.

After the show, Dallas needed to say a quick goodbye to his parents and to Cassie and the kids, who were staying at J.I. while Dallas went to New York with Matt for the interview. They were in the hallway just outside his dressing room.

Cassie kissed him sweetly. Dallas wished they could sneak back inside, and told her so. He ended with, "I'll be back before you know it," and touched Jade's blonde curls delicately. Ry got a happy hug and a promise that he could do a song in the next big show.

Dallas picked Hunter up and held him in front of Matt so Matt could say goodbye too. "Keep an eye on those wild horses for us, Hunter," he ordered.

Hunter was sleepy. He wiped his eyes with a fist and yawned. "My daddy said the howses keep an eye on us."

Neither Matt nor Dallas could speak all the way to the waiting limo.

In the car, in the darkness, Matt cleared his throat. "And that, my friend," he said, "is the universe's best kept secret."

"Told to us by a four-year-old," Dallas tossed in as a reminder.

"Sounds like a song to me," Matt said.

"Yep," Dallas said. "Just like a song."

It was a rainy Calgary night. When the limo pulled away, it glistened underneath the rainbow of lights under which it passed, one after the other after the other. As one beam ran its course, another began, so that the lights were all connected; so that together they became one continuous beam.

Matt was staring out of one window, Dallas out of another. Both were thinking the same thing—that life was like that, each person a light that touched another and then another, before letting go and going dark.

"Never really completely dark, though," Matt thought, picturing Jessie the last moment he saw her tonight, leaning against the door frame of her dressing room, eyes damp, arms crossed, watching him go. The pain of loving her sometimes brought him darkness, but overall she was a great, great light.

"Not so dark," Dallas thought, picturing the loss of Dale, renewed through his child. He considered holding Hunter at bedtime, the two of them looking through the photographs Dale took of the wild horses. It hit him again that Hunter had a long road ahead, likely to become harder as he grew older, having to come to terms with his father's secret life and with his suicide.

Leaning back, Dallas closed his eyes and said out loud, "I'm glad you're here, Matt. I'm really glad you're here."

Next to him, Matt let the image of Jessie fade. He replaced the sorrow she always caused him with the love of a very special child. *Hunter*, he thought, and closed his eyes, and smiled.

Out loud to Dallas he said, "You won't be glad I'm here when I wake you up at four in the morning for the interview."

Dallas sank back into his seat and raked a tired hand through his long hair. Grinning at the knowledge that Matt had told him he was staying on as his security chief, Dallas said to himself, *Wanna bet, old man?*

Matt caught the grin, and punched his friend in the arm.

Dallas yelped and rubbed his arm before he punched him back. "Hey Matt," he said after a bit, "this last while has got me thinking a lot about brothers."

"And?" Matt asked.

"You have one. You have a brother."

"I do. Michael."

"Are you two good?"

"Sure. Yeah. Michael's happy."

"He had his own tragedy."

"His wife and daughter, yes. A long time ago now. He's remarried, and he's good now."

"What about the rest of your family? Maybe it's your turn to reconnect with your past."

"Our parents are gone now. Michael and I stay in touch; we see each other at shows, and a few other times each year when we can. I'm good on the childhood family front, Dallas, but thanks for thinking of me."

"I'm not sure any of us really age without some ghosts from our pasts haunting us, Matt."

"You know most of mine."

"What don't I know? What brought you to Jessie in the first place, all those years ago?"

Matt hesitated. "Desperation, I think. A need to do something different. I thought she'd be an easy babysitting gig." A sardonic laugh was followed by a quick, "Boy, was I wrong."

"Why did you need something different? What was so bad about your life? You had a good job."

Matt frowned and rested an elbow on the door beneath the window. "Police work. Yes." He took in a long breath. "I suppose you could say I left policing in a hurry. I left a few stones unturned. I suppose that's a part of my past I've never quite made peace with."

"Maybe you should. Maybe then you wouldn't need Jessie so badly."

Outside, a damaged streetlight blinked on and off, on and off.

The car slid past it like a snake hunting prey.

Matt didn't answer.

Dallas said, "I get the two of you now, but it scares me. You need her like an addict needs a drug. She's not good for you."

"I just walked away from her, Dal. Again."

"Not your heart. Your heart didn't."

"And it never will. Drop it." Momentarily, Matt ducked his head and ran a finger over a thumbnail. "Please," he entreated quietly.

Dallas dropped a reassuring hand on his shoulder, then went back to looking out of the window on his side of the luxury vehicle.

Inside, the friends each disappeared deeper into thoughts of the loved ones they were leaving behind.

The big sleek SUV slipped through the night with the utmost of grace, at times benevolent, at other times daring as it moved amongst fast-moving traffic in the busy city. Somewhere in the night, not far off the busy highway, Ethel switched off her television and stood alone in the semi-darkness of her small living room. She'd just watched Dallas deliver healing to millions of viewers worldwide who streamed his concert live. In the minds of many, Dallas was a hero tonight.

In Ethel's mind, Dale was every bit as present on stage as Dallas, and was also a hero. To some, Dale lost his battle with life. To others, he won. After all, he wrestled life until it simply got too big for him. Until it got too hard to breathe.

And that, to Ethel, was the true making of a hero—to journey as far as one can through life. Period. Especially when life gets hard. Especially when it hurts. To just keep trying until there just ain't no more trying left.

Reaching up, Ethel pulled on a small gold chain and switched off the living room light. Humming the last song she heard Dallas sing tonight, the happy one, she waded off to bed in the darkness with Dale, Maria, and Hunter safe and secure in her heart.

Back at the theatre, Boone and Doris and the J.I. gang slipped into their vehicles. One by one, following each other, they headed towards their mountain sanctuary. In his truck, Boone turned on the CD player and rested his big, work-callused paw on the gear shift.

Dallas' confident guitar strums filled the cab, and then his voice was there, too, singing one of Dale's old favourite tunes from Dallas' very first album—a pleasant song about family, and childhood, and the special bond between brothers.

Boone's eyes filled again. It seemed that tonight he just couldn't stop a constant flood of emotion from pouring out. Smiling through the rain of tears, he looked over at Doris, his trusted love and partner for so many years.

"That song?" he said, pointing at the lit-up dash. "That's our sons right there." Letting go of the gear shift, he lifted his hand and wrapped his strong fingers around his wife's. "Doris…that's our sons."

She laid a hand over his, and smiled. "'Bout time you figured that out, you stubborn old coot. Now drive. It's time to go home."

The end.

Thank you!

If you liked this book, please take a few moments to leave a review on Amazon or Goodreads, and consider sharing your thoughts on social media. Self-published authors like myself count on your support to help us continue our writing journeys!

Have a wonderful day ☺

Susan

Join the *Drifters* and *Dallas White* Series family by signing up at **www.susanrodgersauthor.com**.

As a welcome gift, I'll send you a free bonus/deleted chapter from book one of the *Drifters* series, *A Song For Josh*. Happy reading!

www.susanrodgersauthor.com

Facebook: search **Susan Rodgers, Writer** and **StillTheWatermovie**

Twitter: **@srbluemountain**

Instagram: **SusanDrifters**

Pinterest: **Susan Rodgers**

email: **fatcat@pei.sympatico.ca**

About the Author

Susan Rodgers' first novel *A Certain Kind of Freedom* was a Finalist in the Writers' Federation of Nova Scotia Atlantic Writing Awards for unpublished manuscripts. Her short story from the novel of the same name, published in two anthologies, has received rave reviews, as have the Drifters novels, Susan's all-time favourite books to write.

Owner/Operator of Bluemountain Entertainment, Susan is a 'Diploma With Honours' graduate of Vancouver Film School. She produces mostly documentary style client films and short dramas with plans to one day shoot a Feature Drama based on the novel Atlantic Blue.

Formerly a Museum Curator, in winter Susan lives with her partner Steve and her striped cat Oliver (Lucy Maud Montgomery once said the only good cat is a striped cat) in Summerside, Prince Edward Island, Canada. In summer, she hides in a small trailer in Darnley, P.E.I., where she writes novels, paddles kayaks, and crafts sandcastles on the beach. She makes frequent trips to Vancouver to visit her son Christopher, where she enjoys life in the hippie city while listening to great music and sipping on good espresso.

Books by Susan Rodgers

Dallas White series:

Castles In The Sand

Like A Song

Drifters series:

A Song For Josh

Promises

No Greater Love

Riptide

Whispers of Home

And Then There Was Silence

Let the Music Cry

If I Could Sing You Home

After the Rain

Into the Blue

A Sacred Peace

Watch Over Me

The Light In Me

When The West Wind Moves

Listen To The River

Feature Screenplays:

The Story of Jack & Emma

Still the Water

Beautiful Jane

They Were Dreamers (adapted)

Short Stories:

S12

A Certain Kind of Freedom

A Gentle Peace

Steve and I on the actual Snip and Lady, on the clear-
cut across from J.I. Mountain just moments before
our own gentle Alberta cowboy got bucked off.